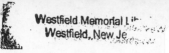

WHAT HOLDS US TOGETHER

WHAT HOLDS US TOGETHER

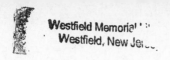

WHAT HOLDS US TOGETHER

SANDI WARD

THORNDIKE PRESS

A part of Gale, a Cengage Company

LIBRARY OF CONGRESS CIP DATA ON FILE.
CATALOGUING IN PUBLICATION FOR THIS BOOK
IS AVAILABLE FROM THE LIBRARY OF CONGRESS

ISBN-13: 978-1-4328-7778-1 (softcover alk. paper)

Published in 2020 by arrangement with Kensington Books, an imprint of Kensington Publishing Corp.

Printed in Mexico
Print Number: 01   Print Year: 2020

In loving memory of Laura

THE JOURNAL

ANNIKA

My own flesh and blood has stolen from me.

That infuriating excuse for a sixteen-year-old has swiped his father's journal from a drawer in my bedside cabinet. I should have known he'd take the diary for himself if he ever found it. I hope he hasn't read very far yet.

I love him, but Donovan is a problem. And I'm not sure what to do about it.

I grip the steering wheel tighter as I drive Delilah downtown to do a few errands. I'm dying to ask her what Donovan is up to, and where he has squirreled away Peter's journal, but I don't want to force her to choose sides.

The kids don't look alike, but they're still twins. It's hard for Del to choose a side that's not her brother's.

We pull up to the mom-and-pop drugstore. In the display window is a fading American flag and a cheap blue plastic beach shovel that was never taken down at the end of the summer.

"Okay if I run over to the penny candy store?" Delilah is leaning forward to look out the windshield, rubbing her mittens together. We've got the heat blasting and seat warmers on, but we're still freezing. I'm sorry Delilah has inherited my poor circulation. She has a red knitted hat pulled down over her forehead all the way to her dark eyebrows. "I'll meet you back here in ten minutes."

"Sure, sweetie." I hand her a few dollars, and she's off.

I head toward the drugstore, pulling my purse strap up on my shoulder. As I yank open the door, I hear the bell start to clang in the steeple of the Congregational church up the road; it must be four o'clock.

I'm just intending to pick up my Xanax prescription, but as I round the corner to turn down aisle two, I freeze. Because lo and behold — there is my son.

The thief.

I had no idea he was downtown. Delilah mentioned he went out after school with a "friend." But now I see that the friend is a petite girl with long, straight dark hair and

8

a mischievous smile who I've never seen before.

I duck behind a display of ceramic Christmas tree ornaments: snowmen, trains, and golden retrievers wearing red scarves. I take another quick look to make sure my eyes aren't deceiving me.

Nope, that's him. No other boys around here have a blond ponytail. If he grew a beard to cover his baby face — and I doubt he could, even if he tried — he'd look like a young Viking. He and the girl are side by side, holding hands, fingers intertwined. They talk quietly, and when she looks up at him, Donovan smiles. Lately, it's rare to see him happy. My heart skips a beat.

The girl pivots so she's facing him, her body nearly touching his. Her down jacket is unzipped and she's wearing a shirt so tight it could be a ballet leotard. She reaches up to smooth a loose strand of hair back behind his ear with her fingertips. It's a tender gesture, warm and familiar. As she gazes up at him, she smiles with a flirtatious tip of her head. Obviously these two know each other well.

So why have I never met this girl? Why has Donovan never mentioned her to me?

I don't dare interrupt them. Donovan and I have been fighting so much that I'm sure

9

he wouldn't be pleased to see me. I decide to leave him alone.

And there are only a few things a teenage couple could possibly need in a drugstore. I hope they came in for a bottle of water. I chew on my lip and decide I'd better not think too hard about it.

I go out to the car empty-handed. Delilah is waiting for me and looks puzzled. "Something wrong?"

I wave that thought away and shake my head. I'll get my prescription another time. "No, no, I just remembered they've got better prices at Brown's. Let's head over there, because we need milk, anyway."

As we walk to the supermarket, Delilah digs into a small brown paper bag and hands me candy — my favorites: a square of dark chocolate and a few meltaway mints in pastel green, yellow and pink.

"What are you eating? It smells amazing."

She shows me the wrapper. "Strawberry taffy."

"Hmm. I might have to get that next time." I try to keep my mouth shut about her brother, but it's no use. "Delilah, do you know who Donovan was going out with after school?"

She just shrugs, her eyes wide and innocent. "He didn't say." Del is two inches taller than I am, just like her brother, and wears a sensible, oversized wool coat. She sticks the rest of the candy in her pocket and locks arms with me as we stroll down the sidewalk, huddled together for warmth.

I'm sure she knows who Donovan is with. I warn myself for the second time to back off. But I can't seem to stop asking questions before they blurt out of my mouth.

"Del, you know what's strange? Your dad's journal is missing from my bedside table. Do you know if Donovan happened to borrow it?"

I glance over at her. Her face doesn't give anything away.

"I dunno, Mom. Maybe he did. I can ask him for you if you want."

"Thanks, baby." I squeeze her arm tighter. "I appreciate it."

"Maybe he took it because he really misses Dad."

"I know he does. We all do."

In the sixteen months since Peter died, Donovan's behavior has deteriorated. He wants nothing to do with me, but at least he still listens to his sister. Delilah personifies all of Peter's best qualities, which makes it easy for Donovan and me to cling to her for support.

Once we enter the supermarket, I grab a

11

basket and head for the dairy aisle. Delilah follows me and scours the ice-cream choices in the freezer case while I look at yogurt, but I can't focus.

"Are we stocking up for the storm?" Delilah points at something behind the glass. "Can I get ice cream? Rocky road?"

"The storm?"

She scoffs. "Yeah, Mom. Not following the news much, huh?"

I shrug. I hate watching the news — too depressing. "It'll be fine. You'll see. They always get it wrong." I watch her dig out a pint of ice cream from the back of the case. It's coated in freezer burn, but she doesn't seem to care. "You have a terrible sweet tooth, you know that?"

"I know." She grins back at me.

The worst thing is, I don't know what's in that journal. It's a navy-blue leather book that was essentially Peter's diary. He started keeping it when he was a teenager, about the age Donovan is now; then he put it away for many years. A couple of years ago Peter found it in the bottom of his closet, was thrilled to discover it, and started adding to it before he died. He never showed it to me or invited me to read it, although it wasn't a secret or anything like that. I would often find him at night tucked into bed, scribbling a few lines with a black pen or sketching with a pencil. I haven't decided yet whether or not I'm ready to read it. So instead, it's been shelved away for safekeeping.

Until now.

For all I know, Donovan has already started to read the journal, parsing it word by word. Studying his father's innermost thoughts.

"Hey, Emmy!" Delilah calls to a girl her own age who is just coming around the corner at the end of the aisle.

Emmy wears her hair up in a bun and comes jogging over in uniform. "Basketball tryouts today." She gives Del a high five.

"You think you made it?"

Emmy smiles. "Our school is so small that literally *everyone* makes the team. So yes, I do."

I'm startled when a woman who followed a few steps behind the girl sticks her hand out at me. "I'm Emmy's mom. Olivia."

"Oh." I switch the basket I'm holding into my opposite hand so I can shake hers. "Annika."

A strand of her sleek black hair falls artfully over one eye, but she tosses her head to get it out of the way. "You're new in town, Emmy tells me . . . ?" Olivia's outfit is cute — turtleneck under a ski jacket,

13

light-blue jeans, and duck boots. Honestly, I try my best, but I worry that in comparison I look like a mess.

"No — I mean, yes, we're new. I grew up here and now I'm back. The kids and I are staying at my parents' house for a while." I realize this probably sounds like I'm dealing with a divorce, but I go to great lengths to avoid talking about Peter's death.

"Will we see you at the PTO spring fundraiser? Invites go out just after the holidays," she continues, with an encouraging smile.

"Hmmm. I don't know. Maybe I can come." I don't want to say too much in front of Delilah, but in my mind, Manchester is just a temporary stop.

I suppose I could offer to buy the cottage from my parents. But lately I've decided that Manchester isn't going to be good enough. Getting out of the house where Peter died was a step in the right direction, but this town drenches me in old memories, and I don't think we can stay.

"Where did you move here from?"

The waistband of my skirt starts to itch, and I shift my weight. These questions are starting to feel intrusive. But when I glance over and see Del and her new friend are deep in conversation, I try to keep up.

"Southern Connecticut."

"Very nice."

I can't tell from her tone if she thinks much of Connecticut or not.

"It was fine. I mean, we were on the water. Lots of woods and rolling hills, with stone walls dividing up the properties. So not that different from here, I suppose." I think about it. "My husband enjoyed being so close to New York City, but I never quite warmed up to it. It never really felt like home, the way Massachusetts does for me."

"Oh, for sure," she says, exhaling as if she'd been holding her breath while waiting to find out what I *really* thought. "It must be *so nice* to be back with your parents."

"Yes. Well. Actually, they retired to Maine. I asked them if they'd keep our old house off the market so the kids and I could move in for a while. So it's just me and the twins."

"Delilah has a twin? I had no idea. Amazing." She brightens, with a quick glance at the girls.

"They're fraternal, not identical. Her brother is Donovan. You'd never know it. They don't look exactly alike."

Her expression changes, and I can't quite figure out what she's thinking. "Oh, right. Right, right, right. Donovan. Emmy mentioned him." Olivia leans in and lowers her voice to a whisper. "He's very fond of his

15

girlfriend, as I hear it." She holds up a hand and crosses her fingers. "She says they inseparable."

I nod, at first slowly and then rapidly, as if I'm familiar with the whole situation. "Well, you know." I put a hand on my hip. "Boys. Hormones. The whole thing. I can't tell him what to do, and without his father around . . ."

"Oh, I completely understand." She tips her head sympathetically. "I have girls, no boys. But I can only imagine the trouble."

"Yes." I sigh. "Thank goodness for my Xanax prescription."

She laughs and winks at me. "Ha ha." She thinks I'm joking.

I grip my shopping basket tighter as it grows heavy. I didn't move here so my son could cause problems.

I enrolled my kids at Manchester High School so they could walk the halls that Peter and I did before we graduated. I longed to pop into the old library downtown, have the kids pick out some books that are slightly damp, and show them how to shake sand out from between the pages. I yearned to hear the distant foghorn on a rainy day, and breathe in the cool, salty air. I was excited to take them for a box of hot fried clams on a humid summer night, imagining we'd gaze at the fishing boats in the harbor while sitting on a wooden bench.

We did all of those things this summer, and it was a tonic for my soul. A short reprieve. But as soon as school started and I tried going back to work, everything got out of whack again.

"It was nice to meet you," Olivia says. "Hope this storm isn't as bad as they're predicting."

"Bye," Del calls to Emmy, who gives a wave.

The entire exchange has exhausted me. I just want to get home and make a cup of tea. "Come on, let's see what else we need," I say to Delilah. But my day isn't over yet.

It's a shock when, yet again, I run into someone I'm not expecting to see. Delilah and I decide to grab a box of cereal, and we're just turning down an aisle in the middle of the store when someone catches my eye.

I let Delilah go ahead of me and I squint down toward the deli. Is that who I think it is? Sure enough, it's two dark-haired men — Sam Parsons with a man who I believe is one of his older brothers, Danny.

I freeze, hoping they don't see me. My heart starts to pound and heat creeps into my face. The long coat I'm wearing feels ridiculously heavy all of a sudden, and I wonder why they've got the temperature cranked up so high in the breakfast foods aisle.

Sam hasn't changed much since high school. I bet he still fits into his varsity football jacket. Some men transform dramatically over the decades as their waistlines expand and hair recedes, but I guess the Parsonses are blessed with good genes.

I watch Sam and Danny talk and laugh while waiting for their order at the deli counter, wearing winter parkas and hiking boots. I fight the urge to flee the store, like a skittish teenager seeing her crush from afar.

Sam had not one but two older brothers. It's hard to imagine three boys growing up in one house without nearly killing each other. And there were more: Sam's older sisters, Diana and Andi. The five of them lived in a ranch house with their parents down on Ancient County Way. I remember they had two Saint Bernards — huge dogs, the size of ponies. It must have been sheer madness living in that house. Not that I ever heard Sam complain. On the contrary, I got the impression he worshipped his older siblings from the way he talked about them.

He was the youngest, the baby of the family.

I take a last glance at Sam. I want to talk to him, and yet I don't. Not right now.

I catch up to Delilah. "You know what? I'm exhausted. Pick out what you'd like and let's get going."

"Yes, Mother," she teases me. "Sorry, I didn't know we were in a rush."

We successfully check out and exit the store without Sam seeing me. It's a relief, but as Delilah fiddles with the car radio, I still spend a moment daydreaming about him. Sam was the kind of boyfriend any teenage girl would love to have, kind and attentive. I don't know why I'm so nervous about the prospect of talking to him.

No — I take that back. I have my reasons.

Lost in my reverie, I've forgotten to turn on the heat. Delilah reaches to click the knob for the fan up to the highest setting.

"Thanks, Del."

She smiles. "Don't worry. I won't let us freeze."

I turn my thoughts to Donovan as we drive home. I suppose I could call my parents and ask them what to do about him. But I don't want them to hear the sadness in my voice, which will be inevitable when I confess that Donovan misses his father so much, he's decided to punish me for it. Although my parents had their own trouble-making kid to deal with — my headstrong, older sister Lisa — they never had a boy who lost his father. I'm in a unique situation here.

Besides, I don't want to explain to anyone that Peter had a journal, and I never read it. The truth is, I'm afraid to read it. Peter's gone, so why dig up the past? Why hash over his musings and feelings and longings and grievances now? What disappointments might I find? I don't feel ready to look at words Peter wrote by hand on lined pages. I may never be ready to read it.

I don't think Donovan should read it either. Whatever Peter wrote was obviously private. It wasn't meant for public consumption, and may not be appropriate for a sixteen-year-old kid to read. I don't think it's right.

Maybe we could read it together in ten years. But now, so soon after his death? I'm sure it's wrong. It feels like a violation of Peter's trust.

Is Donovan ready for whatever he finds there?

Am I?

HIS SPIRIT DID NOT WANT TO GO

LUNA

Peter is gone, and yet he is not.

Peter died in our big, beautiful home overlooking the ocean. It was all on one level, with a huge deck that ran the entire length of the house. We lived in a brilliant world of sun glancing off of rocky cliffs, the sea air tickling our noses and sand shifting underfoot. We lived *large,* as Peter liked to say, and his quick laugh filled the house with joy. For that home to turn into the place of his death was jarring and changed my view of everything.

Once his body was removed from the house, Peter's scent remained on everything. I detected him on the couches, the chairs, the bedsheets. He was a vibrant person, and his spirit did not want to go.

In the days that followed, I felt haunted. I heard Peter's voice in the way Donovan demanded his mother help him with the laundry. I saw his gaze when Delilah raised an eyebrow at a story her brother was telling. Sometimes, I closed my eyes and imagined Peter talking with a few friends in our living room: a man playing guitar, a woman chattering, Peter pouring a drink. But once Peter was gone, the house grew quiet, and rooms that once were inviting became stale and hard to recognize. Strange shapes, odd shadows. Nothing pleased me anymore.

The summer dragged by, blending into a long autumn where I felt numb much of the time. Peter was gone. Gone! And yet he was everywhere, in our thoughts and memories. His black razor remained in the bathroom for weeks. His scuffed-up sneakers sat at the front door for months.

Annika paced around the house feverishly and with no purpose, as if she had lost something she could not find. She often pulled on one of Peter's old T-shirts and cried. Grabbing a handful of the material and pressing it to her face, she breathed in to try to calm herself, but dissolved and began sobbing again. She could not let go, and neither could I. I began to howl at odd hours, jumping from chair to table to kitchen counter, distressed by Annika's strange behavior.

I followed Annika around the house like a needy kitten. I tried to provide my humans with comfort while feeling stressed myself. The twins kept up their routine, but they weren't happy about it. Delilah gave me treats and brushed me every night. I gazed up into her face and let her reassure me that everything would be okay. But I worried about Donovan. He had no desire for companionship, and spent more and more time holed up in his bedroom.

A dark and dreary winter passed, spring emerged again, and Annika packed everything up into boxes. She folded the shirts infused with Peter's scent. She sorted his underwear and socks, and put away his books. His old typewriter went into a case with some papers, and Donovan took it from his mother, insisting he must keep it. Two men came and inspected Peter's piano and took it away.

And then we moved to this cottage. I had never been here before, although Annika's scent is everywhere. We are working on making a new life here.

I stare at a photo of Peter and remember. His hair, the color of sand, soft to touch with my paws when I batted him awake in the morning. His expression of amusement when he listened to a story, as he tipped his head until the light hit his cheekbone. His groan when Donovan told him a terrible joke. His arms, strong and sure, when Delilah needed a hug. His sigh, when Annika asked him for the third time to turn off the music and come to bed.

Annika has been suffering, too. When we first moved to this new house, she spent hours curled up on the couch with a blanket, staring at nothing. Her phone rang, and she did not answer it. She grew thin and pale, and for a time I feared I might lose another family member.

But lately, I see signs that give me hope. This cottage is small but comfortable. Annika gets up, showers, and gets dressed in the morning. Anyone seeing her from afar would presume she was happy and healthy. But she does not go to work. Instead, Annika spends her day with her coffee and reads books, speaking to no one.

Despite the new house, I still feel uneasy. My guilt about how Peter died hovers over me like a hawk, causing me to dart under tables and beds for safety and security. I remember that when Peter played the piano, I would run for cover because I didn't like the noise — but oh! What I would give to have Peter back, to hear him play, to see him smile. I would try to tolerate that piano, if we still had it.

Sometimes when I'm in a bad mood, I stalk Annika, meowing and voicing my protest. *Fix this!* I yowl at her. But, of course, it is hard to say how things can be fixed at this point. Peter is dead. That's a fact we cannot change.

But the children are still walking and breathing and growing and learning. For their sake, we need to keep up the motions of a normal family. A happy family.

What I miss the most about Peter is his way of teaching the children about the world. He was a fantastic storyteller. I heard him tell the twins amazing tales over the years, often at bedtime. So I have learned all about the wide world beyond our neighborhood. I know all about gnomes, dragons, giants, witches, hobbits, and every sort of odd creature that exists on this planet. Peter's recounting of how the world works expanded my view. I like to think of myself as more sophisticated than your average cat, thanks to his teachings. There is so much I have never seen and perhaps I will never see — I have no desire to explore beyond the edge of our woods. But there is so much out there!

Lately, I have seen flickers of movement in dark corners, here and there. I have come to the conclusion that Peter's spirit has followed us to this house. I wonder if I am the only one who has noticed traces of Peter lingering in strange places. Lately, I sense him every day.

Of course, I heard Peter tell Delilah and Donovan ghost stories many times. So I know what a ghost is. It is when the body of a living creature dies, but the soul remains behind.

I puzzle over it: If Peter is actually here, why has he stayed? Perhaps there is some unfinished business he needs to take care of. I would like to see Peter achieve his goal, whatever it may be.

But for the life of me, I can't figure out what it is.

BOARDING SCHOOL

ANNIKA

Delilah arranges photos on the kitchen counter. She places one down at a time, as if dealing from a deck of cards.

The cottage kitchen is exactly the same as it was when I was in high school, never updated, with a black soapstone countertop and cherry-stained cabinets. My mom left a rack of dried herbs and flowers on the wall: safflower, yarrow, thyme, mint, and lavender. Delilah and I frequently joke that we're going to actually use some of the herbs while cooking, but just end up admiring them and breathing in the scent, afraid to touch any of it.

"This was a great night," she says with a smile, pointing to a photo of food and drink on a long, dark table. "Grandmommy and Granddaddy took us out for a beer tasting."

I instinctively frown, but force myself to relax and open my eyes wider.

27

"Wow, that sounds like fun."

I try to mirror her enthusiasm level, but I'm really thinking: That sounds ridiculous. Even scandalous. Should sixteen-year-olds be drinking beer? With their grandparents? Honestly. I'm sure the kids couldn't tolerate the taste of it, although they probably put up a brave front.

It was terrifying to let the kids go to Germany with Peter's parents, Judith and Frank. The twins had never been away from me for so long — ten whole days. But I couldn't say no to the Kuhns, because they miss Peter, too. His death was devastating for them; he was their only child.

Peter fought with his parents and felt a lot of pressure to live up to their expectations, but I understood why they clung to him so fiercely. After we had the twins, they even moved to Connecticut to be closer to their grandchildren. So when Judith and Frank said they wanted to show off the kids to extended family and offered to take them to see where Peter attended school for several years, I had to say, *Yes, of course they can go.*

"Here we are with Jannik," Delilah goes on, pointing to another photo. She grins, and I can tell she liked him.

Jannik is their second cousin. I've never

met him in person. I can see he's a large, young man and has shaved his hair quite short. For all I know he can chug a pint of beer in ten seconds flat.

Fantastic.

Donovan wanders in and heads straight for the refrigerator. I brace myself for a complaint. He's unhappy about the fact that we moved here to Massachusetts.

Well, that makes two of us. It's not helping as much as I hoped it would.

I think about Peter every day, and my future feels empty. He'll always be in my heart, but I thought the pain might start to fade by now. Sadly, my plan to get a fresh start has backfired, because being in Manchester makes me dwell on Peter more than ever. I don't know why I'm surprised. After all, this is where our love story began.

At least the house is familiar and comfortable. We vacationed here with my parents for a week every summer since the twins were born. And I loved growing up here. Sure, the cottage is a little cramped, but it's cozy; it has a fireplace in the back room and a woodstove in the front sitting room. Either spot is perfect for curling up with a blanket.

Yet Donovan manages to find something new to critique every day. He's let me know the kitchen is dark, the floral wallpaper is ugly, and his bedroom is stuffy. The TV is old, the microwave is crap, and the windows jam when he tries to force them open. I wonder what he's found to grumble about today.

I hold my breath. But Donovan doesn't say a word to us. It's like we're not even here.

"Delilah just got her photos printed," I announce in the most cheerful voice I can muster. "They're amazing. Seems you guys had a fantastic time. Want to take a look?"

"I'm busy," he says, his tone flat. "I'm grabbing a snack and going back upstairs to do homework."

Okay. I get the message.

This probably isn't the right time to quiz him about Peter's diary. But as usual, I can't help it.

"Donovan, I assume you took your father's journal, because it's missing. I'm not exactly sure how you found it in the first place, because that would mean you were snooping around in my room."

He snorts. "It wasn't that hard to find. I mean, you practically made a shrine to Dad with his photos and stuff all in one place."

"A shrine? Let's not —" I shake my head. "Look. At any rate, you're not in trouble, but I don't think you should be reading the journal by yourself. Can you please bring it downstairs and we'll look at it together?"

There's a long pause. He stares into the refrigerator.

Donovan grabs a bag of baby carrots from a shelf, shuts the refrigerator, and looks at me with a calm air of superiority. "Why can't I read it? You don't own Dad's journal. It's mine, too."

I gape at him. What an entitled brat! He is driving me crazy.

"Because IT'S PRIVATE, sweetheart, and I'd like to see what your dad wrote first to make sure it's appropriate for you to read."

I wait, hand on my hip. He'd better not reply with a snappy, sarcastic comeback. I have really had enough.

But his mouth quivers. His eyes go wet, and it catches me off guard.

"Mom." He folds his arms and looks down. I can see the scar on the side of his neck from when he fell off his skateboard three years ago. "You've had sixteen months to read the journal. If you haven't looked at it yet, I doubt you're ever going to." He exhales, looking pale now that his summer tan has completely faded. "I can't wait anymore, okay? He's gone and he's not coming back. Dad is gone. And that journal is all I have left."

31

My heart collapses in my chest, and the anger drains out of me. I want to tell Donovan I'm sorry. But for once, the words don't come out.

I glance at Delilah, who casts me a sympathetic look. But when I turn back to Donovan, it's like there's a shade drawn between us. He won't even look at me.

After a pause, Donovan opens the door to the refrigerator again. "Where's the celery?"

"What?"

"Didn't you go to the store earlier? Can't you even get the shopping list straight? Dad never forgot what I asked for. It's not like you're busy with a job."

I bristle as a critical edge seeps back into his voice. Donovan may as well just come right out and say it: Peter was a better parent. He was closer to the kids than I was. It's not a big secret. Peter worked from home and took care of the twins when I was on the road for work. I'm not going to deny what we all know is true.

"Put it on the list. I made a new list on the refrigerator."

Donovan rolls his eyes. "Never mind. I have to go. I have a lot of geometry problems to do. Are we done here?"

Donovan knows that a mention of geometry is going to get my attention. I love math so much that I devoted my career to it as a professor.

As much as I enjoy it, I'm not working right now. I tried going back to work at New York University after Peter died, but it seems I wasn't quite ready. I lasted only two weeks. It turns out that breaking into sobs over silly little things like a computer mouse that won't work properly is frowned upon in the math department. Poor Mrs. Wetzel stated that in her opinion I was having a "nervous breakdown." I explained to her that there's no such thing; I told her it isn't an actual clinical diagnosis, and she could feel free to ask around among my colleagues in the psychiatry department if she didn't believe me. But she wasn't having it.

Once we moved here to Manchester, I tried going back again for the fall semester. I took a new position at a small local community college, and I really thought I was prepared to do the job. This time I lasted a little longer, about six weeks. But I quit to save myself the humiliation of being fired. My mind was always elsewhere. At one time, I was a very organized and motivated person, but I found myself muddled. I was constantly worrying about things at home: Did I buy the right groceries? When was I going to do the laundry? Did I forget to pay the electric bill again? Would I get home in time to give Delilah a ride to debate club? Peter used to take care of things at home, and once I had to do everything myself, I started to realize the extent of what he'd accomplished and how overwhelmed I really was.

"Sweetheart," I sigh. "Okay. Sure. Go do your homework."

I turn back to the photos, but don't really feel like looking at them anymore. I am not going to win this battle with Donovan. I should just resign myself to that fact right now.

Delilah puts an arm around my shoulder. "It's okay." She leans her head against mine. "Do you want me to steal the journal back for you?"

"No, you don't have to do that. Just let him stew for a while. I'll try to talk to him again later." I run the palm of my hand down Delilah's hair, which is coarse and the color of tree bark, like mine.

Donovan, on the other hand, inherited his father's fine blond hair. His hair is as long as his sister's, which I still find hard to believe. He grew it out for years. Every time I'd get the urge to tell Donovan to cut his hair, Peter would tell me to leave Donovan alone; he'd start in with a lecture about how in Germany no one would care, and Americans are too rigid in their expectations. Donovan thought it was amusing to get us into this argument repeatedly, so I learned to keep my mouth shut.

"I could give you some ammunition," Delilah suggests, lowering her voice. "If you think you might need it."

I turn to look at her. I'm skeptical — but tempted. "What?"

She takes in a deep breath. "Well . . ." Her eyebrow raises and she traces the outline of a photo with her finger. "You want me to tell you a little about Donovan's girlfriend? It's getting serious. He's been posting photos of her on his social media accounts."

I don't mention that I saw him with the girl in the drugstore, or that Emmy's mom already brought it up. But I'm relieved one of the twins finally told me. I suppose it's possible I could use the information against Donovan in some way. Maybe I should forbid him from seeing her until he returns the journal . . . ? No, that would backfire. There would be no way to enforce it, and it would just make him angrier. But maybe if I ask him about this new relationship, I could win him over. I am genuinely interested, after all. It might be a way I could re-earn his trust.

"Is that what makes it serious? The fact that he's been posting photos on social media?"

She scrunches up her nose and smiles. "Yeah, it makes it official."

I sigh.

"Darling Donovan." That was my nickname for him when he was a baby. He's got the same bright smile his father had, and an open, boyish face. I need to keep a closer eye on him. Pretty soon he won't be sipping beer with his grandparents; he'll be asking college kids to buy it for him.

"I think it's a little crazy that Donovan has only been at Manchester High School for three months and he already has a girlfriend." Delilah taps one finger against her bottom lip. "I feel like he jumped into a relationship kinda fast."

"Well, you know, it makes all the girls take a second look, not knowing anything about a new boy and wondering what his story is. It makes him seem kind of mysterious and intriguing."

I remember. Peter was once the "new boy" at my high school, having just arrived from Germany. I recall staring at the back of his head sometimes in art class and wondering what he was drawing. I contemplated the white sneakers and shorts he wore those first weeks of school, which looked very European to me. The boys talked about how Peter was a natural at soccer, and from the look of his thick, muscular legs — a little detail I remember because of his later accident — I believed it. We had no soccer team at that time, in the 1980s, and someone said the gym teacher might have Peter teach us some basic soccer skills.

I didn't talk to Peter much, not at first, but I did notice him. I didn't fall in love with him senior year of high school, because at that time my whole heart belonged to Sam. But Peter stood out because he was different.

"Don't worry, this girl seems okay," Delilah continues. "Her name is —"

"Wait." I hold up a hand. "Don't tell me. Let him tell me himself."

I look over the photos again. It does look like the twins had a very good time in Germany. They're smiling in most of the photos. I suppose it was a nice opportunity for the two of them to get away from me — and my sorrow — and grow up a little.

"Looks like Grandmommy showed you a fantastic time. I'm glad the two of you didn't get lost in the Black Forest. I'm happy you weren't captured and thrown into a witch's oven like Hansel and Gretel."

Delilah laughs. "Nope." She pauses. "You sure you don't want me to steal that journal for you? You could distract Donovan with an apple cider donut or something, and I could search his room."

"Ha ha. No, thanks." I close my eyes briefly. "No, this is between me and him. You don't need to get in the middle of it."

I have to talk Donovan out of reading that journal. I am sure there are things in there I don't want him to know about. Since Peter started his journal back in high school, surely he wrote about the car accident that Peter, Sam, and I were all in on prom night. That would certainly upset Donovan. And there are more recent entries that I'm afraid may also be too personal for Donovan to handle. He's too emotionally damaged right now to handle any more shocks to the system.

I've already tried to steal the journal from him myself. I searched high and low all around the house, but I can't locate it. One way or another, I'm going to get it back.

I shuffle the photos into a pile. "So did you talk to Grandmommy about me while on your trip?"

Delilah looks startled, her big doe eyes widening. "About you?"

"Yes." I square up the photos with the palms of my hands. "I assumed she asked about me."

"Oh. Well." Her shoulders relax a little. "I guess so. She's just worried about you."

"Mmm." *Worrying* about me is not quite exactly what I'd call it. Judith has made it perfectly clear what she thinks of my move to Massachusetts, poor parenting skills, and lack of ability to hold down a job and keep the house running smoothly. Her crisp German efficiency doesn't leave a lot of room for argument.

The twins need structure, Judith had said to me in the women's room at Boston Logan Airport when I picked up the kids after their trip. *They're at a very important time in their lives. They are so smart. So special.*

I know, I'd replied cautiously. I wondered if she was really talking about Peter; he was smart, he was special — but now he was gone. All she had left of him was her grandchildren. I wasn't sure where she was going with this.

But they also don't seem focused on the future. If they're going to get into college, they need guidance.

What do you mean? I'm a college professor, for goodness sake, I'd countered. *I can help*

39

them get into college.

There was a long silence. *You're not a professor anymore, Annika. You're not working anywhere now.* She took some brochures out of her purse and handed them to me. *Look at this beautiful school. Wouldn't this be wonderful for them?*

I couldn't win an argument with Judith, and usually quit trying.

I came to see she meant the twins need guidance from someone who doesn't hole herself up in a cottage in the woods, afraid to leave the shrine she's built to her deceased husband. I get it. I'm not in denial about my inability to deal with my grief. It's been sixteen months, and I agree with her that it's time to get my act together and make some better decisions.

So I have the brochures for The President's Academy tucked away in a kitchen cabinet. The applications have been filled out, signed, and sent in — all by Judith. Frank wrote a check for the spring semester, which the school cashed. The boarding school is only thirty minutes from Judith and Frank's house, so the kids can visit them on weekends if they want to.

But Judith assures me they won't want to, because they'll be very busy. The school offers everything the lost teenager needs to feel direction — the right courses, caring teachers, top-notch clubs and programs. And I assume they have a cafeteria that won't forget to order celery, because apparently that's vitally important and it would be blatant child neglect to forget such a thing.

I tap my fingernail on the kitchen counter. It's already late November. It's time to show the kids the school brochures and share the plan with them. But every day I find some excuse to put it off.

"Did Grandmommy tell you more about that private school near her? She makes it sound so wonderful. I think we should drive down and take a look at the campus next weekend."

"Yeah, it sounds okay. I guess. But I'm not really interested in changing schools again." She narrows her eyes at me. "You haven't seriously forgotten that we're going to be snowed in, though, right? We're not going to be driving anywhere for days."

I shake my head. "I told you, it's going to be fine. The forecast is always wrong."

A little snow is the least of my worries.

A Strange Man Wearing a Black Mask

LUNA

All is quiet, but I can sense something is wrong.

A storm is coming.

I feel nervous. Restless. I decide to go out. I stand on the mat at the sliding glass door in the kitchen and wait patiently.

But there is something sharp and disturbing in the air. My nose catches it right away when Annika opens the door. Frigid air pours in like water topping an overflowing tub, and it sinks down to where I crouch on the tile floor. I feel my muscles tense, ready to run away. This is my first instinct, always: flight.

As the air washes over me, it smells alarming. My whiskers spread to full attention.

I don't mind the cold. It is winter here much of the time, and I seek out bright squares of sunlight and warm heating vents when I need extra comfort.

But this feels different. The chill seeps down to my bones despite my thick winter coat. No, thank you.

"Not going out this time, Luna?" Annika asks me, but she is not enthusiastic about it. She knows what I know. This is no day for woman nor cat to venture outside.

When I glance up, she is studying the tops of the tallest pine trees against the blue of the sky. The beauty of the day is deceptive. The sun is brilliant but not strong enough to warm the air.

Annika examines the one cloud in the sky from under long, feathered eyelashes. I study her face. Her eyes, large and round, appear calm and thoughtful.

Annika takes time to paint her eyes, color her cheeks, and brush her hair, even when she is not going anywhere all day. This is how I know that her morning ritual is something she does for herself and not for others. She always looks wonderful to me. The colors of her clothes don't always match, and sometimes she does strange things with her hair, like piling it up on top of her head. But as far as humans go, I find her lovely.

I believe it is Annika's way of coping with Peter's death. For a long time she was bereft, but now she tries to take care of herself, even when she is alone.

Annika sighs and shivers as she pushes the door closed. "Let's make a cup of peppermint tea."

I follow her back to the stove and plop down in my favorite spot on the kitchen floor. I know I shouldn't worry about the storm. No matter how bad it gets, we won't starve. I watched Annika and Delilah bring bags of food in from the car yesterday. The kids also hauled in several armfuls of chopped wood, which is currently sitting by the fireplace. I don't get too close to the woodpile. The bark is peeling, and splinters stick out in odd directions. But I nose around it at times, attracted by the earthy scent and occasional bug I can turn into a snack.

Annika's shoulders sag as she drops a tea bag into her mug. She has been exhausted. I worry about her health. I wonder if she is eating enough.

It's all because Peter is gone. My heart sinks. I feel guilty for not doing more to save him the day he died.

It's so strange feeling like Peter's ghost is here with us. Sometimes, I think I can even smell him; my nose twitches with the scent of the fresh-peeled clementines he was always eating one slice at a time.

44

What if Peter haunts me forever? I assume it's me he's after, since I'm the only one who senses him. Perhaps he will follow me until the end of my days, until my body is cold and lowered into a shallow grave.

I remember how the family buried Delilah's rabbit Snowball after she died. Peter dug the hole himself. Now it's Peter's body that rests rotting in the earth, while his spirit roams this house.

My back and tail shiver spasmodically. I have spooked myself!

A sharp rap at the front door flattens my ears and causes Annika to jump. She lifts her head and begins to move toward the front door, her fancy shoes clicking on the tile floor. I follow.

On her tiptoes, she peeks through the window high up in the door, then rocks back onto her heels, staring at the doorknob. Hmmm. Must be a stranger. We know the mailman and the package delivery woman. Annika would not hesitate if it were someone she knew.

Finally, she reaches out and swings open the door. The bright sun pours in again and we squint.

And — oh! It is a strange man standing on the top step.

Wearing a black mask that comes up over

45

his nose and mouth.

Frightening! Like an ogre!

I freeze. Men are not my favorite type of human. Most of them strike me as big and clumsy. They talk too much, considering that they are not very sharp thinkers. Peter was an exception, of course, but even he stumbled over me a few times when I was lying on the floor, or he bumped me with a crutch.

Peter needed crutches sometimes because he had one leg made of human flesh, and the other leg — well, it was missing below the knee. Sometimes he wore a mechanical leg called a prosthesis, but when he did not have it on, he needed crutches to help him balance. Peter was like that from the day I met him. It didn't slow him down. With his prosthesis on, he could still put on sneakers and get around like everyone else. He was a little slower with his silver crutches; they cuffed around his forearm just below the elbow and he'd lean down on the handgrips. I always made sure to stay out of the way of those crutches, just in case.

I wish Peter were here right now. I don't like the idea of Annika having to deal with a stranger while she is weak and distracted. The children are in the back room, engrossed in a movie on TV.

Peter, where are you? I think. *Make yourself known to me!*

I glance around, but I get no reply.

Rats. I guess ghosts don't appear on demand.

In addition to the mask, the man at our door wears a bulky black coat, clunky boots that look like they might break a cat's tail, and a hat and gloves. Annika's eyes open wide, but she does not move.

"Hi," he says, almost out of breath, and I can sense that he has been out in the frigid air a long time from the husky tinge to his voice. "Is Rich here?"

Annika tips her head.

"No."

As the man stares at Annika, my momentary panic subsides. The man's eyes — which are essentially all I can see of him — are kind and alert, framed in dark eyebrows. Seeing this human feature calms me.

A moment passes by. It's quiet. No wind. I glance up to watch a leaf falling slowly, like a feather, from the top of a tree.

"Rich and Cindy are in Maine," Annika finally jumps in, putting one hand on her hip as if she is already tired of this conversation. "Permanently. What I mean is, they live there year-round now."

The man hasn't changed his expression.

47

Finally, his eyes crinkle up and if I could only see his mouth, I'd understand better what he was feeling. "Annika?" he finally blurts out.

I take a step back. This man knows my woman?

"Yes?" Thankfully she closes the door a little, because the air is bracing cold.

"Don't — don't you remember me?" He pauses. "From high school?"

"Well." She blinks. A few times. Those long lashes fluttering down and then back up. "I can hardly see you. But your eyes look familiar."

"Oh." He reaches with both hands behind his head and with a *snap!* pulls the mask free. His cheeks and mouth are as pink as raw salmon. "Sam. Remember? Wow. Annika. It's been a long time." His mouth twists up for a moment in amusement. "Sam. Parsons. You must remember." This man has a funny way of talking. It's thick and raspy. Perhaps he is losing his voice in the cold.

I am not around men much anymore, and I have no idea what to expect of this one. I watch him warily. The way he looks at my woman, I believe his intentions are friendly. He seems genuinely pleased to see her. His mouth stays open for a moment in wonder,

48

as if he is looking at snow falling inside our home and cannot believe it.

Annika's face goes pale. "Yes, of course. Of course, I do. Hi, Sam. It's great to see you." She moves back a few inches. She looks almost — anxious. Uncertain. And it really is uncomfortable standing here with the door open. I don't know why she doesn't invite him in out of the cold.

But then, she never invites anyone in.

"I haven't seen you in so long," he blurts out.

Annika frowns. "I know. Since . . . since prom night."

He grins. " 'Goodbye Yellow Brick Road,' am I right?"

She shakes her head. "What?"

"We —" He extends a hand toward her. "Don't you remember? We danced to it at prom. It was our senior class song." When her expression doesn't change, he leans forward slightly. "The vote came down to 'Goodbye Yellow Brick Road' or 'Free Bird.' " He looks pleased with himself. The man waits for her response, and I can see this memory means something to him.

Annika exhales, a long sigh, and seems to relax all at once. She rolls her eyes. "So cliché. Who would want either one of those as their defining class song? Honestly. Those songs are from the seventies, for God's sake. Why not pick a song from the years we were actually in school?"

The man's previously hopeful expression turns pained. I think she has insulted him. "What? Are you serious? They're classics. Absolute classics. They're both fantastic. 'Goodbye Yellow Brick Road' was a great choice."

"Was it?"

"Yes."

"Why?"

The man tips his head, clearly fascinated, as if he has never seen this type of human before. I can see his breath in the air when he exhales. Strands of dark hair poke out from under his hat, and his face is turning a deeper shade of red. Because he's wearing heavy layers, I assume he is both freezing and too hot as my woman keeps him standing on the front step. I saw the same thing happen to the twins when they were younger. They would play outside in the snow and get overheated from the layers of clothes Annika forced them to wear.

"Because," he finally sputters out, "Annie. Because. Look. Think about the lyrics. They *mean* something. That song is about realizing the outside world isn't all it promised it would be. It's about returning home. Like both of us, finding ourselves back here in Manchester after going off to college and the years passing. Right?" He suddenly looks surprised all over again. "I can't believe you're here. If your parents moved, why are you here?"

His face brightens, waiting for her answer.

Annika stares back. Her face is blank. I'm not sure what she's thinking.

He squints at her. "Come on. I know you remember. We danced to —"

"Sam." She shudders, as if coming out of a trance. "Why are you here again? Why are you looking for my dad?"

He sighs. Stuffing his face mask in his coat pocket, he says, "Yeah. Sorry. Okay. Forget it. I suspect the deeper meaning would be lost on you, anyway. You'll never appreciate classic rock, right?" He chuckles. "Well, I'm just here to see if you want your driveway serviced. My dad's company has a standing contract with Rich — I mean, your dad — to plow his driveway, and I was checking in. I had no idea he moved to Maine. He never ended the contract. But I guess he knew you'd be here and need plowing out. They say it's going to be a blizzard with hurricane force winds, so there will definitely be drifting."

"A blizzard? That bad?"

"Yeah, that's what they say. It could be two feet of snow, maybe more. So the way it works is, we'll get everyone done repeatedly on a rotating basis. You might hear us at 11 p.m. tonight and then again at 11 a.m. tomorrow. It all depends on when the snow starts and how fast we can rotate around. We'll plow the driveway and then shovel the walk by hand."

"I'm just staying here for a while. I mean, we might be gone in a month or two. I don't know yet." Annika shivers as the one cloud in the sky begins to cover the sun and the whole day darkens by a shade of gray. "But the plowing sounds fine. I don't care what you do, or how you do it." She wraps her arms around her torso. "I mean — it's not that I don't care. I do care. What I meant to say is, I don't mind. I'm glad. I can't shovel the whole driveway myself. Clearly."

"Okay." The man pulls at his gloves, as if they're not on tight enough. He shifts his weight from foot to foot, and I can see he's feeling the cold right through his thick boots. "Yeah, believe me, you want help for this one. Otherwise you could be trapped here for days. You've got a really long driveway, and that Volvo you've got sitting there isn't going to get far if it's buried in snow. You should put that car in the garage.

52

Didn't you hear the forecast?" He looks around, as if it's already starting to snow and he's trying to show Annika that she just needs to focus in order to see it. But the day is still silent and dry and beautiful, the ground bare with dead leaves and pine needles.

"The car won't fit in the garage. It's full of old junk my parents never got rid of. And yes, I heard the forecast." Annika leans against the door. It's a red door, flawless and shiny, with a brass knocker in the shape of a whale. "I know all about the storm. It sounds nice."

The man's head snaps back to look at her. "Does it? But what —"

"Mm-hm. I'm really looking forward to it. It sounds peaceful. I'm going to take the time to relax and catch up on my reading."

I agree with her! It's going to be wonderful. Snuggled up in the soft blue fleece blanket. Sitting by a roaring fire. Listening to the reassuring drone of the television.

But when I look up at Annika, she actually doesn't look so happy about it. Instead, she suddenly looks rather lost.

In fact, I highly doubt she needs to "catch up on" her reading. She reads all day, every day.

I think the man sees what I see, because

he stops fidgeting. "Well, I just hope you're prepared," he says in a gentler tone. "You went to the grocery store, right? Do you have enough milk and bread for a few days?"

"Sure. I have plenty of food. And I love the snow."

The man stares at her, and his eyes soften, as if he's suddenly reminded of something. "I know," he says quietly. "I know that." He opens his mouth, as if he wants to say more, but nothing comes out.

"I'm sure you're really busy, with this storm coming. Thanks for letting me know you'll plow the driveway. And thanks for coming by, Sam. It's good to see you." Annika shuts the door, turning her head away from him and not bothering to wait for the man to retreat down a step or two.

Annika pauses, leaning back against the closed door and putting a hand over her stomach. Her eyes fill with tears, and her nose crinkles up. I wait, unsure if she feels unwell, or perhaps is about to cry. But then she takes in a sharp breath, thrusts her shoulders back, and looks at me.

" 'Goodbye Yellow Brick Road,' " she mutters, shaking her head and dabbing at her eye. "That's nonsense. I mean — it was, Luna, wasn't it? Total nonsense." I follow her as she strides back to the kitchen.

54

I agree with her. I don't know what in the world that man was talking about. I don't know what he was trying to pull.

Although . . . it's also true that my woman was the one asking most of the questions. I feel sorry for that man. She kept him standing there in the cold too long. He was slow and obviously confused.

When we get to the kitchen, we stare out the sliding glass door to the backyard. The woods look frozen. The maple trees are bare, the pine trees appear brittle, and the world is still. This must be what the humans mean by the "dead of winter."

It's unnatural, and makes me terribly nervous.

And that's when I feel it. I bristle, realizing that Peter's spirit hovers behind me. I turn to look at him. I mean — at his ghost.

Peter is watching Annika with clear blue eyes. He's wearing a worn-out T-shirt and comfy shorts as if it's a lazy summer Sunday instead of the middle of winter. I suppose that's what he was wearing the night he died, in the heat of July. He's also missing his leg, and yet not leaning on his crutches — he's standing as if on two legs!

Lines form on his forehead as he frowns. I bet he's not happy to find himself here, in this cottage in the woods. Peter loved our big house by the sea. He probably doesn't understand why Annika moved. Maybe he'd like us to go back.

"Nineteen degrees, Luna." Annika glances at a small box just outside the door. "That's colder than it was a few hours ago."

Hmm. I crane my neck up and try to catch her eye, but she's scanning the backyard. I wonder if she senses what I do: the danger. It is going to be a terrible storm. I can feel it all over.

But now that Peter's ghost is here, I feel a little better, so I stand my ground. Peter will keep an eye on us, I'm sure of it, but I also know from listening to Peter's stories that there's only so much a ghost can do. A ghost is not capable of the same actions as a living human.

I guess I don't actually know what a ghost can do. Anything helpful? I know that they rattle chains and moan, which are things that I seriously cannot imagine Peter doing even for a minute. But what else can a ghost do? I wish I could ask Annika.

Maybe I can ask Peter.

Why are you here?

He turns and looks at me, which makes me jump.

Annika is holding me here. She's been thinking about me a lot lately — more than ever,

56

now that she's back in Manchester.

Where's your prosthesis?

He smirks. *In my casket? Donated somewhere? I don't know. But I don't need it where I'm going.*

But you're standing without crutches.

Yes, I am. Strange, isn't it?

Why yes, it is.

Before I can ask him more, he fades from view. I look around, but sure enough, he's gone.

It occurs to me that although that man Sam was an unwelcome distraction, perhaps it's best that he will be back. If this storm ends up being fierce, it would be good to have another human know that we're here.

Just in case. Despite the fact that Sam looked like a scruffy troll.

The fact is, our home is in the woods, and the neighbors are not close. We can see the lights from other houses at night, but during the day the houses are hard to discern through the hills, rocks, trees, and brush.

Will Sam definitely come check on us, though? I wonder. My woman did close the door in his face rather abruptly.

I trot to the front room and stare out the picture window until the sun finally sets, melting pink behind the trees, and the sky takes on an eerie glow. My eyes wait for the flutter of a wing or the flick of a chipmunk's tail, but there's nothing to see.

The twins stay up late watching movies and stuffing their mouths with buttered popcorn, as they have already learned they have a "snow day" tomorrow, which means no school. Annika and I go to bed before they do, Annika under the comforter and I on top. Just before sunrise, I wake.

And, I realize with a fluttering in my heart, it has begun. While I cannot see it or hear it, I know the snow has started to fall.

THE SEA SERPENT

LUNA

While I wait for Annika to wake up, I think about how Peter's spirit spoke to me yesterday. I believe his soul was supposed to leave the earth when he died.

So what's gone wrong?

I remember the stories he told to try to figure it out, thinking back to the days when the children were small.

I jump up on Delilah's bed to hear Peter better. This is my favorite time of night, when the children get comfortable so they can listen to Peter tell a story.

"What does Death look like, Daddy? Is he a scary skeleton?"

Peter scoots closer to Delilah. His crutches lean against the wall, nearby. Delilah is wearing a long, red flannel nightgown and has kicked off her white comforter.

"Death?" He kisses her forehead. "Are you

59

thinking about Snowball?"

She nods, sticking her thumb in her mouth. We found Delilah's rabbit dead in her cage one morning last week.

Peter takes Delilah's hand away from her face with the utmost care and holds her hand. "Don't worry about Snowball. She's in Heaven, eating carrots and lettuce."

"But what does Death really look like?" Donovan chimes in. He's wearing striped pajamas. Both of the children have straggly hair that won't stay in place and a variety of odd-sized or missing teeth.

Peter pauses. "No one knows. You see, once you meet Death for the first time, it's also your last time. Because, of course, you're dead! And then your soul is whisked off to Heaven. No one has ever come back from Heaven to tell us what Death looks like."

Donovan rolls around on the foot of the bed. "Everyone knows Death looks like a skeleton. Come on, Daddy." His voice drips with frustration. "Everyone already knows that."

"Well." Peter raises an eyebrow. The glow from the bedside lamp is dim and yellow. "Some say Death looks like a skeleton, cloaked in a black cape and hood, carrying a scythe."

"A what?" the twins ask in unison.

Peter holds his arms up over his head and brings them down in a broad, slicing motion. "A sharp blade for cutting down wheat."

Delilah opens her eyes wide. Donovan's mouth drops open.

"But no, no, no. Personally, I think that's totally wrong." Peter rubs his eyelid with one finger. "Look. If you're going to Heaven, why would God send this character Death who looks like a monster? That makes no sense at all. I think Death must be absolutely beautiful. If you can picture the most amazing, kind, and loving angel in your mind —"

"Boy or girl?" Donovan interrupts.

"Doesn't matter." Peter lifts his chin. "Just imagine a very sweet and benevolent —"

"Bene-what?" Delilah scratches her elbow.

"Someone generous and friendly," Peter continues. "Then that would be Death, I think." He peers at Delilah. "You aren't thinking of Mommy, are you?"

She giggles.

"Because Death doesn't look like Mommy. Just picture a different nice person."

"Woo-hoo!" Donovan howls. "I'm tellin' Mommy you think Death looks like her."

"Nooo," Delilah squeals, but she is not

upset. She clenches the material of her nightgown in her fists. "Don't say that. Please. I'm just picturing a sweet angel."

I get up from where I sit near Donovan and walk over to Peter to take my place in his lap. Sometimes, I climb on his thighs. But tonight, since he is not wearing his mechanical leg, I curl up at the end of his stump on the bed.

He runs a steady hand down my back. "You know, the ancient Egyptians worshipped cats. They turned cats into mummies when they died, just like they did to people, wrapping them up before burial. And they would mummify mice to leave with their bodies."

Excuse me?

I look up at him. Is this true? I always assume everything Peter says is true. I suppose it must be.

"And," he goes on, "humans mourned their deaths just as they would if any family member died."

"But, Daddy!" Delilah is quick to grab his arm. "Of course they did. Who wouldn't?"

Peter shrugs. "I don't know, sweetheart."

"Can we mummify mice for Luna?"

He laughs. "Maybe. Maybe we should."

My goodness! Perhaps the Egyptians worshipped cats, but I certainly worship Peter. He is so smart and knows so much about the world.

"Daddy . . ." Delilah looks up at the ceiling. "When you lost your leg, did you think you might die?"

Peter grows quiet, and for a moment he looks inward and his face shuts down. But he quickly recovers. "No, no, sweetheart." He ruffles her hair. "I lost some blood, and I wasn't thinking straight. I was in pain for a while. But I never thought I would die. I really, really wanted to live. I wanted to marry your mom and meet you guys."

Donovan nods at his father. "Sorry, Daddy."

"There's nothing to be sorry about."

Delilah grabs Peter's hand. "Can't you ask a nice witch to make a spell and give you your leg back?"

"Ah." Peter swallows and takes in a breath. He reaches down to move me out of the way, handing me to Donovan. Then he pulls the comforter up over Delilah's legs and his own, so she's not looking and comparing their legs anymore. "But you see, sweetheart, there's no spell that works like that. I'm sorry if it makes you upset."

Her lip trembles. "It doesn't make me upset, Daddy," she whimpers, starting to tear up. "I don't care if you have a stupid leg or not."

There's a pause. Delilah reaches to hug her father first; then Donovan scrambles over. I jump to get out of the way. I don't want to get hit by little human knees and elbows.

"It's funny," Peter says, "it still feels like my leg is there. I don't remember it's gone until I look down or try to stand up. And I always have two legs in my dreams. I think about playing soccer on a huge green field. But, you know, having two legs? It's not really that important." He holds both children in his arms. "In the big picture, it's just a nuisance not to have it. You guys are what's important."

"Yeah," Delilah agrees. "You don't need it."

"You're still a strong man, right?" Donovan looks up at Peter.

"I can do what I need to do."

"He's strong!" Delilah scolds her brother. "Daddy, squeeze him tighter and show him."

The children start bickering and laughing, but I'm still thinking about Death. I wonder, is that what will happen when I die? God will send a lovely angel, and the humans will wrap up mice for me? Hmm. Interesting. Very good, then! I settle down by myself at the end of the bed, curling up for a nice purr to think about it.

Once they're done being silly, Delilah sighs and lies against her father. "What about ghosts?"

Ghosts? I pick up my head. I don't know what that means.

"Yeah, Dad," Donovan cuts in. "Tell us a ghost story!"

Peter hesitates. "Well, ghost stories can be a little scary sometimes. Maybe I could tell you a great love story instead. Love stories are better, in my opinion."

"Love story?" Donovan starts to gag. "Blech. No way. Just a ghost story."

"Are you sure?"

"Yes!" the twins yell at once.

And so, I hear my first ghost story.

A few weeks later, Delilah asks again how Peter lost his leg. He's told the twins the story many times.

"Daddy. Will you tell us the story about the sea dragon?"

I stretch out, front legs sunk into a soft pink blanket on Delilah's bed. I start to knead my claws to keep them sharp.

Left paw, right paw. Over and over.

Peter puts his crutches aside and sits next to Delilah, and she slides over. He's wearing his favorite sweatshirt, the one that reads BOSTON COLLEGE across the front. It's blood red with rich gold lettering. Peter likes to point out to the children that these were the colors King Arthur used to wear, maroon and gold. Sometimes I wonder, could Peter be a descendent of that king? He knows so much about the Knights of the Round Table, it's almost as if they are members of his own family. We have heard the stories about Camelot and Excalibur many times.

Peter admires Delilah's braids. "You did your hair again the way I like it. Mommy taught you how to do this yourself?"

"Yes," she says, twirling a braid in her hand. "She showed me last week. So now I can do it myself when she's away traveling. It's still wet, but now it will be nice to sleep on and not so messy." She leans against him and flutters her eyelashes. "Will you tell us about the sea dragon, *please,* Daddy?"

"It's not a sea dragon." Donovan bounces on his knees at the foot of her bed. "There's no such thing as a sea dragon. It's a sea SERPENT." He shakes a fist in the air. "SEA SERPENT. GET IT RIGHT."

"Okay, settle down." Peter puts out a hand. "Sit down. Yes, I'll tell the story. So, you remember I encountered the sea serpent in Germany, right? Germany is where I lived with Grandmommy and Granddaddy for a while. There has never been a sea serpent sighting here in Connecticut."

"Say it three times fast — sea serpent sighting, sea serpent sighting, sea serpent sighting," Delilah chants as fast as she can, the words tripping off her tongue.

"I wouldn't want either of you to be afraid to go in the ocean here at home because of sea serpents."

"We're not." Donovan groans. "C'mon, Dad. We already know there's no sea serpents in Connecticut. Everybody knows that."

I can smell baby powder; Delilah likes to shake it on after her bath, and it makes my nose twitch. I sneeze and then gaze up at Peter, ready for the story.

"Okay. Well." Peter folds his arms, and the children grow still. "I encountered the sea serpent when I was swimming out to a dock that was tied up off the beach."

"You were a good swimmer."

"Yes, I was. I loved swimming and spent every summer at the local pool. So when I was seventeen years old, just before we moved back here to the U.S., my parents took me to Ahrenshoop for vacation. We stayed in a beautiful hotel on the water. One morning, I went alone down to the beach very early while everyone was still asleep. And there was a dock far out, maybe a half-mile or so, where I could see a mermaid was stranded. I couldn't believe my eyes! But there she was. Her tail had been injured. Her scales were sparkling in the sun, and there were barnacles on her shoulders, and I thought —"

"Wait, Daddy." Delilah puts a small hand on his arm. "Is this a true story?"

"Well . . ." He shrugs. "It's a *good* story."

Donovan falls onto his back and kicks the wall. The sound makes my ears flatten. "C'mon, Dad. Is this a story, like Santa Claus? Is it pretend?"

Peter's brows knit together, and he pinches his mouth for a moment. "This is a better-than-true story. It's not a story that anyone knows but me. No one else was there."

Delilah gazes up at her father. "What do you mean better-than-true?"

Peter looks tired all of a sudden. "Sometimes, Del, the truth is very dull. It does nothing to enlighten us. And sometimes, it's just unbearable. It makes us sad and wish we had done things differently."

"Yeah." Donovan sighs, sounding older than his years. "I know what you mean."

Delilah is puzzled. She fiddles with the

top of her ear. "The truth can be unbear-able?"

Peter shifts his weight. "Here's the thing. I like to tell the story about how I lost my leg in a way that's entertaining, you see? That's all. This way, it's *my* story. I'm in charge of it. The great thing about telling your own story is that *you* get to decide what hap-pens. You get to tell it any way you want, with monsters or angels or whatever you can think of. Look. When you get older, if you decide that my stories are no longer for you, I'll respect that. But I'm hoping you'll let me tell it my way, at least for a little while longer. To make it exciting. I want you to really enjoy it."

The kids aren't quite sure how to react.

Peter tries again. "Here's the way I look at it. You've got to take charge of your own life. So I lost my leg. That happened, and I can't do anything about it. But I don't have to dwell on the bad stuff. I'd rather give my story a new twist — to think of something amazing and make it mine. It's *my* story, and I'm improving it. Okay?"

Delilah and Donovan look at each other, and seem to make up their minds.

"Yeah, okay. If you want. I still want to hear about the sea dragon, Daddy."

"SEA SERPENT." Donovan's face grows

red. "COME ON. SERPENT. Not a dragon. It was ten feet long. Like a giant snake. Like an eel. Right?"

"Yes." Peter's eyes grow wide with recognition, as if he's seeing it again in his mind's eye. "Yes." He leans to pick me up with a steady hand under my ribs, and pulls me over to hold me to his chest. "If only I'd had a loyal friend like Luna with me, I might still have my leg today. Cats have a sixth sense about danger approaching. Maybe she could've warned me that the serpent was waiting for me."

"Yes, she would have." Delilah reaches out her arms and Peter deposits me in her lap.

But I am not the hero of this story. Peter is. I close my eyes and wait for Peter to continue. I have heard this tale many times.

I can imagine the sparkling deep blue of the sea, the feel of cool spray from the waves hitting Peter's face, the taste of the salt on his lips, and the terror I'd feel if I were him, floundering in the water, unsure of where the sea serpent would strike next. Good thing he had that knife strapped to his waist! Or the serpent might have dragged him down to the watery depths forever.

There's nothing like a good sea serpent tale. Nothing in this world! I snuggle in

70

tight, my wet nose pressed against Delilah's tummy, and enjoy the story.

Hmm. I can't think of anything Peter said to explain why his spirit remains on the earth. The ghost stories he told were mostly tales about spirits haunting houses and scaring people — terrifying and thrilling, but I can't think of how it applies to Peter.

It's the story about losing his leg that has stuck with me the most vividly. Those frightening details. The shock. The surprise. Years later, he still woke up sometimes feeling as if he had two legs, and looked down to find one gone.

I suppose that's the biggest story of his life.

Isn't it?

Bad Advice

Annika

I wake up curled in a tight ball, full of anxiety. I wish Peter were here. If I asked him to spoon me, he would put his arm over my waist and the weight of him against my back would make me feel safe.

Peter had the ability to steady me when I was upset. I think about the first time my parents met his, at his house for dinner. I was stressed out, hoping my parents would be able to impress his mom and dad. Peter held my hand under the table and flashed me that beautiful smile to let me know there was nowhere else he would rather be. He made it easy for me. Honestly, I couldn't wait until dinner was over so we could be alone and relax. We excused ourselves to go up to his bedroom while the parents talked over dessert. Lying on his rug, a pillow propped under his head, he read to me a chapter from one of his favorite books. I closed my eyes to listen to the sound of his voice, and nestled my face into his ear so he would feel my breath on his cheek and know I was listening.

I wish I could hear his voice again now.

Slowly, as I spread out in bed and take a deep breath, my thoughts turn to Sam. That was certainly odd, to find him on my doorstep. Not uncomfortable. Well — I take that back. It was a little uncomfortable for me. The strangest thing is that it didn't seem awkward for Sam at all.

It's odd to see someone after many years have gone by. Those people you knew years ago, back in high school — the jocks, the nerds, the slackers — they're the same, aren't they? And yet, you know they've grown up and changed. They've had experiences you know nothing about and gone through God-knows-how-many life-changing events. And at the same time . . . it's almost as if you can pick up a conversation you started decades ago and keep running with it, and it feels normal.

Sam seemed the same, just older. Warm. Actually happy to see me, which I didn't know would be true. I wish I could have invited him in. But I was afraid we would end up talking about the past, and I'm not ready to do that.

Sam is the first boy I ever loved. For one wonderful yet painful year I was obsessed with him. He was my Romeo, loyal and brave. But I messed everything up. Which is why I avoided him when I saw him in Brown's supermarket.

Sam was with me the night Peter lost his leg. The night I ruined two lives. I somehow, amazingly, managed to salvage something with Peter.

But Sam? I don't know if he forgives me or not.

Luna gets up from where she has camped out at the foot of my bed. I'm not sure why she always insists on plopping down right where my feet are supposed to go. Peter slept on the right side of the bed, and I prefer the left. Despite all the extra room now that Peter's gone, Luna still insists on sleeping on my side of the bed. So I'm forced to curl up in an unnatural way to make room for her. She knows I'm awake now and wants breakfast. She climbs right up on my chest to settle down in a purr, just like she used to with Peter.

Ow. She always places her paws in the most inconvenient places. "Shove off," I tell her, but I'm gentle about picking up each paw and placing it elsewhere. Her purr is incredibly loud. I'm sure her purr has been more therapeutic for me than any medication the doctor could possibly prescribe.

When we get up, I can see that it has started to snow. "Look, Luna." She stands, with her tail held high. I rub my fingers together to entice Luna to jump up onto the loveseat that looks out toward the front of the house from my bedroom. Snow is falling in fat flakes and clumps as big as a quarter; they float down and cling to tree branches. The walkway is perfectly covered in snow. "It looks beautiful."

Luna glances up at me, forlorn. I know she doesn't think it's so great. Now she can't go outside.

Once I'm showered and dressed, Luna curls up in my lap while I read a book. When the kids wake up, I make them breakfast: salty bacon sandwiched between wheat toast. Delilah dips hers in thick maple syrup.

"It's snowing so hard!" Delilah exclaims, sitting on a stool at the kitchen counter and staring out the window. "Snow day. Woohoo!"

"It looks so cool," Donovan chimes in. "Everything is disappearing under the snow." Even he is charmed at the sight of snow pouring down between the trees. Donovan has an eye for beautiful things.

Delilah points her sandwich at me. "Is

Aunt Lisa coming over?"

My older sister, Lisa, is renting the cottage across the street, at the top of a steep hill. When I finally confessed to her that I wasn't coping well with Peter's death and had decided to move back home for a while, she was quick to relocate from New Hampshire and offer help, which I appreciated. Lisa was married for three years when my kids were young, but now she's divorced with no kids of her own. At first, Lisa took a month-to-month lease on an apartment in nearby Beverly. When my older neighbor across the street moved into assisted living a few weeks ago, she took the rental immediately.

"I texted your aunt Lisa. She doesn't have work, but she's going to hold down the fort at home and see how it goes today. Maybe she'll come over when it stops snowing." I put the last of the bacon on a paper towel. "You guys slept late. You must be tired from school."

Donovan clears his throat. "I didn't sleep well."

"Up texting Lexi?" Delilah pokes at his arm with a finger.

He scowls. "No, I mean, yes, but — that wasn't the issue. I wonder if I could have sleep apnea like Dad."

76

I freeze. It never occurred to me that one of the twins might have sleep apnea, as Peter did, unknown to us. But it's highly unlikely, isn't it? I'm sure Donovan is fine.

I immediately shake my head. "No, honey. No, I really doubt it."

"Do you?" He puts down the crust of his sandwich. "You didn't listen to Dad, either, you know that?"

"Sweetheart, I —"

"When Dad said he was tired in the morning, you told him it was because he was working too hard."

"But he was."

"When he asked if his snoring bothered you, you said you didn't hear it because you slept like a rock."

"Again, that's true." I glare at him. I almost get the impression he's rehearsed these lines, like a lawyer putting me on trial. "Have you ever heard the expression hindsight is twenty/twenty?"

Delilah swallows a last bite of bacon, her big eyes darting back and forth between her brother and me.

"In fact," Donovan concludes, folding his arms across his chest, "I looked up sleep apnea on the internet and you missed about a thousand clues. I remember Dad asked you if he should see a doctor because he didn't sleep well. You said the doctor would just give him addictive sleeping pills and he shouldn't bother. You told him to take Advil if he had headaches. And you told him to use fewer blankets if he woke up in a sweat. Seriously, you gave him a lot of bad advice. You're not a doctor."

"She's a doctor of math," Delilah butts in. "Does that count?"

For the love of God. I sigh. What can I say? Donovan is right.

Peter is a man who lost his leg and went right on with his life, never looking back. I thought he was Superman. I thought he could handle absolutely anything. Headaches and snoring weren't enough to concern me.

I didn't know about Peter's sleep apnea. I didn't understand what his symptoms added up to, or that such a thing could be fatal. If I could go back in time, I would.

I'd do a lot of things differently.

I think about it all the time. Maybe I'm not as good a listener as I think I am. What else did I miss? What else did I ignore or misunderstand? What else did Peter try to tell me, only to have me push it aside?

What is wrong with me?

"Okay, you win," I concede. "I killed your father. Are you happy now?"

78

Donovan rolls his eyes. "I'm being serious. Why don't you take responsibility for something you did wrong, for once?" He brings his white plate over to the sink and rinses it off before disappearing upstairs again.

"For once?" I call out after him. "What else did I do wrong?"

I ask this even though I know what else I did wrong. I know why Donovan is still traumatized about Peter's death.

I've tried to bring it up a few times, even though talking about Peter's death hurts me as much as it hurts Donovan. But he refuses to discuss it. Donovan walked away from therapy just as he walks away from me now. Sometimes the shock fades for a while, only to come screaming back when something triggers our memories and we hurt all over again.

Delilah hunches over the counter toward me. "Let him go. He's probably in a bad mood because he doesn't get to see Lexi at school today. Wanna see a photo of her?"

I hesitate. But, of course, I do. "All right."

"Okay, okay, okay," Delilah says, getting excited as I walk over to her. "But do *not* look at Donovan's user name. Don't use this as an excuse to stalk him online."

I balk. "I would never stalk him online.

79

You're the one who offered to show me a photo! Honestly, Del."

"Sorry." She places one hand over the top of her phone, I suppose so I can't see whatever information would allow me to identify Donovan's account. "This is her."

I peer at the photo. I need my reading glasses. She's as I remember: short and cute. "Does she wear that skimpy outfit to school?"

"No, look. She's in her bedroom at home. Can't you tell?"

All I can tell is that she's barely wearing anything. Certainly not a bra. And those might be fake eyelashes. "Donovan took this photo?"

"Noooooo, Mom. No, she took this herself. He just reposted her photo."

Hmm. Terrific. Lexi is pretty — and looks pretty darn proud of it. I guess many kids take photos of themselves these days, but this sort of vanity rubs me the wrong way.

I take a step back. "Is she nice? Is she nice to you?"

Delilah just shrugs, like she can't tell one way or the other. Which I take as a *no.* Or maybe Lexi just hasn't had a chance to get to know Delilah yet. That makes me a little sad, but Del has her own friends.

She watches me. "What's the matter? Why

do you look so worried?"

"I'm not worried." I unfurrow my brow and relax my shoulders. "It's just that Donovan hasn't been in a relationship before. So I don't want him to get hurt."

Especially when he's had such a hard time this year missing his father, I think. But I don't say that out loud. Delilah and I love to talk about Peter, but we have an unspoken rule about keeping our thoughts upbeat and positive.

"Don't worry." She clicks off her phone. "When I see them together at school, she's obviously really into him."

I'd like to ask for a translation of what "really into him" means according to Delilah, but I bite my tongue. I can imagine.

Later, the kids and I put on our winter gear and bring in three more armfuls of wood from the garage. We have days when I wish the garage was attached to the house, but I love the old two-story building — it's as big as a barn — and my parents left it full of enough split wood to last several winters. As we trudge down the walkway, snow is already up to the ankles of our boots.

"Isn't it strange how snow makes everything feel insulated? Almost like it's warm out." Donovan tries to catch snow on his tongue.

"It feels like we're walking in a snow globe." When Delilah exhales, I can see her breath in the air.

I agree with them. The sky isn't dark, like on a rainy day. Rather, it's white. The sun trying to shine through the clouds gives off a weak, smothered glow.

Once the wood is piled up on a mat just inside the front door so we don't track snow down the hallway, I feel tired but also a sense of accomplishment. I light a pine-scented candle and peek in the refrigerator to admire dinner.

"Cod with a little butter, Luna? You're going to help us eat it?"

She blinks at me. That's a yes.

In the late afternoon, I look out the picture window in the front room. A thick layer of snow covers everything. The flakes are smaller, and the wind is beginning to pick up, making the snow swirl. It forms hills like sand dunes as it drifts.

I try standing on tiptoes. The sky is growing dark, and I can't see the street anymore. We're located on one of the several private roads in town, and it's not paved. It's just a winding dirt path through the woods, wide enough for a car.

"Should we be worried, Luna?"

She stares back at me. A sphinx. Hard to read.

I realize this would be a great time to talk to the kids about The President's Academy, because we're not busy. But once again, I chicken out and put it off until tomorrow.

Delilah helps me with dinner by snapping the green beans, setting the table, and pouring the drinks. Donovan arrives at the last minute and slinks into his seat, not contributing to the conversation except for the occasional grunt or shrug.

I've just finished loading the dishwasher when Luna suddenly jumps up onto four paws. I hear it, too, in the distance: a truck engine. The harsh sound of a blade scraping the driveway. The steady beep of a vehicle in reverse.

I'm surprised to find I'm actually excited. "Let's go, Luna!" We both dash down the hall to look out the front window. But there's nothing much to see.

The light post by the driveway doesn't illuminate very far, and the rest of the world is in darkness. I watch headlights flash and sway, shining against the falling snow and the garage. The plow moves slowly, forward and back. At one point, it stops. I hear men yelling against the wind. I suppose they've gotten out to shovel the walkway. Good.

I'm just about to walk away from the window when I see shapes against the white, and it slowly dawns on me that it's two men, up to their knees in snow. Up to their knees! And, inexplicably, they're slowly moving down the walkway toward my front door. Large, hulking figures, all wrapped up like mummies in dark clothes, with just the eyes peeking out.

Even though I know they're coming, I startle when there's a sharp knock. I run to answer, and the wind pushes against the door with such force that I must throw my weight against it to stop it from flying open.

"Annika," croaks Sam, although the two men are dressed in so many layers it's hard to tell them apart at first. "Can we come in for a minute?"

I hesitate, because I'm alone here with the kids and I'm not sure who the man is with Sam. But it's ridiculously cold out there. I can't stand here with the door open another minute. "Of course, come in."

I glance back to see if either of the twins are coming down the stairs to see who's at the door, but neither appears. I imagine them both huddled on Donovan's bed, paging through their father's journal. It makes me shudder, thinking of Donovan looking for more ways I let Peter down — and let him down. If that's the case, Donovan will find what he's looking for. I'd like to get the diary back before he reaches that point.

The men step inside and start to pull off their scarves and gloves. Sam removes his face mask. With every move they make, small pieces of ice scatter like glitter. Luna bats at a chunk of snow with her paw.

Both men are red in the face. Their hands, ears, and cheeks are raw. In contrast, it's toasty in the house because I've got the heat cranked up.

"Thanks, Annie. We have a small problem."

Annie. That's what Sam called me in high school, even though the *A* in Ann-ie is different from the *A* in Ahh-nika.

I look from one to the other. The man to the right of Sam looks like him, with the same thick dark hair and broad shoulders, but he's an inch taller with a more angular face. I can tell he's Danny, Sam's brother, the one I saw in the supermarket. He was three years ahead of us in school.

I wait for Sam to continue, but he doesn't. He looks down, as if baffled by his coat and uncertain how to take it off. I watch his swollen, frozen fingers try to unfasten each snap, a slow process.

85

My curiosity is killing me. "What's the matter?"

He slowly looks up. "It's the truck. The snow is coming down faster than we can keep up with. And we're stuck. The wheels are spinning, but the truck's not moving." When he sees the look on my face, he quickly continues. "It'll be okay, Annie. I don't know what happened. We'll get ourselves out."

Luna bellows a loud *meow!* I don't think she likes all this company, but I ignore her.

Danny unzips his coat with a quick motion. "You ran right into a snow bank because you were cutting at a weird angle. That's when you lost traction." The criticism in his voice confirms for me that he's Sam's older brother. He's got a thicker Boston accent than Sam, which means he probably has lived here in town his whole life. "You've gotta just shovel and let me do the driving. I'm sorry if you're tired of shoveling, buddy, but that's the job."

"Danny," Sam says, raising his voice, "I'm not tired of — Come on. STOP. The way the driveway curves coming down that steep slope? It's not that easy."

"That's why you should've let me drive."

"No, anyone could have made the same mistake. There's no visibility. And I think the driver's side front corner of the truck looks low. I think the tire is going flat."

I bite my lip as I feel my heart starting to race. This situation isn't okay. It's pitch-black outside. A raging storm is enveloping us and sealing us in like in a tomb. I can hear the wind rattling gutters and windows. Their truck is stuck in my driveway, so I can't get my car out? We're all trapped here?

Me and Sam, stuck here together?

When I saw him two days ago, I practically ran out of the supermarket. I don't know how much I can handle all at once.

"Call someone to come help you out. You've got to move that truck."

They just look at me.

"Call someone. To come help you." Do these guys not understand what I'm saying?

Sam looks at me with regret, like he's breaking bad news to a toddler. "I don't think we can. It's late, and the roads are terrible. There's a state of emergency in six counties. All the town plows are busy with the main roads. No other vehicles are allowed out, and I wouldn't want anyone trying to drive up the hill right now anyway."

"We'll get ourselves out. Don't worry. We're pros. We can handle it. We just need a short break. It's freezing out there and the wind chill is wicked bad." The taller man sticks out his hand. "I'm Danny Parsons. We've met before, haven't we? You look kinda familiar. You're Rich's daughter?"

I shake his hand. His skin is freezing cold despite the fact that he had on waterproof gloves. "We met a long time ago. I'm Annika. I remember you from the bus stop."

Sam gestures at me with a hand out and his face lights up, as if he's proudly showing off a new car. "You remember her, for sure. Annika grew up right here, in this house, back in high school. She was in my grade. She's Annika Something-else now," Sam says, raising his eyebrows and glancing at me. "Right? But she used to be Annie Karlsson."

Danny tips his head and looks quizzically at his younger brother for a moment. I can see that something unspoken is communicated between them.

"Ohhh, you're *that* Annika. Karlsson. It's all coming back to me now." He nods in recognition. "Wow. Annie Karlsson. You're *that* girl."

I don't like the sound of this. "Excuse me?"

"Sam's partner in crime. You're a trouble-maker. You got my baby brother in some serious hot water." Danny puts his hands on his hips, looking pleased. "In more ways than one. Ah, yeah, now I remember who you are. The girlfriend. The bad influence, as my dad used to say. I thought your name sounded familiar."

"The bad influence?" I feel my hands clench into fists. "Me?"

Sam immediately steps up. "Wait, no. No. Nothing that happened was her fault. I mean, every time I got in trouble, it was my own fault, believe me —"

"Yes," I jump in, "it wasn't all me. Don't make me out to be some criminal mastermind."

Danny waves at me. "Nah, I'm just kidding around. I'm sure it was all Sam's doing. I seem to remember Sam was the one who got arrested a couple of times, right?"

Sam shrugs, rubbing the back of his neck.

My head starts to hurt. This could be a long night.

"Would it be okay if we get a glass of water?" Sam finally asks.

"I can do better than that. I'll make you some hot coffee. Let me hang up your coats."

I walk past them to slide open the closet door. I catch a glimpse of Peter's silver crutches, which are propped up in the back corner of the closet. Peter's crutches are one of those things I wasn't ready to give away, so they traveled with us to this house. The twins sometimes still take turns trying to walk around the house with them, just for fun. I reach into the closet and touch one of the black handgrips for good luck before turning around to take Danny's winter jacket.

After I get Danny's coat hung up, I grab a hanger and turn to Sam. When he hands me his jacket, it's cold and wet on the outside, but I can feel warmth soaked into the soft fleece lining. I linger with it for a moment, feeling the heaviness of it in my hands. It feels solid. Safe.

Sam watches the way I hesitate. "Can I help you?" he asks so quietly I doubt Danny even hears him.

I nod, and we get the coat onto the hanger together. And it all comes back to me in a rush: *Here we go. Hang on, sweetheart. I've got you.* Words that Sam said to me years ago when I needed him. It startles me, a memory I hadn't thought of in a long time.

I take the coat and stick it in the closet as fast as I can, like it's a hot potato I can no longer stand to touch. "Wipe your wet boots on the mat," I say, distracted, and hurry down the hall to the kitchen.

OCTOBER 1986

ANNIKA

I head down to the kitchen to start the coffee. I'm more of a tea drinker but happen to have a bag of ground hazelnut coffee that Delilah sometimes brews before school. As I fill the pot with water, I think about what Danny just said, because he's right: Sam got in trouble repeatedly senior year of high school, and it was always for my benefit.

I don't like to dwell on my memories of Sam because of how it all ended. But as my mind drifts back, I recognize that there were moments when Sam took my breath away. Days when he revealed how much he loved me, or when I realized that I felt the same way. Those are days that deserve to be remembered.

For example, the first time Sam got arrested, it was for a crime he didn't commit. He turned himself in and confessed, even though he knew I'd done it.

91

The irony is, I didn't commit the crime either.

I snap my gum, loud, and Dana giggles. Dana Mazzanti is my best friend, and we're inseparable. It's 6:45 a.m. and still dark out, but we're fully primped with our hair feathered, lashes coated in black mascara, tight jeans securely buttoned, toes dusted with baby powder, and feet tucked into high-heeled boots. The only exception to my otherwise supercool outfit is my bright blue and yellow pair of mittens. They don't match what I'm wearing, but my grandmother loves to knit winter accessories for me and my sister, Lisa.

Sam sits in the seat across from Dana and I on the bus, headphones on, half asleep as he looks glassy-eyed out the window at the darkness. He's wearing his varsity football jacket and rests his head on one hand until the bus hits a pothole and his head bounces back and hits the seat. He's one of the most popular boys in our grade, but the truth is, he doesn't seem to have many close friends. Sam always sits by himself on the bus.

"We're going to die."

I grip the seat in front of me as best I can with my mittens on. We're in the back of the bus, which is our privilege as seniors, but it's actually the worst place to sit. We feel every bump in the road, and when the bus swerves around a corner, gravity throws us to the side and we crash into each other. There are no seat belts. "This bus driver is a maniac," I continue. "He goes way too fast down Meadows Hill Road. It's criminal."

Our bus driver, Mr. O'Shea, has a strong Scottish accent and a heavy foot on the gas pedal. We always get the sense he's way behind schedule.

Dana nods. "Can you believe that hairpin turn? We're going to go flying off the road one day to our DEATHS." She sits up straighter. She has sleek black hair cut in a bob, and it swings when she turns her head. "What the hell? Let's stage a protest."

"Yeah!" I love this idea. Our favorite history teacher has been talking to us lately about the 1960s and student demonstrations. She's gotten me all fired up. "What if, after school this afternoon, we all just refused to get off the bus at our stops? Then Mr. O'Shea would be forced to take us back to school, and we could march in to the principal's office and demand a change."

"You think kids would really do it?" Dana asks, wrinkling up her nose.

I shrug. "SAM," I call out, leaning into

the aisle.

He slowly turns and pulls off his headphones. "Yeah?"

"You wanna help us with a student protest after school? If you do it, everyone will do it."

He frowns. "I've got football practice every day. Like, every single day, after school. You never noticed that before?" Shaking his head in disgust, he turns away and sticks his headphones back on.

Hmm. I forgot about that. I don't care about football. I've been to a few Friday night games, but only for the bland hot dogs, stale popcorn, and the chance to hang out with Dana. We spend most of each game complaining about how cold and uncomfortable the metal bleachers are under our butts. And we ignore the game, preferring to cheer like crazy for the amusingly terrible marching band.

"Give me a break. He's not going to help." I turn to Dana. "Forget him. He's being an asshole."

"Me Sam. Me play football," she calls over in his direction. "Me big football player." She taps her head. "Cannot think for myself and help the humans."

"Hey." He turns back. "I heard that." He pulls the headphones back off and leans toward us. "What's the problem?"

"Well." I lean over the aisle as if I'm going to whisper and impart a great secret, but I still have to speak loudly to be heard over the noise of the bus. "We want to protest because Mr. O'Shea is a horrible driver. My mom's already called the school to complain twice, but nothing changes. Remember when he stopped on the train tracks that one time?"

Sam looks at me warily. "Yeah."

Dana leans over me, outraged. "We could've been killed!"

He glances at her and then back to me. "But there wasn't a train coming."

"That's not the point." I roll my eyes dramatically. "We could have been. Killed. If a train did come." I get up, cross the aisle, and slide into the seat next to him. "Can you imagine? All the little freshmen, smashed to smithereens? Wouldn't that be sad?"

Something in his face softens once I settle next to him. I make gestures when talking, and he watches the way my hands move around. I assume he's getting my point, even with my big mittens on. At least I know he's amused, because I can see it in his face.

"Okay, okay. Calm down, Karlsson." He squints at me. "So what do I have to do with all this?"

"You have to help protest!" Dana says, leaning toward us and opening her eyes wide. "If you have football after school every day, let's do it tomorrow morning."

"YES!" I point at her with my mitten. "That's even better. When we get to school, we'll refuse to get off the bus. It'll disrupt first period classes. That's perfect." I turn around, back to Sam. "So, you're in?"

He chews on the inside of his mouth a minute. "Sure. Why not?"

"Yay!" I throw my hands in the air in victory.

He laughs in response. Which is rare. Sam is usually too zoned out to talk to us on the way into school in the morning. He reaches into the pocket of his jacket and pulls out a pack of grape gum. "You need more? Or are you already chewing, like, three pieces?"

"I've got plenty, but thanks." I stick out my tongue to show him.

"Gross. Your tongue is bright green."

"Watermelon."

I used to think Sam was being stuck-up when he ignored everyone and didn't chat, like he was too cool for the rest of us. But lately I've started to think that maybe he's just tired from sports and homework and college applications. He's been nice to me,

96

and I would even say we're friends, despite the fact that he clearly thinks I'm weird. Which I kind of am.

The bus jerks to a halt at Mill Street, the last stop before we drive the last mile to school. Mill Street is a nice development of five new houses, all big and beautiful, embedded up on a rocky cliff. Dana immediately runs a hand over her hair and straightens her shirt. Only two kids get on at Mill Street, and one of them is a new senior, Peter Kuhn.

Peter is tall and blond and grabs our attention like a shiny new toy. He's American, but told us he moved here from Germany, where his dad was working for the family business for several years. You can tell Peter is a little different because he wears things that seem slightly out of place in New England, like a headband, or a shirt with bright stripes.

"Ciao, Peter!" Dana calls to him as he comes down the aisle, giving him a friendly wave as if he might not see her — although she's two feet away from him — and he smiles at that.

"Hey, Dana." He turns to look at Sam and I. "Hi, guys. *Was geht ab?*"

We have absolutely no idea what he's said, but Dana and I can't help bursting into giggles. We love it when he speaks German. Peter has gotten used to our inane behavior and just smiles again. I'm sure he thinks we're hopeless. He sits in the row ahead of us and gets out a textbook to study on the way in to school.

When I get off the bus, my sister, Lisa, is waiting for me. She locks my arm in hers so we can walk together. On the bus, she always sits by herself and sleeps her way to school. "Why were you talking to Sam? What are you gals scheming?"

Lisa is older than me, but everyone knows her as my "twin." My parents held her back to repeat third grade when it was clear she was a little overwhelmed by school — in more ways than one. Since we're only eighteen months apart, it meant that Lisa ended up in my grade. Some teachers started referring to us as twins to explain why two sisters were in the same grade, and save Lisa some embarrassment. But it's a small school, and everyone knows the truth.

I wince. Lisa smells like smoke. It permeates all of her clothes. She's wearing bright orange lipstick, a lacy top with a short skirt, and fishnet tights. It hurts my heart a little bit, because on the one hand, I think she looks ridiculous. It's as if she's on her way to audition for a cheesy music video. Who is she kidding?

On the other hand, I'm jealous. Because maybe she really does look cool.

I tell Lisa about our bus protest idea.

"That sounds dumb and completely dorky. But what else is new." She purses her lips. "Did Sam say he'd help you?"

Dana is walking on the other side of me. "Do you want to help out and join us tomorrow?"

"Maybe. I was just wondering if Sam is part of your little plan."

Dana frowns. "So you only care what Sam thinks? You only care if a boy is going to be there?"

Lisa is, in fact, boy crazy. I know she is. She cut out photos of every boy on the football team from last year's yearbook and taped them to the headboard of her bed. Including Sam's photo.

"Sam's cute," she gushes, clutching the strap of her purple backpack. "He has dark eyes."

"His eyes are brown," I correct her. "Just brown."

"His eyes are *dark* and *warm*," she repeats, as if she hasn't heard a word I said. Her hands fly to her hair to adjust her bandana. "You know what I mean."

"Not really," I say, feeling a little uncomfortable with the way she's talking.

Dana and I exchange a look, as we often do when Lisa is acting ridiculous. "Sam's a baby," Dana says. "He's always pouting about something."

Lisa shakes her head. "You have him all wrong." Letting go of me, she reaches in her pocket for her strawberry lip gloss and administers it right over her orange lipstick in one quick swipe. "He doesn't talk too much to you girls because you're annoying and immature. And he's not pouting. He just has a perfect kissy mouth."

Dana scoffs and barks out a short laugh. "Oh, my God. You can have him. He's not my type."

I don't say anything. I don't crush on Sam as hard as some girls do, but I wouldn't exactly say he's *not my type* either. As I mentioned, we've been on friendly terms lately. He even came over to the house a few weeks ago to see if I could give him the math homework problems he forgot to bring home. I'm not sure why, but it was a little embarrassing to have a boy in the house, even if it was just for ten minutes. My dad came out of the den and talked to him about football — ugh. Weird. Humiliating. Thanks, Dad. Meanwhile, Lisa heard Sam's voice and ran from her bedroom to go say hi to him. Which I thought was a little inappropriate.

Okay, so maybe I do have a little crush on Sam. He's so nice. What's not to like? I don't need Lisa telling me how kissy his mouth is, and running downstairs to say hello to him when he comes to visit *me.* I don't want to hear her opinion on him at all. She acts like she's some big expert on boys.

"You care about bus safety, don't you?" Sometimes I wish Lisa would get a little more passionate about the things that I'm excited about. Nothing much fires her up. "You'll join the sit-in, right? And not just because of Sam."

"I guess so. Whatever."

I can tell she doesn't care one way or the other. Which pisses me off.

We stop in front of my locker. We have to split up, because Dana and I have calculus, and Lisa's in algebra. Our teacher lately has been introducing concepts from aeronautical engineering, and it makes everything a little more interesting. I sometimes daydream about being in a spaceship, floating around in space, with only my math skills to get me back to Earth — far away from all of the other humans, in my own peaceful bubble.

"See you later," I say as Lisa walks away. I feel let down. What kind of person doesn't support her own sister? But I can't think about it for too long as I get out my notebook and calculator and head to class.

The next morning, the sit-in starts off with an awkward moment, where Mr. O'Shea pulls up to the school, cranks open the door, and then barks at us to get going. Nobody moves.

Dana and I spread the word on the ride home yesterday, asking all the kids to stay seated when the bus arrived at school. We also made sure to sit in the front row, fearing that the underclassmen might get intimidated and scurry off the bus, leaving the seniors sitting in the back by ourselves.

I buck up my courage and tell Mr. O'Shea that we need to talk to the principal. At first, he balks. But when he sees we're serious, he shuffles off. A teacher comes on and scolds us. When I explain that this is a protest about bus safety, she rolls her eyes. Finally, the vice principal, Mr. Galanes, comes on and threatens us all with detention, which makes my heart start to pound. I'm sure kids are going to bolt. But when I look across the aisle at Sam, though, he's not fazed. He just keeps his headphones on and stares absentmindedly out the window, Walkman in his hand.

"We're staying," I announce calmly, so everyone can hear me. "We'd like to hear what you're going to do to ensure our safety."

Mr. Galanes, who also happens to be an assistant football coach, grunts at Sam. "Hey. What is it you guys want, exactly?"

Sam slides his headphones off and gestures toward me with a thumb. "Ask her. She's in charge."

"Okay, Ms. Karlsson." He narrows his eyes at me. "Name your demands. I don't have all day."

"We want a new bus driver who agrees to go the speed limit, especially on steep hills and dirt roads."

Sam looks up. "How about better music? The music Mr. O'Shea plays is crap."

I gasp. "Nooooo. Sam, I love those pop songs. That music is the only thing that keeps me going in the morning."

"A better driver, that's all we want," Dana interrupts. "Let's get this show on the road."

Mr. Galanes puts his hands on his hips. His tie is crooked and his belt buckle off-center. "All I can do is put in a request at the bus company and see if I can get your driver reassigned to a different route. He'll end up driving too fast with some other kids."

I frown. "But that's not right. That's not good enough. Can't you please just call the bus company and explain the situation? My mom has called them twice to complain, but nothing has changed."

He rolls his tongue in his cheek. "You're ruining my Tuesday, Karlsson."

I shrug. That's exactly the point.

"I'll be back." He pulls the lever to open the door and then glances over at Sam. "Parsons, you realize that student activism died out in the seventies, right? It's 1986. You're not turning into some kind of a hippie freak, are you?"

The ghost of a smile flickers over Sam's face. "Uh, no, sir."

Mr. Galanes nods, satisfied, and steps off the bus.

Lisa, who has been sitting behind us, jumps up and joins Dana and I in the front seat. "I've gotta go."

"Nooo!" Dana reaches across my lap to grab Lisa's arm. "No, Lisa. Please. If you leave, other kids will start to bail. Why do you have to go?"

"Because." She drums her fingers on her knee, impatient. "I've already had lunch detention six times this year for being late to class or cutting out early. You want me to get in trouble for *this*? This is stupid."

I feel anger bubbling up in my chest. She's leaving? "It's not stupid. IT'S IMPORTANT."

I didn't realize she'd had lunch detention six times already. Lisa never said anything to me. I had no idea. Do my parents know about this?

That doesn't even make sense. We take the same bus to school, so how could Lisa possibly ever be late to class?

Where does she go?

"It's okay," Sam says. "She can leave."

I glance over at him. I didn't realize Sam was listening to us. I watch him stand up. Oh, God — he's not going to bail, too, is he?

Sam faces the bus full of kids and clears his throat. "Guys, if you absolutely have to go to class, then go. You'll only be fifteen minutes late. We're staying, though. So if you want to stay with us, we'd appreciate it." He gestures and nods at me. I nod back.

Lisa looks pained after hearing Sam's words. I think she hates to let him down even more than she cares about what I think. Sam is one of the popular kids, and Lisa wastes a lot of energy trying to impress people. I watch her weigh over in her mind what to do.

"Thanks," she finally says to Sam before grabbing her backpack and standing up. "You know, Sam, you don't have to stay and do this."

He shrugs.

Lisa hesitates, taking one last look back at me, and then hurries off.

Slowly, one by one, half the kids get up and exit the bus. A bunch of them stop and tell Sam it was a good idea, even though they have to go. As if it was all Sam's idea! But I don't mind him getting the credit. No one would be staying at all if he weren't here. Sam smiles and talks to each one. I'm impressed. Seriously, he can be friendly when he wants to be.

I look around. There are only about a dozen students left. Ugh.

But I'm happy to say Peter is still here, sitting right behind Sam. When he sees me looking at him, he closes his science textbook.

"Peter, do you need to go to class? I feel bad if you're missing something." I say this despite the fact that I want him to stay, of course.

He raises an eyebrow. "I'm not going anywhere. Don't worry."

"Okay, good."

I feel like I should say something else, but I'm not sure what. He and I stare at each other a moment too long. It's almost like a game of chicken, to see who is going to break eye contact first. His mouth slowly begins to break into a smile. I can't take it anymore and turn back quick.

I sigh and then bounce over to sit with Sam. "Well, this protest is going nowhere fast. But thanks for hanging in there with us." I fold my arms in a huff. "I can't believe Lisa left! She's so lame. To make it sound exciting, I told her we could chant slogans and spray-paint peace signs on the school. But clearly this is too boring for her."

He smirks. "If you gave Lisa a can of spray paint, I doubt a peace sign would be her first choice."

I laugh. "You're right."

"But, look. You're trying. I give you credit for that." Sam looks tired, his face pale.

"What's the matter? You look like you didn't get much sleep last night."

He rubs a thumb over his mouth. "My dad's in the hospital. He had surgery. He has cancer."

Wow. That's alarming. "Oh, my gosh, Sam. Really? Your dad seems too young for that." I don't actually know anyone with cancer. I guess I'm lucky, since everyone in my family is healthy.

"Anyone can get cancer."

"So why are you here, then? Shouldn't you be at home?"

He blinks, and for a moment he's somewhere else, far away. "Nah, there's nothing I can do. My mom's at the hospital with him, and she told me to go to school. The doctor said he'll be okay."

I can only hope that's true, for Sam's sake. "I'm sorry," I whisper.

The bus is getting humid, as it sits baking in the autumn sun. I start to feel like I'm overdressed and wonder if I should pull off my mittens. But I'm also heating up a bit from the way Sam is looking at me, his face close to mine as we're side by side on the bus seat. I suddenly decide that I was right to assume that Sam isn't being snobby when he's staring out the window. Rather, he's been preoccupied. He seems sad, actually. And when he gazes at me, I have to admit Lisa was right about something.

His eyes are dark and warm. Yup. Check that box.

I lean up against him, putting my head down on his shoulder. "Sam." Sometimes I don't know what to say to people.

He rests his head on top of mine. "Annie," he sighs. He always says *Annie* like that, as if he wants to say something more but can only get out my name.

However, today he does say more. He speaks quietly, so only I can hear it.

"I can't believe I'm missing calculus. You're really irritating." But the way he says it, it sounds like he means the opposite.

I laugh again, this time a sharp outburst that bubbles up from my lungs. Dana looks over, like, *what?* But I just smile. I shut my eyes and stay where I am, my head leaning on Sam's shoulder.

Maybe it's just my imagination, but I think I feel Sam tip his face toward mine just a bit, and I swear his mouth is just an inch from my temple and I can feel his breath on my skin, and it's almost like he might kiss me on the forehead. But of course, he doesn't. It's just a weird thought that I have, probably wishful thinking. The idea of a boy kissing me is something I think about a lot, but if it happened in real life, I'm sure it would be too much for me to handle. I'd probably explode and evaporate into thin air.

After ten more minutes, where I almost fall asleep because it's getting hot on the bus and I'm cuddled comfortably up against Sam, the door squeaks open. The VP comes jogging up the two steps to address us. I sit up straight.

Mr. Galanes straightens his jacket. "Look, Annika. They'll talk to your driver about the speed limit and have a supervisor ride along for the rest of the week. That's all I can do. I tried." He clears his throat, then speaks a little louder. "For whoever is left on the bus right now: I'll see all of you in lunch detention today."

Everyone groans.

"Okay, Mr. Galanes." It's not exactly a big win, but we got at least one concession. One little something we can brag about. I turn to Dana. "Sound good?"

She hesitates just a moment and then nods, satisfied. "Yeah, let's go."

I stand up and look at Sam. "Thanks."

"Sure." He stares back, and it's hard for me to know what he's thinking.

"I hope you're not sorry you got detention for such a small victory. Maybe you should've gone to class."

"Nah, I would never abandon you, Karlsson. You're way too cute."

I feel my face get hot, and hurry off the bus. No one ever said anything like that to me before.

It's only when we're in the hallway that Dana says, "I cannot believe your sister didn't stay."

She's right. Lisa wasn't there for me. "I know."

I don't know why it seems like Lisa and I are growing apart, but clearly, we are. I thought sisters were supposed to be close — and stay close. Read each other's minds. Know each other's thoughts. Feel what's in each other's hearts. So . . . why aren't we like that?

Is something wrong with us?

By second period there's some kind of strange energy going on around the school, and the hallways are buzzing with kids moving and talking. Dana and I follow the crowd to the gym and gasp when we enter.

Someone has spray-painted BUS SAFETY SAVES LIVES in blue on the cement brick wall, behind one of the basketball nets. Dana and I burst out laughing because we're both absolutely shocked.

"Who in the world would do that?" Dana has to pat her chest as she chokes on her own laughter. She doubles over and puts her hands on her knees.

"I don't know!" I'm stupefied. I think it's hilarious. Hilariously stupid. I mean, the bus sit-in worked, and now it's over, so what's the point of . . . ?

Oh. And suddenly, I know who did it.

That's when I see Mrs. Evans, the gym teacher, talking to Sam. She's shaking her head, hands on her hips. She's shorter and squatter than Sam is, with big, round glasses, and she looks genuinely hurt and disappointed as she gazes up at him.

I'm confused. When Sam notices me watching him, he comes jogging over.

"Hey," he says, "I told her it was me, so you won't get in trouble. Worst-case scenario, I can't play in the game on Friday night. But I'm exhausted anyway. I don't mind missing one game."

"Worst-case scenario . . . ?" I'm dumbfounded. "Sam, you know it wasn't me who spray-painted this, right? It was probably Lisa." I look around to confirm that my sister is nowhere in sight. "No, it was *definitely* Lisa."

He freezes, mouth partly open. "Really?" For the first time, worry flickers over his face, but then his mouth sets in a grim line. "Whatever. It's fine. At least she was trying to help us out, right? You wanted her to help, and she did. It's actually kind of badass. She did this first period? She could've been caught so easily." He looks back to admire my sister's work on the wall.

I smack his arm. "But I was kidding! I would never spray paint the school. I didn't want anyone to do that."

Two police officers walk into the gym. They approach Mrs. Evans, and she points them in the direction of Sam.

I can see the fear now in Sam's face as he realizes that missing a football game might not actually be the worst of it. I reach out and grab his elbow, and when he turns toward me I throw both arms around him. "Sam," I beg. "Please don't get in trouble for this. Just tell them Lisa did it. Or at least admit it wasn't you. I'll feel horrible if anything bad happens to you."

When I pull away, the worry has melted from Sam's face. His smile is totally sweet and mushy. I don't know how else to describe it. "No way, Karlsson," he says, crinkling up his nose. "I'm not ratting out your sister. No chance. Too late now. You wanted a protest, and you got one. Be happy."

I try to smile. He stands up straighter as the two police officers approach. Be happy? I'm mortified.

"Take it easy," he goes on, looking me over. "Nothing bad is gonna happen to me. Seriously. It was worth it just to see you get so worked up. You never hugged me like *that* before."

Dana and I stand there as Sam leaves the

gym with the cops. I look over the graffiti again. I suppose it can just be painted over. It's not the end of the world.

"What just happened?" Dana whispers to me.

"I'm not sure." I'm still wondering how to wash off or cover the spray paint when I feel her grab my arm.

"He really likes you," she says, in wonder. "Sam Parsons. Huh. I didn't realize he felt that way about you."

And once I stop to think about it, and remember everything that's happened this morning, I realize she might be right.

ACHES, PAINS, OR TELLTALE SIGNS

LUNA

My woman seems to have no choice but to invite Sam and Danny to come in and warm up a bit. They're like werewolves — grungy, disheveled, and unshaven. Disgusting!

Their only saving grace is that they smell fresh, like snow.

Annika has retreated to the kitchen, and I hear the sputtering of the coffeemaker before long. I find it odd that these men are working to remove snow that is falling from the sky. What a strange job.

"We'll be right there," Sam calls out.

Danny puts a hand on Sam's arm to hold him there, pinching him at the elbow. He turns to his little brother, speaking quietly.

"You know, this would be the perfect time to deal with the house. It's ideal. Conditions out there are bad. When's the last time you saw it this bad?"

Sam stares down at his boots. Snow on

the tile has already started to melt into rivulets. "It's been a while." He wipes a hand over his forehead, and I can see he's sweating; a few strands of his hair are wet.

"It's a total whiteout. You know the house is *right there,* next door," Danny continues, with a toss of his head. "Across the creek. We're close. We're so close I can almost see it through the trees."

Sam closes his eyes for a moment. "Danny, you've got to drop it, okay? Just let it go."

"Listen, it'll be fine. Thanks to this snow, it's gonna be a piece of cake. No one's outside. No one's on the road. I'll never get a chance like this again." Danny wipes his bottom lip with his thumb. I notice he has a slight gap between his two front teeth. "It's a great plan, a stroke of genius."

Sam winces. "It's not a *stroke of genius.* It's a stupid thought that popped out of your mouth after you had one too many at the bar last week. I wish you'd never thought of it."

"Nah, it's inspired. It's going to totally put an end to our suffering. And Dad's suffering, too. I have to do it. We need to get things in order."

"Yeah, but —"

"Listen. Do you want Mom and Dad to lose their house?" He pauses, putting his

116

hands on his hips. "And where would you and Brianna go, Sam? You're living there, too."

"I know." Sam hangs his head. "No, of course I don't want them to lose the house."

"Me neither." Danny scratches the back of his head. "So let's see what happens with the storm and I'll figure out the best time to do it."

Sam takes in a sharp inhale, as if he's been holding his breath. "I don't know, Danny. It's just that . . ." He takes a quick glance at his brother and then ducks his head. "But — all right. I mean, maybe it could work. Let me think about it some more."

"Don't think for too long."

Sam stomps his boots to shake the last crystals of snow from the laces.

Hmmm. I'm not sure what to make of this conversation. My whiskers vibrate in warning.

I have no idea what these men are scheming, but it doesn't sound good. They want to "deal with" the house across the creek? I know that house. It's brand-new. No one lives there.

"You know . . ." Danny looks around. "I don't see evidence of a husband, do you? You said Annika was living here now, right? Do you think she's back home because she's

117

getting divorced?"

Sam's face opens up at the mention of Annika's name, and he glances down the hall toward the kitchen. "I don't know. She didn't say anything about —"

We all turn to the sound of footsteps. The stairs wrap around with a sharp turn in the middle, so we don't see Delilah until she is halfway down the stairs. She's wearing flannel pajama pants and an oversized shirt with numbers on it. "Oh," she says, freezing. "I thought I heard people."

Sam stares at her, mouth open.

"Hi there," Danny gives her a polite smile. "We know your mom. I'm Danny Parsons, and this is Sam. We're just taking a little break from clearing the snow."

It seems as if the sight of Delilah has taken Sam's breath away, because it takes him a moment to speak. "Annika is your mother?"

Delilah nods.

"You — you look like her. When she was younger."

"Do I?" Delilah looks them over again, her eyes wide and curious, thick dark hair hanging over one shoulder. "Yeah, people have told me that before. Okay, well, have a good break. I'm Delilah, by the way. Bye." She disappears back up the stairs.

Sam swallows, watching the stairs long

after Delilah has gone.

Danny shoves Sam's arm. "Go on, buddy. Go get something hot to drink. I'll be right there."

Sam nods and heads down the hall, toward the rich scent of coffee brewing. I scamper out of his way, because not everyone looks down before walking, and these men may not be used to stepping over a cat. Danny waits until Sam is out of sight, then takes out his phone and stabs it with his finger.

"Dad. What'd ya need?" Danny stares absentmindedly out the window. "No. Don't say yes to anyone in Gloucester. Do *not* do that. Dad —" He freezes. "No, we don't have time to go over there tonight. We might not even make it to Magnolia until tomorrow." His mouth stays open as he listens. "Because we're busy here. There's a shit ton of snow; the town plows aren't keeping up, and it's taking time. Trung's taking care of Beverly Farms and a couple of —" He drags a hand over his eyes. "Did you hear what I just said? Christ. He can't go in the opposite direction. Do not take on any more customers. Please, Dad, we can't really —" He hangs his head, defeated. "I know. Yeah. Yes. Okay. All right. Dad, stop. Please. I'm hanging up now."

He uses his thumb to press the side of the

phone gently and slips it back into his pants pocket. Hands on his hips, he takes in a deep breath and then lets it out.

I follow Danny when he joins the others in the kitchen, and settle down on the rug under our small kitchen table. This home is full of lovely, plush rugs. Some are soft and thick. Others are fun and stringy. There is one braided with ropes, and I love to feel the lumpy texture as I lay across it.

And then, suddenly, I see Peter again.

He gets more vivid in my mind's eye as I stare at the wall. I can see the slope of his nose and the outline of his body. He's leaning against the floral wallpaper. I wonder how he feels about these men being here in the kitchen. I stare, drinking in the sight of him.

The worst part about Peter's death is how unexpected it was. The day he died, Peter was healthy and vibrant. He swam in the ocean. He ate a sandwich at lunch. He argued with Donovan and asked him to take responsibility for doing more around the house. It was a totally normal day.

Yet I can usually sense death coming for humans. It's true. I have witnessed several deaths.

My first owners were elderly. When my man died, and then my woman perished the next year, I knew it was coming. For days. Weeks, even. I could smell death. I could sense the organs slowing down. I could see the glow of life start to diminish and then quietly go out.

Yet with Peter, I had no clue it was coming. Death descended all at once, like a blanket thrown over his body in a fit of anger.

Peter's ghost flickers. He seems calm. No moaning, no rattling chains, no evil laughter.

How very disappointing. Ghosts in stories usually do *something* dramatic. Maybe he's waiting for the right time to move a lamp, or a pillow, to let Annika know he's here.

Peter nods at me. *You're doing a good job comforting Annika.*

Am I? I'm trying my best! Why are you here again?

He looks over at my woman. *I'm here when Annika thinks about me.*

Oh! It seems that no one can see you but me.

He nods and shrugs. *I know you've heard me tell ghost stories, but most humans don't really believe in ghosts. Even if they sensed a ghost, they'd come up with an excuse not to see it.*

I blink at him. Interesting!

Annika hands each of the men a striped mug. They thank her and huddle over their steaming cups as if before a roaring fire. As the color evens out on their faces, I study the two brothers. Danny has already taken off his coat; he now removes a down vest and then a fleece, tossing them on the kitchen counter until he has stripped down to a thermal shirt. Sam, on the other hand, keeps on his black hooded sweatshirt.

The brothers resemble each other greatly, yet I can see the differences. Danny is a little taller, and more feline around his cheekbones and eyes. I've decided that Danny must be the clever one, as anyone with cat-like features would naturally have to be. Sam, on the other hand, seems more like a dog. Eager to please, glancing at his big brother from time to time to see if he needs anything.

Annika takes a red box of crackers out of a cabinet. She finds a wedge of cheese in the refrigerator and places it on a cutting board with a knife. The men stare at the food but don't reach for it, as if they're not sure if it's for them or not. Annika slices off a piece of cheese and hands it to Sam, who thanks her as a drop of sweat runs down his cheek and he wipes it away.

"You both work for your dad?"

"Yeah," Danny says, reaching for a cracker. "I've worked for him for years. Sam has only been with us for six months. We've also got two more employees, Trung and Hien. They've been with us a long time. They're in the other truck."

Annika taps her lips with one finger. "Wait — you have another truck?" She pauses. "They can't come help you out?"

Danny shakes his head. "They're taking care of our customers over in Beverly Farms. I don't want them to waste time driving all the way over here, and I don't know if they could get up the hill anyway. I don't want them to get stuck, too. Better for them to keep moving for those customers."

"I see."

There's a pause where we listen to the twins upstairs, laughing about something. Annika hands Sam another piece of cheese on a round cracker.

"So." Danny puts his mug down, runs a hand through his hair, and sticks his hands in his jeans pockets. "This is weird, right? You and Sam were high school sweethearts, and you haven't seen each other all this time?"

Sam gives his older brother a warning

look. But Danny looks at Annika, waiting for an answer. She seems caught off guard, unsure of what to say.

"She probably went out with me because she felt sorry for me," Sam jumps in. "She was one of the smart kids. Too smart for me."

"I got good grades," Annika says in a soft voice. "But I didn't always act very smart." She grips her mug tight and stares down at the kitchen counter.

I've never heard my woman speak badly about herself before. These men seem to be affecting her in a strange way.

Danny clears his throat. "And you have a twin sister, right?"

My ears twitch. I realize the man must be talking about Lisa.

"Yes, Lisa. Well — we're not actually twins. We were in the same grade, though, because my parents held her back." Annika takes a sip of her coffee and holds it to her chest with both hands. "Did Sam mention her to you?"

"Yeah, for sure! He said she was a pain in the ass. He told me this one time . . ."

His voice trails off when he sees the look on Sam's face.

The room gets quiet for a moment. "She was the one we were driving home on prom night," Sam finally says.

"Ah, right," Danny says, leaning back against the stove. "Oh — yeah, that's right. It's all coming back to me now. The car crash. Wow, that was ages ago. I remember now. I was at college — failing at college, I should say — and Mom phoned me, crying. She was really broken up. That was a horrible way to end senior year, right? We were all so shocked when that happened."

"Yes." Annika's shoulders slump. "It was my fault. I insisted we take Lisa home. Even though we were all drunk."

Sam's eyes widen before they narrow. He looks Annika up and down, head to toe, his mouth slightly open.

"That's not — don't say that," Sam says, all in a rush. He starts to reach for her elbow, but then seems to think better of it and pulls his hand back. "It wasn't your fault. Maybe we were all to blame. But especially Henry McKean, right?" Sam watches her. When she doesn't look up, he leans closer. "Henry's the one who ran into us. I wish you and I hadn't been fighting, but . . ."

Annika shifts her weight from one leg to the other. "No, it was my fault, Sam, and I'm so sorry —"

"Please don't say that. I don't want you to

think that."

Danny frowns. "Annika. You can't blame yourself. Sam was the one who chose to get behind the wheel when you'd all been drinking. Now, I love Sam, and I could've easily made the same mistake at that age, but —"

"Let's not talk about it now," Sam interrupts. "We don't need to talk about it. We can't go back and change anything."

I lift my head. There! A flickering in the corner, by the sliding glass door. Peter is moving closer. He's listening to this conversation.

Danny clears his throat. "Sorry. I didn't mean to bring up a sore point." He pushes off from the stove to move toward the refrigerator and swings open the door. He makes a big show of looking over the contents. "Hmm. Are you having a party? Is this why you're all dressed up?"

"A party?"

He holds up a chilled dark green bottle. "Yeah. Is that why you're in a skirt and heels? Because I don't think anyone's coming. You canceled, right?"

She shakes her head. "No, there's no party."

"Oh, I see." He turns back to the fridge, and his eyes dart back and forth. "Actually, no. I don't see. Is all this wine for you, then? You went down the packy and stocked up before the blizzard?" He bites his bottom lip. "Don't worry about it. I get it. You like your wine."

Annika glances at Sam. He sighs.

"Danny, knock it off. Quit snooping around."

"It's okay," Annika says with a wave. "No, I actually don't drink. My parents pick up wine from vineyards around New England and left these bottles here when they moved to Maine." She walks up to him and snatches the bottle out of his hand, placing it on the counter.

"You don't drink?" Sam asks.

"Rarely. Once in a great while."

"And yet your parents left you all this good wine?" Danny asks, fascinated.

"Yes, they were afraid the bottles would break if they tried to move them."

There is another silence as Danny takes a quick, furtive glance at his brother.

Honestly, these men are so slow! They don't seem to understand my woman. But she is speaking perfectly plain English.

"Hmmm." Danny strokes his chin with one hand. "I think I might be able to help you out with this situation. I could assist you in clearing out a shelf or two."

Sam's mouth twitches. "Dan. Go easy. We've got a long night ahead of us."

Everyone freezes when a strong gust of wind slams into the house with a howl. The lights flicker.

That's not good. My fur stands on end.

Annika shivers. "It's getting bad out there. Did you feel the house shake?"

Ever since the sun set, the wind has been getting more violent. Every so often it careens into the front window with enough force to make the house rattle and moan in protest.

"It'll be okay," Sam says, stepping closer to my woman, "don't worry." He looks up at the pendant lamp over the sink, which sways slightly. "I hope the power holds."

"Yep." Danny scratches under his chin. "It's bad. We gotta get back out there and dig out the truck. But first." He turns to Annika and gestures toward the wine bottle. "Since you have all this wine . . . a shot of this would warm us up better than the coffee. What do you say?"

She chews her bottom lip for a moment, staring at him. Finally, she nods. "Okay. Fine with me. I'm not going to drink it." When she turns to search through a drawer, Danny rubs his hands together with satisfaction.

It seems Danny is the type of human who can sway others in order to get what he wants. When he notices me looking at him, I decide to get up and say hello. Danny bends down to greet me, so I rub my cheek against the back of his hand. "Hey, girl," he says to me. "Is this a girl?"

"Yes, that's Luna," my woman calls out.

"That's a great name for a cat," Sam says, looking at me for the first time.

"She's named after Luna Lovegood. You know, from *Harry Potter*."

The corner of Sam's mouth twitches up into a smile. "You're still a science fiction fan, I see."

She turns to face him. "Harry Potter is not science fiction, Sam. It's about magic. That's different."

"If you say so."

I push my face against Danny's hand again because he's stopped paying attention to me. *Hey, down here!*

Danny turns his head to admire me, and I blink at him. "This is a pretty cat. But she's almost cross-eyed. Where'd you get her, the pound?"

"The pound? Like, the dog pound? It's called an animal shelter. And yes, that's exactly where she's from."

Danny chuckles and runs his hand down

my back. And that's when I sense it.

I lock eyes with him. Up close, his green eyes are spectacular. But. However. There's something very . . .

Oh.

Oh, dear.

This is not good. Not good at all.

Danny smiles, not a care in the world. But to me, it's as if he's now encased in a fog. Here is the thing that strikes me: He shimmers with illness.

He is sick. Under severe stress. Something is wrong.

I *meow!* If I can get him to pick me up, maybe I can listen to his heart properly through his chest. And that will let me know if he's okay.

"C'mere, funny face." He reaches out to pick me up with two hands so he can hold me while he watches Annika twist a corkscrew into the top of the bottle. He tucks my tail under and curls me against his chest. "You're a cutie." I close my eyes while he rubs the top of my head, between the ears.

I listen. And feel for it. I can sense his heartbeat through the waffle texture of his thermal shirt. The muffled beat.

Thuh-*thump.* Thuh-*thump.* Thuh-*thump.*

Everything sounds okay. Yet . . .

My nose twitches.

I feel dizzy. It's not his heart that's the problem. But I can smell sickness. Something deep in his body is not right.

I bury my head in the cloth of Danny's shirt. This is awful. What in the world is wrong with him?

What if he dies suddenly, like Peter did? Oh! The heartache is too much.

Danny lowers me gently onto the floor so he can take a wineglass from my woman, and I begin pacing. Suddenly the kitchen doesn't feel right to me anymore. I'm agitated and overheated.

I trot away from the humans and slink under a chair. And then I feel it — Peter crouching down next to me. Just remembering he's here helps me calm down considerably.

I know you feel guilty, Luna. But my death isn't your fault.

I was there, Peter. I could have done more. I could have tried to save you. At least Donovan tried, once he found you.

He shakes his head. *No, it's not anyone's fault. It's just something that happened.*

But I should have —

His hand moves down my back, and while I cannot feel his touch, my heartbeat slows. *Luna. You can't cling to guilt the rest of your life. Life is too short for that. Believe me, I should know.*

I peer up at him, wide-eyed. This is all good to hear. But I'm still sorry.

Danny tries to get the others to have wine with him, but they turn him down. "Cheers," he says anyway, lifting the glass before taking a big drink.

"It's nice you guys work together now." Annika looks at Sam. "Last I heard, you went out to UCLA to get an engineering degree."

"Oh, yeah. Well." Sam looks stricken, and the color drains from his face. "I did get that degree. I did. Took me five years. But . . . I got a job in a corporate office, and it wasn't a lot of fun. I was bored and couldn't see myself there long-term. California didn't suit me anyway. So I came back east and started working in the public works department for the town of Newton, which I did for years. But then my dad called and said he needed me to move home to help out." He pauses. "It's not exactly what I imagined for myself back in high school. I mean, it's not really —"

"That's nice, Sam. I'm sure you guys have a great time together. I bet it's fun to be here and work with your family."

He relaxes and smiles. "I guess so. I mean, being back home isn't the worst thing in the world, right?"

Annika beams back at him. It's the first genuine, relaxed smile I've seen her give since the men arrived. "You know what? I'm glad you're here," she says. "I never would have imagined you here in my kitchen in the middle of this snowstorm." She pokes Sam's arm for emphasis. "You're the first person I've run into from high school since moving here. I don't think many of our classmates are left."

"There's a couple. Maybe four or five in town. I can help you connect with a few people, if you want." Sam nudges her with an elbow. He's standing very close to my woman, and — now, this is interesting — she hasn't moved away. "But I'm glad you ran into me first."

Danny watches Sam, an eyebrow raised. When Sam catches his brother staring at him, he adopts a neutral look on his face and slides a few inches away from Annika.

"Maybe we should get back out there, before we get too comfortable in here," Danny suggests gently.

Out? Must they go back out now? I'm worried about Danny. I don't think he should be going back out into the howling bitter wind and snow.

"One more for the road." Danny refills

133

and drinks fast. Sam frowns, but doesn't say a word.

I come out from under the chair and *meow!* But the men start back down the hallway toward the front door. They pull on their coats and begin to bundle up with scarves and hats.

I follow them and *HOWL. Hey! It's too cold!* This is ridiculous. These men shouldn't go out there in this severe weather. Danny is sick, and he seems to have no idea. He should be home, in bed, getting proper care and taking pills, like Annika does when she doesn't feel well. I wonder how it's possible Danny doesn't know his body is damaged. Doesn't he feel it? Aren't there always aches, pains, or telltale signs that let humans know they're sick?

YEOW!

"Luna!" Annika scolds me. "Shhh. They have work to do." She turns toward the men. "Sorry. She's very loud sometimes."

Umm . . . yes, I am. I have something to say!

When Sam yanks open the door, I scamper away. I don't want that cold air biting at my nose and delicate whiskers. I sprint to the front window and perch myself on the windowsill so I can look out. I can hardly see anything. Snow batters the glass and has started to pile up, blocking my view.

Eventually, I see lights flashing. I hear the low grumble of an engine and the sound of men's voices yelling into the wind in the distance.

The house itself is quiet once the men are gone, other than the sound of the twins upstairs. When I touch my nose to the glass, the window is freezing. I'm happy to be inside.

A while later, the red front door swings open, hard. I watch from the couch. Sam lumbers in, wrapped in layers and coated in chunks of snow.

"Everything okay?" Annika strides down the hall from the kitchen.

"Annie, does Rich keep any sand or salt in the garage? We ran out."

Annika rubs her hands together. "I have no idea. I'm sorry." She pauses. "You can call me Annika now. I don't really go by Annie anymore."

Sam stops short. "Oh. Sure. Sorry." Delilah's voice carries down the stairs as she talks to Donovan about something with enthusiasm. "Do you think we could get a bucket of water? Lukewarm? The handle on the truck is frozen."

I feel bad. Sam is making a lot of requests.

135

Annika likes things quiet, not chaotic. I don't appreciate Sam stressing her out.

But after I take another glance at Sam's face, my heart softens. After all, his older brother is ill. And from the way Sam looks at my woman, I can see he needs her help. He's covered in ice, like a snowman.

"Of course." Her heels click on the tile as she walks down to the kitchen. "I'm sorry this has turned into such an ordeal," she calls over her shoulder.

Hopefully the men will get their truck going and be on their way shortly. But I know in my heart that this storm is a long way from over.

PRONE TO EXAGGERATION

ANNIKA

I can't believe Sam Parsons is standing on my front mat, melting snow dripping from his boots and gloves.

He yells to me, "Do you need anything? Milk or bread? If we get the truck going, I can bring you whatever you need tomorrow."

I glance down at Luna, who sits at my feet by the kitchen sink. She watches me warily. I understand how put out she must feel. We don't usually have strangers in the house.

"No, thanks, I think we're okay," I shout, so Sam can hear me. I roll up my sleeves, locate a bucket under the sink, and fill it.

I make my way back toward the front door, where Sam is looking down into his phone. It gives me a moment to study him.

Sam has taken off his hat and face mask. When he was in high school, he had a mop of brown hair, a little too long. It's now shorter, and I can see more of his face. I always thought he was good looking. It's hard to be popular in high school without being attractive in some way, isn't that true? Objectively speaking, he's fine to look at. Yet it took me a while to fall in love with him. When you've known a boy since kindergarten, he seldom becomes appealing to you personally, I suppose because you know all of his quirks and faults. I could see why some girls thought he was cute; but at the same time, I couldn't see it — not at first, anyway — because my history with him got in the way.

Oh, for the love of God. Why am I thinking about this now? Sam is older, that's the truth. He's the same person, with more years on him. There's some gray in his hair, there are wrinkles around his eyes, and I'm sure he has a wife and five kids and that's that.

When he sees me coming, waddling as I try to carry the heavy bucket with two hands, Sam puts the phone back in his pocket and starts to pull his gloves on. "Thanks." He steps up to take the bucket from me. "I've gotta get back out there. Danny is going to give me hell if I spend too much time in here warming up with you."

I glance out the front window and see the truck headlights in the distance. But I'm not sure the headlights have actually moved since the last time I checked. "How's it going with the truck?"

He shakes his head. "Not great." Sam shifts the bucket from one hand to the other and puts it down at his feet. "Look, Annika. While we have a minute, I just want to say — I'm sorry. For the way things went on prom night. I was stupid. And what I said before still stands. We don't have to talk about it. But I just want you to know I missed you so much after I left. I had regrets. But it was a long time ago. I'm just really sorry."

As he stares at me, looking forlorn, my heart loosens up a bit. And then it starts to open, my protective layers peeling back.

I loved Sam so much when we were together that it's hard to look at him now and not feel something. He's standing on the front mat in the same spot where he once hugged me good night and called me sweetheart for the first time so many years ago.

"Sam. You're right — it was a long time ago. Everything's fine. I don't want you to worry about it."

I have a sudden memory of getting frustrated with Sam in high school sometimes.

139

But that's what happens when the stakes are high and you really care for a person, isn't it? You get stressed out when things aren't going perfectly.

"Is Lisa doing okay? I mean, did everything turn out all right with her?"

"She's fine. She was living in New Hampshire, but when we moved here this summer, she rented the house across the street. I'm sure you'll see her around town soon, if you haven't already." I pull at a strand of my hair, anxiety gripping my stomach.

"Are you guys getting along these days?"

"Sure," I say, although I don't know how convincing I sound. "Honestly, we had a falling out for many years. But I'm trying to reconnect and be a better person now. A better sister."

"You always were a good sister. And I get it. I'm the same way. I'm always trying to be a better person. I feel like . . ."

Sam's mouth opens, but he doesn't go on. It makes me want to rush over to him. I want to make him feel better and smooth things over, just as I always did. With Sam, I always had the sensation of wanting to run to him, to chase after him, even when he was standing right in front of me.

"Never mind." He nods at me. "I'm really happy to see you."

"I'm happy to see you, too."

He smiles. His eyes are still dark and warm, just as they were in high school.

There's a noise behind me, and I turn. It's Donovan, coming down the stairs. I can see he's not ready for bed yet, as he's still wearing jeans and a sweater. "Hey," he says cautiously to Sam.

"Hi." Sam's eyes light up. "I'm Sam." He turns to me. "Your son?"

Donovan and I both nod. I fight off the urge to put my arm around Donovan when he stands right beside me, shoulder to shoulder. I don't know if Donovan would find that insulting, like I'm trying to protect him from something. Which is silly, because he's taller and bigger than me.

"I heard you guys talking." Donovan's face is calm, but I know there's discontent simmering right below the surface.

Delilah comes running down the stairs next. She nearly runs into her brother. "Hi! Again." Delilah looks back up at Sam. "So, this is Donovan. We're twins. Even though we don't look alike. So you're Sam? Like, Sam from high school?"

I study her. She's breathless with excitement.

I never mentioned that I knew a Sam in high school to her. Did I?

141

What are these two up to?

"Yeah, that's me." Sam smiles at her. "Sam from high school. And the neighborhood. And the school bus. I lived just two blocks from here."

"So." Delilah holds her hands behind her back. "You were Mom's *boyfriend*?" She puts so much emphasis on this last word that it sounds like something shocking or illegal.

Sam is caught off guard. "Uhh . . ."

He glances at me. I shrug.

"Yes, I was her boyfriend."

"Was it serious? Like, a serious relationship?"

Sam hesitates. "Yes, it was. But it was also a really long time ago." He bites his bottom lip. I feel myself squinting, as I try to figure out why Delilah is wearing an expression of glee.

"Wow." Delilah gives a quick shake of her head. "How crazy is that?"

"You look surprised. Am I not her type?"

Delilah thinks about it. "No. No, you're not. You're not her type at all."

Donovan smirks.

"Oh," Sam says, lumbering backward a step, starting to look nervous. "Okay. Well, like I said, it was a long time ago. It was nice to meet both of you."

142

Sam opens the door, picks up the bucket, and makes a quick exit, as he sometimes did back in high school when things got a little too intense. The snow outside the door is deep, and the air that blows in is bracingly cold.

I push the glossy red door to make sure it's fully closed behind him. Delilah grins at me, while Donovan folds his arms across his chest.

"What are you two up to?" I practically shout. "I never told you Sam was my boyfriend in high school. You didn't need to put him on the spot like that. That was rude." I can practically feel my blood pressure rising, as my heart pounds in my chest. "Did you . . . ?" I don't want to ask, but I have to. I can hear a desperate note start to creep into my voice. "Did you read about Sam in your dad's journal?"

The twins take a quick glance at each other.

Delilah licks her top lip. "Actually, I met him earlier tonight. But yeah, Dad did write about him in the journal."

"Dad didn't like Sam." Donovan's voice is hard and indifferent at the same time.

I dig my nails into the palms of my hand. "I don't think that's true. Your dad and Sam didn't hang out together. They barely knew each other in high school. How in the world do you come to that conclusion, with your father not here to explain how he felt, with —"

"How do I come to that conclusion? Hmmm, let's think." Donovan clasps his hands behind his back and looks up, as if the answer is written on the ceiling. "Oh, yeah, that's right. It's because I'm reading Dad's diary and learning THE TRUTH. Dad liked you senior year, and Sam told him to back off. He told Dad he shouldn't talk to you."

Ugh. I remember hearing about that, after the fact.

I don't want Donovan reading that sort of thing. Peter's inner teenage thoughts are not a "story" for Donovan to enjoy as if he's breezing through a comic book.

"Dad didn't like him. And I don't like him either."

I can't decide if I want to strangle Donovan, or grab him and squeeze the life out of him in a bear hug. He looks so much like Peter when he tips his head and the light catches his cheekbone, it wrenches my stomach. "YOU DON'T HAVE TO LIKE HIM. He's just plowing our driveway, for God's sake."

"I kinda like Sam," Delilah jumps in.

"He's a little scruffy, but I bet he cleans up okay." She fiddles with her hair. "He sure likes you, Mom. You should've seen his face when I came down the stairs before to spy on him. He said I looked just like you when you were younger. He was like" — she opens her eyes and mouth to express a dreamy astonishment — "starry-eyed."

I roll my eyes. "Okay. Enough already. You know what? You're prone to exaggeration, just like your father. It's almost eleven. Can you two please go to bed?"

They turn and start up the stairs. But I have one more request.

"Wait. Hold on."

I motion for the kids to come back, and they reluctantly comply. They stand in front of me, as if soldiers ready for inspection.

I decide to just blurt out what I need to say.

"Donovan, first of all, I just want you to know that it's possible, in the heat of the moment, that your dad vented in his journal about something Sam did back in high school. It doesn't mean he didn't *like* Sam. In fact, if you read on, you'd probably see that a few months later . . ."

But I stop, because I don't want to talk about *later*. I don't actually want Donovan to read that far ahead in the journal.

145

"A few months later? Go on, finish your thought."

Just then, Donovan's phone *pings.*

He casually slides his phone out of his back pocket to glance at it. I watch the smile grow on his face as he stares into his phone, a look of bliss. I'm sure it's the girl, and he's clearly smitten. It's good to see him smile. It's good to see any real emotion cross his face, for him to have a feeling he can't suppress, because he spends too much energy trying to tamp everything down and act like he doesn't care.

"Is that — is that Lexi?"

He presses a few buttons with his thumb and then looks up at me. He doesn't answer the question.

I put my hands on my hips. "So Lexi is your girlfriend?"

I don't know if he is going to object to that word — I don't know what the kids call it these days. He just shrugs. "Yeah. So?"

I blink. "So . . . that's nice." I don't believe Donovan has ever had a girlfriend before, and I'm not sure what to say. "What do you like about her?"

"I don't know," he says, taking my question seriously. "I guess we click. Sometimes you just *know,* right?"

"Sure." I study him. "You mean that you

146

have chemistry. That makes sense." He seems okay with this conversation, so I press on. "I'd like to meet her sometime."

He rolls his eyes. "Mom. You'll meet her. When I think you're ready to meet her."

What does *that* mean? I feel a familiar acidic pang in my stomach. This kid fights me on everything. "Why can't I meet her?" I swallow and try to dial it back. "It's just that I'd like — never mind. Just tell me one thing you like about her."

Donovan glances down at the phone again. "Okay. I guess I'd say . . . she's fun. This has been a really shitty year, but she laughs a lot." He stares at her photo. "I just want to be with her all the time. She makes me feel better." His voice trails off. "I love her," he adds, so quietly that I almost miss it.

When he raises his eyes to meet mine, and I see how sincere he is, I feel my eyes quickly well up. But I push the tears back down. I want to be strong right now, not weak.

"That's nice, Donovan. I'm glad." I reach out to rub his elbow, but he instinctively pulls away.

"Is that all?"

I clear my throat. "No, not quite. Sweetheart, I want that journal back. I've had enough. You have until breakfast. Bring it downstairs with you, or I'm coming to get it."

This is it. I'm drawing a line in the sand — or, should I say, in the snow.

I see the glimpse of a sneer cross his face, but he calms his expression. I could swear there's a twinkle in his eye as he processes my challenge, and I can almost see the wheels turning in that clever brain of his as he plans what to say next.

"I'm sorry, but that's going to have to be a no." He stands up straighter. "Are those guys done with the driveway yet, by the way? What's taking them so long? Are they completely incompetent or what?"

For the love of God. I don't want to hear it, so I cut him off before he can say anything more.

"Their truck is stuck, Donovan. You don't happen to know how to help them, do you? I didn't think so. But, listen. I actually have something more important — more pressing — that I need to discuss with both of you." I take in a deep breath. "I want you to know that I spoke to your grandparents and they feel strongly that you should attend The President's Academy next year. I agreed. It looks amazing. And your grandparents offered to pay for it. They sent in a check. You'll start in mid-January, for the spring term."

I've never seen Donovan's face change so quickly before. He goes from arrogant to shocked in the blink of an eye. Delilah is equally surprised.

"What, Mom?" she whispers.

"No." Donovan can barely speak. "No way," he says again, quiet, as if I've knocked the wind out of him.

I wince. "Sure. Your grandmother told me you both toured the campus with her last summer and thought it was beautiful."

"But, Mom." Delilah gasps and puts a hand on her stomach. I worry that I've induced an ulcer. "We took the tour with her just to get out of the house. We told Grandmommy the school sounded good to be *polite*. I don't want to move again. I've just started to make friends here. Please?"

I shake my head. "I can't stay here, Del. I can't. I feel like your father is here with us. This cottage and the whole town have too many memories of him. I just can't do it. I've already told Nana and Poppy to put this cottage up for sale. I'll probably move to Maine to be closer to them, and try to get your aunt Lisa to come, too."

"But, Mom." Tears well up in her eyes. She takes in a shaky breath and regroups.

"Okay. Okay. I hear you. You need another change. But I mean, I'd rather . . ." She flutters her hands out in front of her, unable to get the words out fast enough. "You know, Mom, I haven't mentioned this before, but Grandmommy also asked if I might want to live with Jannik next year. In Germany. Like a year of study abroad, you know? What do you think? Could I do that instead?"

"What?"

I didn't see that coming. I feel my heart freeze up.

A year abroad? In Germany? What is she talking about? Where is this coming from? Going back to Connecticut is one thing, but she wants to go live in Europe for a year?

Why would Peter's mother bring that up? Where does she get off asking Delilah about that without consulting me first?

It's probably too late anyway. Judith already paid for the spring semester at the Academy. I suppose I could call and ask her —

"No." Donovan's voice breaks my concentration. "NOT A CHANCE IN HELL. Are you kidding me? How could you even think about doing that to us, sending us away? You let her pay for school without even asking us?"

"I didn't want to do it, sweetheart. It wasn't my idea. But I think she's right that you two could use more structure. More attention." Doesn't Donovan understand that even hearing Peter's mom bring it up broke my heart? "She said she talked to you guys about it. Didn't she talk to you about the school?"

"Yes," Delilah answers. "But we didn't take it that seriously. We just nodded and let her do all the talking to make her happy."

"But maybe your grandmother's right. Maybe I'm not doing a great job here. Maybe I'm not providing you with enough direction right now."

There's a pause as the twins think about it. I notice that they don't immediately jump in to dispute what I'm saying about doing a bad job at parenting.

"No." Donovan shivers with anger, barely moving, as if I'm a wild animal that might attack him. "No, no, no. Forget it. There's no way I'm leaving Manchester."

"But I won't be here, Donovan. You don't like it here, remember? You hated leaving Connecticut, and now you can go back. You're always complaining about this house. Look, we all have to move on. The Academy could be a fantastic opportunity, sweetie. It's an amazing school. You're so lucky

Grandmommy knows a few people and pulled a few strings to get you guys enrolled in the middle of the year." I wipe my mouth with the back of my hand. This isn't going well. I can see that. "Listen, let's take a break. We can talk about it tomorrow. And, Donovan, please bring that diary downstairs with you in the morning. I promise you and Delilah can both read it, but it's your father's private journal and I think I should look at it first and make sure it's okay for you to read. And then, we can read it together as a family, okay? I love you."

He stares at me, stunned. He obviously thinks I've gone off the deep end. "I'm not leaving Manchester." He shakes his head, then turns to go. "You know, if things were reversed, Dad would never send us away."

I watch him walk up the stairs, and feel like weeping.

"You're right, okay? Your dad was perfect, all right?" I hear myself getting hysterical. "He'd figure out a way to handle it and make it work. The wrong parent died. I HEAR YOU."

I didn't mean to quite say that. I realize I've gone too far. But I don't know how to fix what I've said now.

Donovan hesitates a moment, resting his foot on a stair. He turns his head slightly

152

back toward me and opens his mouth as if to say something. But he seems to change his mind, and keeps ascending. Moving away from me.

"Mom." Delilah tries to smile, but it comes off as anxious. "He doesn't mean that. You know that's not what he means at all. We love you, too. But you don't need to sell the house and rush off anywhere. You don't need to do that. We have to talk about it and make a decision *together.* You're right — let's not get into it tonight. But definitely tomorrow. Okay?"

"Okay, baby. I'm sorry to spring it on you like this." I put a hand on my forehead. I feel somewhat lighter, now that I've told them about the boarding school. I had a sense they'd object, no matter how terrific that school is. But I didn't realize how disappointed I'd be in myself. "Why don't you go ahead up and get ready for bed now."

Delilah tips her head and studies me, I suppose weighing her options. "Okay. To-morrow we'll talk again," she says with a definitive nod, as if it's all settled. She turns to head upstairs.

"Sure. Of course," I promise, although I know nothing will be different tomorrow. At this point, I can't imagine what could possibly happen to change my mind. I know why Donovan is angry with me, and there's nothing I can do to change the past.

It's not just that I missed Peter's symptoms. I also wasn't home when he died.

Warm Summer Night

LUNA

I'm curled up in a corner of the couch, as still and quiet as a mouse. I don't like to hear my humans fighting. I see defeat in Annika's eyes and watch the way her shoulders slump.

I know she's concerned about the children. I'm worried about them, too.

I know what they've been through. A terrible, awful thing.

I went through it myself. I relive the night Peter died, going over and over it in my mind. And I dwell on what I could have done differently.

Peter always has trouble sleeping. There are nights where he tosses and turns, and ends up stumbling half awake to the kitchen with his crutches to pour himself a glass of water. He sinks into the couch with a big sigh, not bothering to turn on the lights. Sometimes

155

he breathes unevenly while he lies in bed, but it doesn't wake him up. Other nights, he sits up suddenly, gasping for breath, holding his chest.

Annika sleeps soundly through most of these episodes, as do the children. They're all heavy sleepers. I am the only witness to Peter's sleep troubles. I'm awake most of the night anyway, so I follow Peter around the house if he goes for a short walk. Once he's back safely in bed, I snuggle under his arm. Sometimes he'll be groggy in the morning, dark circles under his eyes, hardly able to eat his breakfast. But he doesn't complain much about his sleep problems.

The night Peter dies, it's a warm summer night. He's alone in the bed, and snoring while in a deep sleep. The noise wakes me up, so I go for a walk to hunt for crickets. When I return, I jump up to the bed to check on Peter. A damp sheen glistens on his forehead, and his mouth is slightly open. He's lying on his back, so I climb up onto his chest as I have hundreds of times before. As a gentle breeze floats in through the open window, Peter begins to inhale. I feel his chest expand under my paws, but he fails to draw in a full breath; then his rib cage falls again. Not long after, I feel his heart start to go quiet under my paws. His heartbeat sloshes, and the life seeps out of him.

I know it's happening — I know it! He's a healthy man in the prime of his life, and I sense the onset of death. But I do nothing. I am naïve.

A few minutes later, his heart simply stops. And that's that.

It's a quiet and peaceful death.

I should know. I'm right there, lying on top of him.

In the moment, I think it will be okay. Nature is taking its course. I have come across dead chipmunks, possums, and even a large deer in our woods. I have slaughtered many birds, out of instinct, just for fun.

And I've heard Peter talk about Heaven. He doesn't make the afterlife sound so bad — not so bad at all. So at the time, I don't understand the import of Peter's death, and how it will change our lives.

Moonlight pours in through the sliding glass door. Peter and Annika's bedroom opens to the deck that runs the length of the house and overlooks the ocean, and I love lounging out there on breezy afternoons. Sometimes when moonlight hits Peter's face in the middle of the night, he instinctively turns away toward the cooler, darker side of the room. But now, a white beam of light splashes across his face, giving him an eerie glow, and his eyelids do not twitch, and he does not move. I sit heavily on his chest as he lies still.

Of course, later I realize I should have stood and yowled. I could have reached out and slashed Peter's face with my claws to wake him. Or I could have run down the hall and pounced on Delilah to rouse her. Yet I just settle down and try to keep Peter's body warm with my own.

What a fool I am! By morning he is as cold as a stone.

Everything after that is a blur. Delilah wakes first, and peeks in the bedroom door after she doesn't find her father in the kitchen. She comes into the room and can't get Peter to respond. Delilah's voice is low and panicked as she calls for her brother, and I hear the sound of her footsteps as she runs down the long hall to wake him up. Donovan follows her back to the bedroom, rubbing his face. Delilah orders him to call someone on the phone, which he does, his eyes opening wider as he starts to understand the seriousness of the situation. They both climb up onto the bed with Peter, as if there is something they can do. But I know there is not.

Donovan tries pressing on his father's chest over and over, as if he might be able to restart his heart, but it has been still for a long time. A siren wails, and strangers hurry into the house with shiny equipment. I run and hide, staying out of the way.

Once the body is removed — useless and lifeless, yet precious as Donovan clings to Peter's hand and Delilah caresses his face — a woman and a man stay behind.

They stand in the living room with Delilah, who looks gaunt, her cheeks sunken. I hear the woman ask, "How old are you?"

"Fifteen. My brother and I, we're both fifteen."

"Where's your ma?"

"Away." Delilah's complexion is pale, but she speaks with confidence. "She's on a trip. A business trip. In upstate New York. At Cornell."

"She's away?" There's a long pause. I peek out from under the couch to see the man and woman exchange a look. "Do you have any relatives or family friends here in the neighborhood?"

"Sure." Delilah shakes her hands out in front of her, as if trying to get her circulation going. "Yes, I can call my best friend's mom. Our grandparents — my dad's parents — are about forty-five minutes away. Closer to Hartford. I'm sure they'll come right away. And my other grandparents are up in Massachusetts."

"Okay. Can we sit with you and make some calls together?"

"Yeah." Delilah glances toward the kitchen, distracted. Worry passes over her face. But she stands with her shoulders squared and speaks in a calm voice, because she knows what Donovan needs most in that moment. He needs her to take charge and placate these strangers. "Yes, of course. I've got numbers in my phone. I need to call my dad's boss, too."

"That's a good idea."

They all take a seat in the wide, white living room. It's quiet in the house — other than the sound of wailing coming from out back, a howl that surges and wanes like a wounded animal caught in a trap. I pad my way over to the kitchen, where the sliding glass door to the deck is wide open.

When I step outside, the deck is hot to the touch of my paws, but the breeze off the ocean is cool. I can hear waves breaking down at the shoreline. Donovan is kneeling, bent over, hands out flat on the deck in front of him. He sobs and gasps for breath, tears and snot pouring out of him, his forehead down on the deck as if he's wiping his face on it.

I brush my soft fur against Donovan's hip

and arm, for there is no one else to comfort him. He's already yelled at the others to leave him alone. A seagull calls out overhead, a witness to our grief.

It's okay, I try to tell him. *You tried to save him. It was just too late.*

Donovan weeps until he has exhausted himself. The heat from the sun grows intense, and the humidity is uncomfortable, but still I sit with him. After the strangers leave and other adults arrive, Donovan finally takes Delilah's suggestion and drags himself back to his dark bedroom to lie down. By the time Annika gets home, he has retreated inward and barely speaks to her. And as the months go by, I see that when Donovan needs something, he goes to his sister, the only person he feels he can really count on.

In the days that follow Peter's death, I hear in one conversation after another that Peter could have been saved, if only someone had known about his *sleep apnea* and understood it. People say many odd things to my woman, including:

At least he died peacefully.
You didn't know — no one knew!
It's good to know he didn't suffer.
He went in the best way possible: quietly, in

161

his sleep.

But were any of these things true? Peter didn't sleep well, not ever. He was often tired and cranky and not at peace. Someone knew about his sleep problems — *me* — and yet I didn't do anything about it. In my estimation, he did suffer — many nights, when we were alone with the moon and our thoughts. And was that truly the best way to die?

But I suppose what the humans mean is that at the very moment of his death, Peter slept in his own comfortable bed, with his favorite cat on top of him. He never had a chance to say goodbye to us, but neither did we have to see him in terrible pain.

I still blame myself for not doing more to save Peter at the time of his death. But I also think what his spirit told me is right; I can't cling to guilt for the rest of my life. It does me no good, and it isn't what Peter wants for me. I look forward to my next meal, my next brushing, my next long nap. Sometimes we must let the past go and allow ourselves to take pleasure in the now.

PETER, THE ONE AND ONLY

LUNA

"What did you do today?" Donovan's voice is soft and low. He's sitting on his bed, leaning against the wall, with his silver phone glued to his ear. I'm spying on him from the hallway.

Donovan had many posters up in his bedroom of our old house: surfers holding their boards on golden sand, clear blue ocean waves, dirt bikes with thick tires covered in mud. But here, his walls are blank and white. It's as if he's left his old life behind and can't remember what interests him.

But there's an open sketchbook and a thick pencil next to him on the bed. He's been working on this drawing for a week with great concentration. It looks like a pretty girl with soft curves who is lying down on a couch. He has several similar drawings of the same girl, with different

163

outfits on. And there are a few drawings where she's wearing no outfit at all.

"It's snowing so hard. Have you been watching out the window? It's exciting, right? I wonder how many days school will be canceled." The soothing tone of his voice is one he only uses on the phone, deeper than usual. "I miss you, too." He sighs, and the expression on his face is serene as he studies his sketch. "Look, I have to tell you that my mom has cooked up some insane plan to send me and Del away to boarding school in Connecticut. Our tuition is already paid for." There's a long pause. "No, it'll be okay. I told her I'm not going. I'd rather jump off a cliff. There's no way I'd go." He pauses, listening. "I know. I miss you so much. I wish you were here, stuck in the snowstorm with me." He slumps down to lie on his bed, tracing the edges of the paper with his fingertips. "I don't know. But it's okay. If she drops me off down in Connecticut, I'll just get on a bus and come right back." He laughs. "Yes, I would. You know I would."

His mood seems calmer. I decide to give him some time.

I hop back down the stairs and find Annika curled up on the old couch that faces the front window, with a novel in her lap. I take my place at her side but can't relax. I feel restless as I listen to the truck engine revving and men hollering outside. I get up several times, ears alert, turning my head to decipher the strange sounds.

My ears twitch at the sound of music coming from upstairs. Delilah has started strumming her guitar.

Finally, the truck lights go out, and all is dark outside. It's an ominous sign.

A sudden gust slams against the house and I watch snow swirl in the glow of the motion-sensor light above the front window. Human shapes move past, outside.

When the door swings open, a freezing burst of air whips through the room. Danny comes in first, ripping off his hat, gloves, coat, boots, and snow pants and throwing them in a heap on the front mat. His face is devoid of expression. I get the impression he's holding something in. I intuitively know they didn't fix whatever jam the truck is in.

Annika stands up and approaches carefully. "Let me hang up some of your wet clothes. Or maybe throw them in the dryer. Here, give me your stuff. Both of you."

Danny sighs loudly, but reaches down to fish his hat and gloves out of the pile of clothes. Sam slowly takes the hat from his head and gloves from his hands and places them directly in Annika's arms, looking embarrassed, as if he's done something wrong.

Danny follows Annika as she walks down the hall to the kitchen, and I scamper behind. Somehow, I get the feeling he's not trailing her to tell her what temperature to set the dryer on.

"Do you have more of that wine?" he asks, his face bright and flushed from the cold.

"You know I do," she answers. "I don't suppose you want some?"

I take a seat on the little rubber mat by the stove, looking up at the humans from my spot on the floor. The dryer is in a closet in the kitchen. Annika throws everything in the machine and turns the knob. When she turns back around, Danny is already picking up his wineglass, which she fills.

"Cheers." He carefully clinks his glass against her coffee mug.

"Are you sure you should be drinking so much? Don't you still have more driveways to clear tonight?" Her gaze wanders to the hallway, and I believe she's waiting for Sam to appear.

"I'm sure."

Sam comes into the kitchen, and he brightens when he sees Annika arranging mugs on the counter.

166

"I made another pot of coffee. It's hot."

"Thanks." He watches Annika pour. "My back is killing me. And my hands are frozen. I couldn't even hold the shovel anymore." He lifts a hand to show her, his fingers curled as if holding a tennis ball.

Annika gently cups his hand with hers. "You're not kidding."

He stares down at the way she holds his fingers. "Your hand feels hot."

"It does?" She hesitates. "In a good way, or in a bad way?"

He looks up, surprised. "In a good way."

Annika smiles. Sam's shoulders relax.

"Look at this," he goes on, moving slightly closer to her, "I can't even move these two fingers."

She inspects his hand as if it's fascinating, but there's nothing to see as far as I can tell. "How did it go, by the way? Is the truck okay?"

I know the truck is still stuck. But no one has said otherwise. I look from human to human, waiting for the truth.

"Did you say your back is killing you, Sam?" Danny asks, his voice louder. "Wow. That's a shame. Because if you think you're tired now, imagine how you're going to feel when you have to dig that truck out at the crack of dawn tomorrow morning."

167

"Tomorrow morning?" Annika lets go of Sam's hand.

"I screwed up, okay?" Sam says, swinging around to face his older brother. His cheeks and nose glow as his body adjusts to the warmth of the kitchen. "It's a blizzard. What do you want me to do, Dan?"

Danny takes a swallow of his wine and shakes his head. He turns toward Annika. "The wind is whipping the snow into drifts and boxing us in. We can't dig out the truck fast enough because the snow blows right back where it was. And since Sam drove the truck over a rock or something —"

"Dan, I didn't see —"

Danny puts a hand on Sam's shoulder. "I told you, Sam. I've told you this before. You shouldn't drive the truck. Ever. I should be at the wheel at all times. You're good at paper and pencils and not driving a god-damn snowplow. How many times do I have to tell you? You don't listen. You never change. You always have to do everything your way."

Sam glares at his brother. "Come on. I'm here to help you, and all you do is complain about it. I quit my job — a job I actually liked — and came here to help."

"I didn't ask you to do that," Danny says, his eyes opening wide. He throws a hand out to the side and gestures toward the front yard, where the truck sits abandoned. "DAD ASKED YOU. It was Dad who wanted you to come help. Not me. Don't forget that."

Sam makes a face like he's tasted something bitter. "Well, obviously he thinks you need help. He called me and asked me to quit my job for A REASON. I know the finances are a mess —" But he stops short, with a quick glance at Annika.

I slink over to sit under a dining room chair. I don't like raised voices. It fills me with alarm and makes my fur stand on end.

Danny lays his hands flat on the kitchen counter. "That's Dad's fault, not mine. The company has Trung. And Hien. WE DO NOT NEED YOU, Sam. I wish you never quit your job. That wasn't what I wanted. Now we're one truck down. And that's a brand-new truck, by the way. I hope it's not damaged. Truck repairs are the last thing we can afford." He grabs his phone from the back pocket of his jeans and holds it up. "I called Trung and told him to go home and sleep for a few hours, and gave him the list of people we can't get to tonight. If we lose customers due to this fiasco, it's on you."

"Take it easy." Annika holds a hand up.

"My kids are going to wonder what's going on down here."

Sam quiets his voice. "Look, we won't lose customers. Trung works fast. And I'm sorry we're stuck. I think we just need a new tire, but whatever happened, it was an accident. I didn't see a rock. Maybe I drove over something that was covered in snow, but who knows? It's impossible to see where the driveway ends and the yard begins."

Granted, I'm feeling a bit slow. My brain is fuzzy from all the commotion. But what is happening here exactly? If they aren't going to try to get the truck out until morning, then what is the plan . . . ?

Oh.

Seriously?

Annika clears her throat. "So you can't fix the truck tonight?"

They stare down at the kitchen counter. Danny takes a napkin from the caddy and wipes his mouth.

"No, Annie," Sam says softly, peeking up at her with a sweet look. "We'd normally catch a little sleep at this point, seeing as conditions are so bad — a total whiteout — but we can't get home. Can we stay here? We'll get up real early and go. We won't wake you. We'll just sneak out."

My heart squeezes in my chest. Of course.

They need to stay here overnight. And Sam assumes Annika will say yes, because she's known him for a long time, from what I gather.

Well, he did ask nicely.

"Sure," Annika agrees, never taking her eyes off of Sam. "It's no problem. You must be exhausted."

"Sorry — I meant to say Annika." Sam turns to Danny. "No one calls her Annie anymore."

"Oh. I see." Danny tips his head to study her. "Annika, it is, then. You're the boss. I don't want to piss off the nice lady serving me good wine."

Sam says he needs to make a quick phone call. He comes back toward me to sit in a dining room chair. He descends slowly, wincing with pain, and shakes out his hands before trying to use the phone.

Annika watches Sam a moment. "Want to go sit in the den when you're done with your call?"

He turns his attention to her, surprised. "Yeah, definitely. Just give me a minute."

I get up and follow Annika into the back den, which is full of books on shelves surrounding a fireplace. The dust makes me sneeze. Most of the furniture in this room is not ours; it was here when we arrived. The couch is dark blue, and the pillows are white with a starfish design. There's a set of shells on the mantel: a conch, clamshells, and a dried sea urchin. Danny enters the room behind us. I take a seat on the cold bricks of the hearth.

"Is Sam calling his wife?" Annika asks quietly, sitting down on the couch.

"Wife?" Danny is distracted, hunting around the room for something. "No, probably his daughter."

"Oh." Annika's hand flies to her mouth, and she chews on her thumb a moment, lost in thought.

Danny finds a large bottle in a desk drawer. "Hmm. Your dad's got good taste in whiskey." He unscrews the cap and takes a drink right from the bottle, like Donovan chugging chocolate milk.

"What are you doing?"

He wipes his mouth with the back of his hand. "Do you mind? You don't drink, right? I'll replace it. I've known your dad a long time, you know. He used to coach me in rec basketball."

She raises a skeptical eyebrow. "Oh, sure. In that case, make yourself right at home. Help yourself to whatever you like. My dad might have left some cash in the bottom drawer, if you need it."

172

Danny chuckles and sits in a worn-out armchair, covered in a denim material that's faded and fraying at the seams. He almost seems too big for the chair, his legs spread out. "So. Where's the husband? You married? Or did you come back here to Manchester after a divorce?"

Annika tugs at her skirt, which rode up a little as she sat down. "My husband passed away," she says smoothly, as if it is something less important than it really is. "In his sleep. It was unexpected."

"Ah, sorry. You don't hear that every day. That's rough." Danny still has the bottle in his hands. "When did that happen?"

I stare at Danny, my whiskers tingling. He doesn't seem sick. He doesn't look skinny or weak. On the contrary, he looks rugged and confident. But I know what I felt when he held me. The sickness. I can't figure him out.

"About a year and a half ago. Sleep apnea. He went to bed one night and just never woke up."

"What? That's terrible. I'm sorry to hear that." Danny runs a hand through his hair and appears genuinely troubled.

The truth is, it's unusual for a human so young to up and die from random causes. It must make Danny stop and think: Could I be next?

I think that Danny could, in fact, be next.

"How'd you guys meet?"

Annika stares down at her hands. "Peter and I met senior year, when he transferred to Manchester High School. He moved here from —"

The wood floor creaks as someone comes into the room. "You're talking about Peter?"

Sam moves rapidly toward them, and Danny sits up straight when he sees the look on his brother's face.

"Yes. My husband, Peter."

"Peter. Wait — Peter from high school is your husband?"

"Yes, that Peter. The one and only." She turns to explain it to Danny. "As I was saying, he moved here from Germany."

"Did ya know him, Sam?" Danny tips his head. "It's a really small high school. You must have known him, right?"

Sam doesn't respond. He looks suspicious, as if Annika is pulling an elaborate joke on him.

Annika takes in a deep breath. Just like she used to do when she was trying to get herself to stop crying over Peter's death.

"He was in the car accident with us," Sam says quietly, never taking his eyes off of my woman. He folds his arms and frowns, still puzzled.

Danny's mouth hangs open. "That kid? The one who lost his leg? Whoa. You ended up marrying him?"

"Yes, I did. My parents put a wedding announcement in the local papers. I guess you didn't see it. We didn't get married up here. Peter and I moved to Connecticut after we graduated from college because I got into NYU graduate school and they offered me a job. So the ceremony was down there."

"Connecticut?" Danny is incredulous, and he makes a face. "All of those Yankee fans. How could you stand it?"

Annika tries to smile, but her lips don't quite make it.

"I didn't know about any of that." Sam has gone stiff, his back straight.

"Well, why would you? When we got married, we had no cell phones, computers, or social media, right? It was possible back then to just disconnect and disappear." She swallows. "You did. You disappeared."

Sam presses his lips together tight.

There's a thumping upstairs. The kids must still be awake.

"Okay. That's fair," Sam says slowly. "It's true that after I left for college, I stayed in California for a long time. I lost track of

175

everyone. I didn't think anyone in this town would want to see me." Sam rubs his cheek, as if someone has just slapped him. "But . . . I can't believe you *married* Peter."

Annika waves at him, as if pushing aside that thought. "Well, I didn't know it would turn out that way. Peter and I both went to college in Boston, and we stayed in touch, and —"

"But that summer," Sam interrupts, his voice a little louder. "That summer, right after graduation. Did you start going out with him then?"

Danny looks up at Sam. "Buddy. Calm down." He speaks quietly but firmly, playing the role of the reasonable and patient older brother.

Sam squints and peers around the room, as if expecting to see Peter hiding in some dark corner. "I just — you married him? When I said *take care of him,* Annie, that's not exactly what I meant."

"Sam." Danny stands up. "Goddamn it. HE DIED. He's dead. Shut up before you say something stupid you regret."

It takes Sam a moment to register what Danny is saying. His face goes blank. "What?"

"Shhh. My kids are upstairs." Annika stands, wringing her hands together. "Yes, he died. Look. I'm sorry if you're not happy I married him, Sam. But what's done is done. There's no point in getting upset over what happened a long time ago."

We all freeze as the lights flicker again. I lift my head.

Sam puts a hand up to his chest as if checking to make sure his heart is still beating. I jump up on all paws. Is he okay?

"Wait," he says. "Hold on. Let me just back up a minute." He turns to his brother. "Dan, could you give us a minute? Maybe call Dad?"

"I actually already . . ." He pauses. "Yeah, you know what? I talked to Dad, but I can check in on Mom. Excuse me a minute."

Annika and Sam watch him go. There are footsteps overhead, which sound to me like Delilah heading down the hall to Donovan's room.

They're quiet for a moment. Sam finally walks around to sit on the couch next to Annika. He stares into the fireplace, eyes glazed over. Annika has logs stacked in there, ready to go, but hasn't had a fire in a week or two. Cold ash has accumulated in the corners.

"I'm sorry." Sam lowers his voice and folds his hands together as if getting ready to pray, turning toward Annika. He speaks

177

slowly, carefully choosing each word. "I didn't know you married him, and I didn't know he'd passed away."

"It's okay, Sam. I should've mentioned it sooner." Annika settles into the couch, slumping back.

"How long ago did he die?"

"About a year and a half. Sixteen months. He died in his sleep. Of sleep apnea. It was —" She shakes her head, unable to go on.

"Wow. That's terrible. I can't imagine waking up next to him in the morning. It must have been such a shock."

"No, no, no." She cuts him off. "I wasn't even home, and I can't talk about that right now." Annika rubs her forehead, and her hand is trembling. "I've been a mess, Sam. A total disaster. Please talk to me about something else. Not that. Anything else." She lifts her chin. "Tell me about you."

He inhales, then gives her a shy smile. "Me? There's not much to tell. Look, we're all a mess. You're not the only one." His licks his bottom lip and thinks about it. "Life is never perfect. I've only been working with Danny for six months, and I miss my old job. I wish our dad hadn't asked me to quit."

"I'm sorry to hear that."

"It's fine. I'm happy to see you." Sam's

face lights up with a thought. "If my dad hadn't asked me to move back here and work for him, I might not have run into you. But now you're here, and suddenly this town doesn't look so bad."

She smiles. And then laughs.

He goes on, encouraged. "You know, I can't believe you're here, in this house. And you've got two great kids."

"I do." Her voice softens. "Danny said you have a daughter? But you're not married?"

"No, I'm not married. I had a girlfriend for a long time, but we never made it official. My daughter lives with me right now, at my parents' house." He raises an eyebrow. "Like I said, it's not perfect. But it's okay."

"You don't have to say it's okay if it's not." Annika's voice is nearly a whisper. "I'm a terrible single parent. I'm truly a complete failure. The worst mom in the history of the world."

"You are?" Sam chuckles. "Yeah, okay. I know that's not true. I'm sure you're better than you think. You were always great at everything." He studies her. "You still look the same. You look amazing. It's like no time has gone by at all."

Annika shakes her head. There's a flush on her face and gleam in her eye. "That's not true. That can't possibly be true. But thank you. It's nice of you to say." She sighs. "I just wish I wasn't so tired all the time. Do you feel that way, too?"

"Sure. My knee is about ready to fall apart. My back gets sore. But getting older isn't all bad. There's good stuff, too. I feel more relaxed when things don't go my way. Problems don't bother me like they used to. I've got a lot more perspective." Sam tips his head. "Man. I was really crazy about you. I'm still mad at my dad for sending me away after the accident. I mean, I guess he had to do it. But I was never happy about it."

My whiskers tingle as I watch Sam. He's growing on me. At first I thought he looked like a scruffy hobbit or something. But he does have a certain charm. I appreciate the way he admires my woman. Maybe he'll turn out to be like a frog who turns into a handsome prince.

Of course, I have an overactive imagination. I'm perfectly aware of that.

Annika looks him over. "A lot of time has gone by. It's time to forgive your dad."

"I know, but . . ." He pauses, looking down at Annika's hands, perhaps studying the way her diamond ring reflects the light. "It killed me to leave you. I never stopped thinking about you."

180

"Sam?"

He considers her for a moment.

She considers him back.

When he leans forward, she waits for him to come to her and embraces him in a hug. Relief washes over Annika's face and she looks radiant, with her arms thrown around him. They sit that way for a good minute, while wind batters and shakes the house, and a draft of cold air floods down the chimney. The floorboards above us creak as the twins walk from one room to the next. And the next thing I know, Sam has turned his head, and his mouth is near hers, and I think he is going to kiss her.

What? My tail twitches with surprise.

I suppose that is, in fact, how you turn a frog into a prince. With a kiss. If I'm being literal about it.

"Wait, wait." She puts a hand on his shoulder.

"Annie."

"You left me."

"No, my dad sent me away."

"Because of what you did."

His eyes study her face. "I know. Sweetheart, believe me, I've thought about it so many times." He strokes her hair, and she lets him hold her, although she now seems skittish, like a bird about to take flight.

"Sam, it was awful. I'm relieved you forgive me. I can't even tell you how glad I am, but now . . ."

"Don't worry about all that. If you need me, I'm here. If you need someone. You don't have to be alone."

She shakes her head. "It wasn't fair," she whispers. "It wasn't fair what you did."

My whiskers spread. What in the world did he do?

"I'm sorry. Do you think we could —" He sighs. "Could we pick up where we left off?"

"Left off?" She pulls away, and he lets her go. "No. Sam, Peter just died."

"Sixteen months ago."

"Yes, but . . . I'm not staying in Manchester. The kids and I need to move on. I'm only here for another month or two."

"That's all?" He frowns. "No, you should stay. Stay a while. Don't you like it here?"

Annika takes in a quick breath. "I don't know if I do." She stands, looking suddenly startled, as if coming out of a deep sleep and surprised to find herself here. "Sam, I can't. Too much has happened."

"But, sweetheart, I want —"

"Don't call me sweetheart. You just can't. My kids will hear it, and . . ." Her head swivels right and left, as if she's afraid someone is watching. "I have to go to bed.

You and Danny can make yourselves at home on the couches. There are a bunch of throw blankets folded up on the footstool in the front room. Good night."

Well! She retreats, and I trot after her. I'm glad she came to her senses.

Annika goes to each of the twins, in their separate rooms, to explain that the men are stuck and must stay overnight. Donovan accepts the news stoically and turns away from his mother to face the wall. Delilah seems to find it exciting, eyes bright, as if this is all a great adventure.

As she's getting into bed, Annika grabs a photo of Peter from her nightstand and kisses it. At bedtime, Peter usually took off his prosthetic leg, settled down in bed, and threw his arm over her, and the two of them fell asleep right away curled up in a ball.

I nestle behind her knee. We loved Peter, and we miss him. I'll do my best to keep Annika warm, but it's never really enough. It can't ever be enough.

February 1987

ANNIKA

As I fall asleep, I think about the second time Sam got arrested. This time, it was in fact my fault.

I didn't realize how much trouble he was going to get into. And I didn't expect him to lose his temper. Sometimes, when you're hurtling toward love at breakneck speed, you make mistakes.

"It's snowing!" Dana runs up to me at recess and twirls around in a circle. I'm sure she's freezing, but she loves wearing the acid-washed jean jacket her mom bought her at the mall even though it has no lining. At least she's got on the hand-knitted mittens I gave her for her birthday — pink and orange stripes, her favorite colors.

I've got on my high-top sneakers. There's four inches of snow on the grass from last week, but the school staff has shoveled and sanded the blacktop pretty well. Still, I would have worn boots if I had known that it was going to snow again and we were going to get kicked out of the cafeteria.

We were ejected because our grade was causing mayhem. The weather's been freezing cold, and most of us are still waiting to hear from colleges, so the seniors are getting stir-crazy. Everyone was on the verge of a food fight, with a couple of kids from band lobbing ketchup and mustard packets at each other. So the vice principal ordered us to go outside for twenty minutes to "get the crazies out," as he put it.

Dana laughs. "I love it. More snow." She has a dark mole on her left cheek, which matches her glossy black hair and stands out against her pale skin. Like everyone else, she looks older this year. Her face has taken on a new seriousness now that she has lost her baby fat and her acne has cleared up. She's also become a grade-A flirt.

The new blond kid is just walking by and Dana waves wildly at him to get his attention. "Peter! *Guten tag!*"

He smiles and walks over. I've noticed Peter has got a great smile, kinda flashy and crooked. And when I say that I've *noticed,* I don't mean that I'm, like, taking notes in a journal or anything. I just mean that over

185

the past few months I've started to realize that I get a good feeling when Peter smiles. It's as if he's got this great secret he's hiding, but it's something he's not ready to share yet.

"Hi, Dana. Hi, Annika." He's got his hands shoved deep in the pockets of his expensive winter jacket. *"Guten tag."*

We both laugh. We still love that he's got a real German accent, to die for, and always demand that he speak it to us. I feel like we don't know Peter as well as we should, because it's senior year and we're sentimentally focused on our oldest friendships. In some other circumstance, we'd probably know him better by now.

But I do know that Peter's a nice kid. In art class, we got paired up to draw portraits. Peter told me he was terrible at faces, so he was going to try something a little different. When he drew me, he had me face away from him, and put great detail into sketching the braids hanging down my back. I was surprised how much I loved it, and I asked him if I could keep it.

"I showed my mom the sketch you made of me," I tell him. "She thought it was so good she wants to have it framed."

"Really? Wow. That's cool." He looks down at the ground, as if checking out my sneakers, and then up again. From the way his gaze finds mine, I can tell he's just acting coy. He's not really a shy person.

"You can draw better than you said you could. You told me you were awful."

"I'm not that good," he says with a shrug. "I just got lucky on that one."

"No, it was excellent. I think you have talent."

"I think so, too!" Dana chimes in. She bounces on her toes, practically shimmering with enthusiasm. "That drawing was amazing."

"Thanks." He looks back at me. "Well, of course, I had a beautiful subject to draw, so that probably made it easier."

I laugh. "Peter! Honestly. That's not true. I only braid my hair because it's usually a mess of tangles, and I'm trying to keep it out of my face." It occurs to me that I've never learned how to accept a compliment.

He smiles back at me. "You know, I could make another sketch of you. If you want. We could sit in the art room, or wherever, and I could give it another try —"

"Annie," someone calls out, and we all look. Sam is just coming out of the school.

At the same time, a group of boys call Peter over from the edge of the tennis court. He tosses his head to get his bangs out of his eyes and gives us a quick salute. "Sorry, girls. Gotta roll." He looks at me and then nods at Dana. *"Tschüss."*

"Auf wiedersehen," Dana sings as he walks off. We watch him go for a moment. "You know," she says, turning to me, "I can imagine him as a cute ski instructor at a mountain in Vermont. Can't you see it?"

I laugh. "Yeah, maybe."

"Come back! I want you to *tschüss* with me," she calls out, but he's out of earshot already. Thank God.

I turn as Sam approaches with a Styrofoam cup. Now that it's winter, Sam has traded in his varsity jacket for a navy peacoat, which he told me was a hand-me-down from his brother Danny. One of the buttons is missing, and I have to fight the urge to reach out and pull the loose string. "I got you a hot chocolate from the cafeteria. The lunch ladies are being nice because it's Valentine's Day and they're giving out free drinks."

"Thanks." I take it from him carefully, afraid it might slip from my bulky mittens.

"I love a man bearing gifts," Dana says. She puts her hands on her hips. "So, where's mine? Thanks a lot, Sam."

He shrugs and looks down at the blacktop. "Sorry. They only gave me one."

I peel the lid off the cup and steam pours out into the cold air. The scent of the chocolate is rich and sweet, and when it mixes with the crisp aroma of snow in the air I could almost faint from happiness. I press the lid back on to keep it warm. "This smells so good. Thanks."

Sam nods. He watches me, putting a hand out in case I need help balancing the cup.

Dana looks at me, then at Sam, and tosses her head. "Fine. Whatever. It's fine. So I'm gonna . . . I'm gonna go get my own hot chocolate. I'll be back." She stomps off.

Dana's current theory is that Sam is going to ask me out any day now, so I guess she's trying to give us some privacy. I've already told her that's not possible. I'm sure he thinks I'm a total geek.

But Sam has been awfully nice to me lately. That I can't deny. Maybe he's just being mature and polite now that he's a senior, in addition to being an inch taller than last year.

He's actually not just taller. He also has nice posture. And I have to admit I agree that he does have a kissy mouth, as my sister likes to remind me.

Not that I want to kiss Sam. I mean, not that I'd *mind* kissing him. By which I mean, if he kissed me first, and it was really amazing, which I'm sure it would be, then yes, I would kiss him back. I think about that a lot, actually.

Oh, boy. I think I'm in trouble.

"I made you something," he says as soon as Dana is gone. He pulls a cassette tape out of his pocket. "I know you hate classic rock. But these are great songs, the best songs I could think of, my top ten. I taped them off the radio. Maybe this will change your mind."

I have to juggle to get the hot chocolate into my left hand, so I can grab the tape with my right. I'm starting to regret wearing these mittens. "It's not going to work," I warn him. "You're fighting a losing battle. You're not going to win me over. Unless the B-52's are on here."

He blinks once, slowly. A snowflake lands on his eyelashes and he shakes his head. "Listen. Here you've got some Kansas, Boston, Rolling Stones, AC/DC, and a bunch of other stuff that an educated person like yourself should probably be aware of."

I hold the tape away from me a bit, as if it might be contaminated. "Okay. Sounds . . . interesting." I'm not convinced, but I'm willing to give it a listen. "How's your dad doing, by the way?"

190

Sam shrugs with one shoulder. "He's okay, but not back to work yet. My mom's spending all her time taking care of him. So they're stressed out, you know?"

"What about your brothers? Are they helping out?"

He bats another snowflake from his cheek. "Not a lot. Danny's away at college. My oldest brother, Greg, has his own stuff to worry about. My sister Andi lives at home right now, but she's getting married this summer. Everyone's busy, and I'm just in the way. I'm sure my parents wish they were rid of me already." He shuffles his feet. "My dad thinks I can't do anything right. Anyway, what do they need me for? They already had two boys, and then two girls. I think I was a mistake. Obviously they couldn't afford to have me."

"Oh." I've never heard Sam say anything like that before. I guess that despite having a big family, Sam must feel alone sometimes. "You need a hug or something?"

He slowly breaks into a smile. "Yeah, I do."

I wasn't expecting that answer.

"Hold on." I place the hot chocolate down on the pavement and balance the cassette tape on top of it. When I straighten back up, Sam is waiting and he reaches out and hugs me. And this is how I find myself in a huge embrace with Sam Parsons, in the middle of the school day on the blacktop outside the gym, on Valentine's Day in a snow shower. Which is romantic, no matter what way you look at it, even if we're just friends. He buries his face in my hair, and I give him a squeeze. I hope I'm doing this right, because I'd be embarrassed if I weren't. He holds me tight, and I try to give him a real, comforting, adult-like hug, using one hand to rub his shoulder blade. I hang on tight for a moment, feeling good and gushy as I press against him, like my insides are melting. When he lifts his head, he looks right at me before letting go, and HOLY COW, no one has ever looked at me like that. His eyes are so sweet and his face is a little flushed from the intensity of it. So that's something incredible right there.

Dana's suddenly back, and she clears her throat. "Hey, guys," she says, looking at us and then looking away.

"Hi." I lean down to grab my hot chocolate and cassette tape from the ground.

"Annie, I . . . I'll talk to you later," Sam says, heading off to go find his friends, I guess.

"Later," I call out after him.

"Well. That was an abrupt departure. I

192

thought he was about to kiss you. Sorry I scared him off." Dana sips her hot chocolate and winces. "Ugh. This is so hot. I just burned my tongue."

"I'm sure it wasn't you. And I'm sorry you burned your tongue." I haven't even started mine. Some of the heat seeps through my thick mitten and I feel my fingers warming up.

She glances at my hand. "Is that what I think it is? He made you a mixtape?"

I nod. I know what she's going to say. "It's just some rock songs. It's not, like, love songs or something."

"Doesn't matter." She pushes her hair back from her face and tucks a strand behind her ear. "He gave it to you on Valentine's Day. Think about it. And now you're getting all huggy together." She squeals. "Ooh, you guys are *so* sitting in a tree. Soon enough you'll be K-I-S-S-I —"

"Shut up," I say with a laugh.

Just then, I see Lisa walking toward us. She's wearing the hood of her coat up, the fur trim hiding her forehead, and I realize that's a good idea. I can't believe I've been letting the snow land in my hair. I'm going to look like a drowned rat later. I pop my own hood up. "Hey, Lisa."

"Was that Sam?" She looks over my shoulder. "Why was he hugging you?"

A strong scent hits me, and I realize she's just come from the smoking area around the corner. "No reason. It's just that his dad has been sick. It's nothing."

"Yeah, I know his dad is sick. That doesn't mean you should throw yourself at him. So . . ." Her eyes dart back and forth. "What's up with the tape?"

"This?" I shove it in my coat pocket. "It's a tape of the holiday band concert. From Mark Tindall. He thought I might want to hear it, since I missed the concert. Whatever. Maybe I'll listen to it later."

"So why'd Sam give it to you?"

Good question. For once, Lisa is being very perceptive. Luckily, Dana comes to my rescue.

"He was delivering it for Mark, because Mark likes to hang out in the band room instead of coming outside," Dana insists, in a tone that leaves no room for discussion.

"Super. Mark is such a dork." Lisa shrugs and turns to me. "You know what would be fun? If you went with Mark to prom, and I went with Sam."

I nod. "Sure. That would be totally fun." I glance around, desperate to change the subject. I don't love lying to Lisa about how I feel about Sam . . . although I have, several

194

times lately. I always feel like she's fishing for information, and no matter what I tell her, she's not very nice about it.

"Where'd you come up with that idea?" Dana asks Lisa, suspicious.

"I don't know. No one's asked me yet, and Sam's a nice guy. He's nice to *me*, anyway, not like most of the useless loser boys in our grade. And I highly doubt anyone's going to want to go with Mark, so he'll need a date."

Dana and I glance at each other. That's the dumbest thing I've ever heard. Mark is a super-nice guy, and he's got lots of friends.

"What's the matter?" Lisa laughs at our sour faces. "It would be great. Although I guess Sam will take Patty."

I'm afraid to ask. "Why do you think Sam is going to take Patty?"

She shrugs. "Because they went out, right? When I was at Cheryl's party Saturday night, I heard Sam and Craig weren't there because they took Michelle and Patty to the movies. It's just what I heard."

Oh. That's fantastic.

Not that it means anything. They might have just gone as a group of friends, right? Or maybe I'm just kidding myself.

Last Saturday night, Lisa found out one of the cheerleaders was having a party after the basketball game. Lisa told our parents she was going to sleep over at a friend's house after the game. Instead, she went to the party in our mom's car, got drunk, and then slept in the car in the beach parking lot.

I wasn't impressed. But yes — I was jealous. Lisa never told me about the party until after the fact. So she didn't just lie to Mom and Dad. She lied to me, too.

"Maybe I should ask Peter Kuhn," Dana says, looking around to see where he went. "He'd look good in a tux."

I open my eyes wide. "Really? You wanna ask him?"

"Maybe."

Lisa taps her mouth with one finger, seriously considering it. "Yeah, I could see that. He'd make a good date. But you'd have to ask him early, before someone else gets to him. I mean, let's be real — he's kinda out of your league. You probably wouldn't be his first choice. But I think he'd be too polite to say no."

Dana gives Lisa a death stare. I shake my head. Lisa can be so rude.

"You know," I say, trying to shake off this whole conversation, "We haven't pulled any senior class pranks since Christmas."

Dana smacks my arm. "You're right!

196

What's wrong with us?" Her eyes glisten as she scans the yard. "Let's get everyone to run over the hill to the golf course, and we'll make snow angels and snowmen."

I laugh. It sounds so innocent and fun when she puts it that way. "Yeah, that's good. I like that."

"No," Lisa says, shifting her weight from foot to foot. "No, you guys. That's so babyish. I'm not doing that."

"Come on." I roll my eyes. "You are such a spoilsport."

She purses her lips. "I guess it would be funny to see Mr. Galanes in a panic."

"Sure." Dana is already taking a step back, looking around to see who might join us in this venture. "If that guy loses the senior class, after forcing us to come outside while it's snowing, he deserves it."

Lisa's hood obscures much of her face, but I can see she's frowning. "But I can't afford to get detention again. One more time and I probably won't graduate."

"Don't worry. Galanes will come looking for us and find us within five minutes," I reassure her.

Dana nods in agreement. "It's a wicked good prank. Let's go."

I start to walk after Dana, but pull up short when I see Lisa hasn't moved. "Oh, c'mon, Lisa. Seriously. Come with us. Senior class spirit! Rah-rah-rah, you know?"

She stares down at her feet. "I'm cold. I can't feel my toes. I'm gonna go in."

"No — look, I don't even have boots on! Let's just go for a few minutes."

But it's no use. Lisa turns toward the double doors to head inside. I feel disappointed. Angry. Let down.

Fine. I don't need her.

But at the last minute, I run to catch up to her. "Here. Take my hot chocolate. I haven't had any of it yet."

She nods and takes it. And then she turns back toward the school.

Dana rounds up most everyone, which is maybe thirty-five kids at this point. I estimate we have about half the senior class right here, with everyone else out sick or in the library, band room, or lunch detention. It seems like a good number to get involved in a prank. I check and make sure Sam is in the group. Sure enough, he's standing there waiting for me.

There's no way he's seriously interested in Patty. Right?

I've never seen him hug Patty on the blacktop.

He's definitely never hugged Patty on Valentine's Day while snow falls romantically around them. I can at least say that much.

"C'mon, you guys, let's go!" Dana points toward the golf course. "Head straight for the scoreboard, and we'll go right over the hill."

We all trudge across the football field, moving about as quickly as can be done in four inches of snow. Everyone walks quietly but steadily as one cohesive group, feet sinking in the white powder, and there's a feeling of glee in the air. Dana and I lean on each other, giggling and whispering, and we run up the hill.

At the top of the rise, some boys start laughing and hollering, and roll down the other side. There's no one on the golf course, naturally. Someone lobs a snowball, and there's plenty of room for us to have a free-for-all snowball fight, every man for himself. Ice gets under my pants and sticks to my ankles as I run around. It's so cold on my skin that it burns. But I'm having too much fun to stop and think about it. Sam hits me in the back with a nice lob because I'm too busy watching the snowball to actually run away fast enough.

He laughs. "Sorry. I didn't mean to actually hit you. You're supposed to run away from the snowball."

199

"Shut up, Sam. I know what I'm supposed to do."

I feel a hand brushing the snow off my back. When I turn, it's Peter.

"Hey," he says, "I got it."

I feel my cheeks start to flush a little at the sudden attention. "Oh. Thanks."

"Sure. I like your mittens."

I don't even know what to say to that. No one has ever complimented my weird mittens before.

I jump when Peter yells, "Look out!" He ducks, laughs, and runs off. That's when I realize Sam has thrown a snowball at him. From the look on Sam's face, he's not kidding around, either.

I get in a few more good throws at random kids. It's only when I see a police car at the top of the hill, where the road passes by the fifth hole of the golf course, that I freeze and turn to Dana. The car parks and the flashing lights turn off. An officer opens the passenger side door, and another comes around the front of the car from the driver's side.

I suddenly realize I'm holding my breath. "Hey. What time is it?"

"I dunno." Dana pivots to see what I'm staring at. "Oh, shit." A big snowball sits loosely in her hand, and she lets it drop to the ground. "You know . . . I guess it has been a while."

My heart starts beating double time. "I wasn't even thinking about it."

"Guys. HEY, YOU GUYS." Dana's voice cuts through the thick air like a carving knife through soft butter. She gets it from her mother, who can holler like no one I've ever heard.

The golf course grows silent. Kids stop running and talking.

We're like deer, suddenly caught in the scope of a rifle. Everyone looks up the ridge to the cops, who are staring back at us.

All the while, the snow keeps falling. The blood pounding through my veins suddenly feels electrified. And when I turn to make eye contact with Sam, my mind flies back to the blacktop for a moment.

All I can think of is how Sam brought me hot chocolate, and he needed to be comforted, and I gave him the best hug I could while the snow fell around us. As we gaze at each other, the snow drops in big flakes, and in that moment I decide that snow is more romantic than shooting stars or a meteor shower or fireworks, because it's *right here* landing on us; we can touch it and smell it and taste it. And it strikes me that that's all I want in this moment: to be back hugging Sam, to touch him and smell him and taste him. I want to kiss him for real. Which is all just to say that I think I love Sam — or something like that. If only I knew what love really was.

I'm starting to realize that I don't have a crush on Sam. A crush is something silly and frivolous and temporary.

What I feel for Sam is something else, something deeper and more powerful. I can't put a name on it. Maybe desire. But desire sounds very adult and scary. So I'm not sure what to call it.

And perhaps that hug foolishly made me feel invincible. But I'm not powerful. I'm just young and stupid. And now I've gotten us all into trouble.

Sam takes a step toward me. "Annie. It's okay. Don't panic."

"But —"

"Galanes is the one who sent us outside in the first place. So we came outside. We just did what he told us to do."

"Not exactly, Sam." I swallow, and my throat feels dry. "I lost track of time. This is bad. Really bad."

He shakes his head. "No, it's fine. Round everyone up, and you guys go in. I'll talk to the cops and explain that it's just a senior prank. It'll be totally fine." Craig is standing

202

nearby, and Sam looks at him. "Everyone should head in, and if Galanes is there, tell him this was my idea, okay?"

"You sure?" Craig squints at Sam.

"Yeah, definitely. No big deal —"

"We can say we all thought of it," I interrupt. I don't want Sam to get in trouble. "Let's just say we all agreed to it."

"All right," Craig agrees, pulling his wool ski hat down farther on his forehead. "Guys, let's go. Hurry up."

I stare at Sam for a moment, and I'm tempted to say more, but he looks so sure of himself. He doesn't look scared, but I *feel* scared. I hardly noticed the temperature a minute ago, but suddenly I can feel how bracingly cold the air is on my face. My hands and feet are numb and damp, so I nod and follow Craig.

We walk toward the school in a pack. Over my shoulder I watch Sam trudge away toward the cops. It's a long walk through the untouched snow across the fairway, and soon he's just a figure in a navy-blue coat moving slowly, far away, a trail of footsteps behind him. I feel it, the distance between us, and it starts an ache in my heart.

When we get back, Galanes is waiting for us. We all get lunch detention tomorrow. He doesn't seem mad exactly, but he's upset. I would almost say he seems a little scared, as if he didn't think we were capable of walking away from school and disappearing like that. Frankly, I didn't know we were capable of it, either, until it just sort of happened.

My heart drops when Craig comes jogging up to Dana and me at the end of the day while we're standing at our lockers, shoving books into our backpacks. "Hi," he says. "Did you guys hear?" I know from his face that it's bad news.

"What? What's wrong?"

"Sam got into a fight with those cops."

"Why — what do you mean?" I drop my backpack in a heap on the tile floor.

"Yeah, I guess he just snapped. They gave him a hard time, and he started yelling at them. They took him to the police station. I overheard Mrs. Rollo telling some of the other teachers. I'm worried he's gonna get suspended or something."

Dana's shoulders sag and I slam my locker closed. I rub my forehead. "Why would he do that?"

"You know he works four nights a week at the butcher shop downtown because his dad's not working, right? And his mom yells at him all the time. Maybe he's tired. Don't you know that? I thought you guys were

204

friends."

I sigh. "I do know, but . . . he never complains about it to me."

Craig puts a hand on my shoulder. "Don't worry, Karlsson. If Sam gets suspended, it might be good for him. He'll get the break he needs. Maybe he can sleep it off at home for a couple of days."

Sure enough, Sam is out of school Wednesday and Thursday. I would try to call his house, but from everything he's told me about his parents, I'm sure he's in big trouble and they probably wouldn't let him come to the phone. And I don't want to bother his dad if he's really sick.

The day Sam is supposed to be back, I don't see him on the bus, and I start to get worried. He's already in school when I get there, and I run right up to him at his locker, breathless.

"Hey, Sam. What —"

"Don't worry, Karlsson." He gives me a quick hug; then I feel his hot hand grab mine. "I covered for you."

I search his face. "I know, but —"

"Annie. Look, my dad is pissed. He thinks I can't do anything right. I've never been suspended before. Last time, Galanes just gave me detention. And the cops are involved again. I'm in big trouble."

"I'm sorry this turned into a mess. I wish I'd been the one to go talk to the police."

"No, it's okay. I wanted to do it."

He moves closer, and I hold my breath. Sam is radiating from the inside out, and I can feel his pulse in the palm of his hand. His chest rises and falls as he tries to keep his breath steady. He wants to kiss me. His eyes give him away. Nothing has ever been so obvious to me in my life.

But he wavers.

And then he drops my hand. "I can't. I gotta go." Sam looks sorry about it, but he still turns to walk away and head to calculus.

And then we don't talk again for two weeks. I don't know if I'm embarrassed, disappointed, or angry — or all three.

I hear through the grapevine that Sam's dad is letting Sam use his truck while he's out of work and getting cancer treatment. So the good news is that now Sam can get to his job at the butcher shop without having to ride his bike in the snow. The bad news is that Sam starts driving to school every day in the truck, so I see him even less. I feel like a loser, a little kid still stuck on the bus. At least I have Dana to ride with me.

Sam not only stops talking to me; he stops talking to everyone. Dana doesn't tease me about him, and I turn my focus to other things. I try to get Lisa to go sledding or ice skating with me to take my mind off of Sam and maybe have some fun, but she's not interested. She just grunts out a no and closes her bedroom door. Great. We're the worst sisters in the world.

Sometimes I look at Sam during math class and I wish he'd kissed me on that blacktop in the snowstorm. I worry that it's too late, and I don't know how to fix it.

Two weeks later, an entire lifetime in my teenage brain, it's late on a Sunday afternoon. It's a lazy day, not much going on. When there's a knock at the front door, I'm up in my room reading a book, but I volunteer to get it. I sweep open the door to find Sam standing there on the doorstep, hands in his pockets, a look on his face I don't recognize. He seems — I don't know. Sad. Lost. But also hopeful.

"Hey, Karlsson. I need the science homework."

I blink, as if my eyes are deceiving me. He's the last person I expected to find standing at the door. My heart soars.

Sam's face is dark, covered in stubble. It dawns on me that he hasn't shaved all weekend.

And then, I think: Sam shaves every morning, like my *dad*? I feel my stomach clench. When did he turn into a man, while I still feel like a girl?

I'm a mess. I'm wearing a huge old T-shirt and sweatpants. At least I have on one cool thing: the friendship bracelet that Dana wove for me in pink and green thread. I glance down at my wrist to make sure I'm not imagining it, because I'm convinced it's the only redeemable aspect to my appearance at the moment.

I'm instantly furious at Sam.

"What do you mean you need the science homework?" I scowl at him. "She handed the papers out on Friday."

"I know, but I don't have it."

"I saw you take the packet."

"Yeah, but I lost it."

"Why do you lose everything? What's so hard about keeping track of a few papers?" I regret the words as soon as they leave my mouth. I don't mean to lash out. I can't explain what's gotten hold of me, other than to say that the past two weeks have been awful. I missed Sam so much it hurt.

"You sound like my mom." I watch as one corner of his mouth twitches. "What's up with your hair?"

I feel my hand fly up to touch my hair.

208

My hair? Oh, right.

Oh, God.

"It's in two braids. And then I just twirled them up onto my head. Who cares?"

He raises an eyebrow. "So, like . . . *Star Wars*?"

"Yes." I double down and stand up straighter. Good for him. He recognizes my hairstyle. Whatever. I don't have to explain myself. I often wear my hair in braids anyway. I just happened to pin them up today.

I don't notice Lisa approaching until she's right behind me. "Hey, Samuel," she says with a grin. "Why are you here?"

He nods at me. "Princess Leia has the science homework, and I need it."

"Come in, then." Lisa reaches out and grabs his arm and pulls him inside. He lets her do this, with a sheepish glance at me.

I fetch the science homework while Lisa chats with Sam, and return to the front door. I thrust it at him.

"Here. Copy the questions down at home, and then you can stick it back in my mailbox. It's already done, so . . . you'll just have to ignore the answers."

"Or you can copy the answers, too," Lisa suggests, as if that wasn't an obvious option. But Sam's not the type to do that.

"Thanks," Sam says, "I appreciate it. I'll get it back in your mailbox soon."

I refuse to look at him. I want to. Desperately. But for some reason, I just can't. "Great."

"Karlsson, don't be mad at me. But I've been busy working. My dad told me I have to focus on school and work right now."

I whirl around, desperately wanting to push him out the door. "I'm not mad! What would I be mad about?"

He opens his mouth, but Lisa clucks before he can say anything. "Oooh, are you two in a spat? I didn't know. What about?"

"Nothing," I say, begging her with my eyes to cut it out.

"I've missed talking to you," he tries. "I've been meaning to ask you how you like the tape. I'm sorry we haven't had time to hang out."

"Really, Sam? You see me every day. In school. You could try talking to me there."

Sam shakes his head slightly, and I know there's more he wants to say, but he lets himself out. "I . . . I'll see you tomorrow. Thanks."

Lisa leans back against the front door when he's gone and sighs dramatically. "The lovebirds are fighting."

"Why are you saying we're lovebirds,

when you told me he likes Patty? Besides. We're not fighting." I cross my arms over my chest and think about it. "How can we fight, when we're not even talking?"

"Annika." She pushes her frizzy hair back out of her face with one hand. "Jeez. First of all, don't worry about Sam when he gets quiet. He doesn't talk much anyway. Half the boys in our grade went mute when we entered high school for some reason. Second, just because he went out with Patty doesn't mean he likes her. He obviously likes *you*." Her top lip curls up in a sneer. "I knew he was the one who made you that tape. And the way he looks at you? Ugh." She moans. "It seriously makes me sick."

"Don't get sick on my account."

"I'm so jealous. I hate you."

I freeze. Lisa has never said that to me before. Or anything like it. I mean — yeah, she's said *I hate you* before. I know that means nothing in the heat of the moment.

But *jealous*? She's jealous of me? Since when?

"Don't be jealous. There's absolutely nothing going on with me and Sam. And there never will be. Sadly. Pathetically. It's completely tragic."

Pushing off from the door, Lisa tosses her head and puts her hands on her hips. "Yeah,

211

I didn't think so." She looks me over and smiles as she looks at my hair. "Sam's normal, and you're so weird. He probably knows that if he asked you out, it would mean the end of his social life."

Good old Lisa. Thanks a million.

I storm off to my room to agonize over Sam in peace.

What Sam doesn't know is that I took Lisa's advice and asked Mark Tindall to the prom. Mark and I have been friends since second grade. There's nothing romantic between us; we'd been talking for months about possibly going to the prom together if we didn't have other dates. So, of course, Mark said yes. Sam will find out soon enough.

THE STORM, THE MEN, THE PLOW

LUNA

Sometime in the night, the cottage stops breathing. The vents stop producing warm air, and all goes quiet and still.

In the morning, I wake in my usual spot at the end of the bed and tuck my paws under me to stay cozy. There's a draft from the window, and my nose is cold.

Peter's ghost stands near Annika, so I assume she is having a dream about him. He looks calm but concerned, as if he wishes he could tell her something. Finally, he lies down and curls around her, as if trying to keep her warm. That's probably impossible for a ghost to do since he can't actually touch her, but it's thoughtful of him to try.

She lifts her head when there's a gentle knock at the door. Peter shimmers and then disappears.

"Annika," Sam calls out, in a low, scratchy voice. "Can I bother you for a minute?"

From the weak light coming in the window, I can tell it's early. The sun has started to rise. I can see through the blinds that it's still snowing.

I roll over and yawn. Annika's eyes snap open as it all comes back to her. The storm. The men. The plow. Telling the twins about boarding school. Her fight with Donovan. Her conversation with Sam.

And then, the new development: It's freezing in the house.

"Hang on." Annika rolls out of bed and sticks her feet into shearling slippers. She grabs Peter's red sweatshirt out of the closet, yanks it on over her long flannel nightgown, and pushes her hair back from her face.

She cracks open the door, and Sam is there with his winter coat on.

"No heat?"

He shakes his head. "Where's your furnace?"

"It's in the middle of the house."

Annika pads down the stairs, following Sam. I bring up the rear. Danny is waiting for them in the hallway.

"You guys know anything about furnaces? I don't want to panic." Danny breathes on his hands, which are white from the cold. "Maybe it's something simple, like the pilot

214

light went out. I'm not sure why it would, but it's possible."

Annika leads them to the furnace, which is in a small closet off of the hallway. They take turns looking at it, removing a panel to peer inside. Sam kneels and tries, with no luck, to restart the pilot light near the bottom of the furnace with the lighter Danny has handed him.

"I think the gas valve has shut off. At least the electricity is still on," Sam offers as he stands up.

Annika wraps her arms around her torso. "True. That's good. At least we have that." But she doesn't sound happy about it.

Sam shifts his weight from one foot to the other. "You know, something like this happened at our parents' house a few years ago, in a storm. You remember that, Dan?"

Danny nods. "Sure. The wind rattled the exhaust chimney, which triggered a shutdown. It's a safety feature on these newer furnaces."

"So . . ." Annika chews the inside of her mouth. "How did your parents fix it?" She turns to Danny, eager to hear his reply.

But he closes his eyes and shakes his head. "They had to have someone come out and service it. I don't remember how they got it started again. It wasn't like flipping a switch or anything."

I smash my face up against Annika's leg. I wish there was something I could do.

She takes her phone out of her sweatshirt pocket and checks the screen. "Hmm. My sister, Lisa, texted me early this morning. She has no heat or power."

Sam frowns. "Right across the street?"

"Yes." She puts the phone up to her ear for a moment. "But now she's not answering. Maybe her phone died."

"Let's go get her," Sam offers, perking up. "I haven't seen Lisa in a long time. It'll be fun."

"Sure, okay. Let's do it. If you think we can get up that hill. It's still snowing, you know."

Danny put his hands on his hips. "That sounds like a plan. Why don't you two go get Lisa while I dig out the truck."

Sam shivers. "Do you just want to wait until I get back?"

"Nah," Danny says, his voice suddenly sharp. "Go socialize. I slept on it and decided I don't want you near my truck. You've done enough damage."

"Screw you."

"Shut up. You're not in charge. I am."

I jump back, fur bristling along my spine. I hate sudden outbursts.

Danny sees Annika's face. "Sorry. I didn't sleep well. I'm cold. And hungry. And I quit smoking three months ago. So I'm a little cranky. I'm gonna get a glass of water." He heads off to the kitchen.

Sam and Annika are left alone in the hallway. She puts a hand on his arm. "Could you do me a favor, Sam?"

"Of course. What do you need?" His expression breaks open, and he looks eager to help. There's a depth of feeling in Sam that I'm beginning to recognize. He's a good listener, unlike most humans, who prefer to talk.

"I'll try to get my kids to come with us while Danny starts shoveling. On the way back, maybe you could distract the kids and keep them outside so I can sneak back in the house and steal a journal out of Donovan's room."

He leans forward. "Steal a journal? From your own son?"

She clears her throat. "It's not his. *He* stole it from *me.* It belonged to Peter. I don't want him to read it. I think Donovan has got it hidden in his room."

Sam raises an eyebrow. "Did you already ask him for it?"

"Yes, many times. Please," she says. "I'm desperate. There are things in there that I

217

don't want him reading. Including from high school."

"From high school? The diary goes that far back?"

She nods. "That's when Peter started it. He set it aside for many years and then started it up again. I don't know exactly what's in it. But —" Her voice falters.

Sam stares down toward his feet. "It's okay. I understand. You don't want him to read about the accident."

"Well, among other things, yes. I don't know to what degree Peter wrote about the details of losing his leg. He always put on a brave face in public, but in truth, he was traumatized for a time, and the journal might be where he poured out all of his despair. It could be upsetting for the kids to read, especially so soon after his death. Donovan isn't in the best frame of mind right now. He hasn't been coping well. I mean, I'm not much better off. But I don't need him getting hurt all over again. And then . . . there's the rest of it. You remember."

"I get it. Of course I'll help." He looks at my woman like he would run a marathon in a handstand if she asked him to. Ready to take any action needed.

"I've felt guilty. All this time. All these years."

He nods. "I have, too."

"My worst nightmare would be if Peter's parents knew the truth of it, Sam." She shudders at the thought. "Peter's mom has already made it very clear that —"

Danny clears his throat, which makes us all jump. Sam and Annika move apart. The smell of burning toast tickles my nose.

"I'm sorry to interrupt, but maybe we should get something to eat and keep moving." He gestures toward the front door. "There are people who depend on us to plow their driveways. Doctors. Cops. Electricians. People who have to be able to get out of their homes. And sick people who need to know an ambulance could reach them if needed."

Annika bows her head. "Of course. You guys have work to do. I understand."

"Have you heard from Trung?" Sam asks.

Danny stands up straighter. "Yeah, he's been working around the clock. He's doing a bang-up job. But it would be good if we could get out of here to help him. He only got four hours of sleep last night."

"Okay." Annika starts to move toward the kitchen. "Maybe you'll be able to get the truck out now that it's daylight."

I trail her. I watch as she pours dry food into my bowl, but then I turn to stare at Danny. I'm still worried about him.

"Not hungry?" she asks me.

No, I'm hungry. But I'm also concerned.

The humans slice up bananas and put them on top of cereal. Sam and Danny eat with ferocity, as if the feat of chewing will keep them warm. Annika rubs her arms and gulps down hot coffee.

Danny disappears for a moment and comes back with the whiskey bottle. He pours some of the amber liquid into his glass and offers it around. "Sam? It'll keep you warm."

But Sam declines it. Instead, he watches Annika with care, as if she's a fragile vase that might suddenly tip over and crash into a million pieces.

It's funny, because at one time, Annika was a strong person. It's true that for months she's been hiding in this cottage, avoiding people. But I've been hoping that eventually she's going to get back to her old self. She used to work, and travel, and had so much energy! I imagine she's just taking a long break and will reemerge at some point.

As if to prove my point, she gives Sam a confident nod. "I'll get the twins." She sticks her mug in the sink after giving it a quick rinse, breezes past the two men, and walks to the bottom of the stairs. I scramble after her.

"Kids? Hey, Del and Donovan. Wake up. WAKE UP, WAKE UP." I hear a bed creak and someone's feet hit the floor. "Hey guys, come on down here. Your aunt Lisa needs us. I want you to come with me when I go get her." She puts a cupped hand to her mouth. "HEY, KIDS. I NEED YOU TO —"

She's startled when Donovan comes quickly down the stairs, followed by Delilah. All in a rush.

"We're going to see Aunt Lisa?" Donovan is pulling his hair into a ponytail. "Good, good. I want to see her."

Annika's mouth hangs open. "You do?"

"Yeah," Delilah announces. She's wearing furry pink slippers and a big white robe that used to belong to Peter. "I wanna come, too. Definitely. We need to talk to her."

Annika looks confused. She checks them over. They stare back.

I am also perplexed. I imagined the kids would sleep late this morning. There's no school, and no rush to do anything. But they seem raring to go.

Curious.

"Well, okay. I'm glad you're coming. Go

back up and dress warm. Very warm. Lots of layers." Annika folds her arms and frowns at Donovan. "No journal? I said I wanted it back this morning. But honestly, I'm not surprised."

Donovan's face falls. "You don't get it, do you?" He shakes his head. "You think it's all about you. You think you're the only one who's suffering. That you're the only one who misses Dad. And you want to keep everything perfectly preserved and un-touched on your shrine."

"What? What are you even talking about? I never —"

"It's okay," Delilah interrupts, with a warning look at her brother. "What Dono-van means is that the journal has all kinds of great stuff in it. Things we didn't know. Like last night we were just reading about a piano recital that Dad was in when he lived in Germany." Delilah begins to speed up her words, something she does when she's nervous, just like her mother. "So when we're reading it, it feels like we're right there with him. Okay? So it's just that we're not done with it yet. We'll go get ready. Be right back."

Delilah turns, grabbing her brother's arm and pulling him back up the stairs. Annika watches them go with a wary eye.

222

I notice that somehow "*Donovan* is reading the journal" has become "*we* are reading the journal." That spells trouble, because once Donovan convinces Delilah to take his side, nothing comes between the twins. And Annika knows it.

Sam comes down the hall. "Something wrong?"

Annika taps her mouth with one finger. "I don't know. They seem excited to go. I guess that's a good thing." She nods at Sam. "Give me five minutes." She starts up the stairs.

Danny comes down the hall and puts a hand on Sam's shoulder to steer him over to the middle of the sitting room at the front of the house. He speaks in a quiet voice. "If the snow keeps coming down today, I'm doing it. I've gotta do it soon, before the town plows this road. I wanna get a look inside Rich's garage and see if there's anything I can use to get it started."

Sam's face darkens. "No, you can't do it with all these people here. Can't you just leave it alone? We'll figure out something else to do."

"Sam. Please. Like what? What other choices do we have?"

Sam shakes his head. "It's a terrible idea. I told you that."

My whiskers stand at alert. I don't like it when these two start going at it. My tail twitches, as I ready myself to spring away if necessary.

"Look." Danny lowers his head. "I've got a confession to make."

Sam winces, as if something is poking his side. "You do? What do you mean?"

Danny peers up at his brother, and hesitates. "The truth is, Dad didn't want you to come back here just for him. I've got it, too."

"Got what, too?"

"Cancer." Danny points to the middle of his chest. "Mine's lung cancer. Don't get worked up — it's early stage. But I haven't started treatment because there's no money for it. I need to figure out how I'm going to pay for it."

Aha! I knew something was wrong with him.

I walk over and rub my face against Danny's boot. He smells like smoke from a woodstove, a pleasant mellow scent.

I don't know this word, *cancer,* but I assume it describes Danny's illness from the way he pointed to his rib cage when he said the word.

Danny has nothing to fear, if his illness is fatal. I heard Peter tell the twins that Death is beautiful and benevolent, a shining and glittering angel who escorts souls to Heaven. That's exactly what Peter said. So there's nothing Danny needs to worry about.

It's the people he leaves behind who will suffer. I should know.

"Early stage?" Sam takes a step toward the couch and sits near the woodstove. He picks up the throw pillow next to him and hugs it to his chest. "Danny, why didn't you tell me? Dad knows, but I don't?" He takes in a shaky breath and exhales.

"Yeah, Sam. Dad knows. And I've been meaning to tell you. But I don't want you to worry. You've got enough on your plate right now."

"I don't understand." Sam's voice is muffled as he buries his face in the pillow for a moment. "It doesn't make sense. You're healthy. You've been working construction and shoveling snow."

"I'm sorry. It's the reason Dad wanted you to quit your job, Sam. He needed you to come back here and help him out, in case I need to quit for a while."

"You both lied to me. You didn't tell me."

Danny sits next to Sam on the couch. "But this is why I've gotta do this and take that new house off of Dad's plate. We need the money. Not just for my medical bills, but to take care of my girls. Look, I know you don't like it. I'm gonna do it all myself. You just stay here and distract Annika."

Sam rubs his eyes. "Distract her how?"

"You know how." Danny sighs. "Look, she's your ex-girlfriend. She's lonely, obviously. And so are you." Danny glances toward the stairs and then back at Sam. "You could use someone like her in your life. You should reconnect with her. I mean, it looks like you're doing fine so far. Just keep talking to her."

Well! I agree that Sam has already "reconnected" with her. What that could add up to, I'm not sure yet.

After all, what Danny says is true. Annika is lonely. Which is why she might be vulnerable to some sort of foolishness. I wonder what Danny is planning to do.

"I don't want to involve Annika," Sam says. "In any way."

Danny dismisses this with a wave. "She won't have anything to do with it. She won't have a clue." Danny starts to get up, but then relaxes again. "Did you talk to Annika about Peter? I mean, she married that guy? What happened there? I'd like to know." He clucks his tongue. "Or maybe it's better not to know, I guess. That must have been a shock, when you heard that. Are you okay?"

Sam clenches his jaw. "I'm fine. Just —

don't bring up Peter again, okay? If she married him after I left, it's none of my business. I'm actually glad. That guy deserved all the happiness in the world. And Annika's right. I disappeared, and that's my fault."

Danny looks at his little brother with pity. "It happened a long time ago, buddy. You were young. Anyone could've done the same thing. You've gotta stop blaming yourself."

I pad my way over to jump up and sit on the love seat overlooking the front yard. I think Sam has killed the truck. Its carcass sits outside, silent and half-buried under the deep snow. I can't imagine how they will get it out now.

Annika comes down the stairs in a few minutes, as promised. She's dressed in an orange sweater, leggings, and fuzzy socks. She's woven her hair into two braids. The men follow her lead and start to get on their own gear as Annika pulls black snow pants out of a box on the floor of the front closet.

"So," Danny asks, clearing his throat, "do you have a shovel in that closet?"

Annika hesitates. "No, my dad didn't keep shovels in here."

"So your shovels are . . ." Danny lifts his head. "Ah." He begins to smile. "So Rich's shovels are in the stand-alone garage, way the hell over there on the other side of the

227

yard?" He pulls up the zipper of his winter coat, transforming into a strange puffy creature. "Whoops," he chuckles.

Annika bites her lip. "Yes."

"That might have been good to know last night. But no worries. We can trudge through the snow." He pauses. "Can I get inside that garage, though, to grab a shovel and see if there's anything else I could use, like a brush?"

Danny and Sam exchange a quick look.

"Sure." Annika puts her hands on her hips. "Where are *your* shovels, by the way?"

Sam raises his eyebrows. He's sitting on the floor, pulling on a boot. "We left them in our truck. So don't worry about it. We're no better. We weren't thinking straight last night."

"Yeah," Danny says, kicking his brother's leg gently. "Too busy chatting up a cute old girlfriend, right?"

Sam starts tying up his shoelaces a little faster. He grunts an incomprehensible reply and doesn't look up at his brother.

"So . . . the garage is unlocked?" Danny asks, putting on his hat and not looking at Annika. "Maybe your dad also has some sand, salt, ice melt, or whatever."

Annika shrugs. "Yes, just go in the back door."

"Great." Danny clasps Sam on the shoulder. "You ready?"

"We'll be out in a minute," Sam grumbles, having trouble with a boot.

ROWR! Hey!

I leap forward and pat Danny's leg with my paw. I want to tell him to stay inside and let Sam do the heavy lifting. Danny still trails the scent of intense stress. Going out in the freezing cold to shovel deep snow seems like a bad idea.

Sam agrees with me. I know it from the way his brow furrows as he watches his brother reach down and touch my head.

"I'll miss you, too, loudmouth. Maybe I'll be back, if the truck won't budge."

He's not listening to me. I look up into his green eyes. *WOWWWR-ROWR. Don't be crazy. Stay inside.*

"Yeah, I know it's cold. Nothin' I can do about that. You're lucky you've got a fur coat."

Danny swings open the front door, and frozen air pours in. But at least it's fresh; the indoor air is starting to feel stale and uncomfortable. The house is too quiet without the *whoosh* of the furnace.

Danny laughs and curses as he forces himself to step into and through the deep snow, which the wind has blasted up against the door. It is up to his waist at first and then midway up his thigh after he takes a few halting steps. Annika shuts the door behind him.

"You have a lot of layers?" Sam asks Annika, his voice kind and concerned. "Hat, hood, mittens?"

"Yeah, of course. It's freezing. I grew up here the same as you, remember?" Annika kneels next to him on the tile and shakes little orange packets at him. "I've even got hand warmers."

His mouth hangs open. "Ooooh. Nice. You're prepared."

While I don't think Sam's brown eyes are as spectacular as Danny's green ones, I'm warming up to him. I watch as Annika offers to help him with his boot. He watches her hands work and smiles when she looks up at him.

I wonder, could Sam be someone Annika might care for, in the same way she loved Peter? Maybe Sam could cure her loneliness, which seems to be like a chronic disease that she can't manage. If that happened, would we have a lovely, bustling, fun house once again? Full of talking and eating and laughing and all of the activity humans engage in when they're happy?

But perhaps Sam and his brother are up

230

to no good. Can we trust them? I know nothing about Sam, other than the fact that Annika knows him from the past. He may have changed over the years.

And anyway, I heard what Annika told Sam last night: We're not staying in Manchester.

I just want Annika to be at peace, above all. That's what Peter would want, too.

And that's when I feel it. Peter stands behind me. When I turn my head, he's by the front window looking at the wood-burning stove, as if trying to decide if Annika has brought in enough wood or not. The stove still stands empty and cold, but she will need it later to get through the night.

When I make eye contact with him, he nods. *You'll be okay,* he assures me. *There's plenty of firewood.*

My whiskers spread as I drink him in. *Peter, is she thinking of you right now?*

Peter turns to look at Annika and Sam as they prepare to go out. He watches them with interest, his eyes bright and taking everything in.

Peter nods. *She worries too much. About the kids. About the future. Sam reminds her of me sometimes. She's thinking about our past. She seems to like Sam. You're not jealous*

231

that he's here?

He thinks about it. *No. She married me, not him. I had a lifetime with her. And it was everything I wanted it to be.* Peter pauses. *I want her to be happy again. But she doesn't think she deserves it.*

The kids come jogging down the stairs and pull on their big, shiny, waterproof snow pants, zip up their padded jackets, and hunt in the bottom of the closet for boots. With a swift yank, the door is opened, and they all plunge out into the bright white front yard.

I'm left alone in the house with Peter. He stands facing the closed front door. I still can't get used to him being able to stand on one leg without his crutch. His soul flickers as he lingers between this world and the next, simmering, waiting for *something.* He looks at me, and I stare back.

What are you trying to do?

I'm not trying to do anything, he explains. *Annika won't let me go. Her guilt anchors me here. She needs to understand that I forgive her. That, actually, there's nothing to forgive. I can't leave until she does.*

Oh! *Forgive her for what?*

But he has no answer for me.

Peter, do you want to go?

I have to go at some point. And I want her

232

to know that I was happy. She needs to really know that, in her heart. He studies me closely. *Do you think you could help? Me? Of course. Tell me what to do.*

He tells me what he has in mind. And then as Annika gets farther from the house, he fades away once again.

EVERYTHING ABOUT YOU

ANNIKA

We trudge across the front yard, snow pouring down around us like confetti at a New Year's Eve ball. The kids bound ahead, while Sam and I lag behind. Trying to stomp through the snow is harder than I expected. It's heavy, like wading through a strong current of water.

After crossing the unplowed street, we glance up. The house Lisa is renting is at the top of a steep hill. We decide to go straight up rather than walk around to the curving driveway, and it's going to be a tough climb.

"Hey, wait," Danny yells. We stop as he drags over a long, red plastic sled. "I found this in the garage." He's out of breath by the time he reaches us. "Maybe the kids want to slide down the back side of the hill."

I nod, appreciative. "Thanks. That looks like fun." I try to sound enthusiastic, despite how tired I am. The sled is exactly the sort of thing that might distract the twins while I look for the journal later.

Because Danny grew up here, he knows as well as I do that behind Lisa's house is a sharp drop into a field. My neighbors keep two horses there, but I'm sure the animals will be in their stable. Delilah takes the yellow cord from Danny's hand and pulls the sled behind her.

I keep my head down, trying to keep the snow out of my eyes. Sam has his face mask on, and I have a scarf up over my mouth. The wind has died down, but the cold and humidity sting my eyes. Once we get under the trees, the snowfall lightens, which is a relief. But moving up the incline is a challenge. There are rocks, bushes, and brush under the snow. We have to zigzag around obstacles. Sometimes my foot sinks deeper than I expect it to, or hardly drops at all as I step onto something buried below the snow. When Sam extends a hand, I gladly take it to help keep my balance.

About halfway up the hill, Sam stops in front of a large rock, big enough to be a kitchen table. He leans back against it and motions for me to do the same.

"You guys are out of shape," Delilah calls down to us. She's almost at the top of the hill. Donovan is right behind her.

"Go take a few runs on the sled," I yell up to them. "We'll meet you up there."

Sam and I watch them go. They don't look back.

"Hey. I just wanted to say again that I'm sorry," Sam says as soon as they disappear over the crest of the hill, yanking off his face mask. "I didn't react as I should have last night when you told me you married Peter. I didn't mean to get upset. I was just surprised. I had no idea."

"Sam, it's okay." I push my scarf down from my mouth. "You don't have to keep apologizing."

"Yes, I do. I hadn't heard anything about you in so long. It's such a strange concept to me that you ended up with Peter, after all that happened." He glances up toward Lisa's house, but then turns back to me. "I'm sorry he passed away. Really sorry."

I swallow, and try to lighten the conversation with a breezy tone.

"It's okay," I say. "Look, Peter and I turned into good friends after you left. He asked me to drive him to his physical therapy sessions because his parents were driving him crazy. His mother is a piece of work sometimes. Judith is very demanding. And then we both went to school in Boston.

Sometimes these things just happen."

Sometimes, you fall in love when you're not looking.

Sam nods in agreement.

When he looks at me, something deep inside my chest heats up as my heart twists into knots. For a moment, I wonder why I didn't let Sam kiss me last night.

I mean, I have plenty of reasons. Number one, I'm planning to leave Manchester. But also, maybe it's just too soon. Who's to say if sixteen months is too soon or not? Who's to say I'll ever want another relationship again? And — what would the kids think? For that matter, what would Judith think? It would probably be one more thing she could add to her list of ways in which I'm a terrible single parent.

The forest is incredibly still, other than the snow settling into the pine needles above our heads. It's funny how snow is so incredibly quiet. While it falls, there's never a peep from a bird or an insect. All of nature shuts up tight. But the stillness is a façade. Life waits right under the ice, ready to resume with the thaw.

Sam reaches up and tugs at his ski hat, pulling it off, and looks me in the eye. "What . . . what was your marriage like? Good?"

I take in a deep breath. I want to give him an honest answer. "Yes."

"I remember Peter loved music." Sam's lips are chapped from the cold, and his nose is turning pink. "Did he become a musician?"

I reach up to pull a braid out from where it's stuck under the collar of my ski jacket. "No, his parents were very unhappy with the thought of him trying to pursue music as a career. They steered him hard toward business. So he got about halfway through college and decided he agreed with them. He didn't want to live a life of uncertainty, you know? He wanted to make money, like his dad did, and went into sales. Peter was great at it. He spoke two languages; he was charming. And it allowed him to work from home a lot, which was good because the truth is, he did have a little trouble getting around sometimes. I know he had some degree of pain, although he didn't talk about it much." I swallow. My chest feels hot in my ski jacket at the same time my cheeks sting from the cold. "So he didn't pursue his passion. Instead, he provided for his family. I don't know if you'll think that's a life wasted or one well-spent."

I'm not really sure myself what I think about it. I did receive the benefits of Peter's decision. He made money so that he could spend and enjoy it. He chose the house overlooking the ocean, the nice cars, and most of the big-ticket items. I never cared much about those things, but they seemed to make Peter happy at the time.

"His life wasn't wasted," Sam insists, with more passion than I expected. "Not at all. He did the right thing, taking care of his family."

"I'm glad you think so. I'm not as sure as you are. Maybe he died full of regret. Maybe his life was empty without music."

Sam shakes his head. "No, I'm sure he still enjoyed music in his free time, right? And he died knowing he took care of you guys. I'm sure that's what he cared about the most. I mean — not that you need anyone to take care of you. But I'm sure Peter did everything right. I can see now that you two were meant to be together. I think it was fate."

"You do? Listen, I really don't think it was divine intervention that we ended up married."

"Maybe it was." He raises an eyebrow. "He seems just right for you. He seems perfect."

"He was a beautiful person, but no one's perfect, Sam."

Sam shakes his head. "Give me one way he wasn't perfect then." He folds his arms, waiting to see if I'll meet this challenge.

"Okay. Well —"

"And I mean something real. Not something, like, he left his socks on the floor. Because every guy does that."

I bow my head and think. "This isn't his fault, but there was a woman he worked with who was in love with him."

This gets Sam's attention. "Really? How do you know?"

I spread my hands out in front of me, starting to use my hands as I talk, an old habit I used to fall into when I was passionate about something, although I haven't done it much lately. "Peter worked from home most days, but commuted into a corporate office in Boston twice a month. There was a team he worked with for years. And I found notes in a book he left on his desk. Nothing too personal, you know, just little notes and cards this woman left for him. Clearly she adored him. Honestly, I don't blame her."

Sam chews the inside of his mouth. "Huh. Do you think anything happened between them?"

"No." I tip my head. "I don't think so. Peter was very . . . I know this sounds old-fashioned, but he was honorable. And he wouldn't have enjoyed the stress of something like that. He'd had enough drama in his life already. Like I said, he wanted to take care of his family, and he did."

Sam sighs, seemingly satisfied. "Yeah, I'm sure you're right. He seemed like a good guy, from what I remember."

"I wouldn't blame him, though."

"What?"

"Well, it's just that . . ." I throw my hands up in the air. "I'm coming to the conclusion that I wasn't a very good listener. Donovan laid out all the ways I brushed Peter off when he tried to tell me the symptoms of his sleep apnea. Donovan has a fair point. Peter liked to talk and tell stories, and sometimes I didn't listen as closely as I should have." I shrug. "I wouldn't be surprised if Peter sought out someone else to talk to. This is another reason I'm worried about that journal. What if Peter was unhappy and wrote about it?"

"I don't think —"

"Sam. It's possible he regretted not pursuing a career in music, and resented having a family to take care of. Maybe he was lonely when I was away traveling, and *did* think about that woman. And what if he was frustrated that I dismissed his health con-

241

cerns and didn't think I was such a great wife? I wasn't even home the night he died. But he'd told me he wasn't sleeping well. What if any of that — or all of it — is in the diary? Maybe if I'd been paying better attention, I'd have figured out that he had sleep apnea."

Sam taps me on the arm. "That's crazy talk. Please don't do that. I'm sure he was happy. Don't turn everything around and make his death your fault. You didn't know. There's no way it was your fault."

"Okay." I'd rather concede and change the subject than dwell on it right now. "What about you?"

"What?"

"Why didn't you marry that girlfriend of yours?"

Reflexively, Sam holds both hands up, as if to say *stop right there.* "It just wasn't in the cards for me. I fell for the wrong girl. I picked the wrong company to work for. There was a lot of that going on in my life for a while. Bad decisions." He gives me a weak smile.

"Was it because of me? Because of us and our breakup?"

"No, of course not. I was going out to UCLA anyway for a scholarship, remember?"

"Yes, but . . ."

"So I met the wrong people. That's all on me. Los Angeles isn't a great place for a New Englander to settle down anyway. Too many distractions. The weather's too damn warm and sunny all the time. It smells like flowers. Everywhere. Ugh."

I can't help but smile. "What about Danny? Is he married?"

"Divorced. Three girls." Sam scratches his head. "He's not in good health. He just found out recently."

"Oh?"

"He has cancer," Sam says slowly, as if he's saying the words for the first time and isn't sure if he's saying them correctly. "Lung cancer."

"Sam, I'm sorry. That's awful." I shake my head. "I remember when your dad was diagnosed with cancer back when we were in high school."

"Yeah. I guess it runs in my family. But my dad has been very lucky, living so long. Maybe Dan can beat it, too." We're standing nose to nose, and Sam gives me a look. "You never did tell me one thing about Peter that wasn't perfect, you know." He's genuinely disappointed. "Some woman having a crush on him doesn't count."

"You're right." I pull my scarf back up

over my chin and tighten it. "Honestly, he was pretty perfect."

Sam nudges my elbow with his. "I knew it." Taking one of my braids in his hand, he pulls it gently and runs his fingers down the length of it. "I remember you wearing your hair like this back in high school," he says. "I don't know if I ever told you, but I always liked it."

I realize it's no accident that I braided my hair this morning. "I know," I say through my scarf. "I mean, I knew it. I knew everything about you, Sam."

He turns his head toward the pale light filtering in through the trees. His skin is olive, just as I remember it, but with darker spots mottling the edges of his cheeks, and lines set in the corners of his eyes. Sam's shoulders are heavier and broader than they were, and his hair isn't as thick and dark. He's not my young brown-eyed boy anymore, although his gaze is still bright and attentive.

I know he wants to say something. But I remember that Sam moves slowly in all things, and I have no choice but to wait.

"Is it getting easier?" he finally asks.

"A little. I try to appreciate small things. Like the smell of garlic in a sauté pan. Or the weight of a snowball in my hand. Or the heat from a hot shower. Peter will never get to enjoy those things again, and it hurts to think about that. I still think about him all the time."

Sam nods, with a respectful silence.

What I don't say is that six months of anti-depressants seemed to help, but eventually stopped working. Delilah went to therapy once a week for a year. She loves to talk, and came out of her sessions feeling re-newed. Donovan tried therapy once and refused to go back, and I let him be. Every-one grieves differently. Donovan spent a lot of time out on the soccer field last summer, practicing by himself, and I hoped he was working things through in his own way.

I've read articles on bereavement. Shock, anguish, loss, guilt, regret. Grief can be complicated.

"Maybe I could help you out," Sam says. "You know, around the house. Or with er-rands. Or giving your kids a ride if they need it."

"But I told you, we're not staying in Man-chester."

"Annie," Sam sighs, as he did when we were eighteen. I recognize that look. And I feel something shift inside me. Is it possible for your heart to change in a moment based on the way someone looks at you? Sam makes me think so. He makes me want to stay.

And so we need to go. Right now.

I pat his arm. "Let's get Lisa."

Sam pulls his hat back on. We continue on our way, one step at a time. At the top of the hill, I grab tree branches to haul myself up. There's movement in the window and a flash of auburn hair. As soon as we step onto her front porch, Lisa opens the door to greet us.

"Hey!" she calls out. "You've come to rescue me. I'm fine, you know. I could've come down to you."

"I got your text. I tried to call. Is your phone dead?"

She looks us both over: first me. Then Sam. Then me again. Confusion washes over her face. But then she stills herself and lifts her chin. She doesn't look thrilled to see Sam.

I wait for her to answer me, sweating under my down coat. When she doesn't say anything more, I interject. "So you're out of power? No heat?" I can see behind her that the house is in shadows. I don't see lights on, or any sign of life.

She runs a hand through her glossy hair and lets it fall over her shoulders. "Sam and Annika." She rests one hand on her doorknob. "Wow. Together again. You guys look like an old married couple. Like you could be my nice neighbors. You did always make a cute couple in high school. You still look good together." She doesn't sound thrilled about this fact.

I sigh. I should've known it would go like this.

"Can I come in?"

"Sure. You too, Samuel. I haven't seen you in ages." Lisa reaches out to grab his arm and pull him in, and I have a flashback of her doing the same thing in high school.

As soon as I step inside after them, I can feel that the air is cold in the house, although at least it's dry and we're out of the snow for a minute.

Sam pushes the door shut behind us and the house gets dark, with the only light coming from the front windows. Lisa is wrapped in a large, bulky white cardigan that ties around her waist, but it doesn't look like she's shivering. She stands there silently, as if waiting for an explanation of why I'm here.

I force myself to ask what I came here to ask. "Do you want to come down the hill to stay with us until power is restored?"

She smirks. "Man, I remember Sam in his football uniform, and you wearing those obnoxious striped mittens. It's all coming back to me. The good old days. You guys used to spend so much time together on that bench under the library stairs."

I'm not sure how to respond to that. Sam and I did, in fact, hang out on that bench a lot. I know Lisa resented it, how close Sam and I became, but I didn't understand it completely until it was too late.

"How would you know? Weren't you always skipping school?" I wince, hearing myself. I sound like a snotty teenager again.

"We were probably studying," Sam responds in a mild voice, pulling off his gloves. "Or just talking."

Lisa runs her fingers over her large, chunky necklace, a series of blue stones, and turns to Sam. "What are you doing with yourself these days, Sam?"

"I live with my parents right now. I'm helping out my dad, working with my brother Danny. We do construction, landscaping, snowplowing. I've only been back in town about six months."

Lisa pinches her lips together. "You've got a wife? Kids?"

"No wife," he says. "One kid. My daughter goes to the high school here now. She's a junior."

That fact makes my head spin. Sam's

daughter goes to the same high school we went to? The one where I enrolled my own children as sophomores? Of course, now that he says it, it makes sense. But it's still hard to believe.

I wonder if Sam's daughter sits on the bench under the stairs with any cute boys.

I wonder if she sits on the bench under the library stairs with one particular boy with dark eyes and asks him to promise to be on her debate team when they pair up later in English class. I wonder if that boy agrees immediately because he is too honest and lovesick to answer any other way. I wonder if she walks away surprised at herself, walking on air, feeling light and powerful.

I wonder if that bench is still there. I believe I carved my initials on it at one point.

"Is your daughter as good at math as you were?" Lisa asks. "I seem to remember that was your favorite subject. Just like Annika."

"Ummm . . ." Sam stamps a foot, sending chunks of snow from his boot onto the mat below. "Yeah, I think so. She likes math. She's autistic, so we don't always — that is, we can't quite exactly measure her progress against other kids her age. But yeah, her math scores are impressive."

Lisa leans forward to put a hand on Sam's arm. "I'm sure you couldn't find a better school for her than Manchester. I've heard the staff is fantastic."

"Thanks." Sam exhales, seeming to relax at her words.

Lisa's sudden shift to a serious tone impresses me. Just when I think she's the same old Lisa, she proves to me that she's changed at least a little over the years.

I wish I knew what to say to Sam. And I wish I knew something about autism, but I don't.

"What's your daughter's name?" I finally ask, my mouth dry.

"Brianna," he answers, his voice quiet in the still house.

The fact that Sam has a daughter in high school who I know absolutely nothing about hits me hard. So much has happened in the years since I saw him last. I suddenly understand how Sam felt when he heard I married Peter. It's stunning how time has flown by and how much has happened.

We stand for a moment, and the house feels wrong and stale. No hum of a furnace, no whir of a ceiling fan, no electric buzz of a lamp. My equilibrium feels off. I have a sudden urge to fling open the door and wait on the front step, taking in a deep breath of the cold, crisp air.

Sam must feel it, too, the need to get out of here. He shifts his weight and kicks the toe of his boot on the mat again. "If you're coming with us, Lisa, you should go turn your faucets on to a slow drip so the pipes don't freeze."

"Okay."

"Then bundle up as best you can, with lots of layers. We lost heat, but at least we still have power and we can cook."

"We?" She narrows her eyes. "Are you staying with Annika now?"

"Uh . . . sort of. Just last night. I mean . . . it's not what it sounds like. It's me and my brother Danny. Our plow got stuck."

"Oh, did it now?"

Sam's face turns pink. "Yeah. So. Anyway. Maybe you could pack a bag with a few things to eat. A loaf of bread, a jar of peanut butter, that sort of thing? We have a small crowd at the house, and this one" — he gestures toward me — "we're going to eat her out of house and home. We could use reinforcements."

"Okay. I'll be right back."

As soon as Lisa has disappeared down the dark hall, I close my eyes. I feel a tremendous ache, a longing for our high school days when I could sit with Sam on that bench under the stairs, when everything was pure and simple. And now, here Sam is, a middle-aged man with a teenage daughter I've never met.

Life is so strange sometimes. Disappointing, I guess. Sam is right next to me. He's offered me a chance to reconnect. So why am I hesitating?

I promised him in high school that everything would be okay. And it wasn't.

Sam told me he loved me, and I pledged my love back to him. And we never had the chance to sit with that, to enjoy and experience it for very long. The car accident cut everything short.

I suddenly realize that life isn't what is disappointing here. No, it's me. I'm the disappointment. After Sam moved away, we didn't stay in touch. Here's what happened: I told Sam I loved him; then I fell in love with Peter the minute Sam left. Why wouldn't he feel betrayed when he heard I married Peter?

Lisa soon has her things together, and we're just about to head back out into the storm, when the kids burst in. They're coated in snow, their pale faces flushed red from exertion.

"Aunt Lisa," Donovan blurts out, a black ski hat covering his head, ponytail hanging behind. "Did you know my mom enrolled us at The President's Academy?"

"Yeah!" Delilah shakes violently to get the snow off of her arms. The hood of her bright pink coat is ringed in soft fur, and she flips it back. "Did you know and not tell us?"

Lisa holds up one finger. "Excuse me. When did the two of you turn into accusatory detectives? Hmm? How about some concern for me, trapped alone here during a blizzard?"

I feel the blood drain out of my face. I'd mentioned boarding school to Lisa, but hadn't confessed to her yet that it was a done deal.

Donovan frowns. "She enrolled us. Our grandmother already paid for it."

Sam takes a step back. "Maybe I should go —"

"No," Lisa says. "Stay. You're here to rescue me, remember?" She narrows her eyes. "What school are we talking about?"

"The . . . the boarding school near Peter's parents. In Connecticut." I clench my fists in my wool mittens. "It's a terrific opportunity."

She makes a face. "In Connecticut? You just escaped from there. We have perfectly good private schools here in Massachusetts if you want to waste your money."

253

"It's an excellent school," I huff. "It's hard to get in. They offer honors-level classes and every activity you could ever want. Judith and Frank pulled some strings, and they're paying the tuition, for both kids. It costs a fortune."

Lisa folds her arms. "So it's a fancy, expensive school. Big deal. Is that supposed to impress me?"

I feel my heart start pounding in my chest. I need Lisa to take my side — I was hoping she'd help me convince the twins to go.

"Aunt Lisa, can I live with you? I don't want to go to boarding school." Donovan pulls the hat off his head and looks down at Lisa with pleading eyes. He's taller than her, but I can see the child in his face. "Can we both stay here in Manchester with you? You could use us in a situation like this. So you're not alone in a snowstorm."

"Sorry, Mom," Del says, turning to me. "But I want to stay, too."

I close my eyes. I cannot believe my kids are trying to undo my plans, right in front of me. Donovan has clearly recruited Delilah to his side, which makes this even harder.

"Well . . ." Lisa puts her hands on her hips. "This is all news to me. I'm just renting here. What's happening with the cottage?"

The cottage?

"Oh. Well." I clear my throat. Lisa waits for my answer.

I notice Sam is listening, too.

"My plan is to move out so Mom and Dad can sell it."

Lisa nods. "Hmm. Okay. That's very interesting. I can work with that. I'd be happy to live in the cottage with the kids. I hope you know I've been waiting forever for that house. I was going to move in myself after Mom and Dad retired to Maine, but you cut the line."

What? "I didn't know that."

"Really? You didn't?"

I rack my brain — has Lisa ever mentioned to me she wanted to move into the cottage after our parents moved out? Yes, maybe. Possibly once or twice over the years. But after Peter died, that's not the kind of thing that was top of mind.

Delilah tries to smile, but falters. I can see she's as confused as I am at this new information. "Okay. You know what? We can talk about it when we get home." She opens the door.

Sam picks up Lisa's bag from the floor and then helps her take a big first step into

255

the deep snow. I feel like I've lost my way for a moment. When I step outside, Sam pulls the front door shut behind us and I stand on Lisa's front porch, squinting as the sun glances off the snow.

Lisa is shocked when she sees what Delilah has leaned up against the house. "Hey! That's our old red sled."

"Sure. You want to take a few runs with it? I'm sure Del will go with you."

"Yeah, Aunt Lisa, let's go." Delilah's face is crimson with the cold, but she's still up for a little excitement. Lisa follows her around to the back of the house.

Donovan, unfortunately, starts back down toward our cottage. I was hoping to keep him out of the house a few more minutes so I can search for Peter's journal. Now that he's recruited Delilah to read it with him, he's probably looking for any kind of information that he can use against me.

I hesitate, because as much as I want to get ahead of Donovan, I'm not looking forward to stumbling down the steep and rocky hill. Climbing up was hard enough; going down will be tricky.

Sam puts a hand out toward me to help me step off the porch. "One step at a time, okay?"

I nod and put my hand in his. I hold his

hand all the way down the steep part of the hill, trying to keep my balance. When Donovan whips his head around to see where I am, I drop Sam's hand and move away from him. But Donovan already saw I was holding Sam's hand, and he frowns at me with disapproval.

At first, I'm embarrassed. But a burning sensation in my chest grows as my frustration with Donovan surges.

I drag my feet, stewing as I wonder what to do, and I'm the last one down the hill. Sam waits for me at the side of the road. I tighten the scarf around my neck. The snowfall is beautiful, but my toes are starting to get numb and my ears are ringing with pain from the cold.

"Sorry. I'm falling behind."

He shrugs. "There's no rush. Too bad we don't have the sled. I could have pulled you the rest of the way, like a horse and sleigh."

I smile. "Ha ha. Thanks, but I'll make it. Eventually."

"Come on. We're almost there." When he reaches out his hand, I take it again. We cross the street, kicking aside the deep snow.

"So . . ." He raises an eyebrow. "Lisa hasn't changed much, huh?"

I wasn't expecting him to say that, and I laugh. "Umm . . . well, maybe not so much.

She's still the same Lisa at heart."

Fortunately, Donovan has made his way over to Danny. It looks like Danny has asked him to climb up onto the hood of the truck so he can knock snow off the roof. He's pushing snow aside with one hand.

Good. This is my chance.

"Make sure everyone stays out here for a minute," I say to Sam.

He looks over at Donovan. "Don't worry about it. Go do what you need to do."

"Thanks, Sam. I can always count on you." It comes out of my mouth before I think about it, and I'm embarrassed when I realize what I've said.

But I don't take it back. It's always been true. I hurry through the snow to get inside.

PETER'S TYPEWRITER

LUNA

I'm sleeping on the kitchen rug when I hear someone enter the house and pad up the stairs.

There are footsteps coming from Donovan's room, but I can tell it's not one of the twins. The twins stomp and run around, but Annika moves with a lighter, slower step. When I enter the bedroom, Annika is searching, opening drawers and checking under the mattress. My woman still wears all of her winter gear, although she has taken off her boots so I can see her fluffy socks. Dust disperses into the air and hangs there, particles floating in the faint light flooding in from the snow-ringed window. Although the room is sparsely decorated, there are dirty clothes and papers on the floor, and Annika has to walk carefully to step around the mess.

She pulls something out from under Donovan's pillow — his sketchpad. Annika pauses, curious, and I think she might open it and look at the drawings. But she's also in a rush, so she shoves it back under the pillow.

I trot over to my woman and rub my head against her calf. As soon as she looks down at me, I dive under the bed and crawl to the far corner.

ROWR! Come get me!

Soon she's kneeling on the floor. I wiggle back, until I'm right against Peter's typewriter case. Annika leans down, sees me, and frowns. "Watch out," she warns, then reaches for the handle, pulling the case out from under the bed. I follow the case, dragging clumps of dust in my fur. No matter. I'll clean it later.

She clicks open the case. "Hmmm," she hums softly, looking at the old typewriter. "Do you think anything's in here, Luna?" There is a thick roll of paper held together with a rubber band that she takes out of the case and sets on the rug. I step forward gingerly to touch my nose to the papers.

Peter.

There's a feeling — a presence — hovering near us.

I crane my head to look up at him. Peter's ghost hovers, looking down at the typewriter. He smiles.

I've been waiting for her to find this.

Annika presses down one key, then the next. It makes a *clack! Click! Clack!*

I remember Peter using this thing. He liked to play with it on lazy days off, when he would sit in a chair, lean back with his arms folded, and think. His fingers did the work to make it go. He pressed the buttons and zipped the paper out when it was ready.

She carefully pulls the rubber band off the roll of papers and unfurls them. I watch her eyes go back and forth as she reads. Suddenly her face bursts into an expression of shock at something she has found there.

Annika reads the paper for a few minutes, unable to tear her eyes away, but then puts it down. The typewriter case is closed and slid under the bed, but Annika takes the roll of papers with her and heads downstairs.

What is that? I ask Peter. *I know that's not your journal.*

No, it's not my journal. He grins at me, wrinkles forming around his eyes. *But it's something I'd been hoping she'd find. Thanks for leading her to it. Maybe it will ease her pain, just a little. Let's see.*

I walk up to his leg, trying to brush my scent against him, but stumble and fall right through him.

Oh! How embarrassing.
Go on, he says to me. *Go see for yourself what she found.*
So I go.

MARCH 1987

ANNIKA

I walk to the picture window, clutching the heavy stack of Peter's papers to my chest. I feel like I'm carrying a living thing, Peter's thoughts and feelings, and it feels appropriate to hold them close to my heart. I close my eyes and I can almost feel Peter here with me.

But when I open my eyes, I see Sam, Danny, and Donovan in the driveway. I watch Sam coach Donovan on how to jump down from the truck roof into the snow, and Danny says something that makes all three laugh.

As I wait for them to come inside, I remember the third time the police questioned Sam. It was yet again for something he didn't do. But the pattern of his behavior was becoming clear. I didn't know what to make of it — or how to stop it.

■ ■ ■ ■

I'm the only one still awake when I hear the front door swoosh open. It's late. Lisa went out with a friend to the mall, and our parents are already asleep.

I almost don't bother to get up and go say hello to Lisa, because I'm enjoying a funny movie on TV in the back room. But at the last minute I decide to let Lisa know that she should come join me, rather than go straight up to bed.

When I enter the hallway, I'm confused for a moment when I realize there are two figures huddled together in the shadows by the front door. I startle when someone looks over at me and I see it's Sam, his face lit up only by the amber glow of a lamp from the living room. He's with Lisa.

"Annika!" He calls to me in a loud whisper. "Help me out."

But I don't move.

Sam and Lisa were somewhere together? It's one in the morning. He just gave her a ride home in his car? He has his arm around her, and he's holding her up?

I feel my stomach start to churn.

"Sam," Lisa slurs, "I feel sick."

I snap to attention and hurry over. "Is she

drunk?"

Sam has one arm around her waist and holds her other arm around his neck. "Quick, where's the bathroom?"

"This way." I lead them down the hall, and the three of us can barely squeeze into the bathroom together. Lisa falls on her knees and hovers over the toilet.

"Hold my hair back," she commands. I wince, but with two hands I gather her hair and gently pull it back out of the way.

We wait. I feel awkward. Sam puts his hands in his coat pockets.

"Where were you guys?" I finally ask Sam.

"At a party. Craig's parents are away tonight. When I arrived, your sister was already playing beer pong. Then she did shots in the kitchen. She's totally wasted."

When I hear retching sounds begin, I cringe. Lisa starts to heave violently, and I hear the water splash. When the smell of vomit hits my nostrils, I gag and turn my head. Sam begins to make some really funny faces; it breaks the ice and I can't help but smile. This is completely disgusting, but Sam isn't the kind of guy to judge — or run away, leaving me to deal with this myself — which I appreciate.

I desperately want to ask Sam how the party was, and why I never knew about it, although my sister certainly did, and what exactly was going on there. But I don't. I tell myself to preserve my dignity and pretend I don't care.

It takes a few minutes, but then Lisa flushes and declares she's done. "I feel ill."

"Do you want to lay her down on a couch somewhere?" Sam asks me.

I look down at my sister, still on her hands and knees on the floor. "No, I'd rather get her into bed so she can just stay there until morning."

"Your parents are asleep?"

"Yeah, they went up a while ago."

So Sam and I help Lisa stand up and walk back down the hall. "I'll wait for you," Sam offers, as Lisa begins to miserably shuffle upstairs and I start to follow her.

"You don't have to do that, Sam. But thanks for bringing her home. I guess I'll have to go get my mom's car in the morning."

"I'll just stay to make sure she's okay. And to see if you need anything."

I stare at him a moment. He has such a sweet face, and I do want to talk to him. "Okay." I turn to catch up to Lisa.

I ask Lisa if she wants to wash her face or brush her teeth, but she shakes her head no. The most she'll let me do is help her get

266

under her sheet and blanket, and lie down. She is quickly asleep — or maybe passed out. I go get a little paper cup of water and leave it on her bedside table.

I slink back down the stairs. Sam is standing by the front door, waiting for me.

I slow down once I get close to him. "Thanks."

He just shrugs. "I figured I'd better give her a ride so she didn't try to drive or end up . . . I don't know. Somewhere else. Somewhere bad."

The house is quiet, other than the murmur from the television set I left on in the back room. There aren't any lights on but that one lamp.

"Were you drinking, too?" I just want to know. I'm curious. I've never been to a party where kids are drinking. And I don't know what Sam does outside of school, other than work a lot.

"I had one beer. I'm not drunk. Your sister takes drinking to a whole new level."

I play with the hem of my T-shirt. "You've seen her drunk before?"

"Yeah, a few times." Sam steps slightly closer to me. "And I hear things. But I know you'll take care of her."

Why is he so sure I'll take care of her, when I'm not? I have no idea what to do about my sister.

When Sam doesn't speak, and doesn't turn to leave, I start to get a funny feeling. I wonder if Sam volunteered to bring Lisa home not only because he's a good guy, but also because he hoped he might run into me. I think he's waiting for me to say something, but I have no idea what to say.

"Lisa wants to go to prom with you," I suddenly blurt out.

I can't believe I just said that. Is that the best I can do? How mortifying.

Sam nods, as if he already knew that. "You know, she mentioned in the car that you were going to prom with Mark. Why'd you make plans so early?"

Good question. "Oh, I don't know. I just thought I'd get it buttoned up now rather than wait. One less thing to worry about, you know?" I can hear myself talking way too fast. "And Lisa thought someone would have asked her by now, but no one has, and she mentioned you. I mean, that is, if you don't already have a date. If you're not going with Patty."

"Patty? No. Why did you want to go with Mark? Are you guys going out now?" He tips his head to one side, as if genuinely puzzled; it's similar to the way he looked at a long, impossible math equation that Mr.

Jones wrote on the chalkboard last week. But there's also *something else* in his voice. Maybe disappointment.

Oh, God. Is he upset?

Have I messed everything up?

"Oh! No, Mark and I are just friends. It's not that I had some great desire to go with him. I just wanted to make plans ahead of time so I didn't have to worry about it."

I didn't want to suffer with anxiety wondering if you were going to ask me, is what I don't say. *Because whether you did ask me — or you didn't — it would have been painful and terrifying waiting to find out. Because I love you.*

"Okay," he says quietly, resigned. "I'll take Lisa. We could all go together, I guess."

I have the most intense sensation of wanting desperately to reach out and touch Sam, to hug him, to kiss him, to tell him I'm sorry for lining up another date. It's so powerful it unnerves me. I can't believe he's here, in my house, in my dark hallway, bundled up in his peacoat — the same one he was wearing on Valentine's Day.

Sam is like one of those black holes we studied in science, sucking me in to the point where I can focus on nothing else.

"Yeah, let's do that." I give him a bit of smile, the most I can handle in my nervous state. "Maybe you and I can even dance to 'Hotel California,' or something equally horrendous."

He searches my face, looking for something I don't know how to give him. "Okay, Karlsson, it's a date. Don't forget. 'Hotel California.' You have to promise not to roll your eyes during the song, though."

"I promise." I wring my hands together down by my belly button and feel my insides all tie up in knots. "I wouldn't dream of it."

"No, wait," he says, starting to smile. "I changed my mind. 'Stairway to Heaven.' That should be our song. I'm gonna request it. Although I'm sure they'll play it anyway."

"Why 'Stairway to Heaven'?"

He glances down at the floor for a minute. "Because it's, like, eight minutes long. It's longer than 'Hotel California.' " He takes in a deep breath and looks back up at me.

I have no reply. I'm useless. Dumbfounded.

Sam reaches into his pocket and pulls out his keys. He licks his lips and hesitates. "I guess I should go. Bye." He suddenly reaches over and gives me a hug, and as soon as his arms envelop me, I feel tremendous relief.

I'm so grateful I squeeze him extra hard.

"Bye. Thanks, Sam. Thanks for bringing Lisa home."

"Sure." He rests his head on my shoulder. When he doesn't make any motion to move away, I start to smile. "Is this okay?" he asks.

"Yes," I laugh. I cling to him like he's the last human on earth. He feels warm and solid. I press up against him and just breathe. In and out. I don't want him to go.

It's definitely way too long to be just a friendly embrace. We stand there for ages. Yet it's absolutely not long enough.

This time, when he pulls back, I put my hand on his face. I am not letting him get away this time. "Sam," I beg. He knows how I feel about him, doesn't he? He must know. I don't have the right words to tell him.

He gathers me back into him again. I feel him bury his face in my hair, and it tickles. He smells like cotton sheets right out of the dryer. "Sweetheart."

Finally! I know it's not a kiss, but — God, just to hear that one word makes my heart soar. "Sam," I sigh, and he squeezes me tight.

"I wish you were going to prom with me and not Mark. I wanted to ask you. I thought we could go together."

I sigh.

"It'll be fine," I whisper. "It'll be good.

We'll all be there together, just like you said. I promise."

I don't let go. I know we only have three months until graduation, and about five months until we leave for college. But on a teenage clock, that's a lifetime. And I'm ready to dedicate every remaining moment to Sam. I put my hand on his head. His hair is soft and his breath is warm on my neck. I feel more alive than I ever have before, like I could do something crazy.

When we finally separate, he clings to my waist with one hand. "Do you want me to pick you up on Monday morning so you don't have to ride the bus to school?"

"Yes, of course!"

"Okay. Seven fifteen. I'll be in the driveway. Bye," he calls out a little too energetically as he walks out the door.

"Shhh," I remind him, and shut the door.

I go back into the living room and lie on the couch. I can't possibly get back into watching the movie at this point. I've missed a bunch of scenes, and frankly, I don't care anymore. I hug a pillow and close my eyes, wondering at the strangeness of it all. If Sam doesn't kiss me soon, I am going to die. My heart is going to stop and I am going to literally die. I am quite sure of it.

Finally, I go upstairs to check on Lisa.

She's breathing in a funny way, as if she's wheezing. She cannot possibly be comfortable lying on her stomach like that. I take a hairbrush and gently stroke her hair away and out of her face. There's a bottle of baby lotion on the floor, and I rub a little on her hands, which feel dry and scaly, and it takes a little of the bad smell away. I turn her onto her side and hope that makes her more comfortable. Then I go down and spray the bathroom with lemon-scented disinfectant, flushing the toilet again.

I'm not sure what's wrong with Lisa. My parents seem oblivious. My dad is busy with work and hasn't said much about her. My mom seems to assume she's just "being Lisa" and a "typical teenager," by which she means a little ornery, a little difficult, a little obnoxious. Is that all it is, though?

I wonder.

Two weeks later, Sam and I stay after school for a few minutes talking in the hallway. Sam plays lacrosse in the spring, but practice is cancelled for the day because the coaches have a meeting to attend. I don't run for the bus, assuming Sam can give me a ride home.

Sam has been giving me a ride to school every morning in the truck, and it's been great not to have to wait out at the bus stop anymore. We spend every minute fighting about what type of music we should play on the radio. He advocates for classic rock, while I argue for alternative or pop songs. The rides are fun, but the best part is walking into school with Sam and having everyone milling around the parking lot or the front door see us together. It makes me feel special, to be honest. It makes it official — Sam is my boyfriend, although it's not like there was a big announcement or anything — at least, I *think* he is, although we haven't talked about it and we haven't kissed or anything.

But still.

The hallway is almost empty of students when Craig comes running up to us and hesitates a moment. "Uh . . . guys. Maybe you should come outside. Annika, your sister is on the roof."

"What?" I'm not sure what he means. Our school doesn't have a balcony or deck or anything.

"The roof. Come on."

Sam and I look at each other, then follow Craig down the hall, through the gym, and outside. The sun is shining bright, and I shield my eyes. It's a nice spring day, starting to warm up. Massachusetts is usually cold most of the month of April.

Members of the girls' softball team file past in their uniforms and gear. Craig points up at the gutter at the corner of the school. "She's up there," he says. "I saw her go up the ladder with a bottle. She invited me to go up with her, but . . ." He glances up, squinting. "I dunno. I'm a little afraid of your sister, Karlsson," he admits with a nervous laugh. "I'm worried she's going to try to jump off and break her ankle or something."

Sam nods at the custodian's ladder, which is propped up against the brick wall. "Come on," he says to me. Craig stands as a lookout while we climb up quickly.

There's nothing on the roof of the school. This wing of the school is just one story tall, and the roof is flat and black and boring. But there's Lisa, sitting with her legs spread out, drinking from a big bottle.

"Hey, Lisa," Sam says casually, and goes to stand next to her, as if this is all perfectly normal.

"Go away, SAM," she says, taking a swig and swallowing. "Freakin' gross lovebirds. You drive me crazy."

"What are you drinking?" I ask her, but I can probably guess.

"Shut up. You left me alone on the bus.

Both of you. You stink."

I can't help but scoff. "You're not alone on the bus. You can sit with Dana."

She shakes her head in an exaggerated motion. "She's *your* best friend, not mine. By the way, you left Dana, too. Now she sits with no one."

I frown. I guess I never really thought about what Dana and Lisa would do on the bus without me. Usually when Sam arrives in my driveway in the morning, I run out the door to meet him. I've never invited Lisa to tag along. And I've never asked him to pick up Dana, either, because I like having a few minutes alone with Sam.

It's true that Sam and I have retreated into our own little world. Isn't that okay, though? Aren't I allowed to do that, just for a little while? Do I have to be responsible for everyone's happiness?

Sam shrugs and sits down next to Lisa. I watch as he reaches out, and Lisa hands him the bottle. He sniffs it and immediately shakes his head.

"Really?" He glances down at the label. From where I'm standing, I can't quite see what it says.

"Go on, lovebird. DRINK."

Sam starts to smile, and surprises me by actually tipping the bottle back and drinking from it. His skin is just starting to tan, and I watch him wipe his mouth with the back of his hand.

"HA." Lisa looks very happy. I can see her fishnet stockings are ripped up and her hair is a mess, yet something in her face is content. She's glad we're here with her.

Lisa reaches into her jacket pocket and takes out a pack of cigarettes. She hands one to Sam, who takes it and leans toward her when Lisa offers up her lighter.

"Who *are* you?" I ask him, kicking his leg, then can't help laughing.

"Both of my sisters smoke," he says. "My brother Danny, too."

When he hands the cigarette up to me, I reach down to take it from him and then go ahead and take a drag. I feel glamorous for about three seconds, but end up coughing and fighting the sensation there's ash in my lungs.

"It's terrible, right?" Sam scrunches up his nose when I sit down next to him. "I don't get the appeal."

"I'd rather drink," I admit. After I hand the cigarette to Lisa, Sam gives me the bottle. I take a swallow. Just one. It burns the back of my mouth. I try not to gag, but the taste reminds me of nail polish remover.

Here we are, senior year. Pretending to be

adults, I guess. I'm not sure if I want to be an adult just yet, though.

We sit there with Lisa, just soaking in the sunlight for a while. Sam holds my hand, intertwining his fingers with mine, something he's never done before. The softball team takes the field, going out to warm up before the first inning. I focus on our hands. I feel like Sam and I are tethered together.

"You guys have it so easy," Lisa says, and I recognize that her mood is darkening.

Sam rolls his tongue in his cheek. "If you think I have it easy, Lisa, you're wrong." He squeezes my hand. "You already know what my life is like. My dad has cancer. He's not working. My parents are both in a bad mood all the time, and we're out of money. We're lucky to have enough for groceries."

"Boo-hoo. So what. It's the same for a lot of people." She turns away from him. "You're still going to college, aren't you?"

"Either I'm going to college or I'm getting the hell out of here some other way."

I've never heard Sam say anything like that before. It makes my stomach clench.

"Sam," I ask, "where do you think you'll go?" I know he applied to four schools and got into three of them.

He looks down at his lap. "Only one college offered me a full scholarship, so I have to go there. I have no choice. I mean, I can't complain. It's a great school. UCLA," he mumbles.

UCLA. Our math teacher, Mr. Jones, is an alumnus, and he wrote Sam an amazing letter of recommendation. Sam showed me the brochure; it looks sunny and warm with palm trees, like a vacation destination. I'm sure it's a terrific opportunity, but it's so far away. On the West Coast. And plane tickets are expensive. Sam will never come home.

"I mean, I want to go there, but . . ." His voice trails off.

I suddenly realize what he's trying to tell me, and how short our relationship is really going to be.

In one quick movement, I put my free hand on Sam's face and kiss him. I *really* kiss him, for the first time, right on his stupid, delicious mouth. He closes his eyes and maybe it's the spring day, or the fact that we're acting crazy on the roof, or just the realization that we don't have much time, but he leans in and it turns into a gorgeous, long, passionate kiss where I can hardly breathe and time stands still, continuing until Lisa yells at us.

"STOP! Jesus. Ugh," she moans. "Get a room. Don't come up here to SAVE me and then IGNORE me. I hate you guys."

279

Sam smiles at me and I smile back, and I feel possibly the happiest I've ever been.

It doesn't last long.

Soon we hear a car pull up on the side of the school, tires crunching on gravel, and then the beep and static of a walkie-talkie. There's a cheer from the softball game, off in the distance. I can hear two men talking on the ground below, near the ladder.

"Ummmm . . . Lisa." I wince. "Did you . . . ? Did you do something?" I already know the answer. Suddenly, I feel a little light-headed. "Why did you actually come up here?"

"Yeah, I did something. I'm hiding out." She reaches into her skirt pocket and pulls out a wad of cash. "I took this from the cheerleaders. They're doing these idiotic fund-raisers, you know, the flower sale and car wash? But they left the box of money sitting on a bench in the gym. They're a bunch of airheads. What do you need the money for, seriously? New pom-poms? This is for you." She lays the money on Sam's lap. He just stares at it. "Take it. Because you're starving. And you're the only boy who is actually nice to me at this goddamn school."

Sam drops his head. He considers the money, but only for a moment.

280

"No, Lisa." His eyes fill with tears, and I'm caught off guard at his sudden burst of emotion. "Oh, my God. Look, I totally appreciate it. I know you mean well in your own twisted way. But . . . I can't take this money. I can't." He lets go of my hand and stands up, carefully straightening the bills into a stack.

Lisa kicks her foot like a toddler. "I'm a criminal. I'm going to get suspended and maybe kicked out. With two months to go. Whaddya think of that? Will I make a good high school dropout?" Her voice cracks; then she starts to cry.

"What is wrong with you?" I feel hot, and angry, and confused. I want to strangle her. I was so happy a minute ago, and now she's ruined it. "Can't you just keep it together for a little while longer, until we graduate?"

Sam takes in a deep breath. "Shhh. Guys. Quiet." He walks toward the ladder. "Lisa, you're not dropping out or getting suspended. Let me handle it. I'll just go to Mr. Galanes and say some kid gave me this money to turn back in. I'm a good student and he likes me. He'll believe me."

"No, Sam," I whisper. "That's not a great idea. Please. Lisa needs to —"

"Hey." An adult male voice calls up to Sam. "What're you doing? Get down here."

Sam looks at Lisa. "Hey, Lisa. You know what? We did come up here to save you. And I have never ignored you. Annika is right. Try to get it together."

Stay here, he mouths silently to me, then descends the ladder.

Lisa keeps crying, and I stay up on the roof with her, despite my urge to run after Sam and try to explain everything to the cops. I realize that Sam has been trying to look out for Lisa all along — out of loyalty to me — and he thinks that's what I want. But the truth is, my impulse is to abandon her and protect him.

I am officially the worst sister in the world.

And is this really helpful to Lisa, covering for her when she messes up? I'm not so sure.

I am also officially the worst girlfriend in the world, of course.

Who lets her boyfriend take credit for her sister's stupidity, when he's already stressed out about college? What if the police arrest him, and UCLA hears about it and decides they don't want him anymore? And what girlfriend doesn't even know that her boyfriend gets hungry because there isn't enough for him to eat at home?

Once the cops have disappeared into the school, bringing Sam with them, I bend down and shake Lisa. She's my sister. I need to take more responsibility for her. Maybe I can talk some sense into her.

"Why did you let him do that?" I demand, as her sniffling finally comes to a halt. "Sam can't afford to get in trouble any more than you can. Are you trying to wreck his life on purpose, when he's so nice to you?"

"He enjoys helping me out." Lisa wipes her nose with the side of her hand. "He likes looking after me."

I feel my hands clench. I have to fight the urge to punch her, or kick her leg. But I know she's speaking the truth. Sam likes helping people, to the point where he gets himself into ridiculous situations. And I don't understand it at all. "I sincerely doubt he enjoys looking after you. You ruin everything."

"No, it's true. Whoa — ouch. Don't pinch me." She shakes her head. "He does enjoy it. Sam thinks he's doing you a favor. He likes to be your hero."

"I know." I cover my eyes with my hand. "You're right."

She wipes dirt off her hands. "You know what else I think it is? With me, he gets to play 'big brother,' you know? He gets to feel competent. Instead of like at home, where he's the baby of the family and they shit on him all the time."

I pick my head up and stare at her. Hmm. She might be right about that, too.

I manage to get Lisa down the ladder, and we walk home so she has time to sober up. I tell her how horrible she is for stealing money, but she's in no mood to hear it.

"Don't worry," she says to me, when she sees I'm still stewing. "Sam would do anything for you. He loves you. You're lucky. You're so goddamn lucky."

I don't know what to say to that. "I *am* lucky." I cross my arms over my chest, feeling the weight of my heavy backpack pull at my shoulders as we walk under a flowering tree. I feel a headache coming on. "You're absolutely right about that."

Sam doesn't confess that he stole the money, but he doesn't blame it on Lisa either. He just says a kid stole it, felt guilty, and handed it off to him to turn back in. Our principal pressures him to give up a name, but he won't. The police question him, but Sam isn't arrested. He still gets suspended again. Mr. Galanes tells Sam he's sorry to do it, but he has no choice. I think Sam has a blind spot where he doesn't realize how much trouble he could potentially get into when things happen. So now just one more suspension and Sam will be expelled or sent to another school, even though we only have two months to go.

I'm not sure what punishment Sam gets at home. He won't talk about it — he stubbornly refuses to. But he holds my hand a little tighter when we're together, his palms sweaty. He hugs me after school when he has to go to lacrosse practice and I have to run for the bus. Sam seems stressed, almost as if he's unraveling, but at least this time he doesn't run from me. If anything, he runs toward me. I tell him I'm sorry he got into trouble on Lisa's account, but he always waves that off. "I don't care about getting suspended. I'm just sorry to disappoint my dad. My dad is important," he tells me. "And you're important. Not that other stuff."

We start spending all of our time together. Although we can't get together at his house because he's grounded, he manages to stop by my house after work a few nights to watch TV with me. On the rare occasion when Lisa isn't home and my parents go up to bed, he kisses me. Sam takes everything slowly, which seems to have the perverse result of making me more frantic to spend every minute with him. My short time alone with Sam is never enough. As spring emerges, the days getting longer and warmer and greener, I start to feel like everything is going to be okay.

Even when I know perfectly well it's not.

GIRL TROUBLE

LUNA

Sam enters the house with Lisa and Delilah. They're covered in snow and pat themselves to get the snow to fall off in clumps.

I've always liked Lisa. She doesn't always play by the rules; she feeds me scraps of chicken or fish under the table when no one is looking. Lisa doesn't take off her puffy coat, but she does slip off her wet boots and put on a pair of shearling slippers she brought with her in a large bag. I watch as a white feather emerges from a small rip in her coat, and I chase it down the hall.

Sam starts a fire in the old stone and brick fireplace in the back room. Annika throws logs into the woodstove in the living room at the front of the house, and Delilah brings a small electric space heater downstairs to the kitchen and plugs it in. All of these sources of heat make the cottage tolerable — not exactly *warm,* but okay, and better than outside, where the air is crisp and raw.

Later, I hear the front door swing open again and Danny and Donovan enter. They're deep in conversation. I walk over to greet them.

"So, you don't know any classic rock?" Danny makes a face of disgust. "No Led Zeppelin at all? How is that even possible?" He reaches down to ruffle the fur on my head.

"I don't know. My mom sometimes plays some of that music in the car, but —"

"Do you at least know some eighties pop bands? The Police? Talking Heads?"

Donovan unzips his coat and exhales. "Look, my dad played classical piano. He spent a lot of his teenage years in Germany, and I don't know what he listened to. What can I tell you? He liked the Beatles. Does that count?"

"That's good, but no. That's definitely a solid no. I'm talking about classic eighties bands. Man, my girls love that stuff."

Donovan smiles. "Well, what should I listen to, then?"

Danny throws his gloves on the mat. "I'm gonna make you a list."

Annika approaches the front door. She watches them take their hats and mittens off. My woman looks eager to hear their news, hands gripping the end of one braid.

"Did you find anything you could use in the garage?"

Danny is reaching down toward his boots but wavers when she mentions the garage. Without looking at Annika, he continues his downward motion to unlace his frozen shoelaces, coated in ice. "I found two shovels, but that's it. The amount of wood that your dad has got stacked up in there is impressive."

"I helped him dig out around the truck," Donovan volunteers. He throws a soggy glove onto the floor. "It's kinda strange, though. The front driver's side tire is definitely punctured. Almost like it hit something super sharp. But I didn't see anything that could have done that kind of damage. Maybe you guys drove over something in the road before you got to our house?"

Danny shrugs. "We could have." He clears his throat as Sam and Lisa come down the hall. He stands up straight, watching them approach. "Hey. I remember you from high school," Danny says, his green eyes opening wide at the sight of Lisa.

"I remember you, too," she says. "You were a senior when we were freshman. I seem to recall we had lunch detention together a few times."

"That's it!" He points at her. "That's where I know you from."

Annika shakes her head. "C'mon." She taps Lisa's arm. "Let's see what we can throw together to eat." They head back to the kitchen, and soon I hear a pan being slid out of a drawer.

Danny stands up straight and folds his arms. "The tire is flat. It has a big tear. Almost as if it was slashed. Don't you think that's weird?"

"Weird?" Sam has a blank look on his face.

Danny scratches his chin. "Yeah, weird."

Sam's face starts to turn pink. He squirms in his boots. "No . . . what . . . what do you mean?"

"I mean," Danny says, tipping his head toward his brother, "maybe it's divine intervention. It's God's way of stranding us here and telling me my plan to deal with Dad's house is a good one."

Sam cringes. "Well, I don't think —"

"Or, it means *you're* helping me. And you slashed the tire."

"What?"

"Come on. Is this your way of helping me out?"

Sam holds up both hands. "No, no way, Dan. You're reading too much into it. I told you, I don't like your plan, and I mean it."

290

He swallows. "And you know I wouldn't mess with Dad's new truck."

Danny stares at his little brother and rolls his tongue in his cheek. I can hear Lisa talking excitedly in the kitchen, along with the sound of clinking plates and silverware.

"Okay," Danny says, putting a hand on Sam's shoulder. "Fine."

"I'm not secretly trying to help you." He pushes his brother's hand away. "Do you realize you smell like gasoline? You'd better wash up. What is wrong with you? Can't you smell it?" Sam walks back toward the kitchen.

"Hey. I'm not dumb. I told Donovan that I spilled — Hey, are you listening to me?"

But Sam is gone.

Danny and I are left alone. He crouches down and extends a hand. A sharp chemical scent tickles my nostrils. I still touch my nose to his fingers and allow him to pet me. I can sense his stress, and I know the illness is eating him from the inside out. His hand shakes slightly as he runs it down my back.

You'd better slow down. You need to concentrate on finding a cure for your illness.

He nods at me, as if he agrees.

The kids retreat upstairs. Annika makes the adults grilled cheese, using a loaf of bread that Lisa brought with her. The humans stand around the stove, occasionally pacing or pulling their coats tighter to stay warm, and I join them. The smell of butter melting and browning gets me worked up, and I throw my body against legs indiscriminately.

"Did you find the journal?" Sam asks Annika quietly, sliding a sandwich from a spatula onto a plate.

"No, but I did find something else interesting." She points to a stack of papers on the kitchen counter.

"What's this?" Lisa leans over the counter. I watch her eyes scan the paper. "Did Peter . . . Is this a story?"

"Yes, I believe it's a novel. Luna dove under Donovan's bed, and when I went to look, I noticed Peter's old typewriter in the back corner. This was in the case."

"Your husband wrote a book?" Danny takes a step closer and peers over Lisa's shoulder.

Lisa whirls around. "I didn't know Peter was writing a novel."

Annika shrugs. "Neither did I." She slides another grilled cheese onto a plate and slices it in half. Steam rises into the cool air.

Lisa is baffled. "Holy crap." Her lips move slightly as she reads. "This is like finding buried treasure under the floorboards."

"I can't believe he was writing a book."

Lisa purses her lips and studies her sister. "Why's it so hard to believe? He was a musician. He was creative, of course." She picks up the top page and starts to read the second. "It's not bad. Did you read this first page? He's got an exciting scene going here. A lot of action."

My ears twitch. Peter was an excellent storyteller!

Are you here, Peter?

I glance around. Ah — there he is. Standing near the refrigerator, listening.

"I don't think I can read it. The thing is . . ." Annika chews the inside of her mouth, thinking. "I mean, he fooled around on the typewriter from time to time. But a novel? Why didn't he tell me? Maybe he wanted to finish before he showed it to me." She taps her fingernails on the table, then bites her thumb. "Oh, gosh. I don't know if I can handle reading it. It'll make me too sad. It's not about King Arthur, is it? He loved the Middle Ages. I mean, I can't even tell you . . ." Her eyes tear up, and she stops herself.

Sam hands her a glass of water. She thanks him quietly.

Lisa keeps scanning the pages and holds

up one finger. "It looks like it's a story about a knight — who is a woman in this case — on a ship, going on a quest."

"Ohhh," my woman sighs. "A knight. I knew it. I know him too well."

Lisa goes on. "There's also a young sailor who is accompanying our hero on her journey." She picks up a glass of lemonade and raises it, as if in a toast. "He's probably the love interest."

Annika rocks back on her heels. "Lisa, will you read the novel for me? Can you read the whole thing and let me know what happens? I just don't know if I can do it right now."

"Of course. I'd love to read it. I'm sure it will be fantastic." She still holds her glass, and I watch the lemon pulp floating in it. "I'm a fan of the knight already. She's fighting a giant sea serpent while navigating rough waters, right on page two."

Ooh — a battle with a sea serpent! I remember Peter telling that story to the twins many times.

Annika looks like she's seen a ghost. I mean . . . not Peter's actual ghost. But she looks pale. She heard Peter tell the sea serpent story to the children sometimes while she was in the next room brushing her teeth.

"Oh, boy. Well. Okay. Thank you."

Sam walks over to the stove to peer into a big black pot. I notice the way my woman turns her shoulder so she can watch him as he reaches for a wooden spoon to stir the soup. Sam is like the magnet Delilah used to drag across the counter, attracting paper clips; Annika can't help but turn to face him.

"This looks ready." I watched as earlier Sam poured cans of tomato soup into a pan. It has been heating on the stove, and the savory scent tickles my nose. Using a ladle, he carefully distributes it into several bowls. Lisa carries two bowls to the table, and Sam brings two more.

Annika goes to the bottom of the stairs and yells for the kids to come down for lunch. She has their sandwiches piled on a plate, where they're getting cold.

"NOW," Annika yells.

"We'll be down in a few minutes," Delilah calls back.

Once all of the adults are seated at the kitchen table, it almost seems cozy. Annika yawns.

And then, something changes. The house, which was already unusually quiet, goes dark.

Lisa startles. "Did . . . did we just lose

power?"

Danny turns to look. The space heater has stopped rotating. The digital clock on the stove is off. The lamp has gone dark. "Yes." He turns to Annika. "You have candles?"

"Sure."

My woman gets up, shuddering, and opens a drawer in the long hutch. She takes out several large candles and a box of matches.

I get up onto my feet.

Peter! Where'd you go?

I spot him; he's still in the kitchen. He watches Annika as she places a short white candle into a jar.

Although Peter is still wearing a T-shirt and shorts, the clothes he died in, he does not shiver or rub his bare arms. His body is just an illusion, so the cold does not bother him. His face is smooth and his blue eyes bright.

It'll be okay, he tells me. *Don't worry about the electricity. There are plenty of people here. They'll figure out what to do. I'm glad Annika isn't alone with the kids.*

He's right. I agree.

What is Annika thinking now? I've become used to speaking with this ghost, and trot right up to him. *Is she thinking about you?*

She wants to read my book, but she's afraid

it would be too painful. I wish she would read it. It's an adventure story, and a love story. I thought it would help her see how happy I was. He scowls, defeated.

Everyone eats their soup faster, I suppose because they want to consume it while it's still hot. They stop talking and focus on their lunch.

Once everyone is done, Annika washes the bowls in the kitchen sink. From the steam rising, I see that we at least still have hot water. But that's about all we have left of modern conveniences. Annika works by the light of a candle and the weak sunlight coming in through a window.

"Everyone should power down their phones," Danny suggests, taking a spoon from Annika and drying it. "We're going to run out of battery power and have no way to recharge."

Sam goes into the back room to make sure the fire is roaring by throwing lots of logs on and moving them with the poker until the flames grow high. I walk over to try to soak up a little warmth. Snow still falls outside the window.

Danny comes in and corners Sam by the hearth. I sit at their feet, craning my head up to watch them carefully.

"So everything looks good. I got what I

need from the garage. I'll do it today."

Sam doesn't respond. He looks worried. I watch him rub his fingers together. "Hey, look, again . . . I'm sorry about the tire. I don't know what I hit or ran over. I'll pay for the new tire."

"Yeah, yeah. Don't worry about that. I'm not worried about that shit now." Danny glances over at the entrance to the kitchen. "Look, I talked to Trung and he said the town plows are struggling to keep the main roads open. They can't keep up with the snow. He doesn't think anyone with a big truck is going to get up into this neighborhood and the secondary roads until at least very late tonight or tomorrow. So today's my best opportunity."

Sam gazes at his brother, but his eyes quickly move away, back to the floor. "So you've got at least the rest of the day free and clear until a truck can get up here." His expression goes mild for a moment, and he looks hopeful. "That's not bad. It would give you time. But there's still a lot that could go wrong."

"Lemme check my weather app." Danny consults his phone. "It says the snow will stop in the late afternoon. Right about the time the sun starts to go down." He rubs his chin. "That'll be perfect."

"You're going to leave tracks in the snow. They'll see you crossed the creek."

"If anyone sees my footprints, I'll say I went over there to try and help out." Danny grinds his teeth a moment, thinking. "You'll have to think of something to keep everyone busy. Maybe Lisa will read Peter's book. But we know Annika doesn't want to. So just keep her occupied."

Sam rubs his fingers over his mouth. He suddenly seems itchy all over, scratching his forehead and then his side. He winces. "You shouldn't have to go by yourself."

Both men stand there with sleeves pulled down over the knuckles of their hands to try to keep them warm. Danny turns and looks at me.

"What's the matter with you?"

Me? He's finally ready to listen to me?

ROWR! Whatever you're scheming, Annika will find you out, I want to tell him. *She's a very smart human.*

"Go easy," Danny tells me. "I don't have any food, if that's what you're looking for."

Food? That's the last thing on my mind.

I hear footsteps, and it sounds like the children are running down the stairs. I sprint over to the doorway to the kitchen to say hello.

Donovan comes bursting in and stops

short just in front of Annika and Lisa. Delilah follows close behind.

"I have to go," he says, breathless.

"Go where? Donovan, you haven't even had lunch yet." My woman grabs his hand. "You're still cold from sledding."

He shakes his head. "I'm cold because it's freezing upstairs. But I have to go. Right now. I'll be back."

Annika and Lisa turn to Delilah, who startles at finding herself the object of attention. But then she realizes they're counting on her to explain why Donovan wants to leave. She puts a hand on her brother's elbow. "Donovan, show them the photo."

"No, no, it's —"

"Lexi just posted a photo with a boy. He's a senior who lives down the street from her. But I'm sure it doesn't mean anything."

"A senior boy? A friend of hers?" Annika wipes her hands on a dishtowel.

"Not exactly." Delilah bites her lip and takes a quick glance at Donovan. "We tracked her on maps and they're at her house. It's probably no big deal. I told Donovan that I bet Steve was just bored, so he went over and offered to help shovel her out. It's not like it's anything serious."

Lisa squints. "Who is Lexi?"

Annika raises an eyebrow. "She's Donovan's girlfriend." She says this with care, as if announcing an important decree.

"Ohhhhh. I see. And you guys tracked her on a map? What kind of insidious, clever, scheming prosecutors have you turned into? Good Lord." She grabs a stack of dry bowls to put away in the cabinet. "What are you planning to do, Donovan? Go running over there, just because your girlfriend posted a photo with another guy? That's a terrible idea. It's probably completely innocent, and that would make you look jealous and desperate."

"Thank you," Annika says, gesturing toward Lisa. "You should listen to Aunt Lisa. There's no sense in rushing to conclusions. And it's still snowing. You can't even get down the street."

"*He* did. Steve got down the street. I mean, he lives a lot closer to her, but . . ." Donovan is staring at the phone. He sounds younger, and his cheeks are flushed bright pink, like bubblegum. "Why didn't I think to go to her house? I should be there to see if she needs anything."

Delilah puts a hand on her hip. "She doesn't *need* anything, Donovan. Her whole family is there. Obviously. Everyone is stuck."

"I have to go." Donovan clicks off the

301

phone. "I have to go right now."

Sam comes into the kitchen. He looks back and forth to try to figure out what's going on. "Everything okay?"

"We're having a crisis." Lisa gestures toward Donovan, who frowns at her, clearly unhappy at this description. "This hothead needs to rush over to his girlfriend's house."

"Well . . ." Annika reaches up to smooth Donovan's hair back from his forehead, but he doesn't see her hand coming and flinches. "Sorry, sweetheart. Why don't you call her instead?"

"But that kid might still be there."

"What's the matter?" Danny asks as he enters the kitchen, pulling on one glove. He has his coat on, and it looks like he's getting ready to go back out.

"Girl trouble," Annika sighs. "Donovan wants to go over to his girlfriend's house to make sure she's not . . . that she's not hanging out with another boy? Is that it? But he really can't go anywhere safely in this weather, can he?"

Donovan clenches his jaw. He looks about ready to lose his grip. "I have to go. It's just snow. We just walked through it to Aunt Lisa's house, Mom. It's no big deal."

Danny raises an eyebrow. "Hey, man, your girl is two-timing you? I think you better haul ass and get over there."

"DANNY." Annika's mouth hangs open. "No, I just said no."

"It's too far to walk in the snow," Delilah chimes in. "She lives downtown. And I really don't think Lexi meant anything by it. That photo is probably just meant to show that she's having fun during the blizzard, you know?"

"Lexi," Danny chuckles, pulling on his other glove. "That's a funny name. I have a daughter named Alexis."

Sam and Annika exchange a look.

Danny looks up, and his expression hardens. "Wait a minute . . . What grade did you say you were in again?"

Donovan freezes, mouth partly open. His eyes dilate, as if he sees a snake on the kitchen floor. He and Danny stare each other down for a moment. Each thinking carefully about his next move.

"No, no, no," Delilah practically yelps, a look of relief on her face. "Her last name is DiGiovanni. Not Parsons."

Danny's face darkens and he stands up straighter. Donovan moves slightly toward his mother under Danny's withering assessment.

"Yeah, that's her mom's last name. My girls live with my ex-wife during the week."

Danny takes a few steps toward Donovan, who flinches. "You're seeing Alexis? Since when?"

"Since . . ." Donovan glances quickly around the room, as if suddenly unsure of the answer. "I mean, I guess about two months?"

"Two months?" Danny huffs. "Wow. Those girls don't tell me anything. And she's with another guy right now? Show me the photo."

Donovan hesitates.

"Show it to me," Danny insists, an edge to his voice.

Donovan peers at his phone, hits a button, and then holds it up for Danny to study. Danny's forehead furrows as he tries to focus.

"Goddamn it." He pushes the phone back toward Donovan and walks over to Sam. "It's this jackass named Steve. He thinks he's God's gift to every girl in town. I can't seem to get rid of that guy. I told Alexis: No boys at the house." He runs a hand through his hair. "You know what that douchebag did?"

Sam folds his arms across his chest. "No. What'd he do?"

"This kid —" He can barely get out the words. "Last year, when he was a junior, he hooked up with this poor, innocent fresh-

304

man girl. And then Monday went into school and told everybody. My ex told me he just went in and practically shouted it out on a megaphone. He may as well have added it to the morning announcements: *In football, Manchester beat Ipswich 14 to 7; and in other news, Alexis DiGiovanni gave Steve Smith a blow job in the parking lot —*"

"Wait." Sam frowns. "It's Alexis we're talking about?"

"Nnnnnnnnooo." Danny throws up both hands in front of him and waves them frantically. "No, no, no, I'm just using that as an example. But Steve is a scumbag. He's so full of himself. I can't believe Alexis even talks to him."

Sam claps Danny on the shoulder. "Sorry. He sounds like a jerk." He nods at Donovan. "You should be happy she's going out with Donovan now. Maybe he's a better choice."

Danny glances back up at Donovan and squints. "Highly doubtful. Highly."

Annika bristles at that. She moves closer to Donovan, who allows it.

Sam cuts in. "I'm sure Donovan is a good kid, Danny."

Danny sighs. "Maybe." He points at Donovan. "Look, don't worry about Steve — I'll take care of him myself. But *you* can't

305

go over there either."

Donovan frowns. He grips the phone so tightly in his hand I think he might break it. His mouth is pressed tightly closed and he breathes out through his nose like a stag about to charge.

Danny goes on. "Your sister is right. It's too far to walk in this weather. But also, I won't allow it. No boys at the house, and no dating until she's eighteen. That's it. That's my rule. It seems she's clearly broken my rule, so she's gonna be in big trouble. You don't need to call her. I'll tell her it's over."

Donovan swallows. He looks back down at the photo, breathing shallow, eyes starting to tear up. He's clearly unsure what to do. His cheeks and mouth have gone from pink to red despite the cold. I'm concerned because he looks like he's going to be sick.

Donovan, I wish I could tell him. *Make a good choice. Be a good boy. Be the good boy your father always knew you were.*

"You know what else?" Danny looks Donovan over from head to toe, as if seeing him anew. "You should cut your hair. I don't like it."

Oh! That was unnecessary. Annika and I both startle at the same time.

I don't understand what Danny is getting

worked up about. Of course, I also don't really know anything about his daughter, or what kind of trouble she might have gotten herself into in the past with this *Steve* they're talking about.

I think if it were a year ago and Peter was still alive, Donovan would back down. He'd keep his mouth shut and leave the room. But a year has gone by and he has spent a lot of time alone. Donovan is taller, and his shoulders are broader. He is becoming a man who speaks his own mind.

"That's too bad, because Lexi likes it," Donovan says, his voice even. He tips his head back slightly in a motion I immediately recognize to be uniquely Peter's, although when Peter made that gesture it signaled he was listening, whereas I can see for Donovan it is meant to be a challenge. "I didn't have to ask her twice to go out with me. If we can't meet at your house, we'll just find somewhere else to go."

"DONOVAN." Annika holds up a finger in warning, eyes wide.

"You little snot-nosed —"

"Danny, back off," Sam cautions before his brother can react, throwing a hand up in front of him.

"Goddamn it." Danny shakes his head and takes a step back. "This is the last thing

I need right now." He throws his hands up. "I'm going for a walk. And I'm going to call Alexis." Just as he's turning to go, he swings back around to point at Donovan. "Don't screw with me. Back off."

Sam waits, casting a sympathetic eye on Annika and her kids. Donovan stands tall, keeping his face and body still, but his mouth twitches.

Once we hear the front door swing open and slam shut, everyone breathes a sigh of relief. Donovan starts pacing.

He shoves the phone into Delilah's face. "What is this? Why would she post this?" There's a note of despair in his voice.

A funny feeling of unease shivers down my spine, and my fur stands on end. Donovan doesn't usually get emotional. He's always in control.

"I don't know. Honestly." Delilah spreads her hands out in front of her. "Maybe they're just friends. Neighbors. I think that's all it is. Maybe she's just trying to show everyone that she doesn't care what Steve told everyone, and it doesn't bother her. Or maybe she's trying to make you jealous. It's possible she's trying to get you worked up. I don't know."

I sense Peter beside me. He's right beside me, hands on his hips. His brow furrows with concern. I look up at him. *What is happening?*

Love is never easy, Luna. There's always drama. Highs and lows. Peter shakes his head, casting a sympathetic eye on his children. *Remember when Donovan was little, and he thought a love story was going to be dull? But love stories are never boring. When he got older, he enjoyed the stories I told him as much as Delilah did.*

I remember. I flick my tail.

She's going to send the kids away, Peter. To a school your mom recommended. Is that a good idea?

Peter turns his head and looks at me. *I heard. But I can feel she's torn about it. The problem is that Annika thinks I'm the one who held all of us together. She thinks the family has lost its center.*

He crouches down. I have the sensation of him laying his hand on my head.

Peter, weren't you the one who held us together? You were the one who kept everything running at home. You fed me and put the children to bed at night.

No, that's not the whole story. Because Annika held me together. I couldn't have done it without her. She was the one who gave me a reason to keep going through the pain. This family is what gave my life meaning.

I start to purr. I agree with him.

Luna, she's not going to read the novel right now. Do you know where my journal is? Do you think you could bring it to her?

My heart nearly skips a beat.

Because yes, I do know exactly where Donovan has hidden it.

TRIP DOWN MEMORY LANE

ANNIKA

While I cook him another grilled cheese, Donovan paces in the kitchen, ranting to Delilah, who eggs him on and doesn't seem to appreciate that if she'd just talk some sense to him, she could have a calming effect. As his twin, she has a powerful influence on him that sometimes I think she doesn't understand. Donovan would certainly listen to her just as well as — no, definitely more than — he would listen to me. He's being irrational, of course; he can't go anywhere. He'll have to call the girl to get this straightened out. But Donovan and Delilah are both passionate people, and they can't seem to decide whether or not Lexi has broken some unspoken rule. I remember what it was like to be a teenager, when the importance of a look, word, or gesture could be greatly exaggerated.

"Just call her," Delilah suggests.

Donovan gives a curt shake of his head. "And say what?"

Maybe it's the snowstorm that has them agitated. I know we're getting a little stir-crazy with this full house and no heat. We're all wearing sweatshirts and down vests and fleece jackets, hopping from foot to foot to stay warm.

I glance over at the twins as they fill their water bottles at the sink. It sounds like Donovan's new girlfriend might have a little more experience with the opposite sex than he does. Well, who cares? Good for her. I hope Peter talked to Donovan about the birds and the bees. I prodded Peter about it several times, but he always waved me away, implying that he had it covered. I hope he actually did, because I'm quite certain that if I bring up anything to do with sex to Donovan, he'll walk right out the door into the snowstorm and not come back.

I make the twins more hot sandwiches and order them to go sit by the fireplace to keep warm, but instead they take their plates and disappear upstairs again. It's maddening. It must be freezing up there, but they insist on going. I'm sure it's because they want to huddle under their quilts and plan how they're going to sneak Donovan out so he can get to Lexi's house. Or it could be that they want to read more of Peter's journal, although the immediate Lexi crisis is probably taking precedence.

"I'll give Danny a few minutes before I go find him," Sam offers. "Let him cool off."

Lisa takes one look at me, and the way Sam is hovering near me by the sink, and sighs. She picks up the large stack of papers on the kitchen counter and straightens them. "I guess I'll read a chapter of this novel by the fire. I'd like to hear a little more about this quest."

I glance at Sam. "You know, when we moved here, I had to pack everything up and found our old yearbook. Do you want to take a trip down memory lane?"

He breaks into a nervous smile. "I don't know, do I?"

"Sure you do. Maybe you can see if the woodstove in the front room needs to be stoked up. I'll meet you in there in one minute."

"All right."

Once he's gone, I turn to Lisa. "What am I going to do about Donovan?"

She reaches out and taps my arm in solidarity. "He'll be fine. He's got a good head on his shoulders." A wistful look comes over her. "Ah, to be sixteen again. He's got it bad, doesn't he?"

I nod. "I suppose it's a good thing that Donovan is allowing himself to be vulnerable. He's been very guarded since Peter died. At the same time, I don't want him to get hurt."

"Of course you don't." Lisa plays with the blue stones of her necklace. "But our boy is in love. Remember Sam, senior year of high school? No one could have predicted half the stuff he did — least of all *us,* and we knew him best. You'd better be prepared for a little craziness."

She's right. I just have no idea how to get ready for it, especially without Peter here.

"Plus," she adds, "you told him you're shipping him down to Connecticut. He's going to have to leave his new girlfriend. No wonder he's freaking out."

She's right. I rub my forehead.

As I turn to go, she says, "Wait." I turn back. "What are you doing with Sam?"

"What do you mean?"

She purses her lips and lowers her voice. "I see something is going on, Annika."

"Nothing is going on."

She grinds her teeth and glares at me. "Look, you're vulnerable right now. Let's be realistic, okay? Sam will always be the one who got away — while he still could. You always talked about him like he was

314

some hero, but the truth is that he did nothing to support you after he caused a horrific accident. Are you under the impression he's come to save the day? Or is he just going to run away when things get difficult, like he did last time?"

"Stop," I hiss at her. "That's awful. That's not what Sam's all about, and you know it. You know it better than anyone. Be nice and knock it off."

I march out to find Sam waiting for me in the sitting room at the front of the house. While I dig out the yearbook from a cabinet, Sam pushes the couch closer to the burning woodstove. We sit side by side in the middle of the couch and begin to flip through the pages, the book spread out so it's half on my lap and half on his, looking at the photos. The heat being thrown off feels amazing, toasty warm. The afternoon sun doesn't provide a lot of light, but we can still find the flaws in everyone's appearance.

"Look at Margaret's hair." It makes me laugh.

Sam chuckles. "You think *that's* bad? Look at the collar on Craig's shirt."

At one point, I notice Lisa hovering in the doorway, checking on us. She doesn't get farther than the entrance to the room and doesn't say a word. The next time I look up, she's gone.

Luna jumps up on the couch. She pushes her nose into my thigh, almost as if she wants me to get up and feed her, but it's not dinnertime. Or maybe she wants me to move so she can sprawl out. I can't tell.

When we come to the page with Peter's senior photo, I stop for a moment, surprised. For some reason, I forgot I'd be confronted with his eighteen-year-old face. My heart seizes up. I love looking at his photo, but it's hard now that he's gone.

Peter was lightness and fresh air, quick to smile with an easy laugh. He was confident and open. He could be intense when he was teasing someone and when he earnestly wanted something. With Peter, everything was *now, now, now.* He enjoyed life to its fullest.

Next, we get to the page with Sam's photo. Whereas Peter smiled with his teeth, Sam smiles with his eyes. He looks mischievous, as if something about the photographer amuses him. I rub my fingertips over the page. "So handsome," I say, and he snorts.

In high school, Sam moved with caution. He thought before he spoke, considering his next move. His voice was gruff and serious. Sam didn't make many demands of

316

others; he was more about giving.

Peter and Sam were very different people, but I loved both of them.

Luna bats at my leg with her paw. It's strange. I still get the feeling she wants me to get up. But why? She often bugs me at bedtime to let me know it's time to go upstairs, but it's still early afternoon. So what could she want?

Sam nods toward the window, pulling my attention away from Luna. "Who knew we'd be stuck here, right? What do you think? It's kind of romantic, isn't it?"

Oh, boy. He's right. It is.

When I turn to look at him, my stomach clenches. He has the kindest way of looking at me, fully attentive, as if he can't wait to hear what I'm about to say.

"Sam." I bump my shoulder against his. "Why aren't you mad at me?"

"What?" He seems genuinely surprised. "What do you mean? You mean . . . because you married Peter?"

"Not that." I flip the yearbook closed. "Why aren't you mad about what happened back in high school? I let you take credit and get in trouble for so much you didn't do. It wasn't fair. I was a terrible girlfriend. I always worried that I ruined your life after you were sent away."

"Annie." He takes the book from me and places it on the coffee table in front of us. "Annika. You didn't ask me to do any of it. That was all me. And we were both eighteen. I was young and stupid, right? Look . . . whatever mistakes I made in the past aren't your fault. I'm okay with my life the way it is right now."

"I'm not trying to say anything is wrong with your life —"

"Good. Because I know it's not perfect. But it's mine, and I'm comfortable with it. You know how you said you're always trying to be a better person? Well, I am, too. And it's taken a long time." He gives me a look. "But you know me. I'm slow about everything, right?"

He's right. I remember how long it took him to kiss me the first time — I waited for months — and I smile with the memory.

The woodstove crackles. There's a thump as a log on the fire breaks up and falls apart.

"I wish you'd tell me how I could help you. You must need help with something right now." Sam's voice is quiet and he sounds a little sleepy.

"Thank you for offering. But the truth is, I need to get my own act together." I play with the thin gold necklace around my neck, twirling it in my fingers. "I know Peter's

318

gone, but I don't know how to move on, and I'm not even sure I want to. Even now that we've moved to this new house, Peter follows me everywhere, like a ghost."

Luna, who is sitting on the rug a few feet away from us, picks her head up. She gets up on all four paws and stares at me, wide-eyed, pupils round and black.

And suddenly, I can almost *see* Peter. In my mind's eye, he's eighteen again. He's sitting in the empty armchair, lanky and tall. He leans forward, with his elbows on his thighs. Tipping his head to gaze at me, his blond hair falls across his forehead. And he's wearing shorts, so I can see his good leg on the left and the stump on the right. He looks like he did when he'd just lost his leg. A young man, still traumatized from the recent accident.

It gives me a terrible chill.

At the same time, I'm happy to have such a clear vision of him. My eyes start to tear up.

Sam rubs his eyes with the palm of his hand. "Did you and Peter ever talk about prom night? Did he forgive us?"

Just then, the lamps flicker on. The room is bathed in a warm glow. Sam and I both startle, and I feel my face brightening with relief.

But the power goes out again immediately, and the room is thrown into shadow.

PROM NIGHT, 1987

ANNIKA

Did Peter ever forgive us?

That's a question I have no answer to. The answer may lie in the journal, or it may not.

Everything about prom unfolds exactly as I expect it to, at least at first. Sam and Mark arrive at our house at almost the same time. Lisa and I welcome them in, and we're all smiles as our mom helps us pin corsages onto the boys. I can't help but notice that Sam looks nice. But I have no intention of telling him that in front of Mark. That seems rude.

"Your sleeves are too long," I point out to him, tugging at them. "Didn't your mom help you rent this tux?"

"My mom couldn't go, so my brother Danny went with me. I think it's supposed to be like that." He shrugs, all bravado. "Why'd you put your hair up?"

"Why?" My hand flies up to the bun on top of my head. "Because it's prom! That's why. Why are you asking?"

"I dunno." Sam takes a step back to make room for me, because my mom is asking us all to get together for a photo. The four of us gather closer together. "I guess I just imagined you were going to wear it down," he says quietly into my ear.

"Sorry if you imagined it wrong." I lean in and smile at the camera. I really don't care what he *imagined*. Honestly.

But then I wonder if I should, in fact, take my hair down. Even though I spent an hour at the salon getting it to look perfect.

"Do I look like James Bond?" Mark jokes.

"Maybe . . . if he were shorter. And wore glasses," Sam offers.

"I've never worn a tux before. I seriously think I look like James Bond."

Lisa laughs loudly at everything the boys say, which makes me roll my eyes. Honestly, I think she's way too eager to please everyone. Maybe she's just nervous. I don't think boys expect you to be delighted about every word that comes out of their mouths.

As we're about to head out the door, Lisa grabs my arm and pulls me aside.

"Promise me one thing," she says, searching my eyes to make sure I'm listening.

322

"What?"

"Don't get overly mushy with Sam in front of everyone, okay? He's my date tonight. I want everyone in the class to know that. My date. For just one night. Got it?"

I frown and shake my head slightly. "Everyone knows that he's going out with me, Lisa."

She clenches her jaw. "You can't give me one night? You're really selfish, you know that?"

"Hey! I don't think that's fair —"

"Listen. I'm just saying, don't get all lovey-dovey. PLEASE. It would be humiliating. He's my friend, too. Promise me."

I sigh, but I also feel bad. "Okay, okay. Whatever you want. We're not lovey-dovey anyway. We're not like that at all."

"Yeah, right." She lets go of my arm and strides past me. I follow.

We drive over to the school in two cars, since the boys came separately. Mark borrowed his dad's car, and I feel very fancy riding over in it. It has a nice tan leather interior and a cool stereo that plays cassette tapes. We blast a pop song and sing on the ride over. I'm so excited I'm practically dancing in my seat. When we arrive at the school I'm so hyped up that I want to run inside, so I grab Mark's hand and drag him in.

The dinner is okay — a bland chicken in lemon sauce that I push around my plate — but I'm too busy chatting to eat much. When that's over, everyone starts dancing like crazy, until we're all in a sweat.

When "Goodbye Yellow Brick Road" comes on, the song we voted on to be our class song for some God-unknown reason, Sam asks me to dance. It's the first slow dance of the night, and I've never slow danced with a boy before, but I get through it okay. The sleeve of Sam's tux feels scratchy and I wonder how he can stand it. I rest my hands up on his shoulders, and he puts his hands on my waist, and he sings the words of the song to me to make me laugh. It's awkward but very nice all the same. I'm happy Sam asked me to dance to the first slow song. I hope that someone else has asked Lisa to dance, but I don't see her anywhere. At least Mark is dancing with someone, and he gives me a wink. I blush but smile back.

I did promise Lisa that Sam and I wouldn't get "lovey-dovey." I hope this doesn't count. But he is my boyfriend, after all.

We're all having a good time until Mrs.

Evans arrives. She's the gym teacher who Sam "confessed" to about spray-painting the basketball court back in the fall, and she's made him feel bad about it all year. She thinks he defaced her precious gym and can't let it go. She seems to make a point of seeking out Sam, glaring at us and shaking her head with disgust.

I can see Sam's mood starting to deteriorate, from the way he rubs his forehead to the fact that he stops socializing and sits back down at the dinner table by himself. He goes from happy to troubled in a matter of minutes.

Dana and I are laughing about something when I spot Sam, and I tell her I'll be right back. Not that it's my job to entertain Sam, but I *am* the one who told him to take my sister to the prom, so I feel a little responsible if he's not having a good time. "Hey," I say to him as I approach the table. "You're not going to let Mrs. Evans ruin your night, are you?" I kick his foot with mine. "Come on."

"Jesus, you'd think she could leave me alone for just one night. I didn't know she'd be here chaperoning, did you?" He pushes his chair away from the table and leans forward, elbows on his knees, as if he's afraid he might be sick. "Ever since the graffiti thing, she's given me a hard time. All year. I can't lose my scholarship, Annie. Why'd she have to come here and remind me how miserable my life is?"

"Your life's not miserable. And you won't lose your scholarship. It's going to be fine. This will all blow over. They're not going to forget about four years of hard work over a few . . . mistakes."

Believe me, I'm consumed with the same concern — is there a chance his college acceptance will be revoked? Sam's counting on that four-year scholarship to UCLA. It's his only option. He can't lose it. I've been in knots with worry, knowing his future is in jeopardy. I'd go to Mr. Galanes and plead Sam's case, but what's done is done. If UCLA has heard about his latest suspension, what can we possibly do about it at this point?

Sam glances up at me, and he tries to smile. But he still looks gloomy.

Grabbing my hand, he suggests, "Do you want to get out of here for a while?"

"What do you mean? Go for a walk outside?"

"Yeah. No. I mean, let's leave. Leave the prom."

I look up and glance around the room. Girls looking pretty in pastel dresses. Boys in tuxedos. A million gold and black balloons on the ceiling and the floor. Dirty plates on tables with silverware piled on top, and dessert next. It's fun here. Why would I want to leave?

But then Sam squeezes my hand. "Annie." And when I turn back, he looks so sad. It's more important to be there for Sam than spend yet another hour dancing, isn't it? Things are winding down anyway.

"But we haven't danced to 'Stairway to Heaven' yet!"

He gazes at me with a serious look on his face and doesn't let go of my hand. "Doesn't matter. I'll play it for you in the car."

"Okay. But Lisa . . ."

"Tell her to get a ride with Tindall, okay? And we'll meet them at Ellie's after party."

I hesitate. "Wait — where do you want to go?"

"The beach." He lights up, for the first time since Mrs. Evans arrived. "There's a full moon. And it's finally a little warm out. We can spin the beach, maybe stop for a while. I don't know. Then we'll go straight to the party, and we won't have to come back here." I must still look uncertain, because he continues. "Please. I'm sick of this school and I just want to get out of here."

"Okay, okay. I'll go tell Lisa. I'll be right back."

Lisa is dancing, her hands up over her head, and she looks like she's having a good time for once. I'm hugely relieved, considering I didn't see her earlier. So rather than bother her, I find Mark.

"Hey," I say, tapping his arm. Mark is standing with a few kids from band. "Would you mind giving Lisa a ride to the after party? Sam and I are gonna go for a ride. Out to the beach."

He adjusts his glasses. "You and Sam, huh? Going for a ride, huh?" he asks loudly, so the whole circle can hear. "Well, well, well. I guess it's about time." Mark laughs. "Have fun, okay? But not too much fun, if you know what I mean."

"It's not like that," I sigh. Although . . . maybe it's *exactly* like that. I guess I'll have to see how it goes.

I find Sam waiting in a corner of the gym. When we burst out through the back door, the clean spring air is refreshing and fills my head with good thoughts. You can tell we had a brief rain shower during dinner by the smell coming off of the newly paved parking lot. I feel special every time I look down at my long, shimmery gown. It's red and silky and I love it so much. This has been a great night so far.

Sam's black car isn't exactly Cinderella's carriage. The scent of mildew and chicken soup hits me as I climb into the low passenger seat. The seats are covered in a fuzzy old fabric, worn from use; it's ripped clear open at one corner so you can see the foam. The rubber mat beneath my feet is dirty with dried mud, and I'm not sure I want to let my brand-new, sparkly shoes touch the icky floor.

Yet at the same time, I'm instantly cocooned in a feeling of comfort and belonging. While riding in his dad's construction truck is fun, I've never been anywhere with Sam in his mom's car, and it feels new and exciting, like we're making a great escape. I crack my window an inch to let in the night air.

Sam turns on the radio to his favorite classic rock station. With four older siblings, I realize Sam knows a lot more about music than I do. But still, this isn't my favorite, and he knows it. I listen to two songs before I can't stand it anymore.

"Can I change the station?" We're just pulling up in a parking space that overlooks one of the smaller beaches on the way out of town. Sam suggested we come here for privacy, assuming the beach downtown is where a lot of other kids will stop on their way to parties. He pulls into a parking space.

"Change it? This is the only good radio station and the only one worth listening to."

"This is *not* the only good station —"

"Don't even start. You know that classic rock —"

"And you know how I feel about listening to this old stuff every time! Who wants to hear the same fifty songs over and over, when there are new and better songs recorded every day?"

"Annie, you're breaking my heart." He shakes his head and turns off the engine. It gets quiet, and I hear a wave crash down on the beach through my open window. "You look gorgeous, by the way. I didn't want to say that in front of Lisa and Mark, but it's true."

"No, I don't." I laugh. "You already criticized my hair."

He tosses the car keys up onto the dashboard. "No, I didn't criticize it. I just imagined you might wear it down, that's all. Because I'd been thinking about it a lot. But it looks good up, too."

I feel myself starting to blush. I have no idea what to say to that, so I change the subject.

"Thanks for going with Lisa to the prom.

She would've been upset if I had a date and she didn't." I still feel bad about the date mix-up. Of course, I would rather have gone with Sam. But, in a way, we did end up going together.

"No big deal. It's just one more thing in a long list of things you've roped me into over the past four years." He waves that thought away. "So, my brother Danny not only helped me rent this tux, he also got me beer for tonight." He climbs up out of his seat and reaches around the floor of the backseat, grabbing a six-pack and hauling it into the front with us.

"So . . . is this why you wanted to go for a drive?" I eyeball the beer suspiciously. "You want to start drinking?" I assume there will be alcohol at the party later, but this surprises me.

"You want one?"

Before I know it, he's pulled a bottle opener from the glove compartment and popped the top off of a bottle. So I take it. It seems rude to refuse. Plus, I don't want to seem super lame. I've never had a beer before, but he doesn't need to know that. That day on the roof was my first time trying alcohol, and I hated it, but this might be better, right? More like a soda?

I take a sip. It's fizzy and bitter. I force

myself to swallow a mouthful, but then put the bottle down in a cupholder. Sam chugs his like it's lemonade. Good Lord. How can he stand it?

"Are you okay?"

Sam shrugs. "No, I'm depressed. I can't believe high school's almost over. And I'm still worried about my scholarship. I can't stop thinking about it. Even though I'm not sure I want to go to California. I don't want to leave."

I give a short laugh. "Sam. You're always so stressed out. I've never met anyone so tightly wound in my life. California's going to be a blast."

"Yeah? Okay. If you say so."

"Look, it's fine to be anxious. It's totally normal. Your dad has been sick, and now you have to move far away, and you've had a lot going on. I just wanted to say . . . I never should have suggested that we go out to the golf course that day of the senior prank. I ruined Valentine's Day."

He takes another drink of his beer and smiles sadly. "But I love that you suggested it. I thought it was a cool idea. That's the pathetic thing. I mean . . . I would do any stupid thing you ask me to. I guess you already know that."

I shrug. "I guess so. I have no idea why

you always go along with everything. And Lisa — God, I don't even want to get into her idiocy. I don't know how you put up with her."

He bites the inside of his mouth for a moment. "Because." He starts to peel the label off of his beer bottle with his thumbnail. "Because I love you."

I peer up at him. Love me?

My mind flies into a panic. I guess he means as friends. He doesn't . . . *love* me, right? I mean, I've been hoping he would say so, but it's terrifying to hear him actually say it.

"What?" It comes out as a whisper. But I need him to repeat it. To clarify.

He puts his beer down next to mine and takes my hand. He squeezes it, so I can't misunderstand, and then intertwines our fingers. "I've always loved you."

I'm incredulous. "No, you haven't." There's no way that's true. I know for a fact that he's gone out with two other girls this year. Nothing serious, but still. He's being dramatic.

My heart starts beating hard. I'm in such denial. I love Sam, too, of course. I was even jealous that Lisa had his yearbook photo taped to the headboard of her bed. I had half a mind to rip it off her bed frame.

"Yes, I have. Annie, come on. You know I have."

"Since when?"

"Since always. Since forever."

And suddenly, I can see it. The way he looks at me. It's not that he's skeptical or critical or hesitant or frustrated or thinks I'm weird. He's swoony.

Oh, God. How did I not get that? I suppose it's because he's Sam Parsons. He's the boy who's good at math and football and is popular in school. He's the one who's *not my type* and out of reach.

Or, maybe, he's exactly my type and easily within my reach. And I didn't understand.

In the moonlight, in his tuxedo, Sam looks handsome and older. I'm not sure I belong here. He can't possibly be talking to me, can he?

It's going to be fine, I tell myself. *He loves you. You can't mess this up.*

I try to force myself to relax, taking in a deep breath and letting it out. I tell myself I can handle this. It's Sam, and I've known him forever.

I pick up the beer with my free hand to take a swig of it, and to my surprise, it tastes better than the first time. I feel it slide down my throat and warm up between my ribs.

This is the craziest night ever. It's definitely living up to all of my prom night expectations. I can't wait to tell Dana.

Of course, I probably shouldn't tell Lisa about any of this. Sam is actually her prom date, and I've stolen him away. Which worries me. What will she think? Is she going to get mad again?

Who am I kidding? I know she is.

Still holding my hand, Sam's watching me, waiting for my response. But I'm not sure what to say. Or do. Is this where I say *I love you* back to him? My throat feels constricted and dry. And before I can get the words out, he starts to move.

Sliding closer, he carefully reaches forward as if to tuck a loose curl of my hair behind my ear. But I know my hair is still perfect, and there's nothing to fix. He just skims his fingers over my neck. I close my eyes, because — holy cow. Sam is touching me so gently. And just as I'm opening my eyes, he leans over and kisses me. It's intense and dreamy, his mouth on mine, tasting malty and sweet like butterscotch. It's like he's kissing me for the first time, all over again. My whole body wants to float forward and meet up with his.

When he pulls back for a moment, I can barely catch my breath. But I don't want him to stop. I feel antsy and suddenly full of energy, so I kiss him right back. I feel a little crazy. I want to climb right out of my seat to get closer to him.

"Sam!" I grab the collar of his jacket, shouting at him even though he's inches away. "Why didn't you tell me you loved me before?"

He chuckles. "Easy, Karlsson. I was hoping to talk to you tonight," he says quietly, his voice low and rumbly. I feel like I've never heard his voice before, and I'm only now realizing how attractive he sounds. "Annie."

I love the way he says my name. I can't help smiling, but he's very serious about it, which just makes me even happier. "Do you want to move to the back?" I blurt out. "We'd have more room."

He nods yes.

The night air is cool when I step out of the car; it drifts up from the shoreline and gives me goose bumps. I can hear the waves crashing on the beach. When I climb into the rear seat, the chill sends me right back into Sam's arms. I feel really good about being with him.

We end up kissing for a long time, madly, intensely. I feel we have to make up for a lot of lost time, like all of the million times when he should have kissed me but didn't.

When we lay down in the back, I laugh because I'm so happy and we don't really fit. He slips a hand under my knee to pull my leg over his so I don't fall off the seat, and — yes, that's even better. My dress rides way up because there's a slit on the side, but I don't care. His whole body against mine feels like it belongs there.

"I've wanted to do this for so long."

"Shut up, Sam. Just kiss me."

When his mouth is on my neck and his hand is way down low on my back, I think I'm going to pass out from how good it feels. I caress every part of his body I can reach and it's still not enough — I want more of him. This is seriously the best thing I've ever done in my life. Our bodies fit perfectly together, and I'm starting to realize that our whole lives fit together, and I have no idea why we've never done this before. Sam spends a long time there, kissing right at the base of my neck, and I hold the back of his head.

"I'm sorry I didn't talk to you for weeks after I got arrested the day of the snowball fight," he blurts out, pulling back for a break.

"Oh." This catches me by surprise. "It's okay. I told you, that was all my fault."

He squeezes me, with his hand on my hip.

"No, it wasn't. We all agreed to go out on the golf course. It was just — I told my dad about you, and I thought he'd be happy for me, but he was mad. He said I had to forget about girls and just focus on making money and getting into college."

"Sam." I grab his shoulder. "It's okay. Just don't let it happen again." I look into his eyes. "Don't listen to your father. He's a terrible influence on you and couldn't be more wrong. I need you totally one hundred percent focused on girls from here on in."

He smiles. "You don't need to worry about that. I think about you all the time. I told you. I love you."

Oh! I pause and squeeze his arm. "You're acting so strange tonight."

"I want you so much."

I flush with embarrassment. "Me? Sam. No, you don't."

I immediately regret saying anything. I seem programmed to second-guess and contradict everything Sam says. But honestly, how could he feel that way about me? I'm silly and immature. And everyone knows it.

He isn't put off by my nervous response. "Yes, I do. Annie. As soon as I saw you tonight, it's all I could think about. How much I wanted to be alone with you. I think about it every day." He holds me tighter. "It keeps me up at night. It wakes me up in the morning. I feel like I'm going crazy."

Oh, God. I must be dreaming. That's really how he feels?

Now I'm the one getting swoony.

I love you is amazing, and it's the best thing Sam's ever said to me, but that's something you could say to your mom, or your best friend, or your cat.

I need you is wonderful, too, but that's something you could say to your lab partner in science class, or your teammate on the softball team.

Only *I want you* is something you say to the object of your romantic affection. It means that your heart has made a choice, and it's reserved for someone special. No one's ever said it to me before. So in combination with *I love you,* it just sends me over the edge.

So how is reality supposed to now live up to these expectations? I fumble around for what to say. "Should I take off my dress?"

He pauses and takes in a deep breath, but doesn't let go. "Do you want to?"

"Yeah." With my arms around him, I feel confident that this is the right decision. "Definitely. For sure," I say, as if I've done it a million times before. The truth is, I don't know if *that's* what he has in mind, but it must be, right? I remember most of sex education from fifth grade, but not everything, not exactly. I would probably pass out if I saw a naked boy. But I'm not one to back down from a challenge. So I double down and reach over for the zipper that runs down my side.

But I only have it unzipped about six inches when he stops my hand.

"Umm . . . Wait. Maybe not tonight." He takes in another deep breath and sighs. "I mean, I want to. Obviously. But I don't have what we need."

"What we need . . . ?" My brain really is muddled, because it takes a minute to click. "Oh. Okay." I smile. "You mean Danny helped you rent a tux and got you a six-pack of beer, but didn't get you condoms?" I sigh dramatically. "What kind of older brother is he? That seems like a serious breach of brotherly obligation. A complete dereliction of duty."

Sam squeezes me tight and kisses my cheek. "Yeah, he's an idiot. He messed up big-time." He nuzzles his face into mine, and I'm overwhelmed.

"I don't care, Sam," I blurt out, and I mean it. "I want to do it anyway."

"No, it's okay. Let's wait. Maybe next

weekend, okay? My parents are supposed to go away overnight, and you can come over."

I nod. "Okay. It's a date." Did I just make a date for sex? Hmm, the rest of my week is officially shot. I will not be able to think about anything else.

"Annie." And for the first time, I fully understand what he means when he says that.

"Sam," I say, smiling and putting my hand on his warm cheek, feeling something in my heart break open. And just like *that,* it becomes easy to say. "I love you, too."

He nods. "Sweetheart, I want you to come to California with me. Transfer out there. Or I'll stay here and forget about UCLA. I guess I could work for my dad."

"Shhh. Sam, you don't want to do that. Don't be insane. I don't want to talk about this right now."

"But long-distance relationships are hard, and California is too far. I don't want you to meet someone else, and —"

"Stop." I smooth down his hair and look into his eyes. "Please stop. I'm not going to meet someone else. We don't need to figure it out this minute."

"Look, just promise me you'll think about it. You could go to school for one year out here and then transfer out to a California school."

"Sam. STOP. I'll think about it, okay? But not right this minute. Please. We're talking about my life and my future —"

"I know. *Our* future."

"This is too much. I can't figure out my entire college path and career and living circumstances right now, in this car. Okay?"

He nods, disappointed.

We spend another hour in the car, losing track of time, kissing and talking, but also sometimes just lying there quietly. He strokes my arm, and I undo a few buttons on his dress shirt so I can touch his chest. It's hard to explain, but I want more of him. I need more, even though he's right next to me, and I don't know how to stop feeling so desperate. I leave my dress unzipped so he can slip his hand in and put his palm right on the skin of my back. It's the most intimate I've ever been with another person in my life, which is scary, but it feels right.

"I love you," he says again.

"What's that? I don't think I heard you the first four times."

When he tickles me, I laugh and nearly fall off the seat. He holds me tight. I never want it to end.

But it's long past midnight, my Cinderella's carriage is already a pumpkin, and my sister is going to be worried about where I went. So eventually we sit up, get back in the front seats, and drive slowly back to the party.

I wish this were the end of my prom night story. I wish I could say Sam takes me home, where my sister is already sound asleep, and he kisses me good night in our driveway. I wish I could say we have a wonderful romantic summer together and say goodbye before we part ways for college; then I bump into Peter somewhere in Boston and it's just chance that we end up together.

Sometimes now, I look back and wish we never drank that beer. It taints my memory of the whole night, because of what happened later.

HIS FINAL DAY

LUNA

I can't believe Annika just said Peter follows her everywhere, like a ghost. Yet she can't see what I see. I wish I could tell her — you're right, Peter is here with us!

Like Annika, I once thought Peter was invincible. I thought nothing could slow him down. He did a good job of convincing me anyway, even though I saw him in vulnerable moments. But he had an inner strength that made it hard to imagine life without him.

Peter's final day before he dies is just a normal day, like any other. The sun shines, the waves crash, the earth turns.

Our home on the beach does not have a second story on top, because it would be hard for Peter to have to go up and down stairs every day. Instead, we have a lovely, sprawling space, just the one level, with

344

magnificent views of the sea below. But there are four wooden stairs that Peter must climb to get up onto the deck after emerging from the path that leads to the ocean.

I sit on a sandy patch of grass, watching Peter taking his time to get himself up the stairs with his crutches. Donovan waits at the bottom of the stairs behind him. They've both been down at the beach for hours, and their bathing suits are wet. Peter's cheeks are pink with exertion. Donovan taps his hand on the railing behind him, a towel around his neck. Donovan is tan and just as tall as his father. He's putting on weight rapidly, eating anything he can get his hands on. Donovan could easily sprint up the steps, but he forces himself to be patient and let his father go first.

"Sorry," Peter mutters over his shoulder as he gets to the top.

"It's okay." Donovan has a bright green board he swims with, and he looks at the way it's lying on the grass. He decides to prop it up against the railing at the bottom of the stairs. "You probably shouldn't go out when it's so rough. We were out there a long time. You look tired."

"I'm fine." Peter wipes his brow. "I need my exercise."

It's the middle of summer, and the air is

heavy with humidity. I sit in the shade of a tall tree, glad that I never sweat. Frankly, perspiration looks gross.

"You swallowed a lot of water, didn't you?" Donovan looks concerned.

"Whatever. I love salt water."

Donovan scowls. "Yeah, right. Why don't you get a waterproof prosthesis? I know they're expensive, but you could afford it."

"Well . . ." Peter pats his chest. "This is good. This is better. To accomplish something without it. I'm glad I don't need a prosthesis for everything."

I've watched the two of them when they go out in the ocean. They are both strong swimmers, and Donovan helps Peter get into and out of the water, leaving the crutches on dry sand.

"Lunch is ready!"

Father and son look up. Annika is calling them from the kitchen window.

Donovan is clearly relieved. "Oh, cool. I'm starving. Lemme just rinse off my feet." He jumps up the steps, two at a time, and heads over to the hose that is sitting coiled on the deck.

Peter takes advantage of the fact that Donovan is busying himself to rest a moment. He leans on his crutches, and his eyes scan the house. I watch as he gives a quick nod, and I assume Annika has seen him from the window.

"Help clean up after lunch today, okay?"

Donovan gathers the hose up in a few messy loops and throws it in a heap. "Yeah, but, Dad . . . I actually told Colin I'd meet him at the park, so I don't have a lot of time."

"Donovan." Peter's voice gets sharp. "You can spend ten minutes helping clean up."

The young man rolls his eyes. He readjusts his hair, which is long and gathered in a bun on the back of his head with an elastic. "Whatever."

"No, it's not *whatever.* I want you to help out. I feel like you're never around anymore. I don't even know where you go half the time. Are you listening? Your mom is leaving today for a whole week, and I want you to spend some time with her. We can't do it without your mom, okay?"

"Can't do what?"

"This." Peter nods up at the house and then looks all around him. "Life. Everything."

The two stand there for a moment. There's a mild breeze coming off the ocean that probably feels good on their bare skin, but how would I know? I'm covered in fur.

I come out from under the shade of the

tree and trot up the steps, moving straight to the sliding screen door that leads into the kitchen. I'd like to see what's being served for lunch. Something smells delicious. But I turn when I hear them still talking.

"You need to help out more, and not disappear with your friends all the time. And you can't just keep taking cash out of my wallet. You're old enough to get a summer job."

"Dad. Not again." There's a note of disgust in the younger man's voice.

"I get frustrated when your mother or I have to drag the trash can to the curb when I've asked you to do it ten times. You know, there are some things that are hard for me to do, and I feel like your mom gets stuck doing too much —"

"DAD. Jesus." Donovan hops back down the stairs so he can pick his body board up and bring it up on the deck and rinse it off. I've noticed Donovan would rather climb or jump than walk. I imagine Peter was the same way when he was young. "Stop talking like that. You're fine. You're PERFECTLY FINE, and you do as much as you can. And I already do a ton. A TON."

"Okay, yes, you've taken on more this past year, but I still think —"

"For Chrissake. We just had a nice morning together and you have to end it by giving me shit? Thanks a lot. I DON'T WANT TO HEAR IT."

Donovan is finished spraying his board and he slams down the hose. He marches over and whips open the sliding screen door so I can enter. But I balk and let him go first. I don't approve of him speaking to his father in that tone of voice. I decide to wait for Peter.

Peter is a magnificent man. He is a teller of great stories. A keeper of world secrets and knowledge. Possibly a descendant of King Arthur himself! And Donovan is rude to him, all the time. It's a shame.

When Peter finally catches up to me, he waits. "Luna. Are you going in?"

I just stare. I know he'd pick me up if he could. But until he puts his mechanical leg on, he needs his hands and arms free for his crutches and for balance. I'm too big and awkward to be picked up without two hands.

Peter leans heavily on the handgrips of his crutches, frown lines around his eyes. I'm sure he's wiped out from swimming. He gets very still, and I wonder if he's replaying his talk with Donovan over in his mind. He also has moments where he disappears into himself, where he shuts down as he fights through pain. I wait, keeping him company.

Just then, Annika appears at the doorway. "Are you coming?"

Peter immediately straightens up. His eyes brighten. He gets that look on his face, the one where my woman is demanding something of him and he needs to respond in the affirmative because he must never, ever disappoint her. I have come to realize that he never allows himself to be seen struggling in any way.

"Yes, I'm coming. My bathing suit's still wet, though. I need to change, but I'll just be a minute."

"Okay." She squints out at the ocean behind him, beyond the rocks and sea grass, and holds a hand over her eyes. The sun sparkles off the dark blue surface. "They said the riptides might be bad today. I wish you wouldn't take Donovan out when they make those announcements. There's no one out there on the beach to even notice if the two of you drowned."

Peter leans one crutch against the wall and wipes a bead of sweat from his temple with the back of his hand. "Don't worry. I know how to deal with a riptide, and so does Donovan. He should've signed up for lifeguard training this year, but he's just being lazy."

She makes a noncommittal sound in the

back of her throat. "Still . . . What if you couldn't get in? I wouldn't want Donovan in the position where he had to save you. Because what if he couldn't?"

Peter rakes a hand through his wet hair. He leans toward her and gives her a *look*. He drops his voice so his words are clearly only meant for her. "Sometimes a man needs to swim in the ocean, and his wife should let him." He reaches with his free hand to touch his fingers to her wrist, as if taking her pulse, and then easily slips his hand into hers. There is something to admire in how expertly he does this, how quickly he transforms himself into a stronger man and convinces Annika to drop her complaints.

Annika stutters her words out. "I . . . I always let you do whatever you want to do, and you know it. I wouldn't dream of trying to stop you. I'm just saying, be careful." She pauses. "Was Donovan being awful? I heard you arguing. You can yell at him if he deserves it, you know. You don't have to spoil him."

Peter makes a face. "Ah, it's all right. I remember my dad yelling at me when I was that age, and I just don't want . . . I think things will sort themselves out in the end. That's all."

"Well, okay. Now, come in here and change."

He still holds her hand. "When do you leave for Cornell?"

"I want to hit the road between three and four. That way I can spend as much of the day with you guys as possible, but also get in a lot of the driving before it gets dark. Then I'll be back next Saturday afternoon."

He sighs. "What kind of deranged college kids take a math class in July?"

She gives a sharp laugh. "Very, very smart ones."

Annika waits while he takes the final step into the house. He kisses her.

"Salty," she says. "You must have swallowed the whole ocean." She turns back toward the kitchen. He follows, at his own pace.

Annika keeps Peter's pictures in frames by her bed. There's one particular photograph of Peter that's my favorite. He is looking away from the camera, clearly amused, with a smile on his face. He's tipping his head the way he did when he was listening to someone talk, and that someone was usually my Annika. For that alone, for the way he gave her his time and attention, I will always love him.

I once heard Annika refer to Peter as Superman. But I know now he was not really a superhero. He did not battle a sea serpent, nor was he actually related to King Arthur. But oh! He could have been. He lived life to the fullest and appreciated what he had.

So, if Peter thinks Annika should have his journal, I will steal it away from Donovan, or find a way to lead her to it.

Luna

Danny reenters the house with a great stomping of his feet. His hands and face are as red as a hot ember from the fire. I expect him to say something about the fact that Sam and Annika are sitting together by the woodstove, but he seems to consider it and then changes his mind. He kicks off his boots.

"Everything's clear from the street to the back of the truck. Good news . . . the snow is tapering off, and the sun is coming out. You could practically get a sunburn out there."

Sam laughs. His gaze turns to the picture window. "I guess it's time to take the old tire off and put the spare on."

"Not right now. I need to warm up again."

Annika clucks her tongue. "Don't you want to be ready for when they plow the street?"

"Look." Danny has taken off his big, padded coat, but left on his fleece and down vest. He comes over to the woodstove and stands near it to warm up. "Trung said the town plows won't get to this neighborhood until after midnight, so we have a little time."

"Are you sure, Dan?" Sam asks. "You were pretty hot on getting a jump on things this morning."

"Yeah, but now that I know it's just the tire, I'm not so worried. Where's that whiskey?"

Annika frowns. "Danny, you shouldn't drink all day."

Lisa enters the room. "I'll have a shot of the whiskey, if you're pouring."

Danny gives Annika a shrug, and she just sighs. The truth is, the humans seem to have run out of things to do, and the relentless cold must be getting to them.

I decide to go fetch that journal, if I can. I really hate to leave the warm fire. Really, *really* hate it. But this is important.

I slink up the stairs, quiet on light paws.

When I reach the top step, I scamper down the carpeting toward Delilah's room, because I hear voices. As I expected, the twins are on top of Delilah's bed. It reminds me of when Peter read books and told us stories every night.

I like Delilah's room better than Donovan's. After they moved into the cottage, Delilah asked her mother to hire someone to paint the room a light yellow. So now, even though the window is blocked by a shade tree, it always feels cheerful and sunny in her room. There's a bulletin board above the bed on which she has pinned colorful papers and photos, and a strand of twinkly lights hang around the window frame. Powered by batteries, the lights sparkle even though we've lost power in the house.

The kids are leaning against the wall, several soft throw blankets over their legs. Donovan holds up a big, clunky flashlight to illuminate the navy-blue leather book that I recognize as Peter's journal. I suppose I will have to wait until Donovan puts it away in its hiding spot, and then drag it with my teeth to Annika. But I'm concerned about how I'm going to actually get to the diary, because the hiding place is in Donovan's room, in the middle of the big geometry textbook Donovan has been reading, and he always buries it under many other thick, heavy books on his bookshelf.

Maybe I can stand near the books and *HOWL* at the top of my lungs. And I'll just hope Annika gets to me before Donovan does. Then I can paw at the books until she inspects them and finds the journal.

Delilah giggles and doubles over.

"God, this is just sappy," Donovan groans. "I can't believe Dad wrote this in high school. I'm cringing."

"Come on." Delilah slaps her brother's arm. "He had a crush on Mom. It's sweet. It's just how he felt. We don't have to read this, you know. Besides, wouldn't you write the same way about Lexi? What would *you* write?"

Donovan puts down the journal next to him on the bed. "I don't know." He rubs his hands together, palms flat, as he thinks about it.

"Actually, why don't you write her something? Like a poem? Or a love letter?"

"Not poetry. Ugh. But . . . you think she'd like it if I wrote something?"

"Sure. Of course, she'd like that. But the thing is, don't just write about how hot she is, or anything superficial like that. She'll like it if you write something from the heart. Something honest about how she makes you feel." Delilah pauses. "I mean, if you were listening to Dad at all while he was alive, you should be able to write a pretty good letter."

"I don't know." He scratches behind his

357

ear. "Lexi might think it's dumb."

Delilah shakes her head, eyes big. "Nah, not if you're sincere. She'd love it."

"Maybe a gift would be better. Christmas is coming and I was planning to get her something anyway. Do you think she'd like a bracelet or a necklace?"

"Yeah, maybe. But isn't jewelry kind of intimate?"

"Why do you say that?"

"Because she has to wear it."

He laughs. "Yeah, I like that. Isn't being intimate kinda the point?" Donovan looks down at his lap, clutching his phone. "Del, I feel like I need to go over to her house right now, and I'm going to explode if I don't. I feel like I'm going to be physically sick if I don't see her. I'm sweating thinking about it. I would walk ten miles in the snow and I don't even care. You have no idea."

She raises an eyebrow. "I have *some* idea. You've been acting pretty strange lately."

"What am I going to do about her dad? And what about Steve? Should I ask about the photo?" His phone *pings!* "Wait — this is her calling me back, finally. Lemme get this."

Donovan hops up, and I duck out of sight. "Hi," he says in a breathy voice, walking out into the dark hallway. He stops to lean against the wall. "Oh, I know, baby, I'm sorry about your dad. He called you?" He closes his eyes tight. "He yelled at you? He said *what*? Jesus. Okay, well — don't worry. Please." Donovan clenches his fist. "Listen, we'll figure out something. We will. I promise we will. Lexi, please don't worry. Don't cry, you know that I —" He turns his face toward the wall and listens. "Okay. Call me back as soon as you can. As soon as you get free."

Donovan heads back into Delilah's room and climbs up on her bed to sit beside her again with legs crossed. He buries his face in his hands and moans. "I don't know what to do."

"What'd she say?" Delilah asks, putting a hand lightly on his shoulder.

I think this is my chance. The kids are distracted.

I leap up onto the bed. Delilah glances at me, but Donovan starts talking and she turns her attention to him. I touch my nose to the journal. The soft leather smells mild and earthy. I think I can sink my teeth into it. But first, I have to get it off the bed.

I bat at it with my paw to see if it moves. It does.

I give it a harder push. The journal slides close to the edge of the bed. A tap, tap, tap

— and it goes falling to the floor. I freeze, expecting a crash.

No.

No?

I walk up to the edge of the bed. The journal landed on a sweater! Perfect! The twins don't notice a thing.

I jump down lickety-split and grab the journal with my teeth. It tastes a bit like salt and sweat. I tug it and off I go. I get it to the hallway, drop it, and stop to rest. I knock it off the top step with my paw. I bite it again and toss my head. Down three more stairs. Wow, who knew? Bonkety-bonk, I clamber down. I push it with my paw. This time, it really tumbles. Almost all the way down. I hoppity-hop and there we are. I snag it proudly in my teeth and get that journal all the way to the bottom of the stairs and across the wood floor and onto the fancy rug and — there! By Annika's feet.

"What in the world . . . ?"

Lisa laughs. She's sitting on the rug near the woodstove, with papers in front of her and a drink in her hand. "What the heck is Luna doing?"

"Oh!" Annika gasps. She reaches down with two hands and snatches it up. Eyes shining, she squeezes it with glee. "Look! Luna brought me Peter's diary. I don't believe it."

Just then, Donovan and Delilah come running down the stairs. They practically crash into each other at the bottom. Donovan hurries over to stand in front of his mother.

He's bewildered. "What just happened? Luna took that from me? She got it all the way downstairs?" Slowly, as he notices how close Annika is sitting to Sam on the couch, his face darkens.

I look up at him. *Sorry, my boy. But your father wanted your mom to have that journal.*

Danny gapes at me in admiration. "That's amazing. I've never seen anything like that before." He knocks back a full swallow of the whiskey in his glass. "I can't believe that cat found the journal when you couldn't."

Donovan spins around. "What do you mean, you couldn't? Mom, were you looking for the journal? Were you in my room?"

Delilah steps up next to her brother. "What the heck? Mom, were you hunting around in Donovan's bedroom?"

"You didn't look at my sketchbook, did y— ?" Donovan stops himself midsentence.

"What?" Annika slumps. "Yes, I was looking in your room, and I'm sorry. You're right. I shouldn't have gone through your stuff. But I asked you for that diary multiple times, Donovan. I gave you many chances to bring it to me yourself."

Donovan throws a hand out toward his mother, and his voice breaks. "This is unbelievable. I'm not done reading that. You have no right to take that from me. It's MINE just the same as it is YOURS. It belongs to ALL OF US." He points at Sam. "And why is he here? Why is Sam still here?" Donovan takes in a deeper breath and his voice gets louder. "Isn't it Sam's fault Dad lost his leg? He was driving the car Dad was in on prom night, right?"

Annika leans forward to try to take his hand. "Sweetheart —"

Donovan yanks his hand away and takes a step back. "I know, I know, there was another kid who crashed into you guys, but Sam was driving, too. I don't understand why you want him here. Would Dad want him here?" A tear rolls down his cheek, and Donovan wipes it away forcefully with the back of his hand. I can see he's embarrassed; but more than that, he's angry. "Why are you guys still friends? It doesn't make any sense."

Sam and Annika steal a glance at each other. And then Annika sits up straighter.

"Donovan, I need to talk to you." Annika looks at Delilah. "You too." She leans forward, holding the journal tight. "You need to know something."

Sam looks wary, nervous about what Annika has to say. The kids brace themselves, perhaps prepared for what they assume is a scolding.

"I know you guys have heard the story about how your father lost his leg in a car crash." She clears her throat, rearranging her thoughts. "I know your father told you that everyone was drunk on prom night except for him. Sam, your aunt Lisa, and I were all drinking that night. Your father was sober, and he was the only one who got seriously injured. Those facts are all true. But there's one part of the story . . ." She sighs, pressing the heel of her hand against her brow, but presses on. "Look. There's something you need to know. And I want to be the one to tell you, before you read about it in the journal."

My whiskers twitch. We wait. And listen.

"Sam wasn't driving the car."

Danny's head turns. He squints at his younger brother, confused. "What? Sam wasn't driving?" He puts his whiskey down on a side table and walks over to the couch to stand next to Delilah. "But the police report . . . and my dad said . . . wait — Then who *was* driving?"

And suddenly — I know who.

AFTER THE PROM, 1987

ANNIKA

I tell them the story. I gloss over some of the details, things the kids don't need to know. But I remember every minute of it.

When we finally arrive at Ellie's after-prom party, I peer through the car window and I'm relieved to see there are still plenty of kids hanging around. They're in the yard, on the front steps, and packed into the front room of the house. One girl leans out the window to talk to someone, and half of her beer sloshes onto a holly bush below. Is it possible no one has missed us?

Sam tries three times to parallel park the car at the curb and still can't get it right.

"I don't think you can fit here." I glance at the Mercedes behind us. If Sam gets this wrong and bumps that car, it's going to be expensive, and I know he can't afford to pay for the damages.

364

At the same time, I trust him. I have no idea why. I don't know if he's such a great driver or not. But he's good at a lot of other things — math and football and, of course, kissing.

Clearly, my brain has turned to mush.

"If we don't park here, we'll have to go way down to the next block and walk a mile. And you're wearing high heels." He shakes his head. "Just give me a minute. I can do it." The way he says this, with a sigh, reminds me that he's used to his family ribbing him and assuming he can't do things right. As the youngest of five kids, he's told me that's just how it is, and I know his dad is critical of him. I press my lips together and vow not to say another word.

He manages to get the car situated after a few more tries. When he turns the car engine off, it's quiet and I realize how exhausted I am. Sam just sits there for a moment, and when he looks over at me, it hits me all over again that I'm sitting in Sam Parsons's car with him. With Sam. All dressed up. In his mom's car. My brain starts to backfire.

I suddenly wonder if I really know him as well as I think I do. He's a popular boy, and he wasn't my date for the prom. He looks troubled, as if something terrible has happened and he doesn't know how to address it, which reflects exactly how I feel. What now?

As everything he said to me comes flooding back into my mind, I feel my face start to flush.

You look gorgeous. No, I don't.

I've always loved you. No, you haven't.

I want you. No, you don't.

I automatically negated everything he said the minute it came out of his mouth. I deleted it. Discounted it. Why did I do that?

I start to panic. Completely panic.

I wonder, did he just say those things in the heat of the moment, and are they meaningless now? Did he only say them because he thought that's what a man is supposed to say in that situation? Were they things he said just to get me to go along, and I've been a gullible fool? We don't hang out in the same cliques, so will we really keep seeing each other over the summer? Is there anything even left to talk about?

I convince myself that whatever was between us tonight is probably over, that the novelty of prom temporarily got the better of us. It's easy for me to jump to the worst possible conclusion, especially when I've had Lisa drilling it into my head for months that Sam would never be really interested in me. I tell myself: *Don't set yourself up for disappointment. Don't be dumb. You have faults, but being dumb isn't one of them.*

I adjust my dress under my bare legs. I'm starting to realize how stiff my fancy shoes are, because my toes are sore.

"Annika." Sam waits for me to say something, his features finally softening into a kind and inviting gaze, but I can't smile back.

"Let's go in. Lisa is probably wondering where I am." That's an understatement. I grab the door handle and hop out of the car as fast as I can.

I can hear Sam's driver's side door open behind me, but I ignore it. My legs move faster as I stride toward the party over someone's lawn, my heels sinking into the grass.

"Annika," Sam calls after me, but I don't turn around.

"Come on," I beg him. "It's late. We're missing everything. Let's go in."

The noise alone lets me know the party is still raging. Kids are talking; there's music playing; someone shrieks in the backyard. Because windows are open, the din spills out into the neighborhood. Spring is finally here, and the pungent scent of newly mown grass overwhelms me as I walk over a small but nicely manicured front lawn. We're downtown, so the homes here are close to each other, and I wonder how long until someone calls the cops. If I'm going to spend any time at this party at all, I have the feeling I'd better get inside.

But as I walk up the front path, I realize my first mistake. Many girls have changed clothes already into leggings and sweatshirts. I'm still wearing my dress. I had other clothes with me, but they were in Mark's car. For a moment, I wonder if Sam had the presence of mind to take off his tuxedo pants and throw them in the back of his car and pull on some jeans, even if he would have had to do it quickly in the street. I hope he did. But I also hope he didn't.

I look back. He's coming up the walk behind me, and he's still dressed up. He smiles, assuming that I'm waiting for him. Oh. My heart skips a beat. I'm really nervous.

He breezes right up to me and takes my hand to help me up the stairs and into the house. I teeter on my high heels but make it in.

We walk into the living room, Sam still holding my hand, which feels strange all of a sudden. Although his hand is warm and comfortable, I have to fight the impulse to pull my hand out of his. He says hi to a few kids, but then turns to me, standing close.

"Let's get a drink."

I follow him to a table where there are bottles and chips set out. I watch as Sam pours us cranberry juice and adds vodka. He takes a long drink. I find it just sweet enough to gulp down. Then I pour myself a refill and drink that, too.

"Maybe I should find my friends," I suggest. It's suddenly hard for me to make eye contact with him. I feel like everyone in the room is watching and judging us, wondering what we've been up to. A quick scan of the room tells me that I'm right; people have noticed that we're together and we've been missing for a few hours, eyes lingering on us for a beat too long. But then they go right back to talking quietly in groups. It's possible I'm making more of this than I should. Who cares if Sam and I left for a while? I know what they're all thinking, but . . . does it really matter now?

When I turn back to Sam, he looks happy. He gazes at me as if I'm the only person in the room.

"What are you smiling about?" I ask him. When he doesn't answer, I continue. "Are you drunk?"

"No," he answers. But his free hand goes

to my waist and he pulls me in for a light kiss. He's gentle and slow about it, and I melt all over again. I can't believe he's kissing me in front of our classmates, and my anxiety finally starts to melt away.

I guess it's the afterglow of everything we've been through tonight, but I feel warmth settling in my chest, and a magnetic pull moving me toward him. I reach over and grab his elbow, feeling the slippery synthetic material of the tux under my fingers, and kiss him back. His mouth is soft, and I melt under the pressure of his hand on my hip. I wish I could wrap myself up with him for the rest of the night, right on until sunrise, and it's a surprise to me to realize that's all I want to do. What in the world have I been so worried about? I don't care anymore who sees us. I'm okay with kissing Sam in front of the whole world, because my heart has expanded by one hundred times. He is sweet, lovely, wonderful. There's no one else on the planet who matters right now. I feel loved, and I'm totally content.

Until I hear my name being called from across the room.

"Annika."

I know the voice before my eyes find her. Lisa gapes at me, mouth slightly open, pink lipstick from earlier in the night settled into a deep stain. Her heavy eye makeup is smudged, and she's in bare feet. An extra-large T-shirt hangs loosely from her shoulders, and she's let her hair down from its high knot so it falls over her shoulders. I have no idea what to say, but instinctively take a step away from Sam. He keeps one hand on my waist, and I can feel him tuck his thumb under my satin belt, as if to ensure that I won't get away. Cool air rushes in between us where just a moment ago there was warmth.

Did she see us together? She must have.

Sam understands as well as anyone that Lisa has issues. But I'm not sure he can see everything she's feeling in her face as well as I do — confusion, hurt, betrayal. All of it, in a flash. And then, upon realizing Sam is watching her, Lisa replaces it with a smooth mask of indifference.

"Where have you LOVEBIRDS been?" She moves toward me in a rush and slaps my bare arm with one hand. Her palm smacks me so hard it aches. Her other hand holds a cup full of amber beer. "I've been freaking out. You've been gone forever." She sneers at Sam. "And, Sam. You're my date, remember?"

"We weren't gone forever," I blurt out to

take her focus off of Sam. "Just . . . just a while. We went for a walk on the beach." I gesture toward Sam, but one look at him tells me he's not going to be any help at all.

"Yeah, a romantic walk on the beach," he echoes, never questioning why I'm lying to my sister's face. He blinks slowly and doesn't say anything else.

Fantastic. He's useless.

"I'm sorry, Lisa. Sam and I needed to talk."

"Talk." Lisa puts her hand on her hip and studies the two of us. "Talk? Really? About what?"

"Fate. The universe." Sam answers her before I can think of what to say. "Our future together forever in California."

"Shut up, Sam," I say, putting my hand right up on his mouth and lightly pushing his face away. I turn back to Lisa. "Please ignore him. He's in a very weird mood."

She looks stricken. It's only a moment too late that I realize I've touched Sam's face in front of Lisa. I've just put my hand on his kissy mouth. It's completely obvious what we were doing in his car, right? Oh, God. And he mentioned our future in California — but I never said I wanted to go there. Ugh. I watch Lisa's face turn pink and get the sensation of something dropping low in my stomach.

"Ow. What?" Sam protests, acting hurt. But the twinkle in his eye lets me know he's amused. "Annika, I love you. Why are you pushing me away?"

And that's it. Those are the words that set Lisa off.

Her eyes flash with anger. She stumbles to one side, and I realize how drunk she is. With a quick glance down at her hand, she seems to make up her mind. She takes her full glass of beer and throws it at me, the cold liquid hitting my torso and splashing up onto my face and hair. I'm instantly drenched. The plastic cup rattles onto the floor.

Sam gives a sharp laugh. "What was that for?" He looks at Lisa, wide-eyed, and then back to me. "What just happened?"

I'm glad he's still in a good mood. Nothing seems to be throwing him off tonight. Lisa doesn't answer. She stalks away.

I shake my head and beads of beer go flying, wet strands of my hair whipping and hitting my face. "I think she's mad we disappeared."

"Clearly."

"No . . . it's more than that. It's because I left with you. You were her prom date. It's like adding insult to injury."

"Yes, but . . . we were all just going as friends, right?"

I search his face. He doesn't get it. Maybe Sam doesn't know how lonely she's been and how desperate she's been to get popular, a goal at which she's failed. Maybe it's better if he doesn't know. "Yeah, of course. But she didn't expect to be stuck at a party without me. I sent her here by herself, and now she's drunk. She doesn't know Mark that well, and probably didn't know who to hang out with. I feel horrible."

Horrible doesn't even begin to explain how I feel. Not only did I abandon her, I left the prom with Sam, the type of boy she's been trying to impress with no luck, and he's one of her only friends. I am the worst sister on the planet.

I feel dizzy.

"I'm sorry," I say quietly. "I have to go find Lisa and bring her home."

"And you should probably get changed before you come back to the party," Sam adds. "I'll give you guys a ride."

Hmmm. That doesn't seem like a great idea. What if Sam tries to kiss me when we get to the house, in front of Lisa? What a disaster that would be. Plus, he's been drinking. His cranberry and vodka drink is right on the table next to us. "No, no, thanks. We'll be fine. Let me ask Mark. He was my date, and I don't want to ditch him again. Stay and have a good time. I'll see you later. I might not come back to the party. If I don't, I'll talk to you on Monday morning, when you pick me up —"

"No," he interrupts. "No, if you don't come back, I'll call you tomorrow."

"Okay." Sam and I have only spoken on the phone a few times. It gives me butterflies to sit in the kitchen talking to him, curling the cord around my hand, while my mom hovers and flits around the stove. "Yes, okay. Call me," I say with a look back at him — but pulling away, knowing I need to make Lisa my priority now.

I stumble through the crowd. Everyone is staring, and not trying to hide it. My gown has big dark splotches down the front where it's wet. I try to keep my head up high. Nothing to see here. Just two idiotic sisters fighting on prom night. I'm a fool.

I find Lisa upstairs, sitting on a bed in what must be Ellie's room, which has ice-blue walls and is overloaded with stuffed penguins. I would find the room amusing if Lisa wasn't beside herself, a puddle of tears, clutching a tissue to her nose. I grab the whole box of tissues, sitting next to her to rub her shoulder.

"I'm sorry." I don't understand how everything could go so right tonight and yet go so wrong.

She's inconsolable. "Why did you leave me? Where did you go? Did you really go to the beach?"

"Yes. I mean, we didn't go to the beach downtown. We went up to White Beach. I'm sorry. Sam just wanted to get away from everyone for a while."

"But why? Did you guys go to . . . ?" She can't say it out loud.

I swallow. I understand. Saying it out loud makes it true. If we don't say it, maybe we can all pretend it doesn't exist for just a little while longer. Maybe just until tomorrow.

"No, we really did go to talk." What am I supposed to say? We didn't have sex, but we did say *I love you* to each other? How does that make it any better? "Never mind. I'm sorry I left you."

"It doesn't matter." She gulps in air. "I know Sam loves you. He's always loved you. But he's one of my only friends. And now I'll be shut out. He's only going to want to hang out with you this summer, not me, now that you're getting all *serious*. Then you guys will disappear to California and have an amazing life and I'm going nowhere." Rubbing her face with the back of her hand, she just ends up making her face more of a mess. "No one is ever going to love me like that."

I shake my head. "No, Lisa. Don't say that. That's silly. Of course, someone will love you. And I'm not going to California. I'm sorry."

"Stop saying sorry." She wipes her nose. "Whatever. I'm already over it. I just thought . . ." Lisa dabs the tissue at her eyes. "I just wish it hadn't all happened tonight, like this."

"Me too."

Great. This will be our lifelong memory of the senior prom. We'll both have to carry these moments around for the rest of our lives. Sam and I disappearing for hours, arriving late to the party, and acting all lovey-dovey exactly like Lisa asked me not to. Lisa devastated, getting drunk, and throwing a beer on me — the smell of which is not going to escape our mother — and crying her eyes out.

In the game of which sister "wins" in high school, I guess I win.

And yet, of course, I don't win. I lose. Because I feel terrible.

"Let's find someone to take us home." I stand and reach out for her hand. "Come on. I'm sure Mark will drive us."

She doesn't take my hand. "I've gotta go to the bathroom and get a drink of water."

"Okay. Maybe wash your face while you're in there." I don't mean to sound critical, but if our parents are waiting up for us, it would be better to have some semblance of normalcy if possible. I'm not looking forward to explaining the whole night to our mom and dad.

She gets up, exits the bedroom, and stumbles down the hall. I turn the other way and almost bump directly into someone tall.

When I look up, it's Peter Kuhn. Blond hair, parted on the side, every strand in place. My partner in art class, the one who sketched my braids in such beautiful detail.

"Hey, Peter. You look nice."

Nice isn't even the word for it. Unlike a lot of the boys who are clearly in cheap rented tuxedos that don't quite fit them correctly, Peter looks perfect. He could be right off a Hollywood red carpet or something.

"Thanks." He shoves his hands into his front pockets. "You look nice yourself."

"Where's Dana?"

"She's hanging out with some of her friends. I'm just wandering aimlessly around. This whole party is bizarre to me."

He looks down over the balcony at the chaos below. "It's funny, because everyone's getting wasted. In Germany, kids our age drink with their parents all the time, so they don't need to go out to a party and chug alcohol until they puke."

"Oh. Yeah, you must think we're all pretty lame." I start thinking about Lisa, and suddenly I'm embarrassed for her — for all of us. "Well, I'm glad you came to the party anyway. Did you see there's a grand piano downstairs? Maybe you should play a few songs."

He smiles. "Yeah, I saw it. But I don't think anyone's going to appreciate it if I turn off Van Halen and start playing Beethoven."

I laugh. "I guess you're right. Say . . . have you seen Mark Tindall? Do you know who I mean?"

Peter nods. "Yeah, he's down in the basement playing beer pong."

"Ugh. Is he drunk?"

"Ummmm . . ." He looks back over his shoulder, as if he might need to see Mark again to really gauge his drunkenness. "Maybe. I mean, he was yelling and running around the table. And he was singing show tunes at the top of his lungs. So I'd say that's a solid maybe."

"Okay." I feel the energy draining out of me. Maybe I can get Mark to just lend me his car, and Mark can catch a ride home with Sam later. I guess I'd be okay to drive.

Peter must see my face fall with this news, because he frowns. "What's the matter?"

I try to lighten up. "I was going to have Mark help me take my sister home. She's super drunk. She's the one who threw a beer at me," I say, gesturing down toward my wet dress. "And she's having an awful night. Thanks to me."

"Thanks to you?" He scoffs. "I doubt it's thanks to you. You're a good student, right? Debate team, math team . . . ?" He squints. "You don't strike me as a big troublemaker."

I laugh again. Wow, he actually knows something about me. I'm flattered. "But I *am* a troublemaker," I say, swatting his arm. "I've been nothing but trouble since I arrived in high school four years ago. You don't know me very well, do you?"

He smirks. "No, I guess I don't know you that well. Not yet, anyway. So, do you want to sit down somewhere and talk? Maybe your sister could just sleep it off on a couch or something." Bowing his head, he leans toward me. "You know, I always meant to make another sketch of you. But we never made plans to get together. Maybe we could meet up this summer."

Something about the way he says this and looks at me makes my cheeks hot. Peter seems more confident than most of the boys in my grade, half of whom can barely put a sentence together. I can't help but smile, and he smiles back.

It's dazzling. Honestly, his smile could stop traffic.

But I have a boyfriend. A very sweet boyfriend.

"We should definitely do another drawing sometime. I'd like that. One day. For sure. But I can't sit and talk. I really need to get Lisa home. Right now." I poke his arm. "Hey. So . . ." I realize that Peter's sober — definitely more sober than Mark or Sam or probably anyone else at this party. "Do you think you could see if Mark will give you his keys and lend you his car for a few minutes?"

And that's how Peter and I end up on either side of Lisa, helping her down the stairs. She's not a big girl, yet she's surprisingly heavy when she suddenly lurches into me and I crash into the railing. Ouch.

Peter goes to the basement to get Mark's car keys from him, and we're almost out the front door when Sam comes hurrying up to us. He grabs my elbow.

"Hey. What . . . ?" He looks Peter over from head to toe, with a skeptical look on his face. "I thought you were going to get a ride from Mark."

"I was, but I ran into Peter. He's sober, so I asked him."

Sam frowns but doesn't say anything. Something passes over his face, and I realize it's the same emotion I saw when he asked me why I was going with Mark to the prom. When I saw it then, I wasn't sure what it was. But now it's magnified, and I recognize surprise. Distress. Jealousy.

Sam steps up, getting right in my face. "Can I talk to you privately for a minute?"

Oh, dear.

"Sorry." I apologize to poor Peter, who is left babysitting Lisa by the front door. "I'll be right back. One quick minute."

"Come back soon, lovebirds," Lisa calls out, slurring her words.

When Sam turns around in the hallway, I unleash on him. "What? What's wrong?"

He gives me a look. "Why are you leaving with that guy? You trust him?"

"Peter? Are you crazy? He's super nice."

Sam steps closer and glares at me. "Is it your plan to drop Lisa off and then come back? You'll be alone in the car with Peter on the drive back here. I don't like it."

It's a little intense, and I stumble back. "My plan? I don't have a plan. For the love of God, Sam. Don't be an idiot. You don't *like* it?"

"I don't want Peter driving you anywhere. I'm sorry, but I just don't. He's obviously interested in you. I know he is."

"Why do you say that?"

He presses his lips together, as if to try to stop himself, but then can't help continuing. "We were talking at lunch one day, and he was asking all about you. I shut it down. I told him to back off. He should know better than to talk to you."

"You what?" I put a hand on my head and pull at my hair, which is starting to fall loose from the tight bun I had it in earlier. I'm sure it got disheveled when I was with Sam in his car earlier, but now it's really a mess. Between that and my wet dress, I'm a wreck. "OH MY GOD. You are so out of bounds. You told Peter he shouldn't TALK to me? What is wrong with you? Why are you ruining everything?"

His eyes grow wet. "Me?" he asks, quieter. "Seriously? You're leaving the party with another guy, and you're asking me why *I'm* ruining everything?" He stops himself, mouth hanging open, like he's too shocked to go on. "I knew it. I just knew it. I knew when you wouldn't even talk about California that —" He turns right, and then left, unable to get out a coherent thought. "The minute I leave, you're going to find someone else, right? You wanna go out with someone like Peter?"

I try to stop myself, but I can't help it. I yell, "NO, of course not. I love you, Sam, but suddenly you want me to change every plan I've made for my life so I can go to California with you? That's not something a person can just decide on the spur of the moment."

His face shows disbelief. "But if you love me . . . why not?"

My head is spinning. I'm overwhelmed and exhausted. "We can't talk about this now. I have to get Lisa home." I whip around and storm off to rejoin Peter.

Sam beats me to the front door and opens it so Peter and I can get Lisa out of the house and down the front steps. I'm not surprised when Sam follows us to the street to help us find Mark's car.

"Sam," I beg, "go back to the party. Just go."

"I want to help. Please, Annika, let me help. I'm Lisa's date. And I'm the one who always helps her out, right? So you don't have to worry about it. I should drive her home. Let me take her. At least, let's take my car. Come on."

"Fine." We turn around and walk the other direction to his mom's crappy, disgusting car. I'm too angry to look at him. After he unlocks the doors, I get Lisa settled in the backseat. She's got her head in her hands, giggling about absolutely nothing. "Give me your keys, Sam. You've had too much to drink."

Sam looks at me, then over at Peter, and back to me again. I can see the heat in his face. But then his voice softens, trying a different angle. "Annika, why didn't you ask me to take you guys home? You didn't have to go find someone else. Peter doesn't need to come with us. We can handle it."

"Noooo, I want Peter," Lisa whines, her arms reaching out to him. "Peter, please ride with us. Keep me company. Don't leave me alone with *them*. I don't want to be alone with the lovebirds. They make me ill."

"Yeah, sure." He smiles at her drunken plea. "It's okay. I'll ride along. No big deal."

I turn to him. "Thank you for coming with us. Can you sit in the back with her? Make sure she's okay?"

Peter looks from me to Sam. "You're sure you don't want me to drive?"

"No," Sam and I say at the same time.

I turn to Peter and put my hand on his arm. "It'll be fine."

I remember this moment. It's crystal clear in my mind. Peter is standing in the street and looking into my eyes and he *believes* me. He hears me say, "It'll be fine," and his eyes agree with me.

It's the last time he stands on two legs.

"Look, I'll drive." I yank the keys out of Sam's hand. I'm so mad at him that I can't even see straight. Sam jumps in the passenger seat when I immediately start the engine. I pull quickly out into the road, to demonstrate to Sam how goddamn incompetent he was in his inability to park the car in the first place, and then start talking to Peter as if everything is completely normal.

Peter seems like such a nice guy. He's a great listener and seems entranced by whatever nonsense I babble at him. It makes me sorry that I haven't made any effort to get to know him better up until this moment. Lisa sits slouched down in the back, sulking and muttering to herself. At one point, she lies down across the backseat and puts her head in Peter's lap, which is awkward. I hope she doesn't completely pass out. The fact that she stretches out means Peter has to slide over and sit right up against the side of the car, his knee touching the door.

Sam keeps glancing over at me as if he doesn't recognize me. He seems confused — worried — by how energetically I'm talking.

Maybe I am talking too fast. But I'm simply trying to be extra perky and friendly to Peter to make up for my sister's completely embarrassing lack of social graces. Peter doesn't know Lisa the way Sam and I do.

Peter is nodding at me, and Sam is watching me talk, when I see the flash of headlights out the back passenger side window, suddenly just behind Peter's head. Henry McKean, hurrying back to the party in his pickup truck after a run home for more liquor, drives through a stop sign and comes flying into us at the intersection of Summer and Beach streets.

The force of impact sends me flying sideways, and my head slams against the window. Miraculously, a concussion is my only injury.

Sam is jolted, and I find out later he dislocated his shoulder. But he's wearing his seat belt and he's also, for the most part, okay.

Peter is not so lucky. He's not wearing a seat belt. I don't think it would have mattered anyway.

He's at the point of impact, and he gets the worst of it. His body absorbs the blow and protects Lisa from injury.

Shattered vertebrae, broken ribs, a severely damaged leg.

In an instant.

After the immediate impact of Henry's truck slamming into Sam's car, Peter doesn't cry out or beg for help. There are no words. He simply gasps desperately for air, as if he is drowning.

That sound. I will never forget that sound. It is the sound of someone in searing pain unlike anything he's ever known.

First, there's the crash, metal exploding on impact. But then I hear Peter breathing heavily, as if it's his lungs that are collapsing and not his leg that is crushed. A tremendous breath in, a staggered breath out. Air in, then out. I glance back, dizzy and terrified. I see his clear eyes open, but focused on nothing. In shock, blinded to anything else but the pain. His breathing is the only sound in the car for a moment, until the rest of us begin to move.

That sound. It still haunts me. A deep gulp as he takes air in. A halting, shaky exhale. Like someone sobbing with no tears.

Like someone scared to death.

Then, the click of a seat belt. A car door opening. Someone bolting out of the car, and the next thing I know, Sam opening my door. His arms are around me and he whispers in my ear: *Here we go. Hang on, sweetheart. I've got you.*

The last time I see Sam, he's standing by my gurney in a hospital hallway. His face is streaked with tears, but he's not crying anymore.

He leans down close and takes my hand. "Are you okay? Listen. Sweetheart. Just listen."

"Where's my mom and dad?"

"They just got here. I asked if I could have a minute to say goodbye."

My head aches. Sam is slightly blurry. "What? Goodbye?"

"I pulled you out of the car before the cops arrived. I told them I was driving," he says near my ear, so no one else around us will hear. "It's my car. They believe me. So it's okay."

"Sam." I grip his hand as tight as I can. "No. Please, no. Not again."

"Lisa was too drunk to remember anything. She was passed out at the time of the accident. And I already spoke to Peter before he went into surgery and he agreed. He understood."

"Surgery?" I try to sit up, alarmed. "What happened?"

"He's injured badly. It's his back and his leg. Henry McKean drove right into us. But you were drinking and so was I. So I gave my statement to the police, and they used the Breathalyzer so they know —"

"No, Sam." I'm dying to get up and straighten this out, but I feel nauseous. I can barely keep my eyes open. "Please don't. Don't do this again."

He opens his eyes wider and leans down to kiss me on the forehead. "It's already done. Get some rest. You might have a concussion. I have to go."

"Go where? You're going home? But are you okay? Did you see a doctor?"

"I want you to relax and do whatever the doctors tell you. Make sure Peter is okay. He and I made an agreement. I was driving. He agreed to tell everyone that, because I told him it can't be you. It just can't. I love you, and I'm sorry I made you upset. So now I want you to help Peter out if he needs it, okay? Promise you'll take care of him if he needs some help."

I start to cry. The tears just stream out of me. I'm still wearing my stupid red prom

390

dress, and it must be three in the morning. Exhaustion weighs on me like a sack of flour. "I will. I love you, too. I don't want it like this."

He takes my hand, but his expression doesn't change. Sam is sober now, and I can see his mind is made up. This is what Sam does. It's how he expresses his love.

He took credit for Lisa's graffiti. He said the school walkout and snowball fight were his idea. He returned the money Lisa stole and wouldn't say who gave it to him.

And now, this. But even in my exhausted state, I know this is different. The consequences are going to be terrible and irreversible, for both Peter and Sam.

"Sam," I try one more time. "Please don't go anywhere. We can still straighten this out."

"Annie," he sighs, shaking his head. "I already did." He kisses my cheek; then he's gone.

Henry McKean is drunk. Clearly. He does not deny it. He fails the sobriety test.

Henry's family has been here in Manchester for three generations. He's a good kid. He played Little League. His mom is a third-grade teacher in town. His dad is a firefighter and town councilman. People shake their heads about Henry. It's a disappointment, for sure.

Sam is also cited for driving under the influence. He's the only one with a police record. The cops have a file on Sam with a list of every time they've come to school on his account. Sam also has a father who is sick and a mother who is at the end of her rope. I find out later that Sam's dad has spoken to the local cops and made an arrangement.

Sam's parents get him out of town as fast as they can.

No Excuse

ANNIKA

The room goes quiet when I finish. The kids will get Peter's side of the story when they read that part of the journal, but for now a quick summary from me is enough.

Delilah looks puzzled, and her face flushes as if it has been scrubbed raw. Donovan stares down at his feet, his expression blank, and I can't tell what he's thinking.

Danny is irritated, shaking a hand out toward Sam. "Are you kidding me? All these years, you never told me, Sam? You let the WHOLE TOWN think you were drunk driving? You let Dad ship you off early to California? You missed graduation?" Then he turns and points at me. "Do you know what you put my brother through? What you put my whole family through?"

"Don't yell at her," Sam snaps. "It was my idea."

I bury my face in my hand. The smoke

393

from the wood fire is starting to make my eyes water. "I'm so sorry to let everyone think Sam was driving. I shouldn't have let that happen. I have no excuse."

"You sure as hell don't."

Sam stands up and pushes Danny's hand away. "I said, knock it off. It was what I wanted. I gave the police a statement without involving Annika. I didn't ask for her permission. It was my choice. Don't blame her."

I remember sensations from the hospital: the smell of ammonia and the musty odor of the giant fish tank in the waiting room. The lights overhead, so harsh and bright they cast no shadows. Sounds echoing down the hallway of the hospital: Sam's mom crying and his dad yelling.

The light from the woodstove reflects off of Lisa's face, giving her an orange glow. "I remember the ambulance ride. I thought they were taking me to pump my stomach."

Sam looks at her. "Right. Henry was drunk and you were passed out in the back, so the only person who knew that Annika was driving was Peter. And I knew he'd say okay if I covered for her. I knew it. He was in no shape for me to even talk to him. He was drugged up before we got to the ER, and then they started prepping him for emergency surgery. But he listened. And he agreed, which I knew he would. Because he liked you, Annie. I knew he did." He stops, glancing at the kids.

"I'm not surprised." Lisa wraps her big white sweater around her tighter. "This all makes total sense. It sounds exactly like something you would have done, Sam." She looks at me. "And you. Unbelievable. Mom and Dad were so supportive while you were getting away with murder. They were so pre-occupied worrying about you after the crash that they barely noticed when I moved out."

"I didn't —"

"No, wait. I'm not done. Because here's the truly crazy part: Peter actually called you. After all that. He *called* you. He still wanted to be with you. You're so lucky. You always get everything, don't you? Everything you want. Including this cottage, the only thing I ever asked Mom and Dad for. As soon as you said you needed it, they said *sure, Annika* and gave it to you."

I don't know what to say. I can't believe Lisa has managed to steer the conversation back to herself. Is that why Lisa moved in across the street, to keep a closer eye on this house? I thought she moved here to help me out. But now I wonder about her motives.

It hits me all over again how hopeless and vulnerable I am without Peter. My stomach feels like an empty pit.

Peter and I kept the secret of Sam's sacrifice all this time and never told anyone the truth of it. The worst part is that I can never talk to Peter about it again. We pretended that Sam drove the car, and it became our reality. We knew what people in this small town would think, how they'd gossip and judge. And we were sure how his parents would react if they knew — badly, incapable of understanding or accepting me. We always had this *thing* hovering over us, a lie we ignored. It was a choice we made to get us through a life marked by challenges because we chose to be together. That was the most important thing.

I never realized I would lose Peter early, and the silence between us on this one topic would extend forever.

Sometimes over the years, late at night, I'd relive the moment of the crash in a waking nightmare and roll over to hold Peter tight as he slept. As if I could squeeze him hard enough to make the memory go away. But I could never bring his leg back.

It doesn't matter, I'd tell myself. It never mattered. Peter's hands were unharmed. He could still play piano. His face was fine. He could still impress anyone with his wide smile. It could have been so much worse. He rebounded from losing a leg as only an eighteen-year-old with a strong spirit can, with determination and resilience. It was a serious injury — but it never stopped him from living his life.

Peter would be the first to tell you that losing his leg didn't ruin his life. He'd say the only way the accident changed his life was that it brought us together. That's the way he always told the story.

Yes, of course there were tears. Difficult days. Pain. Questions. The unfairness of it all. He did cry on my shoulder. Of course, he did. Naturally I comforted him, held his hand, dried his tears, and took him in my arms.

All of that's mixed up in how and why I fell in love with him. How could it not be? It's part of our story. *Our* story. Peter's and mine. That part of our story has nothing to do with Sam.

But I believe Sam would understand my love story with Peter, if I had the chance to tell it to him. And now, I realize, maybe I do want to tell him. Maybe, in some small way, I'd feel better if I did.

Donovan can't even look at me. My poor boy tries, but ends up turning his face slightly toward the dark corner of the room.

"I'm sorry," Sam says quietly. "I wish it had been me. I should've been the one to lose my leg. Not Peter. He didn't deserve it." He shakes his head. "But I'm glad you married him. I'm glad you both were happy."

"We were."

Delilah's wide-set eyes shine as she stares at me, trying to get a handle on this new knowledge. "Why didn't you tell us? Why didn't you and Dad tell us?"

"We wanted to protect you from the truth."

"Protect us? But — it obviously didn't make a difference in the end."

I can see frustration in her eyes and my heart clenches. "No, not in the end. But it was something we didn't talk about. We wanted to forget how it happened."

"But you didn't have to keep it from us. We could've handled it. Oh, my God." Her voice is getting hysterical. "Why in the world did Dad think we shouldn't know?"

I glance at Donovan, but he hasn't said a word.

"Because he loved me, sweetheart." I know this must not make sense to the twins right now, but I hope someday they'll understand. "Sam gave your dad the opportunity to rewrite that part of the story. So he took it. Your dad never wanted our lives to be defined by that accident."

Delilah nods. I know she'll at least try to understand.

I look to my son. Donovan just sticks his hand out. I know what he wants.

"Sweetheart. Why don't you sit down, and —"

He shakes his head. "I don't want to hear it. Just give it to me."

I hesitate. But when I look up at Donovan, his eyes red with disappointment, I decide I owe this much to him. He's right. He deserves to know.

I hand him the journal back.

THE READING HOUR

LUNA

Donovan drags himself up the stairs, the journal in his hand, pressed against his abdomen. I hop up a few steps at a time, watching his feet land, heavy and slow. The air gets chilly as we ascend farther from the woodstove.

Donovan takes a seat on his bed near the window, which is the only light in the room. I leap up and walk over his blue blanket to settle down in his lap and warm him. He allows it, holding the book with two hands over my body.

He flips through pages. When he finally finds the page he wants, he moves me off his lap with care. Grabbing a ruler from his bedside table, he lays the book down flat on the bed and lines the ruler up in the middle. With a slow motion, he rips a page out of the journal, using the ruler to anchor down the book.

I glance over at the drawing. A drawing! I now see that the paper in the book is unlined, and Peter not only wrote words in his diary but also sketched pictures. In this one, a young man with a ponytail stands in a suit of armor. In his right hand, at ease at his side, he holds a sword. With his left hand, he reaches out to stroke the nose of a dragon.

Clearly, the boy in the drawing is supposed to be Donovan. You can see it in the angles of his face.

Donovan considers the drawing for a long time before leaving to walk down the hall to Delilah's room. When he returns, I see he has thumbtacks, and he secures the drawing to the wall above his bed. It's the first thing he has put up on the white walls. Then he returns to the journal, which he places on his lap. I watch his eyes go back and forth as he reads.

Peter liked to write — and rewrite. Tell stories, and embellish them. See in people what others did not.

Perhaps Delilah is now wondering if that is a fault of her father that she hadn't considered before. I could see the confusion in her eyes as she realized Peter never told her the truth.

But for Donovan, portrayed in this draw-

ing not as a sullen and argumentative son,
but rather reimagined as a hero, it may be
the thing that saves him.

OUR LOVE STORY

ANNIKA

As Donovan reads the journal upstairs, I wonder how much Peter wrote about the first few months of our love story.

That summer, after Sam left, I was devastated. Both Sam and Peter missed graduation. Peter went from surgery to a hospital stay to rehab, and I passed many weeks numb and in a daze. My concussion gave me headaches and nausea, but I was sure my depressed mood was more due to the circumstances.

After graduation, Lisa left to work in Vermont for the summer at a bed and breakfast. She'd managed to get into a local community college with the hopes of transferring to UMass one day and would be living with a girl I didn't know in the fall. It was quiet at home, and I was lonely.

When Peter called, out of the blue, to tell me he was home from the hospital and to ask if I wouldn't mind driving him to a few physical therapy sessions because his mom was trying to take over his life, I was surprised and said yes right away. I badly needed a distraction and felt terrible about the accident. Although no one knew I'd been driving, my guilt was crushing. I thought Sam would call or write to me from California, but he never did. So I transferred all of my energy to Peter.

It was shocking at first to see him in a wheelchair without his leg, but it was also surprising how quickly it just became part of who he was. Peter set up a schedule, and I started driving him to therapy all the time. He bought me lunch at the hospital to thank me. I started to see that while the accident was devastating, Peter was a strong and optimistic person, and I liked that about him. It made things easier for me, and the future started to seem brighter. It didn't escape my notice that Peter smiled at every cute nurse he came in contact with, and they all gave him a ton of attention. Peter was eighteen and a handsome kid, after all. If he felt fear, he hid it well. If he felt miserable sometimes, he didn't show it — at least, not in front of his doctors, and not very often in front of me. He had no intention of letting the loss of his leg put a damper on his goal of going to college. He almost seemed to relish the idea of having the chance to overcome this ridiculous obstacle, like it was a new adventure. I'd never met anyone like him before in my life.

That fall, he lived at home and commuted into the city to attend Boston College. I was at Tufts living in the dorm, but I went home most weekends to visit him. We grew to be friends.

One afternoon in November, when we were at his house after a doctor's appointment, he mentioned that his shoulders were sore. He was learning how to use a temporary prosthesis, and it wasn't easy getting his balance and reconditioning his muscles to do what he needed them to do. So I offered to rub his back.

"Really?" His face lit up. "Yeah, that would be great."

We were sitting on a couch in his living room, the wheelchair he was eager to shed nearby. His parents were busy in the kitchen; then we heard them go out to the backyard to rake, so we were alone. I knelt beside him on the couch and started to massage his neck.

After a few minutes, Peter took a quick glance at me over his shoulder before taking one of my hands in his and gently kissing the inside of my wrist. I froze.

It was such a small thing, yet it woke me out of a heavy fog. Although I'd always admired him, and had naturally grown fond of him, I hadn't considered Peter more than a friend up until that moment. He and I had other priorities all summer, healing ourselves. Peter was focused on recovery and learning to walk again, and I was trying to work through my crippling remorse. And now, with this one gesture, I suddenly felt *light*. The misery of missing Sam had made it hard for me to take pleasure from anything for months, but that kiss felt electric. I felt a burning in my chest, and took in a sharp breath.

"Do you still miss Sam?" he asked, and I had to lean forward to hear him. "You haven't mentioned him lately."

He held my arm but did not turn around, waiting for my answer.

I did still miss Sam, but it was a dull ache now that I hadn't seen him in so long. I considered for a moment how to respond.

Sam wasn't coming back. I hadn't spoken to him since June. I knew our fight on prom night was truly, at the heart of it, about nothing but our fear of commitment, fear of heartbreak, and fear of losing each other. And yet, that's exactly what happened. We let our anxieties get the best of us.

I imagined that if I became Peter's girlfriend, he would expect and demand a lot from me. But he'd work hard and give a lot in return. And maybe that was exactly what I needed at the moment. Someone to pull me back into the land of the living.

"I haven't heard from Sam at all. I don't know how to get in touch with him. I don't have an address or phone number."

"I'm sorry to hear that." He held my wrist gently, and I looked at the back of his head. His hair looked silky, and I wondered what it would be like to touch it. "I never thought he was right for you, but he turned out to be okay. I admire what he did for you. I'm sorry he had to leave." Peter turned slightly to glance back at me and meet my gaze, blue eyes flashing up at me. "Well, you know, I'm not *that* sorry. Because now I get to spend time with you."

I felt a fluttering in my stomach. From the way Peter was gently holding my wrist, the soft and vulnerable side up, I knew he wanted to kiss me again.

I'd always thought that the phrase "steal your heart" was silly, but in that moment, I really felt like Peter was trying to steal my heart away from Sam — carefully, consciously, deliberately. And I also knew he was going to get away with it.

Sam was gone. I was clinging to a memory, and I needed someone right now. Why not Peter? I desperately wanted him to forgive me, and — looking beyond the accident for a moment — he was kind of wonderful. It hit me like a lightning bolt.

I did want him to kiss my wrist again. I wanted to see what that felt like. I was curious to see if my heart was open to the idea.

The truth is, I had noticed the width of Peter's shoulders and admired his smile. I'd listened to the cadence of his voice and his slight accent — crisp and lyrical at the same time — and felt a surge of joy. The nurses assumed I was his girlfriend, and I never contradicted them because that role was so easy to play. Unlike Sam, who was often a closed door, with Peter you knew where his passion and opinions lay about everything, right away. But when I did think about Peter, about what it might be like to be closer to him, I'd always pushed those thoughts away to focus on the tasks at hand — the appointments, the wheelchair, his bandages, or whatever needed tending to.

I cleared my throat. "Well. What about my other wrist? You know, my left hand is doing all the work over here."

Peter turned around completely to face

me — not an easy task in those early days, as he was still relearning his balance — but he was highly motivated. His face was excited and he kissed the inside of my other wrist. "*Küssen.* That's how you say kiss in German." There was a pause where we both stared at each other. "Okay, so . . ." He looked me over. "Where should I kiss next?"

I was shocked — okay, maybe not that shocked — and I had to try hard to calm my heartbeat. Arching my brow, I looked up to the ceiling as if thinking about it. "Well, I have a list." I tossed my head as nonchalantly as I could. "Of ten potentially good kissing sites."

His mouth dropped open, just a bit. I grinned as I got the reaction I wanted.

"Fine," he said with a big sigh, as if I was putting him out. "You're very demanding. I can appreciate that. Besides, I owe you one for the back rub." He took a quick glance at the doorway to make sure his parents hadn't come back inside and then rolled his tongue in his cheek. "Okay, come on, I'm waiting. Where should I start?"

I leaned back until I was lying down on the couch, propped up on my elbows. "Hmmm." I slung a leg onto his lap. "My ankle next, maybe?"

Peter took my foot in both hands and

pushed my jeans up a bit to reveal my ankle. But his shoulders slumped, and he paused.

A grandfather clock in the hallway began to chime. I waited as he played with the shoelace on my sneaker and didn't look at me. All of the earlier bravado and confidence drained out of him, and he looked younger in that moment.

Peter frowned.

"What's the matter?" I whispered, worrying that he'd changed his mind.

"Uh . . ." He gave my foot a light squeeze. "Look, Annika. I need to say something first. I've got to be honest with you."

"Okay. Sure. What is it?"

He shut his eyes and briefly pressed a flat palm over his forehead. "I don't know how easily I'm going to be able to get around in the future. Or how this is all going to work out. I don't know if I'm going to need help and care my whole life, and if I'm going to be able to do the things I want to do. I feel like a burden right now. Do you know what I'm saying?" He dropped his hand and squinted open one eye to see if I understood.

I looked him over. As far as I concerned, he was the same boy he was before the accident.

"Peter, don't be silly," I scolded him, making my voice intense so he'd get it through his thick skull. "Don't talk like that. You can do anything you want to do."

He inhaled quickly. "I don't know that yet," he snapped at me, putting my foot down on his lap. He rubbed his hands together, then gestured toward his missing leg.

"I don't know what I'm capable of. Not yet, I don't. I keep having moments of panic where I think I'm going to lose my balance and fall over. Or I wake up and think my leg is still there, and it's only when I try to get up that I realize it's not. I feel achy all the time — my body hates having this leg gone. And my parents are driving me insane, hovering over me constantly. My mom won't leave me the hell alone. Thank God you're here helping, but I wish I knew if you really wanted to be here, or if you just feel sorry for me."

I was alarmed. He didn't usually talk like this.

"Are you still meeting with your therapist?"

"Therapist?" He winced. "Yes, but . . . my therapist can't fix this."

I sat up. I wasn't sure if I should comfort him or reprimand him. So I went with my gut. "Stop making excuses. You can do

411

everything, Peter." I stared at him, but he wouldn't look at me. "It's okay to be scared. But you can handle it. I know you can. I told you — you can do anything you want to. Starting today. Starting right now."

He tipped his head. The sun streaming in from the window made his hair shine and emphasized the angles of his face. I knew he was listening to me. And, just as he did in the street on prom night when I told him *It'll be fine,* I could see he believed me.

At least, he wanted *very badly* to believe me.

So I pressed on, trying to think fast.

"Look, you said it yourself — you owe me *küssen.* I told you I have a list of ten kissing sites, so you need to get started before your parents come back in." When he finally turned to look at me, I started to unbutton my blouse, for emphasis. "And you're going to like what I have in mind, believe me." My fingers flew faster as I undid one more button, seeing that I had his full attention. "Feel sorry for you? Give me a break. Are you gonna figure out a way to make it work, or not?"

Something in his face changed, and he sat up straighter. Peter shook his head slightly and sighed dramatically, for my benefit. "*Fräulein,* why do you torture me like this?"

In a softer voice he said something to me in German, and while I had no idea what he was saying, I knew *exactly* what he was saying. I bit my lip to try to keep a straight face but couldn't do it.

"Come on," I whispered, leaning back on the couch again. "First, my ankle. Get to work."

So he did.

By the time he was done with ten kisses, I was in love.

I didn't mean for it to happen. It just did.

All that time, all of those months, all of those years, Peter knew I'd been the one who not only invited him to ride along, but also drove the car after drinking, the night he lost his leg. And he still called me to ask if I'd take him to therapy, took me home to meet his parents, grew to love me and wanted to marry me, gave me two children, and died in our bed.

And now, I want to read his journal. I need to know more about Peter's perspective. He loved me, despite my faults. If I find any disappointment or regret as part of his story, I can handle it. I'm going to have to learn how to handle it, just as he did when he lost his leg.

Peter and I were thrown together in a

413

traumatic, life-changing accident. The fact that we had a wonderful marriage and two amazing children is the lucky part.

I have many happy memories. Getting married in a garden, surrounded by red roses. Peter kissed me in the coat closet for privacy; we smiled when we heard Peter's cousins calling for him, but they couldn't find him. Years after that, I remember Peter laughing when I tried to build a gingerbread house with the kids, and we ended up eating the gumdrops because the house fell apart. And years after that, Peter made me a hot cup of peppermint tea every Sunday night when it was time for my favorite TV show. There were big things and little things that added up to our great love story.

Peter always told me we had the best love story going. That's what he would whisper to me late at night if I was feeling melancholy; then he'd kiss the inside of my wrist. The only thing is, no one actually *knew* the whole story.

Until now. Because I'm ready to share it.

FIRE

LUNA

The snow tapers off; then the storm is over.
The beauty of the deep new-fallen snow is
deceiving. Despite the magical way the sun
twinkles as it glances off the edges of
snowdrifts, it's still cold outside. And the
humans have work to do if Annika ever
wants to get her car out of that long driveway.

Delilah disappears upstairs. I imagine she
has joined her brother, and they're racing
through the journal to find out more about
Peter's accident. The adults sit in the front
room, quiet and contemplative. I clean my
paws with my rough tongue, perched on an
arm of the couch.

"This day has not gone the way I expected
it to. Not at all," Danny announces, despon-
dent. He is slumped down in an armchair
and holds the big glass bottle of whiskey
with both hands between his legs. He has

consumed quite a bit after the last conversation. "Sam, you're a crazier bastard than I realized."

Sam smiles mildly. "Aw, c'mon. Don't flatter me."

Lisa is sitting on the floor near the woodstove, legs crossed, still reading through Peter's novel one page at a time. She's pulled a soft, fuzzy ski hat on; it's the color of milk. "I'm getting hungry. Are you guys hungry?"

"Nah. I'm going to call Trung to check in." Danny gets up. He stares despondently out the picture window for a moment before leaving the room.

Lisa glances up at Annika, who is still seated on the couch, staring down at her lap. "I'll tell you what. I'll go see if there's anything we can snack on until dinner." She leaves Sam and Annika alone in the room. I remain with them, wanting to stay close to Annika in case she needs a warm cat to cuddle with.

The wind has died down, and the house is still. Three white candles flicker on the coffee table. A small, battery-operated clock on a sideboard counts off at a steady pace: *click-click-click.*

"Annika, can I tell you something?"

"Sure." She waits.

And waits.

"Is everything all right?"

Sam gets up and walks to the window. He throws an arm out to the left. "The house in this direction —" There's a thumping noise as he taps on the glass with one finger. "Do you know the one I mean? The one that my dad is building, on the other side of the creek?"

"The house across the creek? The big one?" Annika stands up, grabbing a blanket from the couch to throw over her shoulders, and walks over to Sam's side. She peers out the window with eyes narrowed, hugging the blanket around her. "I've seen trucks sometimes on the road, but I had no idea your dad was building that house. I haven't been paying any attention. What about it?"

"Well, it's just that . . . that house needs to come down."

"What?"

"Something's wrong with it. So it's gotta come down." He lowers his voice. "Danny wants to burn it down."

Annika turns to face him. "Did you just say burn it down?"

"Yeah." Sam presses on. "Danny wants to burn it down so the insurance company will pay our dad some cash now, and they can start over and build it cheaper in the summer. My dad cut some corners and made

417

some mistakes, and now he can't afford to fix it out of his own pocket. The costs just got away from him, you know? And he can't sell it to another builder this time of year. He's tried." He takes in a deep breath.

I know the house Sam is talking about. It's past the old garage. I don't usually walk in that direction, because I can't cross the stream. But I can see that they cut down some beautiful old trees to make room for that monstrosity. There was a big, fat owl that lost his home and I was sorry to see that happen.

Annika pushes the curtain aside and peers out the window again. "You can't let him do that, Sam," she whispers.

"I know. I know. But I haven't been able to talk him out of it. He's got gasoline, firewood, and kindling."

"But . . . won't someone call nine-one-one, and they'll come put out the fire?"

"The fire trucks won't be able to get up here because the streets aren't plowed."

"I think they'll try to get up here —"

Sam shakes his head as if he's just walked into a cobweb. "Sure, they'll try. But the trucks won't be able to get all the way up the hill. Besides, the hydrants are covered in snow drifts. They'd have trouble finding them and digging them out. And they can't pull water from the creek, because it's frozen and buried in snow. By the time anyone got to the house with any amount of water, it'd be all over."

Annika studies Sam. "Sam, I don't know what to say. You've got to talk him out of it." She winces. "It's a terrible idea. Danny can't do that. You know that, right?"

I'm not sure what Sam is talking about exactly. Fires belong in the fireplace. Anywhere else? They're dangerous.

He nods. "Yeah, I agree. And I've tried to talk him out of it. But it's just that —"

"No, stop. You told me you're trying to be a better person, remember? I am, too. So tell Danny no."

"Sweetheart, Danny is really sick, and it's going to cost a lot of money for treatment. And my parents could lose their house." Sam's eyes tear up.

"I know you want to help them. Believe me, I remember how all you ever wanted to do was fix things." Annika puts a hand on his arm. "If there's one thing I know in my heart about you, Sam, it's that you want to help people who need it. But this is the wrong way to go about it. Please, Sam."

"But . . . just hear me out. Maybe it would be okay. Our dad can just rebuild it. He can do what he wants with his own property, can't he?"

Annika tips her head. "I don't think he can. Wouldn't Danny be committing insurance fraud? Wouldn't they charge him with arson, if they found out? Besides . . ." She takes both of his hands in hers. "What if one of the firefighters got hurt? Or the whole woods caught fire and it spread to more houses, like this one?"

And that's when something changes in the room. I can feel the transfer of energy.

As I've observed, Sam is like a dog and Danny is the alpha of his pack. Until now, Sam has been focused on pleasing his older brother. But I think the prospect of gaining Annika's respect and admiration is a greater pull.

Sam's alliance shifts to her. I can sense it in the air. He looks down at her hands holding his and he seems amazed to find himself in this lucky circumstance. Her touch diminishes his distress and gives him hope.

And when he looks into her eyes — that's when I see he loves her.

"You're right," Sam says with confidence. His shoulders relax. "Yeah, I know you're right. Okay. I'll talk to him again. But what am I going to do about my dad? He's going bankrupt. And Danny needs treatment. I do want to help them, and I don't know how."

"Sell the new truck."

"Our business depends on those trucks."

"I'm sorry. Maybe you will lose your house, then." Annika's face is pink from the warmth from the fire and, I suspect, from standing so close to Sam. "I hate to say that. But, Sam, there's got to be another way. It's terrible to go bankrupt, but it's better than letting Danny do something completely stupid. I'll try and help you, if I can."

He sighs. "Yeah, okay. We'll figure something out." Sam holds her hands tight. "I'm worried my dad asked me to come back here because he wants me to take over the business, since we don't know what's going to happen with Danny. But I really don't want to do that. Maybe for a while, but . . ."

"Sam. Don't do it if you don't want to. Maybe the other men who work for him would be willing to help out more."

Sam nods. "To tell you the truth, I always thought Trung would make a great manager. He could buy the business if Dad wants to retire. As long as Trung keeps the Parsons name on the trucks, people in Manchester will still hire him." He starts to tear up. "I feel bad for Trung. He's saving our asses. He's been working this whole time on almost no sleep. This is all my fault."

The house is strangely quiet. But it's more

than just the lack of electricity humming through the lamps and heat swooshing through the vents.

What happened to the twins? Hmm. They're very quiet all of a sudden.

"Sweetheart," Annika says quietly to Sam, who hangs his head. "It's stopped snowing. Look . . . the sun is out, right? But you don't have much daylight left. You should go outside and change that tire and get some fresh air. Lisa and I will come, too."

Sam takes in a deep but shaky breath and then lets it out. He looks up, defeated, but still searches Annika's face as if she has an answer for him.

She does. She leans forward and gently kisses him right on the mouth. "It's going to be okay. I'll help you. I promise."

Well! I didn't see that coming. I don't think Sam did either, from the look on his face.

Sam's eyes perk up immediately and his face glows. He begins to breathe a little faster.

"Annie," he says, and I start to purr.

"You just have to give me a little time, okay? There's no rush."

"Sweetheart. If you still love Peter, it's okay." He stands up straighter. "It's fine. I understand. I know you still love him. I can tell."

"I do, Sam, but that doesn't mean there isn't any room in my heart for anyone else. I just need to take everything slow."

Sam nods. "Does this mean — Are you thinking about staying in Manchester?"

"I don't know. Let's take it one day at a time."

Sam squares his shoulders and shifts his weight. Letting go of her hands to stretch, he reminds me of a bear coming out of hibernation, shaking off sleep. He swallows and takes in a deep breath, his expression radiant as he gathers his thoughts. "I'm gonna go change that tire. Right now." Walking to the front door with renewed energy, he pulls on his snow pants and winter coat before shoving his feet in his boots. He doesn't bother to lace his boots or zip up the coat, and starts pulling his gloves on.

Annika walks up to Sam and fits the zipper of his coat together at the bottom before pulling up the tab and then fastening the snaps. She palms his cheek while he takes one of her braids in his hand. He gazes at her a moment before gathering her in his arms in a hug. "I'm sorry," he whispers, his face buried in her hair. "I'm sorry I ever —"

"Shhh." She pats his shoulder. "It's okay. You go ahead. I'll find Lisa and we'll be out in a minute," Annika says. And so Sam heads out into the cold, sparkling snow.

Danny comes down the hall. He stops and looks at Annika.

"Where's Sam?"

"He went out to change the tire."

"He did?" Danny scowls and walks to the window to see it for his own eyes.

"Yes, Lisa and I are going to go out and shovel."

Danny tips his head. "You are? I thought you were all going to stay inside and keep warm."

She walks up to him, pulling on her mittens. "Sam told me you're sick. I'm sorry about the cancer, Danny, I really am."

His head snaps back. "He told you about that? I didn't mean for him to go tell everyone about that." His eyes dart away. "Although . . . I guess you're different. I guess that's okay, since it's you."

Annika looks up at him. "I won't tell anyone. I don't want you to worry. I want you to rest. Could you please throw more wood on the fire in the back room and here in the stove?"

He nods and turns to go, passing Lisa, who is just coming from the kitchen.

"What's the matter with him?" Lisa points her thumb in the direction of where Danny went.

"He doesn't feel well," Annika says, taking her coat off a hanger. "Can you come out with me to help shovel the driveway? Sam is changing the tire."

"Shovel? Now?"

"Come on. It's a big job. And I feel like we owe Sam for taking credit for all the dumb stuff we did in high school. Don't you? I wish I could do more for him."

"Yeah, all right," Lisa agrees, pulling her snow pants on and flipping her hair back over her shoulder. "I guess so. The sun's out, anyway. It looks beautiful." She pauses. "So, should we talk about this boarding school thing? I still think it's a big waste of money."

The women keep chatting as they head outside.

And just then, Donovan comes down the stairs. Strange. I didn't hear his footsteps.

Delilah is right behind him.

"Donovan," Delilah says with urgency. "Wait. We can't start a fire. That's insane. How would we even do it, anyway?"

"We've got a whole garage full of firewood."

"Yeah, but . . . do you mean we'd make it

look like someone *accidentally* started a fire?"

Donovan continues to the bottom of the stairs and hunts around for his mittens and boots near the front door. "Yeah, exactly. It should look like an accident. Maybe we could bring some of those wine bottles from the fridge? And . . . sparklers. The ones Mom bought for New Year's Eve. It'll just look like some kids were drinking and playing around in there. We'll think of something."

Delilah makes a face. "No, no, no, we can't. Donovan, think about it. What would Dad say? He was always trying to get you to be more responsible."

"Yeah, but . . ." Donovan turns to face his sister and straightens up. "He also said: *I'd rather give my story a new twist. The great thing about telling your own story is that you can decide what happens.* Remember? He said that to us, Del. And the same kind of stuff is in his journal. You read it." Donovan opens the closet to fetch his coat. "Dad would understand if we wanted to do something heroic, something unexpected. This is a grand gesture. For love. To win Danny over, so I can see Lexi."

Delilah chews on her bottom lip. "I don't think this is exactly the kind of thing Dad had in mind."

"Well, then, think of it this way. We'd be doing Mom a favor. She just said she wants to help Sam. This will help his family."

Delilah folds her arms. "This is to do Mom a favor? Now you're grasping at straws."

When Donovan moves to the bottom of the stairs, he is suddenly transformed into Peter in that moment — Peter's face, his expression, his energy. Donovan throws his arms out in front of him with enthusiasm. "Why do you say that? Dad was always prodding me to get off my ass and do more to help out. This will help *everyone.* But most importantly, Danny needs the money, and he'll be impressed. I'll get to see Lexi when I need to. And, Del, I really need her. I'm gonna go crazy if I can't see her. I'm already out of my mind. I have to see her. Please, help me. Please. Please, Del."

When Donovan reaches a hand up to his sister, I know in my heart that Delilah's going to join him. She hesitates, but he is her twin.

They are determined to find something meaningful in their father's death, one way or another. Together.

She takes one step down toward her brother. And then another. Until she's face-to-face with him. "Okay, fine. I'm not going to get in the way of true love. But listen. You have to do something for me. Let's convince Mom to stay here in Manchester with us. You don't really want to live with Aunt Lisa if you have a choice about it, do you?" She makes a face. "And we need to persuade Mom not to tell Grandmommy and Granddaddy about the fact that she was driving the car the night of Dad's accident. If she tells them, they're going to try even harder to bring us back to Connecticut. You know they will. And I want to stay here. Okay?"

He nods. And in a sudden movement, he gives her a quick hug. "Yeah, of course. That's what I want, too. It's a deal."

She squeezes and then releases him, satisfied. She tips her head the way Peter used to and smiles. "Good. We'll grab matches in the kitchen and go out the back door." And just like that, Delilah takes charge of the operation. She is still giving him orders as they get their winter gear on and head to the back of the house.

TERRIBLE ACCIDENT

ANNIKA

Lisa and I are making good headway on the path from the driveway to the front door. It's slow going, but we take turns with the one shovel we have between us.

"Look, I'm sorry I got mad about the cottage," Lisa tells me. "But I've wanted this place for so long. It was a shock to hear you were moving in here. But I get it. Losing Peter was tough on you guys. You've had a lot on your mind."

I watch her kick the shovel with her boot to force it down under a large block of snow. "It's okay. I should've checked in with you about it."

She straightens. "Look, if you're really moving to Maine, I'll take the house. And I told the twins that if they want to move in with me, they can. They're old enough to decide where they want to go to school and manage their own affairs."

"Manage their own affairs?" I bristle, imagining the twins. Yes, they have the bodies of adults, but when I look at their faces I see the children they were not long ago, before Peter died. "They're still kids, Lisa. They need a lot of supervision and guidance. Every minute of every day. You can't just leave them to their own devices."

"Would I do any worse than the job you're doing right now?" She throws a shovelful of snow to the side. "Seriously?"

I stare down at my snow boots. I don't have an answer to that.

"I didn't mean to steal the cottage from you. You can have it."

"Really?"

I take the shovel from her. "Yes. Look, I've been thinking about the past a lot lately, and I remember I wasn't always the greatest sister to you. In fact, I was pretty awful sometimes. So if it means that much to you —"

"Wait. Do you smell smoke?" I look up to see Lisa tipping her head. She turns her head right and left.

I take in a deep breath of the crisp air. "Yeah, Danny must have thrown a lot of wood on the fire."

Reaching up, she pulls her white ski hat off by the pompom, nose twitching. "No,

430

it's more than —" When she freezes, and her face collapses into a look of panic, I turn to look in the direction she's facing. Past the garage, over the creek, through the trees, a steady stream of gray smoke rises into the darkening blue sky.

My heart freezes up.

"Oh, my God," Lisa whispers. Her face hardens, and she cups two hands around her mouth to yell toward the driveway. "HEY, SAM. Get over here."

Sam comes lumbering toward us as fast as he can through the snow, one big step at a time. "Hey," he croaks out. "The spare tire is on. But — Are you looking at that, over there? It looks like a fire." He stops next to us and observes the smoke billowing from the woods. "That's got to be the house my dad is building. The new one." He points through the trees. "It's on fire. It's seriously on fire. Do you think it has something to do with the power outage?" Sam's voice is quiet, but his face is one of amazement, eyes wide and mouth open.

I feel my heart start to pound. Did Sam start that fire for Danny? Would he do that?

It sure sounds like something he would do.

I wasn't watching Sam the whole time. Could he have snuck away for a few minutes . . . ?

I look back at his face. He's stunned. If he's acting, he's a damn good actor.

He and I make eye contact. He gives me a small shrug, as if to say, *I don't know how it happened.*

Lisa whips out her cell phone and starts scrolling through her contacts. "I'm gonna call Hank. He's the fire chief. It's his sister I'm renting the house from." She puts the phone to her ear. "Hey, Hank, it's Lisa. We've got a fire on the block in an empty house. No one's in there. It's still under construction. Yeah, that's the one."

She starts giving the details, while I look back toward the house. I never saw Danny come outside. I don't understand how he got past us. Did he go out the back door?

Fire engulfs the house within minutes. Soon, it's not just smoke — I can see orange flames through the black trees, against the white snow. We trudge over to the edge of the driveway, and I believe I can actually feel the heat it's throwing off, unless that's just my body temperature rising as my stomach turns.

"Don't worry," Lisa says, seeing the look on my face. "Hank said that homes with a timber frame burn fast. There's no wind, and that property was clear cut so there

432

aren't any trees too close. I think we're safe here. Hank's on his way. He's just on Mill Street. He'll have to walk, but he'll get here eventually. We don't need to go over to the house. We can keep an eye on it from here." She looks around. "They won't be able to get the trucks very close, though."

I take out my phone, hands trembling, and text Delilah. I gulp in a breath of cold air to steady myself. It burns my lungs. IS MR. PARSONS IN THE BACK ROOM?

A minute goes by. Two minutes. YES. HE'S LYING ON THE COUCH BY THE FIRE. HIS EYES ARE CLOSED. WHY?

I glance over at Sam. He stands there, knee deep in snow, hands on his hips.

He doesn't look at me. He looks wary, as if he can't believe there's a fire right in front of his eyes. Which is exactly how I feel.

Yet who else could have done this but him? There are only two suspects here: Sam and Danny. Or the two of them together. This fire did not start itself. There is no way this is a coincidence. For the love of God, we were just talking about it.

I clear my throat. "Do you have anything to say about this?"

Sam squints. "What do you mean? About the fire?" He doesn't have his face mask on because the sun is shining, and in that mo-

433

ment he looks lost. He's gaping at the smoke pouring up from the trees. "I don't know what to think." He pulls his hat off and holds it in both hands, as if not sure what to do with it. "Believe me . . . I don't know what to say."

I'm disappointed. But I don't know why I'm surprised. This is so Sam. He's incredibly predictable. This is exactly the kind of thing he would've done in high school.

I just feel stupid for not seeing it coming.

I can't believe for a moment I was considering staying in Manchester because of Sam. Do I want to get dragged into this insanity all over again? You can't just break the law to help people. Getting yourself kicked out of town, or thrown in jail, helps no one. The truth is, it hurts people in the end.

Sam takes a step away from us. "I'm going to go over there and survey the damage. See if there's anything I can do."

He trudges off in the direction of the fire before I have a chance to ask anything more.

I feel like I'm eighteen again and Sam has just told me he's going to confess to spray-painting graffiti in the gym. He always means well, but it's maddening. He does whatever he feels is the right thing at the time, without thinking through the conse-

434

quences. It drove me crazy back then and amazes me now. But I'm too old to excuse his behavior. Burning a house down is serious business.

That's it. We're leaving Manchester. This is too much.

As dusk descends, we hear the fire engine sirens in the distance, but the trucks never even get close. I later find out they got stuck on the ice and in the snow drifts at the start of our dirt road. Seven men who are bundled up in winter gear hike up the street toward the smoldering remains of the house. They move as fast as they can on foot through the heavy snow, although the fire is, for the most part, over. They have little equipment to utilize anyway, as the trucks can't follow them. I watch their efforts from the driveway, feeling my feet starting to freeze in my boots. My hands are numb and starting to ache. Lisa tells me she's going over to the fire. I'm tempted to get closer to the action, too, but stay where I am, near the kids.

I wonder why the twins haven't come outside, or why they aren't at least watching all of this from an upstairs window. You'd think they'd at least be curious.

The fire quickly diminishes. The firemen poke around the house, although it's past the point where they can do much, and the sun is going down fast. Eventually, they retreat back down the street.

Just as it's getting dark, an older man crosses the frozen creek in his boots, with Sam and Lisa in tow. I wait for them, feeling defeated.

"Let's all go inside for a minute," I say. "I need to check on the twins."

I go in first. The house isn't exactly warm and it's getting dark, but Delilah has left a campfire lantern on for us on the coffee table near the candles, and it feels good to stand in front of the woodstove and soak up the heat. The fire chief follows Lisa into the house with slow, deliberate movements. He's stocky, with salt-and-pepper hair, a full beard, and deep-set wrinkles. He's a man who has clearly seen his share of fires. My palms feel sweaty and my nerves are on edge as he joins me by the stove. I'd offer to take his coat, but it's too cold to undress.

"C'mon, Hank," Lisa teases him. "You've got to do a little more work on the treadmill. You're not gonna make it."

His face is red from the cold. He chuckles. "You're right about that. I don't know why I don't just retire."

"Annika." Lisa turns to me. "Do you remember Hank McKean? Henry's dad."

436

I struggle to figure out who he is, wringing my hands, but then the name rings a bell and I stop fidgeting. "Henry's dad. Oh — yes! It's been a long time."

Wow. I look at him again.

The truth is, I hardly remember Mr. McKean. I'm sure I saw him a few times at events at the high school back in the 1980s. At a football game. Or a band concert.

And in the hospital on prom night, after Henry crashed into us.

He shakes his head. "Annika. It's good to see you. Lisa told me all about you. And Peter! I'm sorry for your loss. I was so happy when I heard you married him. My wife sent money to Peter's parents after his accident, but they wouldn't take it. The truth is, we needed every penny for Henry's lawyer. But it would've made us feel better if they had taken it." He sighs.

"Who's this?" I hear Donovan's voice before I see him.

I turn to see the twins are standing at the bottom of the stairs, and I'm surprised to see them there. They both have their winter coats on, but their faces are flushed like they've been running around.

"The fire chief," Lisa says. "Mr. McKean. There was a fire in that new house, across the creek. Didn't you guys wonder why we were outside so long?"

Delilah's dark eyebrows knit together. I wonder if she recognizes the name *McKean* from what we talked about earlier.

"Well, about that fire." I take in a deep breath, suddenly realizing what I'm going to do and unable to stop myself. "I set the fire. By accident."

"What?" Lisa asks, stunned. "What the hell are you talking about?"

Sam tips his head, puzzled. His brows knit together, and he mouths to me: *What?*

I'm going to help you, I try to communicate to Sam through my expression. It occurs to me that I should have tipped him off earlier that I was going to take the fall this time.

But the truth is, I only knew I had it in me once the words came out of my mouth. It's not something I planned. I just did it. The same way Sam just jumped in and took the blame when he thought I needed help so many years ago.

But this is it. I'm going to absolve myself for my past errors. I owe it to Sam. I appreciate all he did for me, and never expressed it at the time. I feel responsible as the one who sent him on a trajectory where he had to flee Manchester, and never felt at home in Los Angeles — and took a job he didn't like — and fell for the wrong woman —

I stop when I suddenly get the feeling that Peter is here with me. I shudder, because it's so intense, and it brings tears to my eyes. But I can't stop now to worry over whether or not he would approve.

I'm okay, I tell Peter in my head. *I can do this. I'm going to step up and make amends, and give this afternoon a new twist that no one sees coming. I'm going to do exactly what you told us to do — write my own story. I miss you more than I can express, and I desperately wish you were here, but it will be okay. I can handle it. It's fine.*

I clear my throat and forge ahead. "Yes, I set it. It was just a terrible accident. I walked over to the house to make sure no one needed help during the power outage. I wasn't quite sure if anyone had moved in yet, because the house is so new."

"But when — ?"

I give Lisa a stern look, to silence her. "Lisa. Listen, I brought a candle in a lantern with me and accidentally dropped it. Everything caught fire so fast that I had to run for it. That's when I found you shoveling snow on the path."

Lisa squints at me, but she's smart and keeps her mouth shut. I can see the wheels turning in her mind as she glances at Sam.

"So . . . right. That's right. That's when I called Hank."

Donovan walks up right behind me and puts a hand on my back. "Mom. What are you talking about? No one is going to believe that. Why are you making that up?" He sounds amazed, and awfully sure of himself.

"But, sweetheart." I whirl around, shocked that Donovan would call me out. He's hovering, as if he needs to take something dangerous out of my hands. "It was an accident. I didn't mean to do it."

"Mom, please." Donovan shakes his head and turns to Hank. "That's not true. I set the fire. She's just trying to cover for me."

Wait — what? "You set the fire?"

"Yes."

I'm shocked — no, appalled. My son? Started that fire?

But when I see the look on Donovan's face, I soften. He looks grateful, staring at me in admiration. I feel it, the love he's sending me, and it's a relief.

Donovan thinks I was trying to protect him, not Sam.

It's just as well. I would do anything to protect my children. My love for the twins is absolute, no matter how crazy they drive me. I just had no idea it was Donovan who

440

set the fire.

But . . . why in the world would he do such a thing? I think carefully about what my next words should be, aware that Hank is watching us. "Was it an accident?"

"Yeah, Mom." Delilah comes over, closer to us. "It was an accident, like you said, but it was Donovan who started it."

I can see they're not kidding. And it hits me. This is serious. Delilah is somehow involved, too. Oh, God.

I fight back the tears that are welling up. What in the world . . . ?

Delilah quickly approaches and puts her arm around me. "It's okay. We're fine. We're here now."

"You were there, Del?" Lisa asks, narrowing her eyes, putting her hands on her hips. "Why were you kids over there?"

"Yeah, I was there." Delilah nods. "I went to make sure things didn't get out of hand. I knew Donovan was angry, and I didn't want him to accidentally hurt himself." She looks over at Hank. "He didn't mean to burn the whole house down."

Hank adjusts his glasses. "Why don't you let your brother tell me what happened?"

Donovan admits to starting a small fire in the house up on the hill. He explains that he'd wanted to burn his father's journal to punish me, but didn't want to do it in the fireplace at home because he was afraid I might catch him. He tells the story about how Peter died in his sleep, in greater detail than he's ever told me before, and explains that he's blamed me for it ever since, both for brushing off Peter's symptoms and not being home when he died. By the time Donovan is done with this story, clutching the blue leather book to his chest with both arms and explaining that in the end he just couldn't burn the diary but got distracted as the fire spread, he has tears streaming down his cheeks. I haven't seen my son cry like this since the funeral, his face blotchy but his expression typically stoic. Hank can't help but put a hand on Donovan's shoulder in comfort. It's a stunning performance — all the more striking because I'm not sure how much of it is acting. I'm starting to realize Donovan must have heard some of my conversation with Sam, and he had his own reasons for wanting to help Danny out and burn the house down. But a lot of what Donovan is saying is clearly true emotion, the way Donovan really feels. I'm sure Donovan had no intention of burning the journal, but I think he means every word he says about wanting to hurt me.

It only makes me cry, too. Delilah rubs

my back with her hand. It must be clear to her that I have no idea what to do. No one has provided me with directions titled "What to Do If Your Children Burn a House Down." Perhaps there's nothing I can do.

"Don't worry, son," the fire chief says softly. "Accidents happen."

"Don't we all know it," Lisa sighs.

Donovan bites his lip, light and shadows from the fire in the woodstove playing against his face. A shudder goes down my spine as I wonder if I've lost him somehow, if I've let him use his grief to drive a wedge between us.

But then I remember Sam at the same age — sad, confused, and feeling abandoned by his parents. He was never a bad person. On the contrary, Sam was capable of love, humor, and tenderness — if not always the best judgment. It helps to firm up my resolve, and when I reach out a hand to Donovan, he immediately comes to me and lets me put my arms around him. His hair smells like he's been sitting in front of a bonfire.

"Again, I'm so sorry to hear Peter has passed on," Hank says. "He was a good kid who didn't deserve what he got. Losing his leg and all that."

I shake my head. "No, don't you think that. His life wasn't all about the accident. Not at all. He got what he deserved — a family who loved him."

I notice that Danny has now joined us in the room. From the look on his face, I imagine he is suspicious and alarmed about the fire, but he doesn't ask any questions. He stares at my kids, clearly puzzled and tempted to ask more about it. Holding a hand over his mouth, frowning, he sits on the edge of an armchair as if ready to jump into action at any moment. But he sits tight.

"I'm so glad to hear you have two great kids." Hank gestures toward Donovan and Delilah and smiles, as if he's their own proud grandfather. "Twins! You're lucky."

"You know kids, Hank. Sometimes they're great, and sometimes they're just trouble." I laugh and wipe my eye with my thumb.

Hank nods and digs a tissue out of his pants pocket, which he hands to me. "I know." His voice quiets. "Believe me, I know." Hank nods at Lisa. "I'll get this taken care of."

"Thanks."

Lisa offers to walk the fire chief part of the way down the road. They bundle up, she grabs a flashlight, and they head out.

Once the fire chief is gone, Danny jumps

444

up. "I heard everything." He walks up to stand over Donovan, who is now sitting on the couch, but my son is too worn-out to respond. "That was quite an interesting story. We'll have to call the insurance company tomorrow and file a claim." He doesn't take his eyes off Donovan as he paces the length of the couch. "It's so fascinating how that happened. Really amazing. How that all just *happened* in my dad's house. It's almost . . . unbelievable." I'm not sure from his tone if he admires my boy's brio, or is concerned he's now going to be forced to let Donovan visit his daughter because he owes him one.

Either way, I think Donovan has won himself a reprieve. I don't think Danny will object too strenuously if Donovan shows up at his house to visit Lexi this week.

I don't know how to feel about it. Something has gone wrong with my son, and that's my primary concern. I will try again to get him to go back to a therapist. It's clear to me my first priority right now can't be his education; it's got to be his state of mind. Forget boarding school — for now. I'll tell Donovan I want to meet Alexis, and that she's welcome in our home. What I said to Sam is true; I'm trying to be a better person all the time. I just have to coax Donovan to join me on that path, and if Delilah helps, I'm sure we can all get there.

"Donovan," I say, kneeling at his feet in front of the couch. "You don't have to go to The President's Academy. I understand you need to stay, even more than I need to go. So let's just agree that we won't make any big moves right now. We can stay at least through the spring, and then see where we're at. I'll figure out what I'm doing and how to get through this. I will."

Donovan looks at me and nods. Delilah comes right up behind me and almost knocks me over as she bends down to give me a hug. "Thank you," she exclaims. "Thank you, thank you, thank you." She bounces over to sit next to Donovan on the couch.

Sam is standing by the side window, looking out at the darkness. I pat Donovan's hands and get up and go to join Sam.

"I assumed it was you. I didn't know who else it could be," I whisper to him.

He turns to face me. We're so close that his coat rubs against mine. "You were gonna take credit for it? Are you crazy? Donovan's right. Hank would've had a hard time believing it."

I reach out and tap my fingers against his. "Maybe he would have. I wanted to try. I don't want you in trouble. No more. There's been enough."

"Yes, ma'am." He gives me a look. "I hear you."

I glance over to the twins to make sure they're not watching us. I squeeze Sam's hand gently, just for a moment. I'm tired, but that doesn't bother me right now. It feels good, like I've earned it.

When Lisa returns, she assures me that Hank is a good guy, someone she trusts. There will be a police investigation, but Hank has pledged to help sort everything out.

"Thank you. And, Lisa, we're going to stay here for a while."

She clucks her tongue. "Fine. Suit yourself. I'm glad you're not wasting anyone's money on that school."

"If you really want the cottage, of course we'll look for somewhere else in Manchester to live. I'm sure there are many other houses where we'd be comfortable."

She shrugs, looking at the kids, who are draped in random positions over the couch, worn-out to the bone. "Okay, well . . . I mean, that would be nice of you. But I know Delilah already painted and decorated her room. So if you find another house, great.

But I'm not gonna kick you guys out."

"Thanks, Aunt Lisa," Delilah says, putting a hand in the air to acknowledge that she's heard this concession.

Everyone ends up scavenging the kitchen for food; then we go to sit by a roaring fire in the back room, eating cashews, Cheerios, and other assorted random food from a tray I've perched on the coffee table. Delilah and Donovan assign themselves the task of digging everything out of our kitchen cabinets to see if there's anything we can eat that we've missed.

Danny checks his phone. "Trung says the town will definitely plow this road overnight. They're starting to get to the secondary roads anyway. But thanks to that fire, this road is now a priority."

"Good." My stomach grumbles, hopefully not too loud. I'm nibbling on a dry cracker because we've run out of cheese. Sam spreads strawberry jam on another cracker and hands it to me. I smile as I take it from him.

"I hope we get the power back soon," Lisa says. "It'd better not take two weeks for them to fix it."

Delilah comes in and plops down on the bricks in front of the fireplace. She's wearing pink fuzzy slippers, her hair in a bun on top of her head. "So what's this I hear about my dad writing a novel?"

Lisa grabs a fistful of cereal. "Yeah, it's true. It's a fantasy. It's got everything: Dragons. Sea serpents. Magic. A knight on a quest. You're gonna love it."

She perks up. "Did you read it?"

"Some of it. It's excellent. Unfortunately, I flipped to the end, and it ends abruptly in the middle of a scene. I think you're going to have to finish it for him."

Delilah's eyes light up. "What?"

"Sure," Lisa says, sliding forward in her seat. "You've gotta complete it. For your dad. Just read through it and figure out how it should end."

"Oooh, wow." She leans forward. "Okay. I'm up for it. I'll come up with something once I've read the whole thing. I can do that. I get to write the ending? How cool is that?"

"He was a terrific writer. I'm sure you'll be very proud to read his work."

"I'm sure I will." Delilah looks pleased.

Lisa clucks her tongue, watching me. "Del, did you know that when we were in high school I used to call Sam and your mom the *lovebirds*?"

She laughs. "What?"

I immediately straighten up. Sam moves

an inch away from me, looking chastened.

"Yep." Lisa reaches forward to take one cashew and pop it in her mouth. "Love-birds."

"Aww. That's kinda cute."

I can see Delilah gets a kick out of this. I'm sure I'll get a ribbing from her later. I imagine that Sam will grow on her, assuming he and I continue to see each other. He's not Peter, and he won't try to be. Which is for the best. No one can take the place of their father, but that's not to say the twins couldn't use guidance once in a while from other adults I trust.

Standing, I stretch my arms over my head. "I'll be right back."

I find Donovan alone in the front sitting room, lying down flat on his back, sprawled out on the rug in front of the woodstove. His father's journal is on his chest. I sit down next to him and hug my knees, grab-bing an extra blanket from the couch and throwing it over me.

"Aren't you cold?"

"No." He stares at the ceiling, his eyes half closed. "The stove is warm enough." He sighs. The excitement of the afternoon has worn him out. "I hate that you were driving when Dad lost his leg. He didn't need to be in that car with you. You ruined his life."

450

"I made a horrible mistake getting behind the wheel of that car. But I didn't ruin your dad's life, because he didn't let me ruin it."

Donovan's head falls to the side, and he actually looks at me. "I know. Dad didn't care. I read that part in the journal. He didn't blame you for the accident. Dad said it was only Henry's fault, and you were driving fine. He seemed happy about it that you were there. He wrote that it was fate. It was God's plan about how you guys would meet." Donovan rolls his eyes. "What a joke. As if God would want something like a horrific car accident to happen. Dad was just a messed-up teenager with an overactive imagination who went through something traumatic. I mean, when I read between the lines, I can see he was depressed about losing his leg, but he forced himself to be cheerful to impress you. I guess you were good for him."

I don't know how to respond. I haven't read what Donovan has, so I can't interpret it yet. "That sounds about right."

"I still don't forgive you."

That hurts. Donovan must know that hurts. But I take in a shaky breath. "Okay. Fair enough. I don't forgive myself either."

His face wrinkles in confusion, and I can see I've stumped him. "Really? It's been a long time. You married him. You guys must have been happy." He rolls onto his side, and it's to face me rather than to turn away from me, thank goodness. "I think if Dad knew you didn't forgive yourself, he'd be upset about that."

I feel a tear roll down my cheek. "Me too."

Donovan looks at me. He's my baby. He's a smart-ass kid sometimes, but still my baby. And he's got a soft spot for me in that heart of his. I know it.

When I reach out, he has no choice but to sit up and give me a hug. I give him a rough squeeze, wrapping my arms around his broad shoulders, before letting him lie back down.

"Look," he says. "Let's just agree we're okay. With everything. Because Dad didn't blame you, and he's the one who had to live with it. It's dumb for us to keep fighting about everything when he'd want us to be happy. I mean, I'm not exactly happy right now, but I can try to be." There's a pause, and we listen to the fire pop. It will need more wood soon. "Dad did say we couldn't do this without you."

"Do what?"

"This," he says, throwing his arm out from left to right. "Life. Everything." He starts to smile. "He didn't really define it more specifically than that. But you know that dramatic way he had of explaining something." He is still lying down but manages to toss his head and announce dramatically: "THIS. LIFE. EVERYTHING." He laughs.

I want to laugh, too, but I'm drained. I nod and wipe away my tear. "Okay. Thank you."

"You're welcome."

I'm relieved to hear a sincere note in his voice. "Sweetheart." He glances at me again. "I could have done some things differently. Plenty of things. But I wonder if you feel you could have done things differently, too."

His face shuts down again, and he turns his head away from me.

"You two were fighting a lot before he died, but in a perfectly normal way for a dad and his teenager. Your father loved you, and he knew you loved him. He knew it every minute, and he was proud of you. I feel good when I remember the two of you swimming at the beach that summer — you were doing what you loved, together. Even when you were arguing." I put my hand on his arm, and he allows it. "Okay? It was fine."

He pauses, but then gives a tight nod. "Okay," he says, and I have to lean in to hear him.

I let him have a moment to think about it. Because once he's done forgiving me, he also has to forgive himself.

"Mom," he whispers, turning to look at me. "He was happy, I know it. I could tell from what he wrote and from his drawings. We don't have to worry. He was okay. He really was."

I swallow, and realize I've been holding my breath. These are words I've needed to hear. It feels miraculous to hear words of encouragement from Donovan, because I know it has taken him a long time to come to this conclusion.

"Yes, he was happy." And once I say those words out loud, I realize it's true. My heart feels lighter, looser in my chest.

We sit in silence for another minute. Donovan's phone *pings!* He takes it out of his pocket and glances at it.

I nudge Donovan's leg with my toe. "So . . . what's the latest with Lexi? Did you call her yet?"

He turns toward me. "Yeah, she wants me to come over as soon as I can. I know we'll figure out how to deal with her dad. But I'm still not happy about that photo she posted with Steve. I'm trying to decide what to say about it. What's my play here? Am I angry, or does that make me possessive? Am

I jealous, or will I look desperate, like Aunt Lisa said? Am I nonchalant and cool about it, in which case she might think I don't care, even though I do?"

"You tell me."

He chews on the inside of his mouth. A hand goes up to absentmindedly pull his hair out from under his neck. "I dunno."

"I think honesty is the best policy, but it's up to you. It's perfectly okay to be any of the above. It's *your* love story. Only you can write it."

Luna saunters in and brushes up against Donovan's elbow. He scratches between her ears. And I realize: He's finally listening to me.

"Sweetheart, if you don't trust Alexis, I think you should break up with her and not put yourself through heartbreak. If you do trust her, then show it, be supportive, and everyone will admire you for it."

He chews his lip. "I do trust her. I wish I could go over there right now. Del said I should . . . I don't know, write down how I feel, like a love letter or something like that."

A love letter. That's something Peter would have told Donovan to do. I smile to think that Delilah suggested it. Maybe that's sort of how I should think of Peter's journal:

455

a love letter to his family. I can't wait to read it.

I sit up straighter. "You know what? That's not a bad idea. Maybe boys haven't treated her so well in the past, and she needs a knight in shining armor to show her how she deserves to be treated. I'm sure Delilah would help you write something tonight, maybe a poem, and when the roads get cleared tomorrow you can go over to Lexi's house. I can ask Sam to give you a ride over there, so Danny — I mean, Mr. Parsons — won't object."

"A poem? No, I already told Del, no poems. That sounds terrible." He rolls over onto his stomach and rests his chin on a hand. "But I'll write something. I'll think about it." He doesn't sound too enthusiastic, but there's hope in his eyes. I know that look. He's lovesick.

I've seen that look before.

I reach out and brush a stray hair from his forehead. He doesn't flinch or pull away. Instead, he rests his head on my arm. The warmth of his cheek and the weight of his head feels just right. It feels like we're connected.

CONFESSION

LUNA

Danny is the first to go. When he hears the town plow come by in the night, he gets up and gets dressed in the darkness. By the light of a flashlight he locates his snow pants, coats, hats, gloves, and boots. He's soon gone, out to deal with any snow that I imagine the town plow has pushed in his way. Before the sun even comes up, I hear the truck engine start, the headlights flash on, and then he's gone.

Annika and Lisa sleep in the master bedroom, with me between them. They stir when they hear the front door open and close, but go back to sleep.

Later, when my woman gets up, Sam is in such a deep sleep that Annika has to shake him. He's lying on the couch by the wood-stove, and the fire has just about gone out. She throws more logs on and gets the fire started again while he yawns and sits up.

"Danny left you here," she tells him.

He wipes his face with his hand. "Oh, man. I was out cold. I've gotta go. I need to go see Brianna."

"Of course you do." She sits next to Sam on the couch. I wait patiently by her feet, staring at Annika. It's time for my breakfast. But I let them have a minute to talk.

"It's so cold in here. But at the same time, something about the snow makes it feel warmer, you know? It's like insulation."

Annika nods. "Yes, Donovan said the same thing."

Sam drops his head. "I have to confess something." He speaks quietly so as not to wake anyone up.

I see Annika start to wring her hands, and she looks at him nervously. "You do? What else could there be to say? What do you mean?"

"Don't panic. It's nothing too bad." He smiles and drops his voice to a whisper. "I just wanted to be honest. I didn't hit or run over anything with our truck. I slashed the tire because I wanted to get stuck here." My woman's face shows her surprise. "It wasn't easy. It was hard to puncture a tire in a blinding snowstorm with my brother hovering around. I had to really hammer the knife in to get it through the tire. But I wanted to see you and spend time with you so bad, Annie. It was just a stupid, impulsive thing. I don't know why I did it."

She smiles back, and I can see she is genuinely pleased. "And you couldn't wait until after the snowstorm? Are you crazy?"

"But that's just it — the snow." He tips his head toward the window. "It reminds me of you. And us being together." Sam sighs and shrugs. "I'm sorry. Yeah, it was crazy. There's a lot wrong with me."

"Sam, I like everything that's right about you, and everything that's wrong with you."

He chuckles and hides his face in his hand for a moment. I get up and rub my face against his ankle to let Sam know I've decided that I like him, too. In my mind, he never quite made it to handsome prince — at least he hasn't gotten there *yet* — but I also can see that he's not the scruffy ogre I first imagined.

She sighs. "Will you come back and give Donovan a ride to Lexi's house later? If you can. If you have a minute. He'll need a bodyguard to get past Danny."

He takes her hand, moving his fingers until they're intertwined with hers. "Sure. And if he needs a job this summer, if he likes to landscape, we can always use a hand with the lawn mowing. That is, as long as none of us are in jail. For arson or insurance fraud. Or anything like that."

Annika shakes her head. "Sam, I hope not."

He looks fondly at her. "You know what I want?"

"No. What?"

"A do-over. To see if we can work things out. I feel like we could, but we won't know if we don't give it a chance. I think I could make you happy. I wish you'd let me try."

"I hope you do try. I'd be disappointed if you didn't."

He leans over to kiss her. She meets him halfway, her face relaxing, and she puts her free hand on the back of his neck to pull him closer. He says something quietly in her ear, and she nods, but I cannot hear the words. Annika hums as he buries his face under her ear, trusting him and closing her eyes. She puts a hand on his shoulder blade and sighs. I think Sam would like to continue with this, with both hands on her waist and all of his attention on this one task, but Lisa comes down the stairs.

"You guys," she announces. "Hey, lovebirds. The roads are clear. Hallelujah."

The roads are clear. And our hearts are clear. Hallelujah.

READY TO GO

PETER

When Annika is finally alone with the children, once Sam and Lisa have left, the kids relax. All seems well. Delilah is talkative and cheerful, going through the photos of her trip to Germany again while giving Annika details of every chocolate lebkuchen and springerle she ate. Donovan doesn't take long to start telling her about the many German beers he tried, as if he's now an expert. Annika listens patiently. I smile, listening to their conversation.

Luna sits nearby, and I look at her. *Good-bye, Luna, my friend.*

We miss you, Peter. We will miss you forever.

It's a tremendous relief to know Annika will read my journal at last. I was glad to see her hold it in her hands and flip through the pages. There's a lot for her to read in there. So much of myself. I've been waiting

461

a long time for her to read it.

Annika was wondering if I ever forgave her. But there was never anything to forgive.

Having two legs is not what made me a whole person. Having this family is what made me whole, and I'm so grateful for it. I'm sorry it's over for me.

Annika finally understands, now that she has listened to Donovan explain what is in the diary, and she has let me go. I felt her release me. It was sad, but also necessary. I feel my soul being torn from this world, and there's somewhere else I need to go.

She glistens, a shine so bright it's hard to look at her. She's been kind and very patient, waiting all this time.

Okay, I tell her. *I'm ready.*

I get one last glimpse of my family, and then — we're gone.

EPILOGUE

LUNA

The snow has melted, and the small patch of green grass in front of the house emits a fresh, fragrant scent. Donovan has just finished with the old push lawnmower he found in the garage. I sit on the front step and watch a big flatbed truck come down our long driveway, while Donovan waits in the front yard with hands on his hips.

A girl, who I've learned is the Lexi he always speaks to on the phone, nearly leaps out of the truck. She wears a short striped dress and has the grace and long legs of a young cat. "Hi," she calls out with a wave. Donovan hurries to meet her and grabs her hand. They walk down the path between the house and the garage until they're just out of sight of the truck. Donovan takes the girl in his arms and kisses her with such youthful exuberance that he bends her over backward. He plants kisses all over her face and she squeals with excitement. When he releases her, they head off toward the back of the house.

Well! Spring is in the air, after all.

Sam and Danny get out of the truck. There are three young trees in the back of the flatbed, and Danny starts pointing at locations in the wooded part of the yard where they took out old trees last week. The two men have ruddy color in their faces, and I can see they spend more time outside than anyone in my family. Danny is a little thinner, but doesn't look terribly sick, which is good to see. Maybe I'll approach him while he works and see if I can get him to pick me up, so I can assess the situation.

I glance up as Annika opens the front door.

Sam sees her and smiles. "I'll come say hi," he calls out. "In a little while."

Another truck pulls up, and two more men get out. Their truck is full of stinky mulch, which I can smell before I see it.

"Trung, you found the house," Sam says.

"Sure. I had to give Alexis a ride here last week," the man grumbles. "And she sang the whole time. Loudly. At full volume. Can you imagine? She sang. Pop songs. To the radio."

"She sang pop songs?" Danny looks offended. "You had to listen to that garbage?"

"She's happy." Sam grins at his brother.

"Great. That's just great." Danny sighs, and surveys the yard. The sun is intense; he squints and holds a hand up to his eyes for shade. "Okay. So, here's the plan."

I listen to the sound of his voice as it blends in with the birds calling and a leaf blower humming down the street. From inside the screen door, I hear the microwave beep as Annika has gone to heat up hot water for tea. And I hear the *click-clack-click* of Peter's old typewriter, which Delilah insisted on using to finish her father's story.

I'm glad to know Peter's story continues.

He may be gone, but he's always with us.

AUTHOR'S NOTE

Readers often ask authors where they came up with the idea for a particular story. The idea I had in my head when I started writing this novel was that 1) a family would be trapped together in a snowstorm, which would be stressful and (hopefully) lead to truths being spoken and secrets revealed; and 2) my protagonist's high school boyfriend (and first love) would end up getting stuck with her, just long enough for her to remember what she loved about him.

A different theme of *What Holds Us Together* that emerged as I wrote is how families learn to let go of a loved one who has passed on, which can be a slow and difficult process. But I also hoped to bring readers optimism about how a family might "hold together" in the face of loss.

Beyond those themes, I thought I'd share with readers some of the specifics of the book and how they came to me. Some of the book is based on what I learned from research and experience, and some is imagined.

First, as with my previous two cat-narrated novels, there is a nod to J. K. Rowling's world of Harry Potter. In *The Astonishing Thing,* my teenager Jimmy sometimes gives his cat Boo the nicknames Crookshanks and Minerva McGonagall. As Harry Potter fans know, Crookshanks is the name of Hermione Granger's cat, and Minerva McGonagall is the Head of Gryffindor House at Hogwarts, and her Animagus is a cat.

When I was writing *Something Worth Saving,* I saw an online article listing Lily and Luna as among the most popular names for cats in the United States and realized I could carry the Harry Potter references through all three books while still using common cat names.

So in *Something Worth Saving,* the Anderson family's cat is named Lily. She explains that her full name is "Lily J. Potter," which is the name of Harry Potter's mother. And in *What Holds Us Together,* the cat's name is Luna. Annika relates to Sam that her cat is named after Luna Lovegood, a Ravenclaw student and Harry's friend at Hogwarts; she's known for being dreamy and eccentric.

The essence of Luna's character was inspired by a script I was reading at the time I started this novel, *Lettice and Lovage*. My sister-in-law Laura was cast as Lettice in the play at a community theater many years ago, and my husband and I unfortunately weren't able to see her performance. (Laura, who loved the theater, has since passed away from a lifelong illness, and I have dedicated this novel to her.) I always thought the premise of *Lettice and Lovage* sounded fantastic. Lettice Douffet is a tour guide who takes great liberties with historical facts; her motto is Enlarge! Enliven! Enlighten! She sees no point in being boring (at the expense of accuracy). The British actress Maggie Smith originally played the role, and I could hear her voice in my head as I read her lines. So I decided Luna, inspired by Peter, would also be whimsical. She believes in fantastic creatures and loves to hear about great adventures.

Manchester (formally known as Manchester-by-the-Sea) is a real town on Cape Ann, on the northern coast of Massachusetts. It's where I lived from age ten until I left for college, and I still visit a few times a year. When I graduated in 1986, Manchester Jr-Sr high school (grades 7 through 12) was very small, similar to the way it's described in the book. I believe my graduating class had about fifty-five students. Now, they've replaced the old high school with a bigger, modern building and they also educate kids from the neighboring town of Essex.

There was at one time a supermarket in downtown Manchester called Brown's (now it's Crosby's) and there is in fact a drugstore within walking distance. There's also an old stone library downtown, and a harbor where you can sit on a bench and look out at sailboats and fishing boats attached to buoys. Annika mentions sitting with the twins and eating fried clams, but I'm not sure you can actually get take-out fried clams in Manchester (although you certainly can at several places on the main street of Essex, including the famous Woodman's of Essex).

The intersection of Beach Street and Summer Street is a real location in downtown Manchester, but in my mind, the fictional car accident in this book takes place in a quieter and more residential section of town. (I just love the names of those particular streets.) White Beach, where Sam and Annika stop after the prom, is one of the smaller beaches off Route 127 as you head toward Magnolia and Gloucester.

While in the past I have come up with fictional names for my New England towns, I figured if Matt Damon could make a movie called *Manchester by the Sea,* I could also get away with using a real town name in my novel.

I named the boarding school that Judith wants the twins to attend "The President's Academy" because I had in mind The Governor's Academy in Massachusetts. It's the oldest independent boarding prep school in the U.S., originally called Governor Dummer Academy, and my brother attended there for two years.

Fires play a prominent role in some of my stories. My son trained as a volunteer firefighter in high school, which might be one reason fires are sometimes on my mind. After I wrote the first draft of this book, I read on social media about a house in Manchester that burned to the ground when firefighters could not access the house due to a snowstorm. The house was on a steep hill, and the firetrucks could not get up the icy roads and got stuck. The whole house, and everything in it, was lost in an hour (people and pets were safe). That verified for me that the fire scene at the end of this book was a realistic scenario.

In this story, Peter lived for several years

in Germany. I got the idea from my husband's experience; my father-in-law was in the Navy and my husband lived in Stuttgart from age ten to fourteen. My husband also was new to his high school senior year, as was Peter, a tough experience for any kid but made a little easier for someone like Peter (or my husband), who finds it easy to talk to new people.

I did research on using a prosthesis and forearm crutches when writing this story. I gathered some information from an article that appeared in a newsletter for a local hospital here in New Jersey about a dad who lost his leg from the knee down in an accident. I carried the story around in my laptop case for a year so I could refer to it when needed. Peter's story isn't meant to reflect the experience of every amputee; I hope I got the basic facts right, and Peter's emotional journey is his own.

I had one question that went unanswered. Luna describes Peter taking his prosthesis off before bed, and Annika mentions Peter curling up behind her (spooning her), but I wasn't completely sure if he would be comfortable in that position, on his side. In the end, I decided for the sake of this story that Peter would be able to sleep like that, with his weight up against Annika, or at least be able to stay in that position for a short time until Annika fell asleep. I don't think I ever mention in the story which leg he lost (right or left), and I leave that to the reader's imagination.

My brother had a high school classmate who as an adult passed away of sleep apnea, so I knew it was possible for Peter to die in his sleep as a man in his forties. I considered writing the story of Peter's death differently, having Peter drown while out swimming with Donovan, but in the end decided against it. I made Donovan miserable enough without needing to go quite that far, where he'd feel personally responsible for not saving his father at the moment of his death. The way it's written now, Donovan tries CPR, but it's too late to make any difference and he knows that. Also, I wanted to keep the focus on Annika and Peter's original accident, including her guilt for involving him in the car crash.

Finally, a word about ghosts. Personally, I don't believe in ghosts. But they make for very interesting fictional characters.

I appreciate Susan Breen looking at and critiquing this story when it was still a mishmash of ideas, and helping me form it into something that resembled a novel. Thanks very much to Krista Riccioni for offering a thoughtful evaluation of another early draft.

A huge thank-you to my agent Stacy Testa at Writers House for her thoughts, suggestions, and tremendous help in getting the final draft of this story together and her assistance in all things related to writing, publishing, and promotion. I depend on her advice, and I'm thankful for her support!

Thanks very much to my editor at Kensington Books, John Scognamiglio. I'm lucky to be with Kensington, and I'm grateful for the whole tremendous team of people who work on my books in production and promotion: Lulu Martinez, Larissa Ackerman, Lauren Jernigan, Alexandra Nicolajsen, Megan Zimlich, Kristine Mills, and Carly Sommerstein. I hope I have remembered everyone! It's terrific working with people who love books and work so hard to get stories in the hands of readers.

Finally, thank you so much to my family and friends — and, of course, to my readers. I have heard from thoughtful readers who have struggled with some of the same issues my characters have dealt with, whether it's a spouse with mental illness or an alcoholic parent, and I value hearing everyone's story. I've also heard from animal lovers who enjoy reading from the point of view of cats — our best friends and companions. I appreciate it when anyone takes time out of their busy day to read one of my stories, and I hope you enjoyed *What Holds Us Together*! You can visit my website, sandi wardbooks.com, to connect with me, or find me on Instagram, Facebook, or Twitter at @sandiwardbooks. Let me know what kind of story you'd like to read next, and maybe I'll have a recommendation . . . or maybe I can write the story you've been looking for.

■ ■ ■ ■

READING GROUP GUIDE: WHAT HOLDS US TOGETHER

SANDI WARD

■ ■ ■ ■

ABOUT THIS GUIDE

The suggested questions are included to enhance your group's reading of Sandi Ward's *What Holds Us Together*.

DISCUSSION QUESTIONS

1. Some people have multiple romances (and/or marriages) in a lifetime. Do you think everyone has just one great love (the "love of your life") and soul mate, or is it possible to have more than one?

2. What do you think Sam represents for Annika? An idealistic return to the past, or a hopeful future?

3. Delilah and Donovan process their father's death differently, but stay close despite this difference. Do you have members of your own family who reacted to a life-changing event differently? How did that impact their relationship?

4. Peter loses his leg, but he doesn't think of himself as living with a disability and doesn't talk about the accident where he lost his leg. Did you feel this was a coping

mechanism? Was he in denial? Was this a healthy way for him to deal with his loss?

5. Annika's grief overwhelms her to the point where she decides to follow Peter's mother's suggestion and send the twins to boarding school. What do you think would have happened if Sam hadn't shown up? Would she have gone through with it?

6. When the story opens, Peter has already died, yet he plays a role in the book. Have you read other novels where a ghost, lingering spirit, or angel interacts with characters? What do you think about authors using a ghost as a character?

7. Why would Sam consider allowing his brother to burn down the house their father is building? Have you ever watched as a sibling, friend, or colleague did something you thought was a big mistake? Did you try and talk them out of it? Why or why not?

8. Why do you think Danny decided to allow Donovan to keep seeing his daughter? Was it just the fire, or something more?

9. Have you ever been stuck in a debilitat-

ing storm (snow or other type of weather situation)? How did it impact everyone in the house? Do you think losing heat and/or electricity for an extended period of time would change the way your family members interact with each other?

10. Do you have memories from high school that you'd rather forget? Did the mistakes you made as a teenager help you learn and grow, or does it just cause you grief to think about them?

11. The story is told in two points of view: Annika and Luna. Did you relate to one character more than the other? Did you enjoy having two narrators, and did the cat's point of view inform the larger story?